Forgetting YOU

ALSO BY L.A. CASEY

Slater Brothers series

Collins Brothers series

Maji series

Standalone novels

Forgetting
YOU

L.A. CASEY

This is a work of fiction. Names, characters, organizations, places, events, and incidents are either products of the author's imagination or are used fictitiously.

Published by Montlake, Seattle

www.apub.com

Amazon, the Amazon logo, and Montlake are trademarks of Amazon.com, Inc., or its affiliates.

ISBN-13: 9781542022538
ISBN-10: 1542022533

Cover design by Plum5 Limited

Printed in the United States of America

For the real-life heroes who run into danger while everyone else is running away from it.

PROLOGUE
ELLIOT

Fifteen days ago . . .

"Elliot? Elliot? Shit, shit, *shit*! It's his voicemail!"

My world came to a standstill the moment I heard her sweet voice. For a split second, I allowed the familiarity of it to wash over me before reality slammed into me. I hadn't heard that voice on the phone, or in person, in four very long years. The closest I'd got was when I watched old videos that she was in.

"Noah?"

The disbelief in my voice registered with me instantly. I could hear an overwhelming flood of shock and confusion the second I uttered those two little syllables. With my free hand, I lifted my fingers to the silver calla lily pendant that suddenly felt heavy against my chest.

"Help us," she sobbed, the sound causing my heart to clench. "Oh God. Please, I don't know what to do! Bailey, what're we gonna do? It's so dark, put the high beams on."

My grip on my phone tightened and my breathing hitched. I reminded myself that the voicemail came from my sister's phone. Noah was with my sister and I had no idea why. I suddenly felt like I was free-falling and no one was around to catch me. I was standing in the kitchen of the station, staring down at the rice I was cooking. I watched the water bubble through blurred eyes as my senses focused on the call.

"Oh God, oh God!" Noah sobbed. "Bailey, you're going too fast!"

The line began to break up and I clutched my phone to my ear, hoping the call didn't drop.

"Tulse Hill," she whimpered. "Elliot, we're on – Bailey, *slow down*!"

"I'm tryin'!" my sister's panic-laced voice shouted. "I can't stop, it's black ice! We're slidin'!"

"Elliot!" Noah screamed as the line broke up. "Elliot, help us. Tulse Hill . . . Please, please . . . going to kill . . . Bailey! Look out!"

I had never felt true bone-rattling fear until I heard my sister's terror-filled scream as the line went dead. I blindly reached out and gripped on to the counter to keep my knees from buckling. For what seemed like an eternity, I didn't move. I felt like I wasn't in control of my body, like what I was experiencing wasn't real. I swallowed. The haunting silence that filled the room was louder than Bailey's scream. It was deafening. Laughter from the common room seemed to snap me back into reality. I pushed the pot of rice off the burner, switched the hob off, then ran into the room where my friends were gathered.

No one noticed my entrance.

"How long did the electric company say it'd be before they got the grid back up and running?" AJ, my best mate, asked Texas, our friend and co-worker. "It's been years since the whole of bloody London has had no power. Especially not this long – it's been what, four hours now? People must be going crazy without Wi-Fi for Facebook and Instagram."

The tail end of a storm had blown London and a few neighbouring towns into a blackout. We were all on edge; no power meant no lights, and no lights on a winter night could lead to some pretty serious accidents.

Bad things happen in the dark. They always have.

"Fingers crossed it'll all be back on soon," Stitch, the watch manager, said optimistically. "We're lucky this place has a built-in generator. Perks of being firemen, we always need power and we get it."

AJ was about to reply when he caught sight of me. Whatever expression he saw on my face caused him to jump to his feet and hurry over. His hand went to my shoulder, clutching me as his worried eyes locked on mine.

"Irish? What's wrong?"

I couldn't form the words to explain myself, so I lifted my hand and pressed on the screen of my phone. I replayed the voicemail I'd received and put it on speaker for the room to hear. Everyone listened with pensive expressions on their faces.

"Noah and Bailey," I rasped as the message ended. "Somethin' is wrong with them, they're at Tulse Hill. We hav'te go!"

I had barely finished speaking when the familiar sound of a siren echoed throughout the station. Everyone sprang into action; we all knew our positions for the current watch, having been briefed not long after we clocked in. We were well rehearsed, but today I couldn't think straight. My brain wasn't firing on all cylinders.

"Stitch!" I darted my gaze to his. "I can't go. Me sister and Noah, something's wrong. They need me!"

Just as I spoke, the automated, robotic voice that flowed through the speakers of the tannoy system sounded. Everyone went deathly silent as we listened for the nature of the call.

"CHARLIE ONE. ECHO ONE. RTC. PERSONS TRAPPED."

RTC. A car accident. My heart stopped.

I moved before I even realised it. I was right behind Stitch as he ripped off the tip-out sheet from the ribbon printer. I was supposed to already be in my position in the engine. On today's watch, I was BA1. Breathing apparatus one. I was the first one to go into a fire should there be one, but at that moment I couldn't find the willpower to move. I stared at Stitch as he read the report. When he looked at me, I knew what he was going to say.

"The location is Tulse Hill." I held my breath. "Isn't it?"

He nodded. Once.

It was my sister and Noah; they had been in a car accident. They were the people who were trapped and in need of help. In need of *my* help.

"Fuck," I snapped, as adrenaline – and fear – pumped through my veins. "Let's fuckin' *go!*"

We were in the engines and on our way to the scene with the sirens blaring before I could blink. I was a fucking wreck. My heart was pounding, my hands were slick with sweat, and my stomach churned so much I was certain I was going to vomit. I'd struggled getting my gear on even with a friend's help.

"God, please," I said out loud as I clasped my gloved hands together, closed my eyes and lowered my head. "Protect me sister and woman in me absence. Please. Please. Let them be okay. I ask this in your name. Amen."

"Amen." The word was echoed within the truck.

"We're nearly there, Irish." Texas roughly patted my shoulder. "Nearly there, brother."

Every single second felt never-ending. The worst images invaded my mind, of horrifying RTC scenes I had been to before while on watch, and videos and images of others I had seen years ago during my training days. I silently pleaded with God that I wouldn't find the two women who I loved more than life itself in a similar situation to the horrors I had witnessed.

"Fuck," Tank said from the driver's seat minutes later. "The car is on its side, it's smashed right into the exterior of a building. Police are on scene, they'll control the civilians. A crowd has gathered."

"Jesus," I breathed as the truck came to a halt and my sister's car came into view. I jumped out of my side before I even realised it. "Bailey! Noah!"

"Damn it, Irish! Elliot! You can't – *Fuck!*"

I could see the lick of small flames coming from the bonnet of the car. There was fuel pouring from the back end and it had yet to ignite. Its odour was overwhelming. I didn't have long before things changed from dangerous to fatal, and I knew it. I wasn't supposed to go near the car until the situation could be assessed by the watch manager. The risk was too high to my life, to my friends, but I didn't care and I didn't wait for my orders. I heard shouts all around me from people standing idle on the streets, some with their hands over their mouths while others recorded the scene on their phones.

As I ran, I abandoned everything I had ever learned in training. Blind panic took over as I reached the car and scrambled on top of the passenger door without a moment's hesitation. I could feel the heat of the growing fire on my face; I went to adjust the visor on my helmet and realised I wasn't wearing it. Somewhere between my dismount from the engine and reaching Bailey's car, I had knocked it off.

I pushed it from my mind and focused on the scene in front of me, but it was hard. The blaring noise from the car horn made it difficult to think.

I banged on the window of the car. Inside I could see two people, and I separated them immediately based on their hair colour. Noah was in the passenger seat and Bailey was in the driver's. Noah was moving her arms and head slightly; Bailey was utterly still.

My heart was pounding so fast I couldn't hear my friends as they shouted to me and to each other. I yanked on the handle of the car door, but it didn't budge.

"*Fuck!*"

The window was already cracked, so I repositioned my body and used the heel of my boot to smash into the lower right-hand side, where the glass appeared to be at its weakest. It gave way instantly and I heard moaning and soft cries of pain. I assessed Noah straight away; her seat belt was still in place and she was almost dangling in the air. I looked past her to my little sister and felt my stomach drop.

She was still motionless. I couldn't tell if she was breathing or not.

"Bailey!" I shouted, my voice cracking. "Hang on, baby, I'm comin'. D'ye hear me, Bails? I'm comin' for ye!"

I heard my name being hollered, and turned my head in the direction of my friends, who were running towards me. I saw Stitch motion his hands left, right and centre as he shouted orders. My heart felt like it was about to burst with fear. He needed to get the fire under control before a spark touching the poured fuel became a problem. But there was no way I was leaving my girls to help him.

Not a chance.

"AJ!" I roared. "Gimme a knife. I think the seat belt is jammed."

I turned back to Noah and she was mumbling something that I couldn't hear; her eyes were open, and they were on me, but she wasn't looking at me. She was far away – I wasn't sure she even realised I was in front of her. Blood dripped down the side of her face from her temple. I gently turned her head in my direction and instantly swallowed down bile. She had a massive, deep open wound running back into her hairline. I sucked in a breath and repressed the urge to cough as the strong, choking odour of smoke suddenly filled my lungs.

"It's okay, green eyes. I'm right here and I'm gonna get ye outta here. D'ye hear me, Noah? I'm gonna get you outta here."

I was working on her seat belt as her head lolled from side to side. She lifted her hand and slapped it down on Bailey's shoulder and said something inaudible to her. My sister didn't so much as flinch. It was then that I inhaled the metallic tang of blood. I quickly grabbed my torch from its holster and shone it on my sister, and saw that her face was covered in red. Some of her hair was matted to her forehead while the rest of it hung loose to the door, and her nose and jaw appeared to have been crushed against the steering wheel. I realised then that she wasn't wearing her seat belt. A pained cry tore free of my throat when I saw her eyes were wide open and unblinking.

My mind screamed that my baby sister was dead, but I refused to accept it.

"Hold on, Bailey! I'm comin', baby."

I pressed the release clasp on Noah's seat belt and pulled the strap as hard as I could at the same time, and it suddenly gave way. I caught Noah under the armpits and quickly pulled her from the car. Her pain-laced screams made my blood run cold.

"Mum!" she screamed. "*Elliot!* Make it stop."

I hooked an arm under her legs and the other around her back, and I ran with her, shouting for my friends to get the fire under control and for AJ to get into the car and get Bailey free so we could extract her. I noticed an ambulance pulling up just as I set Noah down on the ground. I froze for a second as I looked her over. She had blood all over her – there were bruises, cuts, and her face was swollen – but she was conscious and breathing.

I leaned down and kissed her with relief that she was alive, then I turned and ran back towards the car that AJ and two others were suddenly diving away from. I watched in horror as sparks fell on to the leaked fuel and ignited instantly. I let out a roar for them to help my sister just as the car exploded. The force of it knocked me back as flames flew up into the air and then completely consumed the car.

"Bailey!" I screamed as I scrambled to my feet and ran towards the wall of scorching flames. With my ears ringing and my body swaying, I forced myself to stay on my feet. "Bailey! No! God, no! *Bailey!*"

I was suddenly tackled from the side and then dragged backwards by two sets of hands. I heard voices blend together, but what I heard over them were the pleas and cries that tore from my throat. I fought them, my determination to get to my sister making me swing and kick, but in the end they won and I lost.

I lost everything.

I stared at the flames that swirled and danced with one another, knowing that my baby sister had been claimed by them. She was dead and there was nothing I could do to save her. My world became all the darker, even as orange and blue lights flickered around me. Inside of me there was no light, no peace – just all-consuming sadness, anger and hopelessness.

Things that people normally felt in the dark.

CHAPTER ONE
NOAH

Present day...

Dissonant beeping. That was what I awoke to.

I wasn't sure what the beeping was or where it was coming from, but it was somehow familiar to me. It was as if I'd heard it, or woken up to it, a few times before. I couldn't place the cause of it though, and when I tried to think of what it could be, the pain started. An excruciating sensation pulsed throughout my skull. It was so agonising that I couldn't open my eyes or move my limbs. My body was completely tense and rigid as it braced itself against the pain. I wished for it to go away, but it didn't, it only lessened slightly to the point where I could open my eyes.

My vision was hazy, but slowly a brightly lit room came into view.

An off-white coloured ceiling caught my attention the second my vision could focus. Like the beeping, it was familiar to me, but I had no idea what place it was linked to. For a few minutes, I did nothing but stare at the ceiling as I waited for the pain in my head to fade. It never went away, but eventually the pounding gave way to a throb. Though it was constant and still very painful, I could just about tolerate it. I had no choice but to endure it.

I attempted to say "hello" but my voice didn't sound like my own. The word came out as a slur, barely coherent to my own ears. I tried to say it again, but it felt like my tongue was suddenly too big for my mouth. I wasn't sure how long I was lying there figuring out how to work my tongue, when suddenly the sensation that the muscle was too big just faded away.

"Hello!"

My voice was hoarse and my throat itched, like I needed to down a litre of water to soothe it, but I said the word loud and clear. It felt like a victory of sorts. I tried to clear my throat to scratch the itch, but the action proved to be too painful, so I resisted the urge to cough, even though that was what my body desperately wanted to do. I carefully attempted to sit up, but I couldn't. My body felt like a heavy weight and I wasn't strong enough to lift it. Though I couldn't move all that well, I could turn my head from side to side. I slowly looked to my right and the decor – and machinery – that came into view told me where I was instantly.

A hospital, or medical clinic of some kind.

The beeping I heard seemed to come from a machine that appeared to register my heart rate. I didn't linger on it; the sound was ear-piercing and sharp. Instead, I turned my attention to finding the Call button that every hospital, or medical facility, had. I hoped it wasn't on the wall to the left or right of the bed, because I hadn't got the strength to move my body. I didn't seem to have the strength to do anything.

I was thoroughly exhausted, and before I could attempt to move, my eyes drifted shut and forcibly pulled me into a dreamless slumber.

A throbbing ache in my leg brought me back into awareness. My eyes darted open and once again I found myself staring at the off-white ceiling. It took me a minute to think straight and realise that I wasn't dreaming. I was in a hospital, I reminded myself. I needed to speak to someone. A nurse, a doctor, anyone.

The Call button.

I needed to press that bloody Call button, wherever it was. I moved my arms, jerky movements at first, and felt a pulse reader on the index finger of my right hand. My left hand skimmed over a wire next to my hip. I tugged on it and a remote of some kind came into contact with my hand. Moving hurt more than it should; in fact, my whole body was sore. I bit my lip to focus on feeling the buttons. I couldn't tell what any of them were for so, as best as I could, I tugged it on to my chest. I peered down for a moment and saw a large red button. I wasn't sure what it did, but I pressed it anyway.

I exhaled a deep breath, the simple movements having completely drained me.

For a few seconds, nothing happened, and I worried that I'd pressed the wrong button, but then noises and a voice came from my left. I heard a door opening followed by soft footsteps. A face suddenly appeared over me and it startled me. It was a woman who appeared to be in her mid- to late fifties; she had dark brown skin, and eyes to match.

"Hi there," the lady said. "Can you hear me, sweetheart?"

I winced, the volume of her voice causing the already painful ache in my head to worsen.

"Too loud. My head," I rasped, finding that talking was a little difficult. "It hurts so bad."

The woman frowned and lowered her voice. "I'm going to page your doctor so he can come see you right away. I'll get you pain relief while I'm out there. I'll be back in a minute, okay?"

I didn't want her to leave me, but I urgently needed the pain-killers that she could provide, so I tentatively said, "Okay."

When she disappeared from view, I began to panic. I was terrified that she wouldn't come back and that I'd be stuck in the position I was in with no one to help me. I could barely lift my head or move my body. I didn't know what was wrong with me, or what had happened to put me in the situation I was in, but whatever it was, I knew it wasn't good.

Breathe, I told myself. *Just breathe, Noah. It'll be okay.*

I focused on inhaling and exhaling deep breaths. It helped calm me down, but only just. True to her word, the lady came back to my side within a minute. She had a glass of water in one hand and an IV bag in the other. She saw me eye the bag and said, "It's only paracetamol, but it'll help kill the pain quicker through your IV. The doctor can prescribe something stronger once he gets here."

I started to nod but stopped as soon as I started. The movement was too much – everything at that moment seemed to be all too much. Not only was my head killing me, my body was aching beyond measure. The nurse used a remote to raise the top half of my bed, but not by much, just enough so I could see the plain white room without having to strain to lift my head. She helped me drink some water then, and once I'd had a good few mouthfuls, it made me feel a little more human.

"What happened to me?"

I felt so tired that it was a fight to keep my eyes open.

"You were in an accident," the nurse said, careful to keep her voice low. "You hit your head pretty hard."

An accident? I thought. *I was in an accident?*

Slowly, and with difficulty, I lifted my hand to my forehead, and it was only then that I felt a compressed bandage of some kind wrapped around my skull. I looked at the rest of my body and, though my torso and legs were hidden by a blanket, I could feel padding on different parts of my skin. I lifted the blanket and peered down.

The medical gown I was wearing had ridden up and it gave me a decent view of my battered body. A battered body that was larger than I remembered: my thighs were wider, and I had a flabby gut. I remembered the nurse telling me I'd been in an accident, so I put it down to being swollen from injuries I'd clearly sustained.

I had a bandage on my lower abdomen. My left leg from my knee down was in a black boot cast. It jolted me back to when I'd fractured that same leg in two places when I was twenty-one at a dance studio, and had to wear a similar cast during my recovery.

My arms were destroyed, covered with bruises and minor scrapes; some were scabbed, and others were red lines where scabs had fallen off. My body looked as if it had been to war and back again. I tried to remember what had happened to me, I closed my eyes and forced myself to think about the accident that the nurse had spoken about, but I drew a complete blank.

"I don't remember anything about an accident."

"That's okay," the nurse said with a warm smile. "What's important is that you're conscious and alert, you're moving around beautifully too. I can see it hurts, but movement is good. Can you feel all your fingers and toes?"

"Yes," I answered. "But everywhere . . . hurts. My leg and my head the most."

"I know, love," she said, as she moved to my right and attached the painkiller bag to the IV that was already in my arm. "This will help a little. You'll start to feel some relief in a few minutes."

I hoped she was right.

"Which hospital is this?"

"King's College," she answered.

I nodded; it was my local hospital. It made sense for me to be treated here. I glanced at her name badge and caught the words

"Intensive Care Unit" above her name, and my heart just about stopped. My eyes darted up to hers in an instant.

"ICU?" I said, baffled. "Your name badge says ICU. That's for critically ill patients though. Am I okay?"

Talking so fast made my words sound jumbled together even to my own ears. Fear slammed into me like a train, and the beeping from the machine was faster now and more bothersome than before.

"Now, honey, you need to calm down. This *is* the ICU, but you're okay, you have to listen to me—"

Our attention turned to the door when it suddenly opened. I watched as a middle-aged male doctor walked in and I felt relieved to see him. He had dark brown skin like the nurse, his eyes were soft and his smile was bright. The nurse seemingly didn't have answers to my questions, but maybe he would.

"What happened to me?" I asked as he took a step towards me. "How did I get here? Why am I—"

"Whoa." The doctor raised his hands in front of his chest and chuckled. "Give me a second to look at you, Noah. I'm Doctor Abara, it's wonderful to see you alert."

I tried to relax, but I couldn't.

I was in pain, and the not knowing how I came to be in hospital was stressing me out. The doctor came to my bedside and asked me to do a few things before we could talk. I followed his little penlight, then his finger, then when he touched a part of my body with his pen, he asked me if I could feel it. I told him that I could feel everywhere the pen touched. He asked me to say the names of random objects when he pointed them out. He asked me to move my arms and legs and toes. It pleased him when I completed each task.

"Can you remember anything about your time with us, Noah?" he quizzed, and I noted then that he spoke with an accent. "Anything at all."

"A tiny bit," I answered. "I woke up once before now, but I must have fallen back asleep. I opened my eyes and I was here, but I don't know how I got here. The nurse says I was in an accident but I can't remember any accident."

He nodded and made a note of some sort on the chart in his hand. We went through a series of questions about my well-being, about my pain level from one to ten, and a bunch of other things I didn't really care about. When the examination was over and the doctor had finished making notes on what I now knew was my personal patient chart, he looked up at me and smiled once more.

"I know this is tiresome, but I could go back to jail if I don't follow protocol."

I blinked. "You've been to jail?"

"Once," he answered with a nod. "In Monopoly. It wasn't fun, I'll tell you that much."

I stared at him in silence, then he laughed and looked at the nurse and said, "Tough crowd."

I humoured him when his gaze returned to mine. "Ha ha."

"Sorry." He grinned. "No more bad jokes."

"You can tell me a million of them *after* you answer my questions," I bargained. "How does that sound?"

"Like a deal." The doctor winked. "Fire away."

I had so many questions that I needed the answers to, but I didn't know where to begin. At random, I picked a few and said, "What happened to me? Why don't I remember anything? Why is talking hard?"

The nurse reached over and patted my hand when my voice cracked. I was scared, really scared. Having no memory of how I came to be in the hospital was worse than anything I had ever experienced before. I felt very vulnerable.

"What I'm about to say will sound very scary," Doctor Abara said, "but trust me when I say that, right now, you're okay and you're in the best place receiving the best care."

That doesn't sound very good.

I swallowed. "Okay."

"You were in an accident where you hit your head very hard, so to protect itself your body has been in a coma for fifteen days."

"*What?*" I exclaimed in shocked disbelief. "A coma? *Fifteen days?*"

The machine next to me started beeping rapidly, but one screen-tap from the nurse silenced it.

"I know it must be startling to hear, but you're okay," he stressed gently. "What you need to do right now is take a few calming breaths. Noah, look at me. Noah!"

I lifted my hands to my head and whimpered. The throbbing pain had drastically worsened; it was so bad that I could barely hear anything the doctor was saying. I felt my eyes roll back and my vision started to fade to nothingness, when suddenly my head dropped back against my pillow. I fell into darkness, feeling scared and very much alone.

CHAPTER TWO
NOAH

Eighteen years old . . .

"Noah?" His voice drifted towards me like a song on the wind. "If you're playin' hide and seek, ye picked a rubbish spot to hide, green eyes. I'm already *in* your house, you can't exactly get away from me."

I opened my mouth, not knowing what I was going to say in response, but I didn't have to worry about it when hands clamped down on my waist, making me screech in surprise. Warm, strong arms slid around me to keep me from darting away, and low laughter filled the room.

"Gotcha."

I shivered as his hot breath fanned my ear and neck.

"I wasn't hiding," I said, lifting my chin. "I was just . . . I was just—"

"Ye were just *what*? Lookin' behind the bathroom door for someone else?"

I blew out a big puff of air as frustration gripped me.

"Fine," I grunted. "You caught me; I *was* hiding."

My body turned to face his, and when he nudged under my chin with his finger, encouraging me to look up at him, my stomach burst into a mess of butterflies. I was a tall girl, taller than every girl I went to school with. I stood five foot ten inches, but Elliot's massive six foot five inches dwarfed me and made me feel tiny, feminine.

I *loved* that feeling.

Elliot McKenna, I thought to myself. *Where do I begin with him?*

Elliot had moved to my home town just over seven months ago, in the middle of the school year. His father had opened a new Irish pub in town called McKenna's. Moving to a different country would be daunting, hectic and maybe even a little scary to most people, but not Elliot. He was two months shy of eighteen when I met him, and once he became close friends with a classmate of mine, AJ, we became close too, but in an entirely different way.

Elliot was the first boy that I had ever taken an instant fancy too. The moment I saw him, I felt an attraction . . . and so did every other senior girl in school. He was gloriously tall, had a mop of thick, dark hair, eyes the colour of the ocean, and a dimple in his right cheek when he smiled. He was gorgeous, and to top it off, he had an accent. An Irish one to be exact. He was a Dubliner. I didn't believe he even thought I was a member of the female gender until he kissed me on the night of his eighteenth birthday when we celebrated with him.

That kiss brought us closer; it brought us to now.

"Why were ye hidin' from me, green eyes?"

I swallowed as my palms became slick with sweat. "'Cause I'm nervous."

"About what?"

He was speaking to me, but his ocean blues were on my mouth and so was his thumb, brushing over my lower lip. It was terribly

18

distracting and for a moment or two all I could think about was encircling his neck with my arms, reaching up and crushing my mouth against his. I resisted that urge because it went against what I'd planned to say to Elliot McKenna.

I was breaking up with him . . . and I couldn't kiss him and do that at the same time, or at least I was fairly sure I couldn't. I wasn't entirely certain about the rules when it came to breaking up with a boy who technically was never your boyfriend to begin with. It was new ground that I was covering, so everything was unknown.

It was a complicated mess on a good day but I was certain of one thing: in the span of the few short months that we had been casually dating, I had fallen in love with Elliot, and I didn't want to be strung along and hurt beyond repair, so I had to cut him loose even though I didn't want to. I *had* to, in order to protect myself.

I had always known that I was soft-hearted and more emotional than most people. I took things personally whether I wanted to or not. I grew attached to those I cared about very easily, and that was why Elliot, as a person, terrified me so much. I loved him. I loved him so completely that it scared me. He was someone who could break me without even trying.

We were both young and maybe it was foolish, but I could see a future with Elliot. One where I was in a stable relationship that would give me the security I needed in order to relax and enjoy my life. I desperately wanted that. I didn't want to mess around and spend my early years jumping from guy to guy and have the future be unknown to me. I knew what I wanted and what I wanted was to be Elliot's one and only, the woman he gave his last name to.

I had never thought it was truly possible to find the person I hoped to spend my life with so young, but I believed I had found my future in Elliot . . . and it killed me that he didn't appear to have that kind of faith in me. If he did, he would have already asked me to be his girlfriend.

"I have to tell you something," I said with a firm nod as I straightened my spine. "It's important so you have to listen to me – *Elliot!*"

His laughter burst free as I slapped away the hand that slithered down my back and squeezed my behind.

"I love how ye say me name, *sasanach*." He chuckled. "All prim and proper."

With flaming cheeks, I thumped his chest.

"Don't be touching the merchandise, paddy."

"Am I not allowed to touch what belongs to me?"

A flood of pulsing heat spread from my stomach to between my thighs. My hands moved to Elliot's growing biceps, where I gripped on to him for dear life as I pressed my legs together. I was a simple girl who didn't need a whole lot said, or done, to feel ready to climb Elliot like a tree. It was the virgin in me, and the fact that I'd read one too many Highlander historical romance books that made me weak when a man got deliciously possessive.

Damn those Scotsmen and their bloody kilts.

"No," I squeaked in response. "No, you're not allowed to touch me 'cause I don't belong to *you* or any man. I belong to *me*."

Elliot cocked an eyebrow and I even found that sexy. It was positively mortifying what my hormones were doing to my body. I was glad no one could read my mind, because they'd be having a good laugh at me and my vagina's expense.

"Is that so?" he mused as he pressed me against the bathroom door, pinning me with his hard body. "I wonder why that is? Care to let me know?"

Woman up, Noah. It's now or never.

I cleared my throat and looked at his nose, because I found I didn't have the courage to look him in the eye as I broke my own heart.

"That's why I asked you to come here while my parents are away for the weekend. I need to tell you that I'm breaking up with you."

For long seconds, the room was covered in a veil of silence that prompted me to look up into Elliot's eyes. All playfulness had vanished from those ocean blues, and a flicker of what I gauged to be worry lingered. Time ticked by as he said nothing. He just stared down at me intensely and unblinking. It was like he was trying to answer his unspoken questions with his powerful gaze.

Eventually, he said, "What?"

I blinked repeatedly as I tried to focus on his words and not his touch.

"I'm fed up wi-with you," I stammered, as his hands on my waist squeezed ever so slightly. "We've been going on dates for five months. One, two, three, four, *five* months, and you've not asked me to be your girlfriend yet." I dug my fingers into the muscles of his back as he pressed closer to me. "The trial pe-period is over, you aren't getting a subscription to this body so . . . so we're done."

His shoulders sagged almost instantly, and the fear in his eyes faded and gave way to a teasing glint. "Ye think I don't want you long-term?"

"That's *exactly* what I think . . . You don't have to look so bloody relieved about it either!"

He chuckled. "You're peggin' me all wrong, gorgeous."

"Am I really?" I quizzed. "You look mighty pleased that I'm ending things."

"I'm pleased that ye've got me intentions messed up, otherwise I'd likely be on me knees right now beggin' ye to give me another chance."

My brows shot up with surprise. That was *not* what I'd expected to hear.

"*What?*"

21

He didn't answer me with words; he dipped his head and latched his lips on to my sweet spot instead. My eyes rolled back as Elliot sucked on my neck, using just the right amount of pressure to draw a slight moan from my parted lips. I slid my hands up his back to his neck, and finally tangled them into his thick, inch-long, chocolate-brown hair. He slid his tongue from my neck up to my face, and the second he plunged it into my mouth I was at his mercy.

I lifted one leg and hooked it around the back of his knee, and I felt a thrill dart up and down my spine when I sucked on his hot, wet tongue and heard a slight growl come from his throat. He pulled back enough to break our kiss, but not enough to be out of my reach.

"Elliot," I panted as blood rushed through my veins. "*Please.*"

"D'ye know why I agreed to come over to your house, *knowin'* your parents weren't home this weekend?"

I tried to kiss him again, but he only let me suck on his lower lip, which was hardly enough for me. I wanted more of him. All of him if I could have it.

"D'ye know why?" he pressed, moving his lips out of my reach. "Because they went away last month, and I never came over. Why d'ye think I came over *today*?"

I couldn't think of anything other than dirty, dirty things.

"Tell me," I pleaded as I brought my lips to his neck. "Please."

"Because I wanted to be sure that I loved you."

I froze, my mouth pressed against his skin. I felt his heart beating rapidly as my lips skimmed over a pulsing artery. He pulled back to look down at me, and I stared up at him with wide eyes and my mouth agape. His lips twitched, and his dimple creased in his cheek. He pressed his forehead down against mine and silently waited for me to say something. Anything.

22

"D'you mean it?" I whispered as my eyes stung with sudden tears. "D'you really mean it? Because if you don't, you'd better get out of my house right now, Elliot."

He tightened his hold on me and rubbed the tip of his nose against mine.

"I love ye, *sasanach*. I'm sorry it took me a while to realise it, I've never been in love until I found you. I wanted to be certain about how I was feelin'."

"And you are?" I asked, my heart pounding against my chest. "Certain about how you feel, I mean."

"I am." He smiled gleefully. "I know you like the back of me hand. Ye can be anxious about things that ye can't control and that's not a bad thing, it just means that gettin' reassurance every now and then from people you care about helps ye relax." He brushed strands of hair behind my ear. "I wanted no doubts in my mind about how I feel for you. I wanted to tell ye I loved you, and for *you* to not doubt me when I said the words. I love you, Noah."

His words hit me with the force of a train, and in that moment I knew what true happiness felt like.

"Elliot," I whispered as tears fell from my eyes and meandered down my cheeks. "I love you too."

"You do?" He smiled, the dimple I loved so much deepening. "So much that you're breakin' up with me?"

I laughed and cried at the same time.

"You never asked me to be your gi-girlfriend and I knew I already loved you. I had to pr-protect myself somehow, I didn't want to co-continue as we were until we were together. I feel too much for you to just ca-casually date you, Elliot. I want a future with you, but I wasn't willing to give you my all unless you gave me yours."

"I came to a similar conclusion, which is why I agreed to come by today so I could tell you that I loved ye, *and* to ask ye to be me girlfriend . . . if ye'll have me, that is? This will be a mighty awkward moment if ye still plan on dumpin' me."

I stared up at him for a long, silent moment, then I screamed with joy and jumped on him, wrapping my legs around his hips and my arms around his neck. I just about squeezed the breath out of him.

"Yes," I shouted in delight. "I'll be your girlfriend. Yes, yes, yes!"

Elliot's laughter mingled with my own, and after a few minutes of me near hugging him to death, he set me down on the floor. With my heart pounding in my chest and the butterflies going mental in my stomach, I grabbed his hand and pulled him from the bathroom and into my bedroom. He offered me no resistance as I closed my bedroom door behind us then hurriedly crossed the room and pushed him on to my bed.

"Woah, woah, woah," he said, no longer laughing. "*This* is why I never came here when ye were alone because I *knew* we'd come together like this. Listen to me, Noah. I didn't tell ye I love you just so ye'd let me—"

"I know," I cut him off. "I know it's not only sex you're after. You love me."

"I do," he said, his eyes finding mine. "God knows I do."

"And so do I." I smiled, my heart pounding against my chest. "I love you too."

I hesitated for just a moment before I gripped the hem of my oversized T-shirt and pulled it off over my head, tossing the fabric somewhere on the floor behind me. Elliot froze as his eyes locked on to my bare chest. I never wore a bra when I was at home – I didn't need to because I was barely a B cup, but if I was worried about the size of my breasts before, I wasn't once I saw how Elliot's eyes stared at them with hunger.

My nipples hardened in an instant.

I didn't give him time to blink as I pushed down my pyjama pants, along with my lacy red thong, and kicked them off when they reached my ankles. I let my hair out of the messy bun atop my head and my golden-blonde hair fell down my back in waves. I stood before him naked, vulnerable and very nervous.

"God in Heaven." Elliot swallowed as his gaze lowered to between my thighs. He clenched his hands at his sides into fists. "Have mercy, *sasanach*."

I had never felt more feminine, more empowered, than I did in that moment, as his eyes rolled over me like a gentle wave. He wanted my body, and he loved me. That was all the encouragement I needed to take the next step with him.

"You're wearing way too many clothes," I said, biting my lower lip. "Should I help you undress?"

Elliot looked pained as he nodded and got to his feet; he lowered his head to mine when I neared him, and he kissed me. It was a different kind of kiss, not filled with raw hunger, but instead soft and seductive. It was a lover's kiss. I smiled when he tried to encourage my tongue to dance with his and deepen our kiss. I tugged on his jumper, and in two seconds he had it, and his T-shirt, removed and on the floor.

My eyes dropped to his torso.

"Elliot," I whispered as I stood up on my tiptoes and licked his red, kiss-swollen lips. "Have I ever mentioned how happy I am that you've begun your training to become a fireman? Your body . . . *you* should have mercy on *me*, paddy."

He grinned at the nickname I'd recently christened him with after being called his *sasanach* one too many times.

"I'll show no mercy if it keeps those pretty greens lookin' at me just like they are right now."

His jeans, boxer briefs and socks joined the rest of our clothes seconds later. I pressed my hands against his bare chest and Elliot let me explore him. I ran my fingers over his tight pectorals, down to his abdominal muscles that were *much* harder and more defined since I last saw him shirtless. The V-line at his hips made me swallow, and his dark treasure trail sent another raging pulse between my thighs. He had been taking his training *very* seriously as of late, and I was entirely grateful.

"You're so hard, Elliot."

"Always am when I clap eyes on you, gorgeous."

I laughed.

"I mean your chest and stomach, smooth-talker." I lowered my eyes to his cock and paused when it jumped. "Okay, now I'm nervous again. You're hard in other places too."

I was a virgin, but a realistic virgin who liked to watch porn on occasion, so I had seen just about every size and shaped penis there was, but none of them mattered because they hadn't belonged to Elliot. I hadn't been expecting an anaconda to be hiding in his boxer briefs, but from the length and thickness of it, an anaconda seemed to be exactly what I was getting.

"How many inches is that? Seven, eight? If you say nine, I'm getting dressed right now."

Elliot's laughter was low as his hands touched my back, making me jump. I was tense, and I knew he could feel how wound up I was. One of his hands slid down to my behind and the other up to the back of my neck. He kissed me then, and within seconds I was lost to the sweet taste of him.

"A couple of centimetres shy of eight," he answered against my lips.

The tales about boys measuring their junk was apparently true, and somehow that was very unsurprising.

"Elliot," I hummed. "I've never . . . you *know* I'm a virgin."

"And you know I'm one too."

I had only recently found that bit of information out, when we'd had a conversation about sex and our bodies, and it gave me a thrill to think that I would be the first – and hopefully only – girl he would be with.

I licked his lower lip. "I know, I know. I'm just so bloody nervous."

"Shhh," he whispered. "Let me take care of ye, *sasanach*. It will be *my* pleasure, and *yours*."

He kissed me once more and gently eased me back on to the soft duvet of my bed. He didn't bother to get us under the covers and I was glad. I was suddenly too hot to even consider being covered. The feel of Elliot's skin pressed against mine felt so warm, so comforting, so right.

"I have a condom," he murmured. "Just in case ye ever let me love your body."

"Thank God," I breathed as I sucked his plump lower lip into my mouth. "I feel like I'm on fire, I want you so much."

"Yeah?" He nudged my nose with his. "Ye want me to fuck ye?"

"Yes," I hissed. "Yes, please."

"How about I do a little kissin' first?"

Kissing? He wanted to kiss me? Right now, when I was ready and waiting for him with my thighs wide open?

"Kissing?" I repeated with a shake of my head. "My legs are wide open and I'm practically shoving my fanny in your face, Elliot. You can't get much more of an invitation, paddy."

He laughed as he kissed down my neck and paused at my breasts. When I felt the first touch of his hot, wet tongue on my hardened nipples, I changed my mind.

"Kisses," I moaned. "I *love* kisses."

Elliot's chuckle wasn't long-lasting as he showered my breasts with attention. His thumb brushed the one he wasn't tonguing, and the gentle caress had my toes curling.

"That feels *so* good," I hummed as my back arched slightly. "More, I need more."

Elliot moved his lips down to my navel, then to my pubic bone. Anticipation burned within me like a raging fire. His hands touched the insides of my thighs and pushed against them, spreading my legs as far as they would go.

"*Fuck*, ye smell good."

I hadn't considered what I'd smell like, but I was glad it was a scent he was on board with. I could feel his hot breath on my pussy, then suddenly his lips were pressing kisses to my other lips. I groaned as I balled my hands into fists. He was so close, if he moved just a little, his tongue would be on my clit. The throbbing, delicate petal that needed his attention the most.

"Elliot," I growled, my voice sounding husky and full of need. "Stop teasing me. Please."

"But I like to play," he said, his voice sounding deeper than usual. "Can I play with ye, green eyes?"

"Ye can fuck me, *that's* what ye can do!"

"Tell me what ye like and don't like," he urged, one of his hands massaging the inside of my thigh. "Teach me how to please ye. Teach me how to love you, *sasanach*."

My body was so on edge it was about to burst; I hurt with the need for Elliot to touch me with his tongue. I didn't know what kind of sensation to expect, I had no idea if it would be as good as every woman said it was, but I wanted Elliot to make me come and I didn't care how. The aching place between my trembling legs begged to be touched, licked, kissed, sucked.

"Just kiss me already!"

"You're the boss."

Before I could say another word, Elliot's tongue slid up my slick, wet folds and parted them. The moment he touched the swollen bundle of nerves that was driving my body crazy with need, I

28

cried out in delight. I was so wound up that I could already feel myself nearing the edge of release. My eyes were squeezed shut and my spine was rigid.

"Holy Christ," I shouted. "Oh, fuck! Elliot. Faster! *Yes.*"

I had never experienced such a sensation of pleasure in my life, not even when I touched myself. Elliot's mouth was fastened on to my clit and he wasted no time in drawing out gratification with his hot touch. I was speaking words that to my own ears didn't make sense. The faster that talented tongue curled around the pulsing bud, the louder my moans became.

I was breathless and felt my body rising to a point of no return.

"Yes, Elliot. Fuck! Yes, *don't* stop. Keep that pressure. No, not on my lips, on me clit. *Please.*"

His arms hooked around my hips, and his hands clasped together at the base of my stomach. He applied even more pressure when I began to lose control of my body, and used his strength to keep my arse on the mattress as he feasted on me. His fingers bit into my flesh, and the slight pain mixed with the pleasure his tongue was giving me took me to new heights. I arched my back, threw my head back as my lips parted in a silent scream as celestial sensations slammed into me. My body tensed, and sensation fluttered round and round until my lungs gasped for air.

I sucked in several breaths as I flattened myself back against the mattress. My muscles went lax, and for a second I wasn't sure where I was. I felt soft lips travel upwards on my body, then I felt them on my face and mouth.

"Did I do it right?"

Elliot's voice was hot, raspy and thick with need.

"Yes," I breathed. "Fuck, yes. Do it again."

He laughed as he slipped his tongue into my mouth. I was surprised when I tasted a light, salty tang, then I realised that flavour was *me*. It was incredibly erotic and dirty and I loved every second of it.

"Now," I pleaded as I wrapped my arms around his neck. "Love me now. Please."

He moved off of me for just a few seconds as he grabbed his jeans and fumbled with them. Elliot's eyes were all over me as I lay panting, spread open and waiting for him. His eyes never remained on one location for long. They were on my eyes, my mouth, my breasts, between my shaking thighs.

He licked his lips.

"I've dreamed of ye like this. You're so beautiful," he said as he finally found the condom packet and raised it to his mouth. His teeth had just closed over the foil when he paused and seemed to think better of it. He opened the packet with his fingers instead. "Better safe than sorry," he said, winking.

He was just about to roll it on to his throbbing length when I reached for him. "Let me."

He squeezed his eyes shut for a moment before he approached me and handed me the cherry-scented piece of latex. I reached out and touched Elliot's cock, and heard his barely audible hiss. He was rock hard, but his sensitive skin was silky-soft. I took him in my hand and tentatively pumped up and down, twice. Elliot was rigid as he stood before me, allowing my inexperienced touch to undo him.

"Please," he groaned. "I'll come before I get inside ye, Noah."

I looked up at him; his eyes were hooded with desire, his swollen lips were wet and parted as he breathed heavily in and out. I wanted to taste him, even if it was only for a moment . . . this time. I lowered my head and kissed the tip of his cockhead that leaked with pre-cum. Elliot's shocked gasp turned to a deep, low groan when my lips wrapped around him and gently suckled.

"Christ," he hissed as his hips began to jerk gently back and forth. "Noah. Stop. *Mercy*."

I took him as far into my mouth as I could, and I sucked hard as I pulled back and released him with a pop.

"So fuckin' sinful," he growled. "You're perfect."

I smiled as I carefully pinched the tip of the condom and slowly rolled it down the length of him. I wanted to tease him a little more, not torture him, but I thoroughly enjoyed hearing the sounds that escaped his throat and the faces he made when my lips were wrapped around him. It was thrilling, maybe even a little addictive. But I didn't have the chance to place my mouth on him again, because before I could blink I was on my back, thighs spread wide once more, but this time Elliot's body was nestled securely between them.

"Christ," he hissed as he pressed the head of his cock against me and rubbed it through my wet folds. "I can't wait, Noah. I can't."

The gentle brush of him against my clit had my heart hammering in my chest.

"I can't either," I assured him. "Love me."

"I do," he said, lowering his mouth to mine. "I love you, Noah."

In moments, I was lost in his kiss, then I felt himself nudge my opening and finally he eased inside of me. I resisted the urge to allow my body to tense, and I focused instead on Elliot's mouth. When I felt so full I thought I might burst, there was a moment of slight discomfort. I barely noticed it.

"I'm in," he said, his forehead beaded with sweat. "Christ, you're so tight, and wet, and hot. Ye've no idea how much restraint I'm usin' not to move. This is *so* much better than everythin' I ever imagined."

I smiled up at him, the thick fog of love-making descending upon me slowly but surely.

"We fit together perfectly," I whispered. "We're made for each other."

"Yes," Elliot hissed. "Am I hurtin' ye? Be honest."

"For a split second I felt a tiny bit of an ache, but it's nothing, I just feel *you*. Move, take me to Heaven with you."

With a groan Elliot moved his hips back and then forward, gently easing inside of me again. There was no discomfort, just the sensation of being filled to my core. I wrapped my legs around his hips and attached my lips to his neck. He pressed his forehead against my shoulder and slightly bit down on my skin as he pumped in and out, pivoting his hips with each movement until he found an angle that made me cry out with each thrust.

I could barely breathe as we figured out how to love one another's bodies for the first time.

Coherent thought faded out of existence as Elliot replaced slow, gentle movements with hard, fast, skin-slapping thrusts. My senses heightened, and every slight touch of Elliot's lips, teeth – the gentle breeze of his hot breath blowing on my tender flesh – caused me mind-numbing pleasure. I slid my hands up his muscular back, into his hair, and held him to me as I rolled my hips against his. A moan so low and raw crawled up my throat that I felt it all the way down to my toes.

"Elliot," I panted. "Oh God, harder. Faster. I can al-almost—"

The erotic sway of his hips forced me to the edge of sanity. Elliot gasped, the rhythm of his movements faltering for a moment before his fingers bit into my flesh as his hold on me tightened. In his warm embrace, I looked up and found him staring down at me, his breathing jagged and irregular. His heated gaze stole my breath and his thrusts became harder, faster, wilder.

My eyes rolled back.

He hissed my name, his lips brushing against my mouth. "Look at me, *sasanach*."

32

The moment I locked eyes with him, and saw the intensity of the love and hunger shining in the depths of his big ocean blues, I shattered. A harsh cry climbed up my throat as an unexpected climax hit me. Toe-curling pleasure licked my nerve endings until my muscles were lax and sated. Elliot pressed his lips against mine as his body stiffened, his movements jerking. His moan mixed with my own as he stilled above me.

I wasn't sure how long we stayed in that position, but when I opened my eyes, I realised Elliot's face was now buried in my neck and my body was shaking in the aftermath of what we'd just shared. My heart was pounding, and the weight, and heat, of Elliot on top of me was solid and comforting.

I never wanted the moment to end.

"Oh. My. Sweet. Baby. Jesus."

Elliot's muffled, tired laughter reached my ears and made me laugh too.

"Noah." He lifted his head. "You're mine."

"Always," I answered. "You're mine too."

He covered my mouth with his as he gently slid out of my body. I was surprised when I winced a little, because the act of coming together hadn't hurt other than a slight bit of discomfort. Elliot broke our kiss and frowned at me.

"I hurt ye."

"You didn't," I assured him as he looked down and spotted a tinge of blood on his length and between my thighs, and a little on the bed sheets. I had been so wet that it looked like there was more blood than there actually was. "This is normal. This was perfect."

He looked into my eyes, and when he relaxed I knew he believed me. He quickly discarded the used condom as I closed my eyes and came to terms with the fact that I was no longer a virgin. I had given my virginity to Elliot, my boyfriend who loved me, and he had given his to me. I was positively giddy. I jumped when

I felt something warm and wet between my thighs, and I opened my eyes to find Elliot using a washcloth to tend to me. My heart swelled with even more love for him.

When he finished, he joined me in sliding under the duvet and we wrapped our limbs around each other and sighed in satisfaction, contentment and joy.

"Elliot?"

He kissed my neck and hummed in response.

"When I say I love you, I mean that I love you so much that it scares me."

He was silent for a moment, then he moved his head and kissed my cheek.

"Me too, but isn't that a beautiful thing?"

"What?"

"Being part of a love that terrifies us," he answered as his finger drew lazy circles around my now-hardening nipple. "I don't want a love like everyone else has, I want what me parents have. A love that's so deep, pieces of you become part of the other person. I want us to love each other so much that it'll always scare us . . . that's how we'll know we've got somethin' truly special. Somethin' that's always worth fightin' for."

His words touched me in a way that I could never describe, but I spent the next hour loving his body and showing him exactly how much they – he – meant to me, and how much he always would.

CHAPTER THREE
NOAH

Present day . . .

I awoke to gentle humming and soft singing in a language that I did not recognise. I was pulled away from the delicious memory of my boyfriend claiming my body and heart as his for the first time. With a reluctant sigh, I opened my eyes. An off-white ceiling came into view, and it made me groan as memories assaulted me so rapidly that it made my head spin. It wasn't a night terror after all, then. I was in some sort of accident that put me in the hospital, and I'd just woke up from a fifteen-day coma.

It sounded too far-fetched to be believable, but my gut told me that it was the dreaded truth.

"Noah?"

I stared at the face that was hovering over me. I remembered the man. He'd said he was a doctor, but I couldn't remember what his name was.

"Hello there, Noah." He smiled, his eyes searching mine. "Can you tell me where you are?"

"The hospital."

"Which hospital?"

"King's College Hospital." I grunted. "What happened?"

"Do you remember me, Noah?"

I frowned. "Yes, we were talking then it's just blank."

He flashed his penlight in my eyes then said, "You passed out. Just for twenty minutes or so, you're okay."

Only twenty bloody minutes? It felt like I was out for a lot longer than that; my head was filled with a foggy tiredness that I couldn't seem to shake off.

"I remember you mentioned something about a coma before it was lights out." I swallowed as I grimaced in pain. "Am I really okay?"

"You're really okay," the doctor assured me. "It was a lot to take in, I probably would have fainted too."

His attempt at humour, and his grin, did wonders for me. It actually relaxed me a little even though my brain was screaming that I most definitely was *not* okay. I couldn't explain why, but I trusted this man. He had a warm smile and welcoming manner. He said I was okay, so I put my faith in him and believed him. I just hoped I wouldn't come to regret it.

"My family," I suddenly gasped, thinking of my parents and boyfriend. "My partner. Do they know what happen—"

"They know exactly where you are," the doctor interrupted in his calm, soothing voice. "They've been with you around the clock since you were brought into the hospital. When I came on shift earlier, I convinced them to go home and get some rest, take a shower, get some decent food into them and recharge before coming here again tomorrow to spend the day with you."

"Oh," I said, feeling my muscles go lax with relief as his words hit home. "Are they all okay? They weren't in whatever accident I was in, right?"

"Your parents and partner are all perfectly perfect," he assured me. "They're just tired."

I nodded, slowly. "What was your name again? Doctor . . ."

"Abara," he finished.

He gave me some more water to drink and the liquid felt like Heaven as it slid down my dry, sore throat.

"Right." I shifted in the bed, wincing. "Doctor Abara. You aren't going to tell me about the accident I was in, are you?"

When he mentioned it, there was reluctance in his tone though I wasn't sure why.

"I'm going to leave that to your family," he said gently. "It's not my place."

I wondered why it wasn't his place but I didn't linger on it; I was back to focusing on the pain in my head. I lifted my hand to the temple on the left side of my head and groaned, my eyes closing of their own accord. The doctor asked me the pain level on a scale of one to ten, and I told him it was an eight.

"You're a tough woman, Noah."

I opened my eyes.

"I don't feel very tough, sir. I feel the complete opposite, if I'm being honest with you."

Doctor Abara smiled. "You are very tough, and do you want to know why?"

I managed to give him a one-shoulder shrug.

"You just gave what is likely the worst pain you have ever experienced in your life an eight, *that* is why you're tough."

I felt myself smile at his praise. "Thanks, sir."

I began to feel a little better as the minutes ticked by and the medicine the nurse gave me kicked in and took away the heavy pounding in my head; now I just had a painful ache to deal with rather than a constant throb. The painkillers did nothing for the throbbing in my leg though.

"How injured am I?" I quizzed the doctor. "I seem pretty beat up, and I feel it too."

"You are," he answered as he sat on the chair next to my bed. "This will sound like a lengthy list, but you could have been much worse off."

"I'll take your word for it."

"You fractured your tibia in your left leg and had to have surgery. It was a bit of a mess because you have previously fractured the same bone, just in a different location. The surgery went well, and you're healing. You had some tissue damage to your right thigh that was cleaned and stitched. Your abdomen was pierced with glass or a sharp object of some kind, but luckily it wasn't very deep so there was no organ damage, just some ruined tissue that was stitched back together. There were some deep lacerations on your left arm, but nothing serious once cleaned and stitched. You have a dusting of cuts and bruises over your entire body, and you took a hard knock to your head which resulted in twenty-six stitches from your left temple to behind your left ear."

I blinked. "Fucking hell."

"My sentiments exactly," Doctor Abara chuckled. "You are healing, Noah. Many of the minor wounds have already scabbed over, and your stitches have been removed everywhere. Yesterday your stitches in your head came out, the bandage on now is just for the light bleeding that comes with suture removal. I can remove it now."

I was still as the doctor carefully removed the bandage around my skull. When he was finished, I lifted my hand to my temple and gasped as I gently ran my fingertips along a lengthy, jagged scabbed line that reached back to behind my ear. I realised instantly that half of my hair was shaved down to a buzz cut around the area of the wound. The rest of my hair was shorter too, cut up to my shoulders.

"Does it look really bad?"

I heard in my own voice that I was going to cry.

"No," the doctor answered. "You will think it looks awful though."

His honesty brought on a bubble of light laughter, which fought away my impending tears.

"I can get a mirror if you'd—"

"No," I interrupted. "I think I need more time before I can look at it."

I didn't think I'd ever be ready; what my fingers felt scared me. The closed wound felt huge to touch. I could only imagine how it would look.

"That's okay," he assured me. "Remind yourself that everything in your body is healing and will look bad before it gets better. Things could have been so much worse, so try to remember that when you think of all of the things that are wrong right now. The majority of the damage to your body is only surface scrapes; what has you in the ICU is your brain injury."

I had a fucking *brain* injury.

I nodded, slowly. "I wish I could remember what happened to me, but I just can't. Is that normal? To have no memory at all?"

"It's very normal," he assured me. "Amnesia is a common occurrence when it comes to head injuries. You might remember what happened in an hour, in a week or not at all. We can never tell, it's completely up to your body."

I digested that information. I wanted to remember what had happened to me; the blank spot in my memory wasn't something I liked. It made me feel vulnerable. I tried not to worry about my memory not returning, as the possibility of that truly terrified me.

"Your brain has been through a lot, Noah. It's your body's core and it needs its rest, so don't stress about things that may or may not happen, okay?"

Again, I nodded.

"I need to see my family and my boyfriend," I urged. "What time is it? Is it too late to call them?"

"It's just after midnight, and the nurse has already informed them that you have regained consciousness. I imagine they will be barrelling down the motorway to get to you."

I breathed a small laugh. "I imagine that too." I rested my head back. "I woke up earlier, I'm not sure when, but I fell asleep before I could press the Call button. I'm so tired."

"Again," the doctor said, "that is normal. Each time you wake up, you will stay awake for longer and longer periods."

That calmed me down a little. I relaxed back into my bed and looked at the small plasma television on the wall facing me. I asked the doctor to turn it on and he granted my wish within seconds.

"Is the news okay or do you prefer something else?"

"It's fine," I said. "I just want it for the noise right now. I don't like the silence."

As soon as the words left my mouth, I frowned. Since when did I not like silence? I had always enjoyed the peace and quiet that it brought, but now the very thought of silence made a shiver of fear run the length of my spine and I had no idea why.

It wasn't a pleasant feeling.

I focused on the news and watched it for a few minutes until Boris Johnson, the mayor of London, appeared on screen. He was doing a press conference of some kind outside of Number 10, and it went on for ages but I couldn't make sense of it. I looked at the doctor, who was now standing over by the window, writing on my chart.

"The mayor is getting his money's worth today," I joked. "I've never seen him talk so much."

Doctor Abara looked at the screen on the wall, then back to me with raised eyebrows and said, "He's not the mayor any more – he's the prime minister."

Bemused, I asked, "What happened to David Cameron?"

The doctor opened his mouth to speak, but suddenly closed it. For a handful of seconds, he stared at me, unblinking, then he approached the bed. He sat on the chair next to me again and cleared his throat.

"What is your date of birth, Noah?"

He had already asked me that question earlier, so I frowned at him.

"The sixth of March, 1991."

The doctor looked at his chart, then back to me and said, "And how old are you?"

Blinking, I replied, "Twenty-four."

He looked concerned and I had no idea why.

"What year is it?"

I shook my head, though a sharp pain made me regret it.

I grunted. "Why're you asking me that, sir?"

"Can you answer the question, please?"

I exhaled and said, "It's 2015. Why?"

The doctor frowned deeply, and I became worried.

"Sir . . ." I swallowed. "What aren't you telling me? I know something is wrong, I can see it on your—"

"Noah!"

I jumped when I heard my mother's voice from out in the hallway. Instinctively, I tried to get up, but my body protested and rewarded me with a flood of pain. I fell back against the bed groaning, as Doctor Abara gently leaned over me and placed a hand on my shoulder.

"You'll hurt yourself, Noah. Take it easy."

I looked from him to the door when it swung open. My mother stood in doorway, her hand frozen on the handle as her red, puffy eyes stared into mine.

"Mum," I whispered. "Mum!"

In an instant, she was by my side. Her hands were on my face, and then so were her lips and tears. She kissed me all over and sobbed the entire time. I had a tight grip on her arms as I whimpered. She tried to hug me, but I yelped in pain.

"I'm sorry," she wept, and was now careful where to touch me. "Oh, my baby. You're awake, you're okay."

"I'm okay," I assured her. "I'm okay, Mum."

"My heart." She clung to me. "I was so afraid that we lost you too. My baby."

I leaned into her embrace and inhaled her scent. A mixture of honey and vanilla invaded my senses. She had used the same scented shampoo and body wash since I was a child, and I was glad of it because the smell was familiar. It made me feel safe, secure . . . protected. There was a lingering feeling in the back of my mind that I hadn't felt those things in a long time, and I didn't know why.

"I'm okay," I repeated as I kissed my mum's cheek. She pulled up another empty chair right next to my bed. She didn't sit down, instead she kissed my face again and held me. "I promise."

I wasn't sure how much time passed, but when my mother and I separated, Doctor Abara was no longer in the room. It was just me and Mum.

"Where's Dad?"

"He's here." She lowered herself into the chair as she looked over her shoulder. "John! For God's sake! Get *in* here."

Doctor Abara walked in first and it reminded me of my conversation with him before my mum burst into the room. Something was wrong. I knew it was. I could feel it. He was entirely focused on my mother; he wore a serious expression on his face.

"Mrs Ainsley," he said to my mother. "Your husband would like a quick word outside with you."

Mum shot to her feet. "Our baby is awake, and he's outside wanting to talk—"

"Mrs Ainsley," the doctor interrupted quietly. "*Please*, go speak to your husband."

Mum looked from the doctor to me then back to him. My stomach churned when she slowly walked out of the room. The doctor followed her, and I couldn't hear anything that was being said. I stared at the empty doorway waiting for my parents to come back, and when I heard my mother's gasp, my body tensed. Fear spread through me like wildfire.

"What's wrong?" I shouted, not caring that it caused my head to throb. "Mum! Dad!"

My mother came back into the room, but her face was a shade or two paler.

"Please, Mum, tell me what's wrong. I know something has happened, please. Tell me. I can handle it."

That was a lie if I had ever told one. I could barely handle what bits of information I already knew. My hands were shaking, and I couldn't stop it. Mum, who looked a little unsteady on her feet, looked at the doctor, who nodded in what seemed like encouragement. She cleared her throat, came back to my side, and took my hand in hers. She stared at me for a few lingering moments.

"You're okay," she stressed on a shaky breath. "That's all that matters."

I didn't believe her; she had never been a very good liar.

"Okay."

"Your accident caused your coma, but it seems to have caused some memory loss for you too."

Slowly, I nodded. "Yeah, I can't remember the accident."

"And other things."

"What?" I blinked, confused. "What other things?"

"Baby, you . . . you think it's 2015."

43

Her words weren't much more than a whisper, but I heard them. I wasn't sure how long I stared at her, how long it took for me to comprehend what she had said – but when I did, I swallowed.

"Because it *is* 2015." I frowned deeply. "It's March, tomorrow is St Patrick's Day. Or at least it was, that's the last thing I remember. Fifteen days have passed by since then."

Mum began to cry as she shook her head. She opened her mouth to speak but nothing came out. Instead, she gripped my hand tighter.

"No, honey," she managed to say.

"No?" I swallowed. "What do you mean *no*?"

"It's

I couldn't comprehend what she was saying, and I didn't even attempt to.

"No." I squeezed her hand tightly as I shook my head. "I'm twenty-four. It's the sixteenth of March, tomorrow is the seventeenth – or it was before the accident and my coma. Me and Elliot were coming over for dinner . . . remember? You were gonna cook us a roast, with extra stuffing for Elliot. You remember, Mum, right?"

At the mention of my boyfriend, I prayed that he would show up soon because everything was messed up in my head and I needed him more than I had ever needed him in my life. He was my centre, my rock. I had to have him with me to help me make sense of this. To make sense of what my mum was saying to me.

Mum cried harder and I began to panic.

"Dad!" I shouted. "Daddy!"

I hadn't called him that since I was a child, but the terror I felt allowed for nothing less than the cry of a little girl who needed her father.

"Noah." Mum gripped my hand tight. "Listen to me first—"

"Dad," I gasped when he filled the doorway.

My heart constricted with pain as my eyes rolled over him. He was over six foot tall and had always been a heavyset man with thick black hair and a beard to match. The man across from me now was skinny, bald and freshly shaved. His face was slightly gaunt, and he had aged. He was my dad though; I'd know him anywhere.

"Daddy, what's going on? What happened to you?"

I began to cry, fear latching on to me like an octopus's tentacles.

"Baby girl." He crossed the room, his emerald-green eyes glazed over with tears. "Mummy is telling the truth. It's the third of April, 2020."

"No," I said firmly. "*No!*"

Even as I said this, my heart had already accepted my parents' words as the truth. My father had changed more than a person physically could in just fifteen days, but I didn't want to believe that I had lost five years of my life, just like that. I couldn't have lost that much time.

I couldn't have, I had to fight it – I had to do . . . *something*.

"This can't be real," I said, reeling, my stomach churning with sickness. "It just can't be, this is a nightmare. It's not real, it's not."

"We'll get through this together," Mum sniffled, her thumbs gently stroking my knuckles. "I'm never letting us drift apart ever again."

Again?

"What do you mean, Mum?" I questioned as dread filled me. "We've never drifted apart; we've always been close. Always."

The bond I had with my parents was solid; every decision in my life was made with them in mind. The college I went to so I could remain close to them, the flat I eventually moved into, the job I had. Everything revolved around my family because of how much I loved and adored them.

"We have so much to talk about," Dad said, leaning over and softly brushing his fingers against my cheek. "We'll discuss everything, but right now you need to focus on healing, baby girl."

Something was desperately wrong with him. Everything had changed about him – his appearance, his voice, though not his touch or the love for me that shone in his eyes. The soft brush of his fingers on my cheek held so much tenderness it made me want to sob.

"What aren't you telling me?" I asked, searching his worried eyes that were now filled with so much sadness and pain that it made me feel like I was choking. "I know you're hiding something. Please, just tell me. Are you okay?"

Mum burst into tears once more as my dad took my hand in his. I knew it was serious because he didn't even attempt to comfort her; his focus was entirely on me and me alone.

"I'm sick, baby," Dad said, his voice uneven. "I'm really sick."

I felt my heart stop with fear.

"What?" I whispered. "What d'you mean? How sick? What's wrong with you?"

"I . . ." Dad squeezed my hand. "Jesus, how do I say this to my child?"

He wasn't asking me, or my mum, that question; with his head tilted back and his eyes on the ceiling, I knew his question was put to God.

"Sweetheart." Dad exhaled a deep breath and his gaze returned to mine. "There's no easy way to say this."

"Just say it," I pleaded. "Please."

"I have cancer, Noah."

For a moment, I felt absolutely nothing, then my heart started beating faster and a pain stung the centre of my chest. The throb in my head intensified as my mind screamed in denial of what I was hearing.

"Wh-what?" I stammered. "What d'you mean? You're fine, you're okay. You're *okay*, Dad."

Dad squeezed my hand, which was shaking so badly he held it tightly to keep me still. "I have lung cancer, stage two. Don't you worry about me, I'm responding good and well to treatment. I just knew I'd look very different to you when Doctor Abara mentioned your memory loss. I was diagnosed over a year ago now."

Inside, I was screaming, wailing and pleading for him to tell me it was all a lie. On the outside, I was barely breathing. Tears fell down my cheeks, and my throat burned as sobs tried to claw their way to the surface.

"Please," I whimpered. "Please be okay, don't leave me."

"Never." He wrapped his arms around me, and my mum, as gently as he could. "I'm right here with you, and so is Mummy. We're never leaving you again."

There was that word. *Again*. First Mum said she was never letting us drift apart again, and now Dad was saying they were never leaving me again.

"Where's Elliot?" I sniffled. "Is he okay?"

My parents leaned back, shared a look and I jolted with fear.

"Is he okay?" I demanded, raising my voice. "*Is he?*"

"He's fine," Dad said hurriedly. "Elliot's okay, nothing's wrong with him."

"Then why did you look at each other like that when I asked about him? Please, is he really okay?"

"He is." Dad nodded.

"Noah," Mum began with a sniffle. "You and Elliot. You . . . you broke up years ago, honey. Four years ago tomorrow, now that I think of it."

I felt as if a bucket of ice water had been suddenly poured over my entire body. I opened my mouth to challenge those words, but suddenly a man I had never seen before appeared in the doorway of the room. If I had to guess, I'd peg him at six foot even, and to be around thirty years old. He was lean, with mousy-blond hair

47

and eyes so dark they looked black. He was attractive, but his face wasn't handsome, it was pretty. He was dressed in jeans, boots and a jacket. He was breathing heavily, but his eyes were locked on mine. He seemed to know me, as his face broke out into a wide smile, but I had no idea who he was.

"Anderson," Dad said, his voice firm.

My father stood in front of me as if he were protecting me, but I asked him to move aside, which he did reluctantly. I blinked as I stared at the stranger who looked so happy to see me.

"Noah." He took a few rushed steps forward. "Baby, you're awake."

Baby? I thought to myself. *Who is this man to call me baby?*

I looked from this Anderson stranger to my parents, then back to him. My head thumped as it tried to understand what was happening to me. I couldn't take any more surprises. I just couldn't.

"I'm sorry, mister . . . but who the hell are you?"

"It's me, Noah." The man frowned deeply as he took another step forward. "It's Anderson . . . I'm your husband."

CHAPTER FOUR

ELLIOT

"I'm sorry for your loss, son."

I nodded in the direction of the man who was offering his condolences to me. I had no idea who he was, but that was the way of things as of late. I didn't know most of the people who had spoken to me over the last two weeks, but it didn't matter. All of the words were the same in the end, in a roundabout kind of way.

Sorry for your loss.

She was such a ray of light.

She was too good for this world.

God only takes the best, Eli.

That last one always made me grind my teeth to the point of pain. He only took the best . . . Yeah, He did, and He thought fuck everyone else left behind to mourn them. With a grunt, I downed my second whiskey and signalled to the bartender for another. The tanned-skinned woman with soft hazel eyes flashed me a look of concern, but she said nothing as she refilled my glass.

"Thanks, sweetheart."

With a frown on her face, she turned from me to her next customer. I stared down into the brown liquid and hoped it soon brought the darkness upon me that I craved. I needed the numbness that alcohol brought, I needed to escape from the pain I constantly felt, and as of late, that escape was always at the bottom of a bottle.

Noah.

The simplest thought of Noah Ainsley made my heart pound a little faster.

Once upon a time, she was my entire world and I was hers. I closed my eyes when her face filled my mind's eye. Her hair was the colour of spun gold and hung in thick waves to her waist. Her large doe eyes were a mixture of emerald and jade, and framed by long, dark blonde lashes. Her lips that felt as soft as the inside of a rose were always stretched into a beaming smile. Her skin was fair as porcelain and her heart was as pure as gold. If there was anyone that I ever considered perfect, it was Noah.

She was quiet whereas I was loud. She was soft, welcoming and understanding whereas I tended to have my guard up about a lot of things until I felt at ease enough to lower it. She was day and I was night. In many ways, we were total opposites. She was an optimist and I was a realist. Those differences made me love her all the more. She was pure sweetness and I had never felt calmer than when she was by my side.

I opened my eyes and silently cursed myself for thinking of her in the past tense. She was alive and I told myself over and over that she would remain that way. She had to be okay . . . I didn't know what I would do if she wasn't. I couldn't lose her . . . I'd already lost a piece of my heart – if Noah died, I had no reason for living.

"Dumbarse," I muttered to myself. "She fuckin' hates ye."

Noah was the love of my life, and four years ago I made a mistake that ruined our relationship and her trust in me. In the end, it all led to her marrying another man.

Don't think about it.

I took a gulp of my drink, no longer noticing the liquid burning its way down my throat.

"Irish," a familiar voice behind me said as a hand slid on to my shoulder and squeezed. "My guy, you can't keep doing this do yourself."

I downed the contents of my glass, wishing I was alone so I could wallow in peace.

"I don't need a lecture, AJ." My voice was raspy even to my own ears, but it made my friend sigh. "I need a drinkin' buddy, pull up a stool."

He did as I asked, but he got a glass of water instead of a whiskey and it made me frown. I turned my head and looked at him. He stared right back at me as he picked up his glass of water and drank from it. I'd known Ajax Edwards since I'd moved to Dulwich, South London, with my mother, father and eleven-year-old sister, when I was a couple months shy of eighteen.

Joining school in my senior year in the middle of term made me stick out like a sore thumb, and so did my accent. I was from Southside Dublin, Ireland, and it was something my classmates at school never let me forget. I'd been given the nickname "Leprechaun" three hours into my first day at school by Ajax, and when I punched the shite out of him for it, the nickname quickly changed simply to "Irish". We'd been best friends ever since he laughed and told me I had a good right hook for a paddy as I helped him to his feet.

I looked from AJ back down to my glass and felt my frown deepen. "It's empty, when did that happen?"

"Good, I'm glad it's empty," AJ said with a grunt. "Because this glass of water is *yours*."

I hadn't noticed he'd got two glasses of water off of the bartender. I stared at it then him, and noted the glint of determination in his grey eyes. I took the glass to appease him. I was in no mood for a fight, I hadn't got the energy for it and he seemed to know it too.

"Why're ye not drinkin' the good stuff?" I questioned. "It's Friday night."

"I've been working all day. I finished this evening and was beginning to look forward to four days of relaxing before I'm back on watch. Then your sorry self went and popped into my mind. I was at a late dinner with Dani and she knew I was thinking about you, and she told me to come and find you. It took me two hours and eight different pubs until I spotted you in here. You could have made my mission *much* easier if you'd answered your fuckin' phone, idiot."

I blinked. Slowly.

"It's on vibrate, I didn't feel it ring. Be sure to tell Dani I'm sorry I robbed her of ye."

"Dani knows the drill. We aren't together, we're just fuck buddies."

"Bullshit," I snorted. "Ye warned her not to be off shaggin' other blokes or ye'd kill them."

"So?" AJ grunted. "She told me to steer clear of other women too."

"That sounds an awful lot like a relationship to me."

"Don't be talkin' about relationships, it gives me hives." AJ shivered dramatically. "Just drink your water like a good little lad so I can get you back home. You need to sober up and get your head screwed back on tight so you can come back to work at the station soon. You only got six weeks of compassionate leave because Stitch spoke on your behalf. Once you register time with a counsellor to sort your head out, you'll be back on watch in no time."

The thought of it made me want to vomit.

"Work doesn't matter any more. Nothin' matters."

AJ clapped his hand against my back as he sighed.

"Eli, I know you're hurting, brother. This has got to *stop* though. Your mum and dad have been through hell and back. Your mum can't handle something happening to you and you know it. Bailey wouldn't want this, man."

I closed my eyes and forced myself to remain still. I balled my hands into fists and felt my body go rigid. The sound of her name made every cell in my body tense.

"Don't," I pleaded. "Don't say her name. Just *don't*. Please."

The reason I drank, the reason I craved numbness was *because* of Bailey. Her pretty face flashed across my mind. Blue eyes that matched my own, twin dimples in her cheeks, and pearly whites that'd have a man in love still stop and stare when she smiled. My beautiful, pain-in-the-arse little sister who died fifteen days ago. My little sister who I couldn't save. My little sister who I had to bury long before her time.

My chest constricted with agonising pain every single time her name was mentioned or her sweet face appeared in my mind. I was her big brother; I was supposed to protect her, and I didn't. I chose another over her, and I hated myself for it because there was a part of me that didn't regret my choice.

I had to live with that.

"Fine," AJ grunted. "I'll leave it alone, for now. Has there been any update on Noah?"

My senses seemed to heighten at the mention of her name. The weight of those two syllables on me may as well have been the weight of the entire fucking world. We hadn't spoken to one another in four years, but that changed nothing about how I felt about her. I was still in love with her while she was married to another man.

"No." I swallowed. "The last Mr Ainsley told me was that the MRI and CAT scans showed good activity, so we know she isn't brain-dead. She's just . . . sleepin'. They don't know when she'll wake up from her coma, it's a waitin' game now. It's up to Noah what happens next."

The thought of Noah and what she was currently suffering made me scrub my face with my hands as my mind drifted back to one of the worst nights of my entire life. I couldn't believe it was only fifteen days ago; it seemed like years instead of mere days. I should have known something was going to go wrong. It was night-time when it happened, one of the darkest nights I could remember in a long time.

My worst memories happened at night.

When I was eight, my father had shaken me awake in the early hours to tell me that my grandfather had passed away. Four nights later, he awakened me again to tell me that my grandmother had died in her sleep. When I was ten, a man dressed all in black broke into our house as we slept and tried to hurt my mother before my father saved her and called the guards.

When I got the call from Noah I shouldn't have been surprised, but I was. Everything in my life had changed since that night. Every little thing.

Bad things always happened in the dark.

CHAPTER FIVE

ELLIOT

"Irish?"

I jumped as AJ's voice interrupted my thoughts. I pinched the bridge of my nose as a slight pounding formed in my temples. I felt like crawling under a table and rocking myself back and forth until the images of what I'd seen left my mind, but they never did. They were always there. Silently haunting me.

"You were thinking of that night again, weren't you?"

I drank down another glass of water that appeared in front of me.

"Leave it alone," I said, my voice sounding husky to my own ears. "I don't wanna talk about it, mate. I really don't."

"I know you don't, and that's why you *have* to talk about it," AJ pressed. "You did everything you could, mate. Every little thing. It's not your fault."

But it was my fault. I should have moved faster once I got Noah free, I shouldn't have lingered for those few seconds after I made sure that she was breathing, and I definitely shouldn't have wasted time by kissing her.

"I hovered with Noah when I got her free." I cleared my throat. "Those precious seconds could have saved me sister."

"Elliot." AJ moved closer to me. "You *read* the coroner's report and you saw Bailey for yourself. She died on impact. She was gone long before the fire had the chance to claim her, brother."

I looked into my empty glass.

"If you hadn't of stayed with Noah for those few seconds you'd be dead too, your parents would have buried both of you."

"Please, bud." I swallowed, not being able to listen to his reasoning. "I can't talk about it; it rips me apart inside when I think about her. I'm barely holdin' it together. Please."

"Okay," AJ said, his hand giving my shoulder another squeeze. "Come on, let's get you home. Being here isn't helping you tonight."

Unfortunately, AJ was right about that. Tonight, the drink didn't black out my demons or bring me the numbness I craved. All it seemed to be doing was giving me a headache, and that was one thing I could do without. I downed another glass of water AJ got me then got to my feet. Out of the corner of my eye I watched as AJ held his hands out as if he was preparing to catch me should I fall. I wanted to laugh but found my throat couldn't quite figure out how to do that any more.

"I'm grand, AJ," I sighed as I lifted my arm and patted his. "Barely tipsy. No need to be me shoulder to lean on, the drink didn't hit the spot tonight."

"I'm always here with one to lean on whether you need it or not," he said with a grunt. "I'm always gonna be here for you, mate. You're my brother and I love you."

"I love you too, brother." I gave him a hug. "I'll be okay," I lied with ease. "I'm just in a bad place right now. I've never . . . I've never felt so lost before, man."

Before AJ could say a word, I felt my phone vibrate in my pocket. Hurriedly, I took it out and my pulse spiked when my mother's face flashed across the screen.

"Ma!" I answered, panicked. "What's wrong? Are ye okay?"

"I'm fine," she answered hurriedly. "I'm okay, honey."

I gripped AJ's arm as relief flooded me. "Ma, it's late. What—"

"Elliot," she interrupted tentatively. "Samantha just called me. It's Noah."

Fear just about stopped my heart beating at the mention of Noah. Her mother wouldn't call so late unless it was something serious.

"What, Ma?" I rasped as my free hand clenched into a fist at my side. "Please, don't say it. She can't be dead too. Please."

AJ placed his hands behind his head as he stared at me with unblinking eyes.

"No, she's alive," Ma sniffled. "She's awake, but somethin' awful is wrong with her."

She was alive. I could have vomited with relief. Whatever was wrong with Noah didn't matter because she was alive. I wasn't going to bury her like I'd had to do with Bailey. She was alive.

"What is it?" I demanded. "Is she paralysed?"

"No, physically she's fine. It's her mind, honey."

"Her mind?" My frowned deepened. "What the devil d'ye mean, Ma?"

"She can't remember anythin'." Ma began to cry. "She thinks it's 2015. Samantha and John are so worried."

I tried to digest my mother's words, but it seemed too far-fetched to be real. I shook my head, trying my best to clear it so I could think. I repeated what my mother had said in my head before I spoke out loud.

"2015?" I said, feeling bewildered. "You're tellin' me that Noah can't remember the last *five years* of her life? She thinks she's twenty-four again?"

"Amnesia," AJ muttered, lowering his arms. "She has amnesia."

"Worse than that. She thinks you're still her boyfriend, she had no idea John was sick . . . she doesn't know about the accident that killed . . . that took our Bailey and almost her too. She doesn't even know her own husband. She's doesn't know about anythin' and she's really, *really* scared. She's askin' for *you*, honey. Samantha and John need ye to go to King's College Hospital. Noah needs ye, Elliot. Will ye go to her?"

"I'm comin'," I said as I looked at AJ, who gave me a nod. "I'm comin' to her, Ma."

I wasn't sure who hung up first, me or my mother, and I didn't care.

"My car's outside, Irish," AJ said as he jogged after me. "I'll get you to Noah in twenty minutes, brother."

I didn't answer him or acknowledge what he said in any way. The only person on my mind was Noah – she was hurt, and she needed me. That was all that mattered. I forced all of the scary thoughts of what might happen to her out of my head and focused on the sweet memory that began it all. The moment she became mine without even realising it.

CHAPTER SIX
ELLIOT

Eighteen years old . . .

"Fifty quid says you puke on her instead of kissing her."

I cut AJ a look before I returned my gaze to Noah. She sat across from me at the bonfire looking like a goddess under the orange glow of the flames. She wasn't wearing anything special – blue jeans, a baggy black hoodie and a pair of roughed-up black runners. Her golden locks were pulled up into a ponytail, and wisps of golden-blonde hair hung down around her face as a gentle breeze flowed by.

"I'm shittin' meself." I rubbed my sweaty palms on my jeans. "What if she laughs in me face?"

"Mate," AJ sighed as he passed me a can of cider. "I know women, okay? Trust me. Noah likes you."

I didn't respond but I couldn't stop my heart from leaping at his words. He'd known I was into Noah before I said the words out loud, and a huge part of me wanted to trust his intuition that Noah liked me too, but my stomach was a mess of nerves and I refused to allow myself to hope. I had been playing it cool around her since the moment I first met her, and if she knew what went on inside my head when I thought of her, she'd probably shove her foot up my arse.

"The suspense is killing me and I'm just a bystander," AJ snickered as he took a swig of his drink. "Go over there and kiss her."

My eyes slid to his as I scowled. "I can't just *kiss* her, ye eejit."

AJ hesitated a moment, then said, "Ask her permission first, *then* kiss her."

"That's a bit better," I snorted, shaking my head. "Look, I'm just gonna go and speak to her and ease that I'm interested in her into the conversation. I'm thinkin' practically. Kissin' is like the fifth step or somethin'."

AJ downed his cider and crushed his can in his fist.

"That's your problem – you think too much."

"Says the man who thinks too little."

He punched my arm and I laughed. I felt eyes on me in that moment, and my gut told me they were the colour of emerald and jade. I turned my gaze towards Noah, and when our eyes locked I saw that she visibly flinched, but she didn't look away from me. I realised that this was my moment to speak to her and tell her how I felt. I lifted my hand and crooked my finger at her. Her eyes widened ever so slightly and I felt my lips twitch, and I nodded when she pointed to her chest and mouthed the word "Me?"

"Good luck, bud," AJ murmured as he got to his feet and jogged around to the seat on the log that Noah had vacated. He got stuck into chatting up some girls from our year and forgot all about me. I forgot about him too when my eyes moved back to Noah as she came over and sat in the spot AJ had just left.

"Heya, Elliot."

She didn't look at me as she spoke; she busied herself with adjusting her jumper and clasping her hands together and resting them on her knees, before changing her mind and folding her arms across her chest. I blinked when I realised that she was nervous. This knowledge calmed me immensely.

"Heya," I replied with a chuckle. "Ye looked a little lost over there."

She tucked tendrils of stray hair behind her ear. "I know. I'm friends with a lot of the girls, we just never hang out outside of school. I feel a little awkward being here."

I had noticed that about her. At first, I thought she was being made an outcast by our classmates, but I quickly learned Noah was the one who decided to keep to herself. I only worked my way into her tiny circle because she was table-partnered with AJ in almost every class.

"I'm glad ye came," I told her. "I'd have been sad if ye didn't show up."

The glow of the fire illuminated Noah's cheeks as they flushed a soft red. I felt my pulse increase at the sight. Her blush-stained cheeks only elevated her beauty in my eyes. I wanted to kiss her so badly that it made my throat run dry.

"I'm sure you've said that to all the girls."

She chuckled and still wouldn't make eye contact with me, so before I could stop myself, I reached out and tipped her chin up with my fingers until her eyes snapped to mine.

"Why won't ye look at me?"

She swallowed and parted her lips in a sensual little O.

"I am looking at you," she blurted. "This is me looking at you."

Her entire face was crimson now and it made me smile, which seemed to fluster Noah altogether. That was the moment I began to believe what AJ had been telling me all this time. Noah liked me . . . she liked me like I liked her.

"I have to tell ye somethin', Noah."

Her eyes widened, and before I could say anything else, she exclaimed, "This is for you!"

I dropped my hand to my thigh and blinked as she reached into her hoodie pocket, pulled out a small box and thrust it in my direction. I stared down at it for a moment before I cleared my throat and took the box.

"For me?"

"Of course," Noah said, her voice a little breathless. "You *are* the birthday boy."

"Thank you." I looked up at her. "I love it."

"You . . . you haven't even opened the box, Elliot."

"Doesn't matter," I said. "I still love it."

I looked down at the box again to give her a moment to herself, because her skin was still flushed and she looked completely out of sorts from sitting in front of me. I wanted to calm her like she calmed me.

I lifted the lid of the box and stared down at a little silver flower.

"It's a calla lily, otherwise known as the Easter lily in your country," Noah explained. "I didn't know what you'd like so I got something I liked and put it on a necklace. I love flowers, and I didn't want to get you something as common as a shamrock or a four-leaf clover, so instead I picked a calla lily. I read it's used in Ireland as a symbol of remembrance for those who died in the 1916 Risings."

I brushed my finger over the small pendant.

"You hate it," Noah murmured. "I'm sorry, it was stupid—"

"I love it." I looked up at her. "I absolutely love it. Me great-great-granda almost died in the Risings. He passed away long before I was born, but when me granda was alive, he told me stories about his granda . . . I think of the man I knew through those tales when I look at this. Thank you, *sasanach*."

Noah ducked her head, but I saw her smile.

"Put it on me."

I took the necklace from the box and handed it to her before she could say no. I turned my back to her and waited. Over the laughter and shouting of our friends, I heard Noah's breathing shift as she moved closer to me. I clenched my hands to keep myself still when I felt her hot breath on the back of my neck. She placed the chain around me and carefully secured it with the clasp.

"There."

Her voice was barely a whisper. I turned to face her and found we were face-to-face. I looked down at the lips I wanted to kiss so badly before looking up into the eyes I was coming to adore. I had never felt such an attraction to a girl before, but it wasn't just physical – I liked how quiet she was, how she looked away and smiled when she received a compliment, and I definitely liked that she put so much thought into giving me a gift that had meaning.

"Noah—"

"What does *sasanach* mean?"

I hadn't realised I had called her it.

"It means 'English' in *Gaeilge*. When someone addressed an English person with *sasanach* in the old days, it was usually said with disgust."

Noah raised an eyebrow. "When you call me it, what do you say it with?"

"Fondness," I answered instantly. "Me little *sasanach*."

She exhaled a breath that fanned my face. I smelled mint in the air and I wanted to taste it.

"You're beautiful."

Noah's lips parted.

"You're so beautiful that I can't stop thinkin' about ye. I like how reserved ye are, how thoughtful and at peace ye always seem to be. I *love* your smile. Ye remind me of a still ocean, calm and collected but underneath there is so much more to you."

"Elliot," she whispered.

I lifted my hand to her cheek and gently ran my thumb over her soft, glowing skin.

"Noah," I murmured. "Can I kiss ye? Please?"

She was trembling. "Yes."

The word had barely passed her lips before I covered them with my own. Noah's sharp intake of breath gave me the chance to explore further. I slid my tongue inside her mouth and almost groaned when hers gently moved against mine. Her lips were soft to the touch; I wanted to spend the rest of my days kissing them.

I reached out and gripped her waist and tugged her closer to me. Her hands went to my shoulders before she slowly slid them up my neck and into my hair as she gave up complete control of our kiss to me. I felt her trust in me and I knew that this kiss was going to be one of many. We parted when cheers and whoops sounded. I heard AJ's voice over everyone's, and I silently swore to bash him later for ending the moment I had craved.

"Oh my God."

I pressed my forehead to Noah's, feeling the heat of her skin and basking in it.

"Ignore them," I told her. "I am."

"How? They're all looking at us."

"I only see you."

Noah's eyes shifted to mine. "Elliot . . . I like you so much. I didn't think . . . I had no idea you liked me back."

"Green eyes, I was in the same position. I thought ye didn't know I existed."

"*Me?*" she blinked. "Elliot, I wasn't sure if you knew I was a girl or not. You were always so chill around me."

"I was playin' it cool."

"Cool?" Noah repeated. "More like bloody freezing."

I laughed and so did she. I felt her body relax under my touch as she got used to being close to me while also having an audience. She was still nervous and unsure of herself and the situation, so she lifted her hand to my necklace and played with it. I liked that it seemed to calm her just like she calmed me.

"I had no idea how blue your eyes were," she murmured, more to herself than to me. "Blue like the ocean."

The look on her face as she searched mine made me tense.

"I want another kiss," I almost groaned. "It *is* me birthday, y'know?"

Noah's eyes darted back to mine as laughter and cheering sounded around us. A smile teased the corners of her lips, and with her eyes gleaming, she said, "You can kiss me any time you want, paddy. I could use the luck of the Irish."

CHAPTER SEVEN

NOAH

Present day . . .

All eyes were on me. I felt the stares of everyone in the room burning a hole in me, but I was only focused on one person. This man who stood before me was a stranger, one I had never laid eyes on in the entirety of my life.

"My husband?" I could hear the disbelief in my voice as I spoke the words. "You're not my husband – I've never been married."

He stared at me unblinking, and I watched as confusion filled his dark eyes. I was surprised when an expression of deep hurt marred his features. He shook his head as if not believing what he was hearing. He took a step forward but he looked a little unsteady on his feet.

"Noah, baby."

I flinched at the endearment. I had never liked that pet name, but this man seemed so comfortable with calling me it, like he had done it a million times before. He looked from me to my parents and back again. I didn't look away from him once.

"I'm sorry, but I don't know you, mister."

"Baby," he repeated, his face having lost all colour. "I'm your *husband*."

I nearly collided with my mother as I attempted to sit upright.

"What *is* this?" I demanded, groaning as my arm suddenly stung. I looked down and noticed I had pulled the IV out and was now bleeding.

"She's hurt herself," Mum said to Doctor Abara as she gently eased me back against my bed. The doctor removed the line completely and pressed a cotton ball against the wound and held it in place with a bit of tape.

"A new line will need to be placed in your other arm," he said to me. I nodded and tried to look around him to the stranger who claimed he was my husband.

"Where's Elliot?" I demanded. "Where is he?"

"Elliot?" Anderson almost gaped at me in shock. "Your *ex*?"

Your ex.

"My ex?" I tensed. "What the hell do you mean Elliot is my ex? He's my boyfriend!"

My mother's earlier words echoed in my mind. She'd said Elliot and I broke up four years ago, but that couldn't have been true. It couldn't. Elliot and I were in love. We were planning a future together.

"No, he's n-not!" Anderson stammered, looking completely lost and panicked. "I'm your *husband*. You're Noah Riley. Mr Ainsley, Mrs Ainsley . . . *tell her*."

I looked to my parents and waited for them to deny this man's claim, but they didn't. They looked from him to me and their expressions were ones of sorrow.

"No," I whispered. "Mum, tell me this is a lie. A sick joke. Please."

Fat tears slid down her cheeks. I stared at her, waiting for her to tell me the words I so desperately needed to hear, but she didn't. She took my hand in hers and gave it a comforting squeeze.

"You and Anderson married over three years ago now." She rubbed her thumb over my skin when I stilled. "You and Elliot broke up and never got back together, honey. I'm so sorry, sweetheart."

I felt the moment that my heart broke in two. A pain that was body-consuming stabbed at my chest, and before I knew what was happening, I turned to the side of my bed and vomited until I was dry-heaving. My mother was in a state of panic.

"I want Elliot," I cried as I retched. "I *need* him."

"I already called his mum when I was out in the hallway earlier with your dad. She'll get him here, honey. He'll be here."

"The hell he will!" Anderson spluttered as my father grabbed a tissue to wipe my mouth with. "Noah made it clear years ago that she doesn't want to be anywhere near him. That arsehole isn't getting close to her so he can hurt her again. I won't allow it."

Anderson's words were like a hard slap to my face.

What on earth had happened in my life for me to marry someone other than my Elliot – and worse, to never want to see or be near him again? I stared at Anderson as tears rolled down my cheeks, and I looked at Doctor Abara as he crossed the room, stood in front of Anderson and spoke in hushed tones. Then I looked back at my parents and found their gazes on me. They were worried over me. I could see the fear in their eyes, and it made me feel sick.

I wanted to scream.

In my head, I was comforting myself that this was all wrong, that it was some sort of massive mistake, but everyone in front of me was saying otherwise. My parents had informed me that Elliot and I broke up; my dad said he had cancer and I could see that he was telling the truth based on his appearance. Boris Johnson was no longer the mayor of London, he was now the prime minister of the United Kingdom. Everything that I had heard – and seen – matched up with what everyone was telling me.

I felt like I was a stranger in my own body, in my own life, and I didn't know who to believe because I couldn't even believe myself. The reality I thought I was living was no longer my own. I felt lost. I needed Elliot, I needed to speak to him, but when I looked at Anderson – who was still speaking to my doctor – his words suddenly replayed in my head. He'd said I had made it clear years ago that I didn't want to be near Elliot and that he had hurt me in some way. I was seemingly married to this man, so there had to be a reason why he would say that.

I was so confused. I didn't know who or what to believe.

"Why is this happening to me?" I wept. "What'd I do to deserve this?"

Dad leaned down, careful to avoid the mess I'd made, and gently kissed my head. "Don't do this to yourself. You want someone to blame, something that can make sense of all of this, but sometimes bad things just happen, sweetheart."

I wiped my cheeks. "But this didn't just happen, Dad. I'm not like this because I woke up one morning and just suddenly lost my memory. I was in an accident, an accident I know nothing about, you . . . you *have* to tell me what happened."

My parents shared a look and I didn't miss the expression of dread and worry that passed between them. I didn't think I could handle any more surprises, but I needed to know what had happened to me. Having no memory of what I'd been through left me feeling naked and vulnerable.

"Please," I pressed as my head fell back against my pillow. "I need to know why I'm lying in this bed with an entirely different life than what I think I have. I deserve to know, and you both should be the people to tell me. You're my parents."

"A car accident," Mum suddenly said. "You were in a car accident."

My eyes widened. "But I can't drive . . . can I?"

"No, you can't drive." Dad scrubbed his face with his hands. "You were in the passenger seat of a taxi when the accident occurred. Black ice on the road caused the accident. The driver is fine."

My head swam as I processed what my parents were saying. Questions seemed to pile on top of one another, but before I had a chance to ask one, another person ran into the room. A person who made my whole body respond with a jump.

"Elliot!"

My heart practically burst the second I clapped eyes on him, then an ache took root. My Elliot . . . he looked so different. To me, it felt like I had just seen him, but he wasn't as I remembered him. His chocolate-brown hair that used to be neat all over was longer – shaggy atop of his head while tightly trimmed to the sides of his scalp. He had thick facial hair now and he seemed bulkier, but I wasn't sure if it was weight he'd gained or muscle. He seemed so much bigger, his presence that of a grown man. He looked tired and just as shocked to see me as I was him, but what caught me off guard the most about him were his ocean-blue eyes.

They were no longer lit with a passion for life. They appeared dull, empty . . . dead.

It frightened me.

"Elliot," I repeated. "Everything is so wrong."

He took a step towards me but Anderson got in his way.

"She's confused," Anderson stated. "Don't come in here and take advantage of my wife, McKenna. You *know* she doesn't want you any more."

I gasped, shocked to hear those words leave Anderson's mouth.

"I don't u-understand," I stammered. "Anderson . . . what are you saying?"

"He isn't in your life, baby," he answered me without looking away from Elliot. "He's a piece of shit and I won't let him break your heart again."

Again?

Anderson invaded Elliot's space and shoved him backwards. He was tall, but Elliot had four or five inches on him and was *so* much broader than him. They looked close in age but Elliot just seemed bigger in every way compared to Anderson.

"No!" I shouted, panicked. "No! Please, Elliot. I don't know this man!"

Anderson spun to face me; his face was void of colour. He looked like he was physically hurt by my words, and a sense of remorse washed over me. I didn't know this man, and I didn't understand any of what was being discussed, but he was defending me against Elliot. He believed Elliot was a threat of some kind to me and he clearly didn't want me to get hurt, and because of that I felt somewhat of a connection to him.

"Noah," said Anderson.

"I'm sorry," I said to him hurriedly. "I'm *so* sorry. I don't want to hurt you, I truly don't. I just don't know you – you'll have to . . . you'll have to give me some time because this is all too much and I can't think."

My head ached so badly I placed both hands on my temples and whimpered. My entire skull throbbed to the point where I could hear my own heartbeat in my ears. The pain was so intense I felt as if I couldn't breathe around it.

"Mr Riley, I think it's best if you leave," Doctor Abara said to Anderson. "This is entirely overwhelming for your wife – you must understand."

I couldn't concentrate on what the doctor was saying, I was busy breathing in and out to help the pain in my head. I was so glad the doctor had told him to leave because I didn't think I could do it; he looked so upset and hurt that I didn't know who he was. I didn't want to cause any more pain.

"Should I leave too, Mrs Ainsley?"

My heart just about stopped. I forced my eyes open and focused on Elliot as the room began to sway. I noticed bodies behind him, a nurse and two men in uniform. Security would be my guess.

"Elliot," I rasped. "Please don't leave me."

I was sure I wanted Anderson to leave just so I could have a moment to try to sort out what was happening in my head, but I needed Elliot to stay. Even though he looked very different from how I remembered, he was familiar to me and I needed that at the moment. I needed something, someone, that I knew. I needed my rock.

Elliot closed his eyes as he clenched his hands into fists. To Anderson he said, "She wants me to stay, so I'm stayin'."

"She's *my* wife," Anderson replied. "She'll remember why *I'm* her husband and not you soon enough!"

I watched the interaction between them and I felt the loathing they had for one another. It wasn't simply dislike; it was raw hate, and it was clearly felt by both of them with a passion.

"Until then, I'm stayin' right here." Elliot slowly turned his head and glared at Anderson. "You're upsettin' her by being here, so leave. *Now.*"

Anderson turned to me one final time, looking like he had a million things to say, before he left the room with the two security guards following behind. I watched him go, and part of me felt horrible and cruel. I had no memory of this man, but he knew me as his wife. I had no idea what was going through his head and I selfishly didn't want to know, because I was having a hard enough time trying to figure out how I felt – let alone how everyone else was feeling.

"Elliot," I said. "None of this feels real to me. I can't be married to that man. I don't even know him."

Everyone stood back while nurses entered the room and cleaned up the mess I made from vomiting. I apologised over and over, but they assured me it wasn't a big deal. Elliot took the empty seat to my right when everything was cleaned away, his eyes on the hand I had grabbed without thinking. With his free hand he was rubbing his fingertips over my knuckles, an action he did whenever he felt anxious. It made my heart clench.

His touch on my knuckles felt more intimate than ever, and it seemed touching me still helped to relax him. It comforted me to know that this hadn't changed for Elliot even though we were no longer together and I was married to another man.

I found myself wondering if Elliot's life had changed just as mine had.

"Elliot, why is another man saying he's my husband? Why aren't *you* my husband? I really don't understand any of this. What happened to us?"

Before I got the last word out, the terrible ache spread across my head once again. I moaned and leaned back, covering my forehead with my free hand.

"Noah? Look at me, green eyes."

I opened my eyes as my hand fell away from my face.

"Ye have a lot of questions, you're scared and nothin' is makin' any sense to ye. I know, and I wish I could make it all better for you, but I can't. Ye need to relax and stop puttin' your brain through its paces. It's workin' overtime right now and ye need to give it a minute to get back into the swing of things."

I sniffled as my eyes filled with tears.

"No." Elliot swallowed as he brought his face to mine and wiped away the tears on my cheeks. I smelled whiskey on his breath. "I'm here. Don't be scared, I'm right here."

His closeness made my breath hitch.

"Don't leave me," I pleaded as I put a hand on the back of his neck. "Please, I need you so much."

"I'm not goin' anywhere, Nono. Go ahead and rest. I'll be right here when ye wake up."

"We'll *all* be here, love," Dad said, his tone firm.

"Promise, Dad?"

"Promise."

The mention of rest had my eyelids suddenly feeling heavy and impossible to hold open. I tried my hardest to fight the seductive lure of sleep, but I was no match for it. Every bit of strength I had was drained from me. I let my eyes flutter shut with Elliot's words falling with me into darkness.

"I'm never leavin' ye again, green eyes. I don't care what the hell happens. I've been apart from ye long enough, you're my person. I'll be fuckin' damned if I let ye slip through me fingers again."

CHAPTER EIGHT

ELLIOT

This was real.

I was sitting next to Noah Ainsley – Riley – and holding her soft, supple hand in mine as she slept with the morning sunlight shining on her beautiful face. She'd been asleep for almost ten hours and I couldn't stop looking at her for fear that she'd suddenly up and disappear into thin air. I'd had dreams like this, ones that felt so vivid and lifelike that I wanted to sleep forever to stay in the moment where it was just me and her, like old times. This wasn't a dream though – somehow it was my reality. I couldn't stop staring at her. I noticed things that I remembered about her and things that I didn't.

Her golden-blonde hair was cut up to her shoulders and no longer hung in waves down the length of her back. It was buzzed on the left side of her head, close to her ear to allow her wound to be cleaned and stitched closed. Her thick, fair eyebrows were as I had always known them, but a small, straight scar cut through the right one leaving a tiny gap between the hairs. I wondered how she'd got that scar.

She had a dusting of red and pink little dots and lines on her face. I remembered her having cuts on her face that night in the car; they had since scabbed over and healed, leaving behind little reminders that would eventually fade to white.

Her fair skin looked dull, and I wasn't sure if it had looked like that before her accident or *because* of the accident. The main thing I noticed about her was that she had gained weight. Noah had always been tiny to me; she stood at five foot ten but had always been slim. I often teased her that the only curves she had were when she bent over. I hadn't seen her in person in years, so I wasn't sure when her body had made this change. I'd spotted her now and again for fleeting moments – when I was in Tesco, or driving down the motorway as I passed her and her husband's car – but never close like this.

"Are you okay, Elliot?"

I looked up at Mr Ainsley and my stomach clenched.

I'd known him over a decade and to see him at the place he was at in life hurt me. I visited them often because not long after I'd lost Noah, they lost her too. Anderson Riley was Noah's husband, and though I had no proof, I knew he was the reason she'd turned her back on her family after they got together. That miserable bastard took my heart from me and I hated him for it, but I knew what I hated most was the fact that I'd pushed her into his open arms.

I forced him from my mind.

"Honestly, sir, no," I answered on a sigh. "I'm hurtin' for her, she's so scared and confused. I honestly don't know what I can do for her and I'm worried about it."

"For now, just being here is enough, honey," Mrs Ainsley said.

I found myself nodding. "I can't imagine what she's goin' through . . . to be told she has a whole other life to the one she thinks she had. She must be terrified."

"She is," Mr Ainsley said. "She is scared, and she wanted *you.* Your presence will help her."

"But sir . . . if she thinks it's 2015 then she thinks that I'm—"

"Her boyfriend," Mrs Ainsley finished.

I felt lower than dirt when excitement and hope rippled through me. How many times had I wished that my and Noah's memories could be wiped just so we could turn back time and be together like we were before everything became fucked up? I had got my wish, and the price I had to pay for it wasn't worth it. Nothing was worth my sister's life and Noah's mental and physical health.

Nothing.

I swallowed. "I'm tryin' to figure out in me head how I should approach her, approach the situation. I don't wanna confuse her, and I definitely don't wanna hurt her – but she's married, and I'm not her husband."

Nothing I did could change that fact.

"One day at a time, Elliot." Mrs Ainsley offered me a small smile. "We can do no more than that."

I looked back at Noah. "Does she know about Bailey?"

"No," Mr Ainsley answered. "We told her she was in a car accident in a taxi, but we've not mentioned anything about your sister. I'm afraid, son . . . I don't know how she'll handle it. Doctor Abara is worried. When things get to be too much for her, she faints. Her brain is under a lot of stress right now; the swelling on her brain is causing her headaches that bring her serious pain."

The thought of her being in pain made me feel so helpless.

"I understand," I said. "It's hard for me to say I completely agree, but I understand."

"You think we should tell her, even with the state she's in?"

"It's not that." I rubbed a hand over my face. "It's the keeping-it-from-her part that makes me uneasy. I was always honest with Noah, and the one time I wasn't it blew up in me face and then our relationship ended. It makes me hesitant about keepin' things from her that I *know* she'll want to know."

Mr Ainsley reached out and gave my shoulder a squeeze.

"This is for her own good."

"I know," I relented. "That's why I'm goin' to keep me mouth shut because it's for her benefit. You and the doc are right, it's best to keep it from her until she's stable. She was always close with me sister, and even though she pushed us all away after we broke up, I know she still loved her. Knowin' Bailey is gone will devastate her, even more so when she finds out she was in the wreck *with* her."

"You're right," Mr Ainsley said as he dropped his arm to his side. "This will sound stupid, Eli, but how are you holding up?"

"Not good, sir."

I didn't even try to lie. I had known Noah's parents since I was eighteen, way back when I first met Noah. Not long after we started dating, she introduced me to them and her parents took an instant liking to me, and I formed a strong bond with them both.

"I'm strugglin'," I admitted as I kept my eyes on Noah's face. "I miss me sister more than I ever thought possible. There's this constant ache in me chest. Sometimes it feels like I miss her so much that I can't breathe."

"Elliot," Mrs Ainsley said softly. "Honey, don't keep what you're feeling bottled up. Your mum . . . she told me you've been drinking a lot."

I rubbed my eyes with my free hand and cleared my throat.

"Tryin' to find an escape is all," I answered with a sad smile. "I just dunno what to do. I know everyone says time heals the pain when you lose someone ye love so it's not as body-consumin', but I dunno how to get to a place where I can think of Bailey and still be able to breathe. It's *my* fault. If I was quicker about gettin' Noah out of the car, I could've saved her."

"Elliot." Mr Ainsley locked eyes with me as Mrs Ainsley took my free hand in hers. "Do *not* do this to yourself. You did what your whole crew thought was impossible: you got Noah out of the car before it exploded. You risked your life and went against orders to save my child. It breaks my heart that we lost Bailey, but that's *not* your fault. It was an accident, Bailey just lost control of the car on a patch of black ice. She died on impact – even if you'd got her out of the car, she still wouldn't be here, son."

A huge part of my brain told me that Mr Ainsley was right, but then I thought of the voicemail Noah had left me.

"Ye heard the voicemail though, they were scared of somethin'. Noah was frantic."

"Unless Noah gets her memory back, we'll never know." Mrs Ainsley patted my hand. "There's nothing to indicate it was anything other than an accident – you read the police report."

"I know."

I had read the report multiple times and revisited the scene five days in a row, and everything pointed to Bailey losing control of the car. I'd seen hundreds of accidents like it before, but something about the whole situation didn't sit right with me . . . and it was all because of the voicemail that Noah had left me.

She had said the words "to kill" in her message, and she'd screamed for Bailey to slow down and shouted that she was driving too fast multiple times. There were so many unanswered questions. Why was my sister with Noah in the first place? They had been close once upon a time, like sisters, but that had changed after Noah and I broke up, so them being together was a red flag.

Why was Bailey driving so fast in the middle of a blackout while black ice covered the roads? She wouldn't have unless someone had given her reason to. She wasn't a reckless driver – she was cautious. It was entirely out of character for my sister; she was never in trouble with anyone other than me. Part of me thought Bailey had been helping Noah in some way, I just didn't know what way that was.

Maybe I was grasping at straws, trying to find a reason as to why my sister died. I had to remind myself that there was no reason – if there even was one – that was good enough for my sister to be buried six feet under the ground.

Not a single one.

"I don't want it to have just been an accident, because then I have no one to blame."

"Son." The hand squeezed mine. "You're grieving and you have anger that Bailey was taken from us, and you're trying to find a reason to put the blame on something – someone – to vent that anger. It was an accident."

I exhaled a deep breath. "Maybe you're right . . . me mind is just goin' back to the voicemail and then the dials in me head turn and I think of all sorts."

"That's expected," Mrs Ainsley said. "I'd be worried if you just accepted everything and got on with your life, Elliot. It's normal for you to want to find a reason as to why everything has happened. You're looking for closure."

Closure? So soon after my sister died? I wasn't sure if I agreed with Mrs Ainsley or not. My mind was too messed up to straighten anything out long enough for me to form a coherent thought in regards to the whole situation. Adding Noah and her memory loss to the list was just another ripple in an already unsettled pond.

"I can't help Bailey now," I said, rubbing my thumb over Noah's knuckles. "But I can help Noah, and I promise the both of you that I will do anythin' I can to help get her through this."

"We know you will," Mr Ainsley said with a reassuring smile. "Anderson will be an issue. It's terrible of me to say that about the man, but Noah didn't react well to seeing him. With her currently not remembering him, keeping him away from her for the time being shouldn't be a problem. Doctor Abara agrees that his presence is upsetting for her."

"D'ye *want* to keep him away from her?" I questioned. "Because she won't want that. I know her, she's shocked right now, but when she realises her situation is real, she's gonna want to speak to the man she's married to."

I hated admitting to myself that she was someone else's wife, and speaking the words out loud left a sour taste in my mouth.

"I know." Mr Ainsley nodded. "I just think that, right now, his presence will do more damage than good. He was clearly upset that she didn't remember him, and I feel for him but I have to think of my child first."

"She didn't look like she knew him at all," I admitted, trying not to sound too glad about that fact. "I wasn't sure if I was simply just *hopin'* she didn't because I still have feelings for her, but she looked right through him. I saw it in her eyes, she had no fuckin' clue who he was."

"She has no knowledge of anything that has happened over the last five years. She told me she thought it was the sixteenth of March, 2015. She talked about you and her coming over for dinner on St Patrick's Day."

"March," I repeated. "That was more than a year before we broke up. Jesus, *today* is four years since we broke up!"

Neither of Noah's parents spoke as I tried to make sense of what was happening.

"She really does believe we're still together, doesn't she?"

"Yes," they answered in unison.

"Jesus." I rubbed my face with my free hand. "Just . . . Jesus."

"I know," Mrs Ainsley said with a sad smile. "This is unbelievable and a lot to take in, but we have to accept the cards we've been dealt and go with it. For Noah."

"For Noah," I echoed.

"Don't think too far ahead, Elliot," Mr Ainsley said. "We're taking it minute by minute with her. She doesn't know that she drifted apart from us. She doesn't know Anderson, or the reason you both broke up. She doesn't know about Bailey's passing, or

81

that she herself moved out of town and quit her job. We have to ease her into everything and we have to take baby steps, not just for her, but for us too. We've been given a chance to start over with her . . . We *all* have."

A chance that I would be taking with both hands, because now that I had the opportunity to have Noah back in my life, I wasn't about to let it – or her – go. I had lost Bailey, and I wasn't letting anyone take Noah away from me again. Not even her husband.

CHAPTER NINE

NOAH

Warm fluid snaked down my cheek into the cracked corner of my mouth. I caught the blood with my tongue, and the metallic saltiness invaded my senses. Black dots spotted my vision and my ears rang. I forced myself to stand tall and unflinching as I watched the faceless man's hand swing in a wide arc before it connected with my other cheek.

My head violently jerked to the side, and my neck cracked in protest. Steeling myself not to cry out in pain, I looked forward, stared up into his obscured face, trying to gauge his mood. Many nights just like this one had given me experience – enough that it had taught me that if I cried out, he enjoyed it more, and the beating would last longer.

"Where were you, Noah?" The voice sounded like Elliot's and it was filled with a rage that terrified me. "Tell me!"

"Just taking a walk," I answered, pressing a shaking hand to my throbbing face. "I swear."

"Liar!" he growled, advancing on me. "I'll teach you not to tell me lies!"

I threw my hands up in front of my face just as he swung his closed fist at me and connected with my jaw, bringing me to my knees as a pain-laced scream finally tore free of my throat only to be met with harsh laughter.

I felt hands holding mine before consciousness fully gripped me. As comforting as the touch was, it didn't take away the fear that lingered inside of me. I felt confused, worried and slightly numb. I didn't understand why I'd had a dream that felt as real as it did harsh. I wasn't sure what had brought it on, or why I'd thought of it in the first place – all I knew was that it made me feel scared and incredibly uneasy.

Fingertips brushed over the knuckles of my left hand, and the familiarity of it made my heart thud against my chest. I was aware of where I was before I opened my eyes. Everything came rushing back at me in waves. I lazily lifted my eyelids, and as my head ached it made me groan, filling the silence.

"Mum?"

"Noah?" Mum's voice drew my attention to my right. "You're okay, sweetie. I'm here."

"My head," I murmured as I squinted against the sunlight in the room. "My head. It's bloody killing me."

"I'll get the nurse; the doctor had medication prescribed before the staff rotated this morning."

My eyes followed my father as he walked out of the room, and I was filled with deep concern for him. I remembered that he'd told me he was sick – stage two lung cancer, he had said. I needed to talk to him about it, I needed to talk to my parents about a lot of things. My mind was a mess, I didn't know where to start and who to start with.

"Noah?"

My eyes landed on him before he finished saying my name, and I felt myself smile the moment I looked into his ocean-blue eyes. There was worry dwelling inside of them, but when I smiled it seemed to seep away until the eyes I looked into softened.

"Elliot," I breathed, my relief at seeing him evident in my voice. "I'm so happy you didn't leave."

When I could no longer stay awake the night before, I had been worried that he would leave me. This was a whirlwind of a situation for me and I knew that it was for him too, because he was apparently no longer part of my life. He didn't have to stay with me, but he had done – and I was so thankful because I needed him. That need for him was a tough pill for me to swallow because as much as I hated the fact, everything was different about Elliot and about me. The point I was at in my life apparently had no place for Elliot and I didn't know what to do about that.

To me he was still my person, my safe place . . . but the person I was in 2020 had turned her back on Elliot and I wasn't yet sure whether or not it was for my own good. I thought about the nightmare I had just woken up from – the man who'd hurt me sounded like Elliot, but he had never ever hurt me before . . . not in the memories I had of him, anyway. I struggled with what I should do. Should I push him away like I had clearly already done, or should I kick all my concerns away because his presence, his touch, soothed me so deeply?

I did the only thing I could do – I went with my gut, and my gut told me that Elliot was still the same man I believed he was in my mind and heart. I told myself my dream was just a figment of my imagination, and I prayed that I was right.

"I told ye I wasn't goin' anywhere, green eyes."

"I know." I swallowed. "I was just scared that maybe you'd change your mind."

"I haven't," he said as he gave my hand a squeeze. "And I won't."

I relaxed. "Good. Was I asleep long? It's morning."

"It's just gone five past eleven," Mum answered me. "You fell asleep around one this morning. You were exhausted."

"I still feel like I could sleep for a year," I answered honestly. "I had a weird nightmare. I'm so tired it's hard to think straight."

85

I looked around the room. "I still feel kind of disorientated, if I'm being honest. I can't believe this is happening to me."

"I know, honey." Mum gave my other hand a squeeze. "But we're all here for you. You aren't alone."

"Have you three been here all night?"

"Of course." Mum looked at me as if I'd gone mad. "Where else would we be?"

"Mum." I frowned. "You'll make yourself sick if you don't eat and sleep regularly. Dad looks in no condition to be at my beck and call."

"She's right." Elliot looked at my mum. "I'll stay with her if you and Mr Ainsley want to go and get some rest."

I snorted. "You aren't invincible either, Mr Firefighter." I felt myself suddenly go pale as I stared at Elliot. "Are you even a fireman any more?"

"Yes, I am," he answered, then leaned forward. "What's wrong?"

Unexpected tears fell from my eyes and splashed on to my cheeks.

"I don't know anything about your life now," I sniffled. "Everything is different now. Everything."

Elliot used his hands to wipe away my tears while Mum got up to grab me some tissues.

"Well, that's an easy fix. Start askin' questions, good lookin'. Ye were always good at that."

I managed a laugh as I sniffled again, ignoring the ache in my head.

"Are AJ and everyone else okay?" I questioned. "Your mum, your dad, Bailey? Is everyone okay?"

There was a flicker of something in Elliot's eyes, but before I could guess what it was, it was gone.

"Good as can be," he answered with a smile. "Everyone sends ye well wishes. They've all visited at some point when ye were slee-pin' off your coma, lazy bones."

Hearing everyone was okay was a relief.

"Where is Bails? I'm surprised she's not here with you."

Bailey was like Elliot's shadow; she had been from the time she was little.

"Australia," Elliot said. "She lives in Australia. She moved away two years ago; she has a boyfriend there. We sort of had a fallin' out, we don't speak much any more."

Shock tore through me.

"*What?*" I blinked. "Why? What the hell happened?"

"Things changed, Noah." He shrugged, not looking me in the eye. "Me and me parents weren't happy with her movin' away to be with someone she met online, and she rebelled against us, I guess."

I couldn't believe it.

"Phone her," I demanded. "Let me speak to her."

"Can't." He cleared his throat. "We don't have her number; she calls us when she wants to check in to let us know everything is okay. I . . . I spoke to her briefly yesterday; she won't call again for a few months. That's the way things are right now."

I was flabbergasted beyond belief. That didn't sound a thing like the Bailey I knew. She was close to her family, she adored Elliot, and she loved me just about as much as I loved her. I called her my sister and she called me hers. To think she could have fallen out with her family and moved halfway around the world was unbelievable . . . but the situation I'd awoken to was something I still couldn't believe myself, so I couldn't dismiss what Elliot said about his sister – no matter how much I wanted to.

"This is . . . I can't wrap my head around this."

"You will in time," Elliot said softly. "It's just a change ye weren't expectin'."

He was right about that.

"Has anyone else moved away?" I quizzed. "AJ?"

"AJ leave me side?" Elliot looked at me and grinned. "Not likely. That boy loves me."

I snorted. "I'm glad to hear your bromance is still going strong."

I looked at his face and couldn't get past his beard, and when he noticed he huffed with laughter.

"Go ahead." He waved his hand, amusement dancing in his eyes. "Get the slaggin' underway, I'm sure ye've plenty to say about the beard. Don't hold back, lemme hear it."

With a grin I said, "It looks like a cat up and died on your mush."

Elliot's deep laughter made me smile, and my mum beamed as she came back to my side and handed me a tissue.

"Did ye lose a bet with AJ or something?" I continued, dabbing my cheeks until they were dry. "It seems like something he'd enjoy seeing on your face."

"Ye wound me, woman," he said, still grinning. "Believe it or not, it was me own choice to grow it out."

"Make the choice to shave it off then, or trim it at least. You look like a bloody lumberjack or a Wookiee. Should I call you Chewbacca now?"

Elliot's laughter made my stomach erupt with butterflies. God, I loved his laugh. It was full of life and always brought a smile to my face when I heard it. Even now I was beaming, though my head felt like it was splitting in two. His laughter made me feel better. *He* made me feel better.

"I'll make ye a deal, I'll *trim* me beard and keep up the maintenance if ye promise to take things easy while you're recoverin'. What d'ye say to that, *sasanach*?"

Sasanach. The familiarity of the teasing nickname he'd always called me enveloped me like a warm, cosy blanket.

I winked. "You've got yourself a deal, Chewie."

My dad returned as Elliot began to laugh again; he looked between the pair of us and his whole face seemed to light up. I guessed he liked the fact that Elliot was cheering me up. I liked it too.

"How are we feeling this morning?"

I looked at the doorway as a young nurse entered; her skin was fairer than mine and her hair was a sunset orange, tied up in a bun on the top of her head. She had a bright smile on her freckled face which I found comforting.

"Sore head," I answered.

"Any other pain?"

I hesitated. "Honestly, I'm sore all over but it's my head that's the worst. My leg hurts like the devil too."

"This medication is strong, so it'll likely make you a little drowsy, but that's no harm, you need plenty of rest."

She moved to my right side, hung up an IV bag and connected it to a new line in my arm. A nurse must have put it in after I fell asleep last night.

"Is it normal for me to feel so sleepy?" I yawned. "I've been asleep for over two weeks."

The nurse smiled. "You've been in a coma, honey. That's not a regular sleep; your brain is recovering and the best way for it to do that is for you to—"

"Rest," I finished with a grin. "I've got to get plenty of rest."

"You've got it in one."

I looked back to the hand Elliot was holding. He was squeezing it a little as he watched the nurse. He didn't release his grip until she left the room.

"Hey," I said, causing him to look up. "I'm okay, you know?"

"I know."

He was lying, I could see that he was worried about me. It was in his eyes, and in Mum's and Dad's eyes too. I couldn't imagine what it had been like for them to be told my memory was wiped. They must be feeling like they were walking on eggshells around me.

"Am I still in the ICU?"

"Yes," Dad answered. "You'll be moved to a different ward in a few days if your condition continues to improve."

I nodded slowly, then I shifted and hissed when I felt a slight stinging in between my legs.

"Between my legs." I winced. "What *is* that?"

Elliot lifted up the blanket before I finished speaking. He moved my gown up my legs, but he didn't part my thighs. He relaxed and looked at me.

"Ye have a catheter . . . in you."

Of all of the things for him to see when we were in such a situation . . . it made my face burn.

I groaned. "Bloody hell."

"Hush now," Mum said as she fixed my blanket back around me. "You were in a coma, a catheter is necessary. Don't be embarrassed."

"Easy for you to say." I yawned. "Is the catheter bag in view?"

"It is for me," Elliot answered. "I just noticed it."

I groaned again. "Is it full?"

"Yup." He winked. "Your kidneys are workin' well it appears."

"Pig." I playfully scowled at his teasing. "I think I'm gonna close my eyes for a minute, if the doctor or nurse comes back in, tell them to take it out, okay? I can get to the bathroom by myself now that I'm awake, even if I have to crawl. I know I look broken, but I promise I'm not . . . or not entirely, anyway."

Elliot leaned back in his chair, and his hand let go of mine so he could salute me.

"Anythin' else, boss?"

"Yeah," I murmured, closing my eyes. "Trim the beard, Chewie."

The ache in my head faded away to nothing, allowing me to enjoy the low laughter of the people I loved most in the world as I drifted off into a deep, peaceful slumber.

CHAPTER TEN
ELLIOT

Twenty-one years old . . .

"Bailey McKenna!" I hollered up the stairs. "If you're not down these bleedin' steps in ten seconds or less, I'm gonna—"

"I'm comin'!" My sister's screech cut me off. "I'm comin', ye feckin' ape. Keep your knickers on."

"Give over," Ma called from the kitchen. "The pair of ye."

I crossed my arms over my chest and scowled at the red-headed pixie as she descended the stairs, pulling her hair back into a half-bun thing. I didn't understand it – half of her hair was tied up while the other half was down and curled.

"Your head looks like a pineapple with that hair."

She shoved by me. "Like you'd know *anythin'* about style."

I followed her into the kitchen where our parents were eating lunch.

"What're ye talkin' about?" I quizzed as I held my hands out. "I *am* style. D'ye not see what I'm wearin'?"

I had on a standard grey Calvin Klein tracksuit, paired with brand-new white Nike runners. I looked fresh.

The kid barely glanced my way. "Please, ye've got common MW style."

I blinked. "Common *what* style?"

"MW." She grinned, then mouthed the words "man whore".

I never wanted those words to leave my baby sister's mouth again.

I glared at her. "Let those words slip past your lips again, and I'm staplin' them together."

"Ma! Elliot's threatenin' me!"

"Elliot, don't threaten your sister."

I grinned. "Sorry, baby."

My sister scowled. "I'm *not* a baby, ye hav'te stop callin' me that!"

"Ye'll always be me little baby, *baby*."

Bailey cringed. "Whatever, are ye ready to go?"

"Am *I* ready?" I repeated on a laugh. "I've been waitin' for *you* the last half an hour."

"Ye were rushin' me," she said, scowling. "When ye rush me, it stresses me out and I move slower. Fact."

"The only fact is you're doin' me head in. Get out into me car. Now."

"You're not the boss of me!" she huffed, as she did exactly what I'd told her to do.

She shouted her goodbyes to our parents, then stormed out of the house with me following behind. I smiled as I trotted along after her. This was typical behaviour with my sister; she acted like I was the bane of her existence, but in reality she loved me and always wanted to hang out with me. I had always been close with her, but when we moved from our home in Dublin to London, she didn't take the transition very well and our bond deepened. I was seven years older than her and I had always been protective of her – and that instinct only grew as she got older.

When we got into my car and I reminded her to buckle up, she rolled her eyes. "You're such a loser, Eli. It's always 'buckle up, buckle up'."

I shook my head, not understanding her logic.

"Only losers *don't* wear their seat belt. Ye've no idea how many scenes I've been to that someone could have survived if only they were wearin' one."

Bailey didn't reply, instead she buckled her seat belt.

"I can't even believe I'm doin' this," I grumbled as I put the car in reverse. I put my hand on the back of Bailey's headrest and looked over my shoulder as I backed out of the driveway. "Of all things in the world she wanted to do with me, *why* does it have to be this?"

"Don't be such a bloke," Bailey said, her tone clipped. "Ye love Noah, and she never told ye she wanted to do this, she told me and *I* told you."

"Still," I sighed, putting the car in first gear. "Dance lessons. I'm feckin' dreadin' it."

"Not just any dance lessons." Bailey shimmied her shoulders. "*Salsa* lessons."

I glanced at her as we drove. She looked entirely happy about salsa lessons, and it irked me.

"You're enjoyin' this, aren't ye?"

"More than ye'll ever know, big brother."

I snorted. "She better appreciate this – she bleedin' well better."

It was mine and Noah's three-year anniversary, and up until a few weeks ago I'd had no idea what to do for it. Noah didn't like bags, jewellery or shoes. I had more clothes and runners than she did. The only thing she actively bought was make-up, but I'd checked her dressing table in our bedroom and she was stocked up on everything. Apparently, Superdrug had a half-off sale and she'd gone a bit mad on her way home from work recently, which left me with limited options as to what to get her as a present.

I was stuck, until I happened to mention it to my sister, who then told me that Noah had mentioned that she wanted to take dance lessons with me for fun, but had never told me because she thought I'd say no. She thought right – I would have said no . . . but I'd let my kid sister bully me into arranging four weeks' worth of lessons beginning on the afternoon of our third anniversary.

Today.

"Ye know she'll be happy with anythin' ye get her, Eli," Bailey said. "Noah is so in love with you that if ye picked wildflowers for her, she'd be over the moon."

I smiled. "I know. She's smitten with me, right?"

"Right." My sister chuckled. "But you're equally as smitten with her. I *still* can't believe ye asked the first girl ye've ever liked to be your girlfriend. I didn't think ye had it in ye."

"Ha ha." I grinned when Bailey laughed. "Ye should learn from me. I knew what I wanted and went for it with Noah. There was no point in beatin' around the bush when I knew she was my one."

"*How* did ye know though?" Bailey asked, turning her body slightly to face me. "Was it love at first sight?"

"Love? No. Lust? Yep."

"Ew! I'm fourteen, don't talk to me about how ye sex up Noah. She's practically me *sister*."

She sounded revolted at the very thought.

"Let me finish," I laughed. "I saw her before she saw me. It was me first day in school the week after we moved here, and she was sittin' on the basketball court outside – she was readin' a book and eatin' an apple. I wasn't sure what caught me eye first, how captivated she was by what she was readin' or how her hair seemed to shine like gold as the sun hit it. Either way, I was instantly attracted to her . . . and because I had no clue what to do about it, I ignored her for the first few days at school."

"That was almost poetic until ye got to the end, dumbarse."

I shook my head, amused.

"She liked me too, but I didn't realise it," I continued. "I caught her lookin' at me a few times, and when I started to pal around with AJ and realised she was his friend too, I started to plan ahead."

"What'd ye do?" my sister quizzed. "Bully her until she loved ye?"

"What the hell? *No*. That's toxic, Bailey. No boy will treat ye like shite if he truly likes ye . . . If one ever does, tell me and I'll kill him."

"Yeah, yeah, continue with your story."

"There's not a whole lot to it. We were friends and we grew closer; we had a bonfire on me eighteenth birthday and I kissed her that night. We started casually datin', then I asked her to be me girlfriend a few months later. We haven't looked back since."

"That's like a Wattpad story . . . except nothin' dramatic happened before ye both got together. It's a little anticlimactic, I won't lie."

I laughed. "That's what's perfect about Noah. She doesn't play mind games and she doesn't fight with me just for the hell of it. She calms me in a way I didn't know I needed to be calmed. I've never met anyone like her and I never want to. She's my one."

"I should have brought a bucket," Bailey teased. "All that sweet talkin' may as well be honey drippin' from your lips."

I rolled my eyes. "I don't even know why I'm lettin' ye come along."

"Ye had no choice," Bailey answered as she tapped away on her phone. "Ye need someone to record her face when ye surprise her, and since AJ is on watch at the station today, I'm all ye've got, loser."

"*Stop* callin' me that."

She snorted, then she shamelessly took about twenty-seven selfies before she smiled and bobbed her head happily, obviously liking one out of the whole fucking film reel.

"This one is Instagram-worthy."

I stopped at a red light and glanced at her as she chuckled.

"Oh my God, I posted twenty seconds ago and he's already liked the picture."

My big-brother senses began to tingle as my hands tightened around the steering wheel.

"He?" I repeated. "Who is *he*?"

"A lad from school." She shrugged. "Pretty sure he likes me. He double-taps every picture on me Instagram and always comments . . . Ha! Look, he commented too."

She showed me her phone, and I read the words the little creep wrote.

So sxy.

"He forgot the E, the dumbarse. Stay away from boys who can't spell easy words."

"He's only lookin' at the menu, Elliot, not orderin' from it."

I felt my jaw drop. "Little boys like that can't afford to order what you're sellin' on your menu. Which, let me be very fuckin' clear, is absolutely *nothing*."

My sister giggled, rolled her eyes, then flipped her hair over her shoulder, dismissing me.

"I will *not* be ignored," I protested. "You're fourteen. Ye don't get a menu yet. Your restaurant isn't openin' for *years*."

My sister burst out laughing as a car beeped its horn behind us. I realised the light was green, held my hand up in apology to the car behind, shifted into gear and drove.

"I'm serious, Bailey. Stay away from boys, we're no good at that age . . . at any age, really."

My sister chuckled. "I'll be frigid until I'm eighty if ye get your way."

"Eighty is still too young in my humble opinion."

"You're full of it."

I grinned.

Ten minutes later we parked in town and I rang Noah.

"Hey," she answered on the third ring. "Where are you?"

"Hey, gorgeous, just got into town."

"I'm in the town centre where you told me to meet you. I got off work a bit earlier."

"I'll be right there, don't move."

I hung up as Bailey spotted her.

"She's there," she squealed. "Right there."

I looked to where Bailey was pointing. Noah was standing outside H&M, looking at the outfits on display in the window.

"Sit here on this bench," I said to my sister as we got out of the car. "I'll bring her across usin' the pedestrian crossin', so point your phone that way. Make sure ye start recordin', okay?"

She saluted me. "On it, boss!"

I nodded, turned and jogged across the road, after checking for cars.

"Noah," I called.

She heard me and turned around. When she spotted me, she smiled, and for a moment my breath caught in my throat. She was beautiful with her long, wavy blonde hair, her huge green eyes and her thin but delicate pink lips.

"How did I get to be so lucky to have a girlfriend like you?" I asked her when she reached me and slid her arms around my waist.

"You're Irish." She grinned up at me. "That's all the luck you need."

Amused, I kissed her forehead. "How was work?"

"Not so good." Her smile faltered. "I thought Helen was gonna discuss the manager position with me, but she gave Lesley the promotion instead."

I blinked. "But ye've been workin' at her shop for two years; you're her best worker."

Noah shrugged. "Lesley's older than me by ten years and has more experience."

"That's bollocks," I stated. "Ye came up with fifteen new arrangements for Helen since ye started workin' there. The pieces ye did at that funeral last month were gorgeous, and ye did them by yourself because Lesley was off sick."

Noah smiled up at me. "You're my champion."

"I'm pissed off is what I am." I tucked her hair behind her ear. "Stick it out at the place for a few more years. I've saved up a few grand and I'll save up some more. I'm gonna buy ye your own flower shop one day, one that *you'll* run and call the shots in."

Noah leaned up on her tiptoes and puckered her lips, so I lowered my head the rest of the way and kissed her. She relaxed against me as I deepened our kiss ever so slightly. When I pulled back, I grinned down at her. Her eyes were closed, and she looked happy. That was my Noah – even if she'd had a shitty day, she didn't dwell on it.

"Are ye ready for your surprise?"

Her eyes popped open. "Yes, sir, I am."

"Three years already," I whistled as I took her hand and led her towards the crossing. The light was with us so we crossed the road, and I stood on Noah's left so she wouldn't have a full view of Bailey. "Where has the time gone?"

"I know," Noah chuckled. "I swear it was yesterday when you told me you loved me for the first time."

"Ah," I mused. "The very day ye broke up with me before I even asked ye to be me missus, if I remember correctly."

Noah's cheeks heated as she playfully shoved me. "Don't bring it up."

Smiling, I moved behind her and turned her to face the dance studio.

"Happy anniversary, *sasanach*."

There was a prolonged moment of silence that I wasn't sure was a good or a bad thing.

"We're going to watch a dance?"

"Nope, we're takin' salsa lessons."

"Salsa lessons?" Noah looked over her shoulder and blinked. "Of all things to do on our anniversary, you picked *salsa lessons*?"

I felt my smile drop away and my gut churn.

"But . . . but didn't ye tell Bailey that ye'd love it if we took lessons together but ye never asked because ye figured I'd say no?"

Noah shook her head. "No, never."

I furrowed my brow in confusion, then widened my eyes to the point of pain.

"Bailey McKenna!"

I spun to face her and found her still sitting on the bench a few metres away, her phone pointed in my and Noah's direction.

"Bailey's here?"

"Ye filthy liar!" I shouted at my sister. "Ye stitched me up!"

"Oh," Noah giggled as she moved to my side. "The little devil!"

My sister laughed so hard she fell off the bench and on to her behind, which concerned me for only a moment because she never stopped laughing. In my mind, I was imagining all of the ways I was going to redden her arse for embarrassing me like this in front of my girl, but when I realised that Noah was laughing, I relaxed for about a second.

"It's not funny." I looked at her and frowned. "She lied to me."

"She took the piss outta you, more like," Noah snickered as she moved by me and helped a still-laughing Bailey to her feet. "You got him good."

"I really did, but what's better is ye both actually have to take the classes . . . he already paid two hundred quid for it. No refunds."

My sister jumped behind Noah when I made a play to strangle her then and there. It was hard to be mad at her; she had tears rolling down her face from laughing, and the smile it put on Noah's face made it worth the money, and humiliation. Barely.

"I can't believe this." I rubbed my face with my hands. "Two hundred quid for two lessons a week for four weeks."

"Oh my God." Noah covered her mouth with her hand. "Four weeks? You're mental."

I was beginning to think I was.

"I thought this was what *you* wanted."

Noah lowered her hand to her side. "I know. That's why you're getting lucky tonight."

My mood instantly brightened.

"Vomit." Bailey lowered her phone. "I'm gonna projectile vomit if this conversation continues."

Noah blushed and nudged my sister. "Trickster."

"It was a good one though, wasn't it?" Bailey beamed, certainly pleased with herself. "I didn't think he'd believe me. I've kept a straight face about it for weeks, Nono. *Weeks.*"

"Witch," I growled at her.

Unbothered, Bailey bounced towards the entrance of the studio. "Let's go, ladies! Class starts soon."

Noah was clearly interested, because she hurried after Bailey while I dragged my feet wishing for the day to be over so I could get my hands on Noah and then go to sleep. I was tired of women and it was only three in the afternoon. The day rapidly went from bad to fucking worse. I couldn't do the simplest of steps because they weren't fucking simple at all; it was rocket science in the form of dance and I hated it.

Noah was thoroughly enjoying it, and every time I messed up, Bailey cracked up as she watched from the side of the room. She had recorded so many of my fuck-ups that I warned her I'd break her phone if she didn't put it away. She was on her feet and was copying what the woman was doing with her hips, rolling them from side to side.

"Salsa, Elliot." She shimmied her shoulders. "Let's *salsa*."

I glowered at her, but couldn't stop my lips from twitching when Noah laughed.

"I swear," I growled. "I'll get ye back for this, baby."

Bailey clapped her hands together. "I can't wait."

Looking from her to Noah, I grumbled, "She *always* has to get the last fuckin' word."

My girlfriend wiggled her eyebrows. "Let's *salsa*."

I groaned as Noah laughed and got us back into our starting position. I was a truly horrible dancer – even the instructor told me that to my face halfway through the class, and I was certain she was meant to keep comments like that to herself for the amount of money I was paying her.

"Sorry," I said for the tenth time as I stepped on Noah's foot. "I'm *so* fuckin' bad at this."

"Stop concentrating on your feet and focus on rolling your hips. Your feet will follow."

"The only thing I know how to do good and well with my hips is thrust back and forward. I never learned how to roll anything other than a blunt."

Noah tipped her head back and laughed, and that was it – that was the moment we lost our balance.

One second we were dancing, or trying to dance, the next I was running through the doors of the ER with Bailey hot on my heels, as Noah was wheeled in ahead of us on a trolley with her foot twisted at an unnatural angle. It was broken, I knew it from the second I saw it. My sister was sobbing and had been since the moment I tripped Noah up and we both fell to the ground and she'd heard that godawful crunch.

I jumped when Noah screamed.

"Deep inhales," the paramedic said as he held the tube for the gas back up to her mouth. "Nice, big inhales, Noah."

She listened to him as she was wheeled into a cubicle at the back of the ER. Bailey gripped my hand tightly as we hovered outside the now-closed curtain. I knew each patient was only allowed to have one visitor in the ER, but I wasn't leaving my sister outside on her own so I avoided a few of the nurses' gazes and hugged Bailey to me. She was so short that the top of her head stopped at my chest.

I'd had to leave Noah to go in the ambulance on her own so I could drive my car to the hospital, and Bailey was too terrified to go with her.

"Stop cryin'," I'd told her as they put Noah in the ambulance. "She'll be okay."

"Stop doing that!" Noah moaned. "Oh! I sound like a man . . . why do I sound like a man?"

Bailey had looked up at me, her blue eyes wide with worry.

"What's wrong with her?"

"It's the gas," I answered. "It's numbin' the pain, but it's makin' her all loopy. It's normal."

Now, the paramedics completed their handover of Noah to the care of the hospital, and once they left the cubicle with their gear, Bailey and I hustled inside. Noah was waving her hand in front of her face and staring at it with non-blinking eyes.

"This is *insane*," she shouted. "I've got seventy-four fucking fingers!"

One of the nurses snorted as she cleaned one of Noah's arms and inserted an IV line. Noah didn't flinch, she didn't even notice what the nurse was doing. I was glad of it; she wasn't the best when it came to needles.

"Noah," Bailey said tentatively, her arms still tight around me. "Are ye okay?"

Noah was too wrapped up in her imaginary seventy-four fingers to pay my sister any attention.

"I'm sorry." Bailey rubbed her eyes. "Noah, I'm so sorry."

Noah looked at her and grinned. "What for? I'm having a great time. I love you, baby."

She was *so* stoned.

"I love ye too," my sister said, trying not to laugh as she sniffled.

I rubbed my hand up and down Bailey's back and looked at Noah's leg. Once I looked at it, I couldn't look away. Her foot was kind of twisted upwards, and it almost made me gag. Her shoe had been cut off back at the dance studio, and a brace of some sort was around her leg and foot to protect it. I didn't know what further damage had been done, but it looked like her leg was fucked.

I straightened when a doctor entered the cubicle followed by two nurses.

"We'll be resetting the foot and taking her for an X-ray to assess the damage. We'll be giving her a local . . . the gas won't be sufficient during this process."

Bailey began to sob as Noah began to sing after she sucked in some more gas.

"I have the X factor," she announced. "Where's Simon Cowell when you need him?"

She was a terrible singer.

Bailey and I had to wait outside while Noah was given a local anaesthetic and her foot was reset. I walked Bailey down the hall just so neither of us would hear the noises her leg might make. I could still hear the crunch of the initial injury and it made me feel sick.

We were sitting back in the cubicle an hour later. Noah's foot was reset with a cast plastered on her lower leg. She had inhaled so much gas that she was in and out of consciousness, and when she was awake, she was high as hell from the morphine she was given. She said a lot of weird shit.

A lot.

I looked down at Bailey and glared for the hundredth time when Noah groaned a little in pain as she woke up from another little slumber. My sister turned her eyes to me and sighed. "I said I was sorry . . . How was *I* supposed to know that this day would end with Noah in the hospital with a broken foot?"

"Ye should've guessed what would happen when ye made me dance."

Bailey bit her lower lip. "Da did always say ye were a weapon on the dance floor."

I raised my hand, pretending I was going to whack her, and she laughed and ducked against me. She put her arms around my waist and hugged me. She was tense until I rested my arm around her shoulders.

"You're both so cute," Noah said from her bed. "My likkle wikkle babies."

"Oh God," I grumbled. "Go back to sleep, love. Ye need your rest, okay?"

"Why would I sleep when I feel this powerful?" She suddenly sat up. "Look at my muscles, paddy. *Look at them!*"

Bailey laughed as Noah flexed her thin, not-a-single-muscle-in-sight arms. I got to my feet, approached her, and eased her back until she was lying down once again. Her hands gripped on to my biceps and she waggled her eyebrows.

"Look at *your* muscles," she purred. Literally. Like a damn cat. "You're so sexy, take off your top so I can see you."

"Oh, Christ," Bailey whispered. "She's gone mad."

"She's medicated, not mad."

Noah was in the middle of rubbing her hands over my arms, chest and stomach. I had to angle away from her to keep her from reaching lower. I was about to distract her with a chaste kiss when the doctor who'd reset her foot entered the cubicle.

"Sorry for the delay," he said. "We had a resus."

"No worries, we're not goin' anywhere."

"Elliot," Noah suddenly shouted. "Let's have wild, dirty sex!"

"Oh my God."

I mentally echoed Bailey's whisper.

"I'm sorry," I apologised to the doctor. "She's high as a kite."

The doctor looked like he needed the laugh as he waved his hand.

"Better this than her in pain."

I agreed with a smile. He took out an X-ray image from the folder in his hand and held it up in the air.

"Ah, fuck," I grumbled. "She's gonna need surgery, isn't she?"

I could clearly see the fracture in her leg.

"Unfortunately, yes. She'll need internal fixation," the doctor said. "Which is a fancy way of saying bone fracture repair."

Damn.

I scratched my neck. "Surgery is the only option?"

Noah's hands were back on my stomach, now under my T-shirt, and I left her to poke at my abs and count them out loud to keep her from shouting and causing a scene. Bailey was mortified on her behalf – one look at my sister showed her covering her face with her hands.

"In her case, yes." The doctor nodded as he pointed at the X-ray. "The fracture is quite severe. Her foot is fine, it's actually the bones in her leg she fractured. She has two: one here on the tibia and another here on her fibula. She'll need the aid of some screws, pins and likely a plate to get everything back in working order. The surgery is pretty straightforward; it can take between three and six hours. She'll have a boot cast on when she comes out of surgery, and she'll be able to go home in two days if everything goes well. But she'll be off her feet for six to eight weeks and she'll have to attend physio."

I'd guessed as much.

"Understood." I nodded. "I'll make sure she stays off of it."

While Bailey talked to Noah to distract her, I stepped outside with the doctor. He told me that her surgery wouldn't be until the next morning, as her leg was a little too swollen for his liking. I shook his hand and thanked him just as I caught sight of a familiar face disappearing round the corner.

"AJ?"

He popped his head back and raised his eyebrows.

"Irish, what's wrong? Why're you here?"

He was on watch; he was wearing his uniform minus his jacket and heavy gear.

"Noah fractured her leg in two places." I jabbed my thumb towards her cubicle. "She's gettin' surgery in the mornin'."

"Jesus. Poor Nono."

"Tell me 'bout it." I stretched. "Why're *you* here?"

"We brought in a resus a while ago," AJ explained. "The paramedics needed me to keep up compressions in the ambo."

"Successful resus?"

"So far." AJ nodded. "Fingers crossed he stays on the mend. Cardiac arrest at his grandson's birthday party."

"Shite."

"Yeah. How is Noah?"

"*So* stoned." I shook my head, my lips twitching. "She was tryin' to have sex while the doctor was explainin' to me that she needs surgery. She shouted it. Bailey's mortified."

"The kid's here too?" AJ was suddenly grinning. "Where's she at?"

I snorted. AJ loved to torment my sister, because he – and everyone else – knew how much she fancied him. He was apparently the Dulwich Adonis, according to my sister and her friends.

"Elliot!"

AJ and I darted forward at Bailey's shout. I yanked the blue curtain aside and found my little sister struggling to hold a thrashing Noah down on the bed.

"She said spiders are on her."

Bailey stepped back and AJ and I quickly restrained Noah, who was crying that spiders were in her mouth and crawling in her hair. So AJ and I made a big show of killing all of the imaginary spiders. Noah was a sniffling, snotty mess by the time she calmed down.

AJ handed me a few tissues from the dispenser behind us. I cleaned up Noah's face, and encouraged her to blow her nose like a parent would with their toddler. Then, like the click of my fingers, she was snoring.

I looked at my sister and saw her favouring the right side of her face.

"What's wrong, baby?"

"Noah whacked me by mistake." Bailey rubbed her red cheek. "She didn't mean it, she was scared of the spiders she saw."

"Lemme see."

Bailey dropped her hand and let me tilt her head so I could inspect her cheek. I winced; it was red and starting to swell, and there was already a blue bruise forming around her eye. I leaned down and gave it a gentle kiss.

"She got ye good. I'll get ye an icepack and AJ will bring ye home in me car before he goes back to work, okay?"

Bailey's eyes widened, and her face went scarlet to match her cheek.

"I wanna stay with *you*."

Laughing, I hugged her to me. "He won't tease ye."

"He will," she grumbled. "He always does."

"Are you two talking about me?" AJ questioned. "My ears are burning."

I snorted. "Mind your business, nosey hole."

Bailey giggled. "I guess a whack to the face serves me right for makin' ye take salsa lessons and fracturin' Noah's leg."

"*Excuse me?*"

I squeezed my eyes shut as AJ appeared at my side.

"*Salsa* lessons? *You* fractured Noah's leg?"

"For God's sake! It was a bastard of an accident!"

I launched into a retelling of how Bailey had tricked me and how I'd wound up paying for salsa lessons that Noah had never even asked for, then got to the part about how we tripped, fell and ended up in the hospital. AJ laughed so loud he woke Noah up.

"Shut it," I warned him as I went to her side. "Hey, *sasanach*."

Her face was contorted with pain. "My leg is burning, Elliot."

"I know, love." I brushed her hair back from her eyes. "D'ye remember what happened?"

"Vaguely." She gulped. "Is it bad? My leg?"

"Ye need surgery."

Noah's eyes widened. "Oh, that's not good."

"No," I agreed with a chuckle. "But the worst part is done."

She wouldn't look down at her leg.

"It's reset," I assured her. "Just really swollen and red."

She nodded. "Did you ring my parents?"

I paused. "Shite. No. I was so focused on you."

"I'll ring them," Bailey offered.

Noah looked at her with a grateful smile, then gasped.

"Your face, Bails, what happened?"

Bailey looked at me, and I cringed.

"Ye didn't mean to . . . ye sort of knocked her in the face."

"Oh, Bailey." Noah's lower lip stuck out ever so slightly. "Honey, I'm so sorry."

"I'm fine," Bailey assured her. "Doesn't even hurt."

She was lying. I could tell it hurt her, but AJ had got her an icepack from somewhere and that would help. She dipped out of the cubicle to phone Noah's parents for me.

"Did she admit to anything worth listening to?" AJ quizzed, leaning against the wall. "I love when patients are out of it on gas and morphine."

He wasn't taking this seriously at all, but to humour him, I spilled one of the secrets Noah had let slip.

"She said that she's a member of a secret society of women who knit throw-overs and sell them on the black market."

"Oh God." Noah looked at me with wide, bloodshot eyes. "Elliot, I'm a criminal!"

I tried not to laugh at her because she looked absolutely horrified, but when AJ cracked up, I lost it and laughed into my hand. She wasn't as loopy as earlier, but I could see in her pupils that she was still feeling the effects of the morphine.

"Elliot?"

"*Sasanach*?"

"I wonder if we can get you a refund on those salsa lessons . . . they were fucking rubbish."

My laughter mingled with hers as her hold on me tightened. She was okay, and that was all that mattered. I may have been two hundred pounds down . . . but it would always be an anniversary to remember.

CHAPTER ELEVEN
ELLIOT

Present day...

The walk down the pathway through the cemetery was a long and lonely one even if you were surrounded by people. As I passed by row after row of tombstones, I felt a small sense of comfort in knowing that hundreds of people at some point were feeling pain like I currently was, all because of someone they had to lower into the ground on this very patch of dirt.

I wondered if their pain was still as fresh as mine or if it had faded with time.

I didn't look up as I neared row twenty-three. I absent-mindedly counted each row I passed by, and when I reached the one I was looking for, I passed by eight graves before I came to a stop. I turned to face forward but kept my eyes on my shoes for a long time before I found my voice.

"Hey, baby," I whispered, using the nickname my sister had claimed to hate but I knew she'd secretly loved. I crouched down, cleared my throat and clasped my hands together. "I bet my ugly mug isn't one ye were expectin' to see today, huh?"

I gnawed on my lower lip, took a few steady breaths and forced myself to look up. I had to touch my hand to the ground to keep myself from falling on to my arse. Just being here felt like I'd taken a hundred punches to the gut.

"I'm sorry . . . I'm sorry I haven't been by since your first day here, baby, but I . . . I guess I've been scared to come and see ye. Comin' here made things feel permanent, and I didn't want this to be permanent."

The wind answered me with a low whistle, as a gust of dead leaves blew by my face.

"In me head I've been pretendin' that nothin' has happened to ye, that you're just on holiday or really busy with uni and work. When that hasn't worked I've been tryin' me hardest not to think of ye at all, and I'm so sorry about that, baby."

The backs of my eyes burned, but tears didn't fall.

"I really miss ye, Bailey," I said, my voice cracking as I exhaled a deep breath. "I miss ye so much, ye annoyin' little shite."

I stared at the oak cross with the tiny, polished gold plaque in the centre until I felt my chest burning with pain.

In loving memory of
Bailey McKenna
08.01.1998 – 19.03.2020

The little dash between her birth and death years didn't look like much, but that small line was her whole entire life. It represented everything about her. Everything she ever thought, said or did. Every smile, laugh, and tear she shed. It was all in that tiny black dash. It was my little sister, my Bailey.

As I stared at her name, I thought back to the time of her first heartbreak, when she was just sixteen and felt like her whole world was ending. It was the first of many puppy-love heartbreaks, and one I would always remember.

"Elliot!"

I jumped when the door of my bedroom opened and slammed against the wall. I had the day off after working four days straight. I'd just come off a night shift, but my sister didn't seem to care about that. With a groan, I buried my head in my pillow.

"Bails, I told ye I'd be sleepin' today—"

When sniffles reached my ears, I cut myself off and jumped out of my bed so fast I almost gave myself whiplash. I was in front of my sister with my hands on her shoulders within seconds. When I saw her eyes were swollen and red-rimmed from crying, my gut churned and my jaw clenched.

"Did someone hurt ye?"

If she said yes, I didn't know exactly what I was going to do, but whatever it was would likely get me arrested.

"Toby," she cried. "He cheated on me!"

Her words were spoken on a sob, but I heard her. As she wrapped her arms around my waist and placed her head against my chest, I couldn't help but feel a little relief. I could handle heartache, but someone physically hurting her was a whole other playing field.

I hugged her body to mine and kissed the crown of her head. She cried and cried until I found myself worrying that she would dehydrate herself. I never knew it was possible for someone to have so many tears inside them.

After ten minutes, I spoke.

"I know you're hurtin'," I said gently, trying to choose my words carefully. "And nothin' is gonna make ye feel better right now, but I want you to remember that this boy is *not* worth your tears – or a second of your time, for that matter."

112

Bailey's sobs had reduced to sniffles as she nodded against my chest, letting me know she was listening to me.

"You did nothin' wrong either," I continued. "He's just a stupid boy who didn't realise he had himself a whole queen in you."

I smiled when Bailey snorted. She always found it amusing when I used terms that she and her friends did.

"I feel stupid," she exhaled. "Me friends told me he was a fuckboy and I didn't listen."

I sighed. "Ye should feel sorry for him and the girl he ripped ye off with, because he'll likely do it to her too. What he's done says a lot about him and the person he'll likely become if he keeps this fuckery up."

"Fuckery." Bailey laughed as she pulled away from me and wiped her face with her T-shirt. "I'll have to remember that."

"I think ye dodged a bullet." I brushed her hair back from her face. "If ye want me to batter him, say the word."

Bailey smiled up at me as she hiccupped.

"He's not worth it," she said to me. "You're right – I *am* a queen, and he's not good enough for me."

"Atta girl."

She high-fived me when I raised my hand, then she hugged me once more.

"I love ye, Eli." She visibly relaxed. "Ye always know what to say to make me feel better."

I enveloped her back in my arms.

"I'm your big brother," I said, kissing her forehead. "I'm always gonna be here for ye."

A plane flying overhead brought me back to the present, and instead of looking at my sister's sweet face, I was looking at her grave plot.

"I'm gonna do better," I said to her as I glanced at the upturned dirt that was still in a mound over her grave. The day she was buried there had been dozens of flowers, teddies and cards, but only Bailey's favourite flowers remained: a fresh bouquet of bloomed pink lilies. "I'm gonna visit ye a lot, and I'm gonna talk to ye when I can't come here, just so y'know you're always on me mind. Always."

I scrubbed my face with my hands, my face feeling a little weird. I quickly remembered that I had just come from the barber shop. I was keeping up my end of the bargain that Noah and I had struck yesterday morning. I'd keep a freshly groomed beard, and she would get better.

"I bet I look different to ye," I said to my sister with a snort. "Ye've been houndin' me for months to clean up me beard and I finally did it. Ye have Noah 'Bossy' Ainsley to thank for it. She's awake, baby. She's awake . . . and she's not doin' too good. She has no memory of the last five years, it's all gone. She doesn't know that you're in Heaven and she was involved in the crash that took ye; she just found out she has a husband who's a stranger to her, that her da is sick and that we're no longer together. We're keepin' your passin' from her for now. I think it's best until she gets better."

I could imagine my sister calling me a dumbarse and it made me want to burst into laughter – and tears, because I never knew how much I needed to hear silly words like that from her until I could no longer hear them.

"I need ye to help me look after Noah, Bailey," I pleaded softly. "God knows I can't do it alone. Her parents think I can help her, but I'm a fuckin' wreck meself, sis."

I closed my eyes, then opened them again and looked up at the sky.

"How am I supposed to fix Noah when I'm broken too?"

I wasn't asking my sister that question, but God instead. I had never been a religious man, and even less so since my sister died

114

and I felt like He robbed her from me, but since I got word that Noah was awake and calling for me, I had begun to pray. It was for selfish reasons – I wanted Noah to get better because I couldn't live in a world where she didn't exist.

"Everything is a whole bloody mess, Bails." I shook my head. "The only thing keepin' me breathin' right now is Noah. It's not fair on her that she's the glue keepin' me together, but that's just the way it is. I want to be the man for her, but is it cruel of me to take advantage of her memory loss? She doesn't know Anderson now . . . but she did. I know the answer, it's not fair, but I don't care. No one can love her like I do, not even *him*."

I rubbed my eyes, swiped my hand under my nose then got to my feet.

"I love ye, I miss ye . . . and I wish to God that I still had you with me, but ye'll always be me baby, okay? I'm not givin' up either . . . I know somethin' was wrong that night. I don't know why ye were with Noah or what scared ye both so bad but I'm gonna do me best to find out. I'll get justice for ye, baby. I swear it."

Knowing I would never receive an answer, I leaned down and kissed my sister's name on the plaque and whispered, "I'll see ye later."

I walked back down the same pathway that had taken me to my sister's grave, and I was surprised to find that each step I took didn't feel like it weighed a thousand pounds. Each one was still heavy, and the weight of my sister's passing still sat on my shoulders, but coming by and talking to her, being near her physical body, had helped the pain in my chest to not feel so consuming. For the moment, I could breathe a tiny bit easier.

It wasn't a whole lot, and I didn't know if it would ever feel much different than it did now, but it was a start.

◆ ◆ ◆

"Now wait one fucking second." AJ waved his hand in front of my face as we walked up the stairs of the hospital an hour later. "I've been telling you to tend to that monstrosity on your gob for months, and one word from Noah gets the job done?"

I was too impatient to wait for the elevator. I'd been desperate to see Noah since she sent me – and her parents – home last night to sleep, shower and eat. We were under strict instructions that we weren't allowed to visit her until after ten in the morning every day, and we had to leave by eight in the evening otherwise she'd tell the nurses not to allow us access to her room.

I smiled thinking about it. She was definitely on the mend, and very much acting like the Noah I once knew – giving out orders like a dictator when she could barely stay awake long enough to have a conversation or hold her own head up. Though she was likely to be in the hospital for three or four more weeks, every minute of every day was part of her healing and was pushing her closer to recovery – closer to leaving the hospital altogether and starting a new life. One that I hoped would include me.

"It was a deal we agreed upon," I said to AJ with a chuckle, rubbing my hand over my freshly groomed beard. "She wanted me to trim it and keep up with the maintenance in order for her to take it easy while recoverin'."

"Eli."

I paused mid-stride when AJ suddenly stopped climbing the steps. I looked back at him and raised an eyebrow in question.

"It's good to hear you laugh and to see you smile, brother."

I hadn't realised I'd done either.

"Noah has given me a reason to do both."

"How are you faring amongst all of this change? Really, man?"

"I visited Bailey this mornin'," I answered, earning a whopping smile from AJ. "I haven't been to see her since the funeral, but I went and talked with her for a while. I talked to her about

116

everythin' I was feelin' and thinkin'. I felt better after it. I still feel crushed with pain over losin' her, but I don't know, breathin' was a little easier when I left the cemetery."

I leaned against the stair rail.

"As for Noah, bein' with her is good for me. When I'm with her . . . I don't feel trapped like I was before the wreck. I felt like I was stuck in time while life passed me by, and I hated that, man. Everythin' that happened between me and Noah, it felt like a huge mountain to overcome, but now it feels more like a molehill. It's taken almost fuckin' losin' her to put things into perspective for me. I don't know if it's healthy because I should be able to be on me own and not feel so stuck. All I know is she wants me, *needs* me, next to her, and that's exactly where I'm gonna be until she says otherwise."

Christ, I really hoped she'd never say otherwise.

"But, Irish, man. She doesn't know about *anything* . . . what if she turns you away again when she eventually finds out or remembers on her own?"

Doubt filled my mind. Like a slithering snake, it coiled around me until I thought I might choke. AJ's concern was literally my nightmare. I wanted to be there for Noah like she wanted me to, but I couldn't deny that my stomach was sick with worry that she would suddenly get her memories back and no longer need – or want – me any more. I knew how much it hurt to have her not want me because it had happened once before, and if I was being honest with myself, I didn't know if I had the strength to pick myself up if it happened a second time.

"I can't think about anythin' like that, AJ, I just can't. I'll drive meself mad. I just have to take things as they come."

AJ bobbed his head in understanding. "Just remember that *I'm* here for you. I know I'm not as pretty as Noah, but mate, you'll never have to shoulder anything alone while I'm around."

I gave him a hug, which he returned with a firm pat on my back.

"Thanks, brother."

We continued up the stairs until we made it to the ICU floor. I felt myself grow nervous as I approached the double doors that led to where Noah was. I was terrified that she'd suddenly got all of her memories back and would turn me away again, but I had to force that fear down. I couldn't think about myself, I had to think about Noah. I wanted her to get better. I needed her to.

And if that meant she got all of her memories back, so be it.

The ICU was guarded by security twenty-four hours a day to keep patients' visitors to a minimum. Luckily, the guard didn't seem to be in much of a mood to do his job, because he didn't look up from his phone as we passed him. AJ dropped behind me when I came to a stop outside Noah's room. I gently knocked on the door then opened it. I smiled at her parents, who were sitting and reading as Noah slept.

"How is she?"

"Doing well," Mr Ainsley answered. "She's been asleep since we got here at half nine . . . If she asks, we're saying we came in at ten like she told us to."

I smiled as AJ moved into view beside me.

"Ajax, honey." Mrs Ainsley got to her feet. "Lovely to see you."

She moved across the room and gave him a hug, which he returned with enthusiasm – making Mrs Ainsley giggle as she swatted her hand against his chest.

"Still looking as gorgeous as ever, Mrs A," he said, winking. "Your husband is a lucky man."

"AJ," a voice that brought a smile to my face said. "I know *I'm* stuck in the past, but you should've left those cheesy lines there too."

I laughed as AJ crossed the room and gave Noah the gentlest hug I had ever seen him manage. He was a bear-hugger – even I'd got out of breath once or twice when he squeezed a little too hard – but he was as gentle as a feather with Noah now. I appreciated it, and I know she did too.

"You're a sight for sore eyes, Nono," AJ said to Noah, placing a loud kiss on her forehead. "You scared seven shades of shit outta of me, just so you know. Apologise."

Noah laughed, and so did her parents. I smiled but I also watched her face, noticing how she winced ever so slightly with the action. Her head was still giving her trouble. I looked at her father, and he glanced at me at the same time, seeming to have noticed the same thing. I gestured for him to come out into the hall with me.

"I'm showin' Elliot where the coffee and tea station is," he said.

Noah's eyes dashed to mine and I saw panic fill those pretty greens.

"I'll be right back," I assured her. "Promise."

She relaxed, nodded and looked back at AJ, who was asking her why she hadn't yet apologised to him and making her grin. I left the room with her father while she was distracted, and we walked down the hallway until we were out of earshot.

"The nurse told us she had a bumpy night," Mr Ainsley informed me. "She didn't want us to be called, but her headaches got bad enough that they gave her morphine to kill the pain. She's having another MRI done this afternoon to compare with the earlier scans from when she was in her coma, but as far as the doctors are concerned, she's a miracle. She can talk, her motor skills seem to be normal, and she's engaging in conversation to try to jog her memory. The only obvious brain damage that they can see is the severity of her amnesia."

I digested this as I shifted from foot to foot.

"What if she wakes up and forgets everything again?" I asked nervously. "I've read stories where a person will wake up every day and remember nothing from the day before. Someone like Noah, who hurt their head in an accident."

It scared the life out of me to think something like that could happen to Noah on a daily basis.

"Son, you can't go and worry about every little thing that might go wrong. The list would be never-ending otherwise."

"You're right." I nodded as I scratched my chin. "Of course you're right. I'm sorry. I'm just scared shitless, but I can't show it in front of her. She looks at me like I can make everythin' better and I don't think I can. I'm not the man she thinks I am, sir."

To Noah, I was the man she knew when we were twenty-four, but that man no longer existed. I could see it in her eyes when I looked at her . . . she was in love with me, but not the man I was today; she loved the man she once knew. I couldn't begin to think what I would do if she got her memories back and that love in her eyes faded to nothingness. It was a possibility I had to try to prepare for . . . She'd picked Anderson over me once before, so who was to say that she wouldn't pick him again once she knew everything?

"You're every bit the man she thinks you are and you're *more*. You're the man my child will end up with, I know it in my heart. I call you 'son' for a reason, Elliot." Mr Ainsley embraced me before I could say a word. "Day by day, remember? We'll see our girl back on her feet, just you wait and see."

We separated and I straightened my spine.

"I've one other thing we need to talk about," he continued.

Dread washed over me.

"What is it?"

"It's Anderson. He showed up here in the middle of the night, and when the security guard wouldn't let him in to see Noah, he threatened to file a police report."

"He *what*?" I blinked in disbelief. "A report? On what fuckin' grounds?"

"I'm not entirely sure." Mr Ainsley pinched the bridge of his nose. "Doctor Abara, he's the lead doctor who looks after Noah, he observed the night she awoke in Anderson's presence and he doesn't want him around her right now because of how she reacted to him. Her mental health, and her health overall, is what's important. Anderson seems to believe we're keeping him away from her without her consent."

I clenched my hands into fists.

"He's not thinking of her, only him-fuckin'-self!"

"Try to think of it from his perspective, Eli," Mr Ainsley softly chided. "His wife almost dies in a car accident then is in a fifteen-day coma, and when she wakes up, she has no memory of him, or their marriage, and she still believes she's dating her ex-boyfriend, who he dislikes."

When it was put like that, my anger for Anderson seemed harsh in the situation, but I found it hard to care for his feelings.

"What should we do? We have to let him know that it's not *us* keepin' him away, it's the doctor. He might react differently. If he thinks it's me callin' the shots, he'll blow a fuckin' fuse. He hates me 'cause I'm the big bad ex-boyfriend."

"I don't think he cares *who* is keeping him away, just the fact that he's *being* kept away." Mr Ainsley sighed. "Don't get me wrong, I'm not siding with him. I'm nicer than you are to him because he's my son-in-law, but I don't care for him either. Everything about my relationship with Noah changed once they got together."

I was surprised to hear him say that; I'd always thought I harboured those thoughts for Anderson out of hurt and jealousy because he had Noah, but knowing her father agreed that there was something off about Anderson made me feel less crazy about the whole situation.

"What will we do if she asks about him?" I questioned. "What will I do if she asks why she's with *him* and not *me*?"

"You'll do the only thing you can do, son. Break it down, little by little . . . and tell her the truth."

CHAPTER TWELVE
NOAH

A touch on my wrist brought me awake with a start.

I opened my eyes, blinked a couple of times then stared up at the ceiling. It was different; there was a small vent above me that I wasn't used to seeing. For a moment I wondered why it was different, then I remembered that I was no longer a patient in the ICU. It had been eight days since I'd awoken from my coma, and my status had been downgraded enough that I was no longer required to be in a unit that cared for the most critically ill patients.

Early that morning, I'd been transferred to a regular ward. Even though I was in another private room, I was happy to be among people that needed care but didn't need to be under constant watch. For me and my family it was a massive step on my journey to recovery. I wasn't better by a long shot, and I still had a handful of weeks until I could leave the hospital and live my life again, but it was a step in the right direction.

A layer of bubble wrap had been undone, so to speak.

"Noah?"

I turned my head to the side and blinked. It was night-time and the light in my room hadn't been switched on, so I could only make out the outline of the person sitting next to me. The voice wasn't Elliot's, my dad's, my mum's or even AJ's. My subconscious, however, told me who it was before I could even think.

"Anderson?"

The fingers on my wrist pressed lightly on my skin.

"Yeah, baby, it's me."

I didn't know why, but I wasn't surprised to see him.

"Hi," I said as I pulled myself into an upright position. "Why are you sitting in the dark? Turn on the light."

He hesitated for a moment, then said, "Okay."

He leaned over and flipped the switch on the wall behind me, turning on my bed light. I squeezed my eyes shut against the brightness, then slowly opened them as my vision adjusted. My eyes lifted to Anderson instantly and I found myself staring at him with wide eyes. He looked completely different than when I had first met him.

"Anderson." I scanned his face. "What happened?"

He looked like he hadn't slept in days. His eyes had dark circles under them, his face was covered in a scruffy beard and his skin seemed sickly grey.

"I'm fine," he answered with a smile. "I'm just . . . not coping well with you being so sick."

His words tugged at my heart.

"I'm okay," I told him. "I'm getting better. They moved me out of the ICU."

"I know. Your doctor phoned me this afternoon to give me an update."

I didn't know what to do with myself, so I clasped my hands together as I remained sitting upright. I stared at the man who I was married to and tried to feel . . . something. But all that struck me was confusion. I truly had no memory of this man and it bothered me. I wanted to know what he was to me, how I felt about him.

"I'm sorry."

He blinked. "What for?"

"All of this." I shrugged. "I know I didn't choose it, but I hate that you're getting the short end of this stick. I've tried to remember you, but my mind is completely blank. The doctor says my memory could come back at any time, either whole or in fragments."

"It also may never come back at all."

I shifted. "Yeah, then there's that."

"Maybe seeing me and spending some time with me might help you."

"Maybe." I nodded. "I know Doctor Abara sent you home last week because of my reaction to you. I won't lie and say this is entirely easy for me, but my head is clearer than it was. I'm curious to know you, to know what my life was like with you."

Anderson leaned back in the chair, letting his hand fall away from my wrist. He made himself as comfortable as he could.

"I can tell you how we met, if you'd like?" Anderson offered. "That's light enough. The doctor told me over the phone that major memory triggers were restricted right now because of your brain's inability to process the information without hurting you."

"Yeah," I answered with a sigh. "I've got a lot of questions that can't be answered right now, but what you suggest sounds light enough – as long as I don't think on it too hard."

Anderson nodded, then with a smile he said, "I met you in the florist's where you worked. I was picking out flowers for a friend of mine who recently got a job promotion, and I went with red roses. You asked me if they were for my girlfriend." He chuckled. "When I told you who they were for, you almost passed out. You were adamant that red roses represented love and that I'd be giving my friend the wrong signals if I sent them to her."

I chuckled. "Flowers have meanings: they speak louder than words."

"You said something similar back then," Anderson mused. "You called me a silly billy. I laughed, and when you realised you'd said it out loud, you got all embarrassed. You were shy, I knew that from the start, but you were comfortable when you spoke with me. I asked for your number as you wrapped up yellow roses for me and that was our beginning."

I exhaled a breath, trying to figure out how to process the information I had been given. For some reason, I'd expected to feel something to indicate what Anderson meant to me once I heard of how we came to be, but I felt nothing. It was odd having a man who was my husband tell me how we met. I knew I was supposed to feel love for this man – or at the very least, physical attraction – but I felt nothing.

It felt harsh, because Anderson was clearly going through a tough time because of me. He seemed like a wonderful man, like someone who really cared about me, but my heart didn't know him. He had been wiped from it after my accident. Elliot was the only man who remained, but I found myself wondering if that was just a cruel twist of fate. I wasn't with Elliot for a reason, and Anderson claimed Elliot had broken my heart and that I didn't want him . . . Maybe I was in love with Anderson, and leaving Elliot had been the best choice for me.

My mind was so messed up because trying to think logically hurt my head. My gut told me Elliot was still my person and that Anderson was not, but I didn't know whether I could trust my instincts. Not having my memory meant I couldn't trust anyone, not even myself.

"Did we date right away?" I asked Anderson as I leaned back against my pillow. "What happened next?"

"We texted back and forth for a while before we went on our first date. Only to the cinema to see an Avengers film, but afterwards we went for dinner and then walked around town since it was a beautiful evening. We laughed so much that night over the dumbest of things that we could barely walk. I knew you were special that night and I knew you'd be the one I'd marry."

I had always wanted to be married, to be in a secure and loving relationship. It seemed obvious to me that I must have found love and happiness with Anderson – I wouldn't have married him otherwise – but to the person I was right now, that didn't mean a whole lot. It didn't make me automatically love Anderson, but it did make me a little more open to him. I had shut him down before completely, because of shock and because I couldn't see past Elliot, but I had to be realistic instead of optimistic.

I loved Elliot, but I had to prepare myself for the possibility that we didn't have a future together – no matter how much it hurt me to admit that to myself.

"One of the first things you told me that night was that my eyes reminded you of a black dahlia at first glance, because they're so dark."

I snorted. "Sounds like me."

"You're a visual person." He smiled in agreement. "You can't help but compare people to things you enjoy seeing."

I had never realised that about myself, but Anderson was right. I mostly did that with people's eyes. I always compared the eyes of a person to something visual that I liked. Elliot's eyes reminded me of the ocean, my dad's reminded me of emeralds, my mum's reminded me of the sky, and Anderson's did remind me of black dahlias, now that I had got a good look at them.

"I just learned something new about myself," I said thoughtfully. "I like that."

Anderson leaned forward when I yawned.

"You should rest."

"But I'm enjoying our talk."

126

I wasn't lying, I *was* enjoying our talk, but man, I was exhausted too.

"It's late," he said, reaching out and touching my wrist. "Security is lax now that you're on a regular ward. I only planned to pop in to see you, I didn't think you'd wake up. I don't want to start anything with your doctor or parents, I know they're only doing what's best for you. I'll keep my distance until you're stronger, but I can come back in a few nights to see you again."

I nodded. "I'd like that . . . I'm truly sorry about all of this, Anderson. It's not fair to you."

"It's not fair to *you*," he stressed. "You're the one who's going through hell, but I'll walk through hell with you if it means you get better."

His words touched me.

"Thanks, Anderson."

He surprised me when he leaned in and pressed his lips gently to mine.

"I love you, baby," he said, applying slight pressure to my wrist. "Don't forget that."

When he pulled back, he smiled at me when I nodded. He flicked my light off, bent down to kiss my forehead, then left as quietly as he came. I closed my eyes, trying to find a place in my heart for Anderson. I knew it was going to be a difficult task because no matter what life seemed to throw at me, at the end of the day, the only man who my heart wanted was Elliot McKenna.

CHAPTER THIRTEEN
NOAH

The cycle of being a doted-on patient continued for two days on the regular ward before anyone, including Doctor Abara, would even consider letting me even try to move about – which meant my catheter was removed, but I had to use a bedpan to pee and a commode for number twos. It was humiliating but it was a step in my recovery I had to take. Another step was strengthening my muscles. I now had a physical therapist come into my room and exercise the limbs that were able to move, to keep my strength up; apparently they'd had someone do this during my coma to keep my body as strong as it could be. At first, exhaustion made me meekly listen to my parents, and even Elliot when he suggested I just rest, but I was *done* resting.

I had spent a lot of time sleeping and not enough doing anything else. I knew I needed my strength, but sleeping all the time was extremely tiring. It was a paradox.

I could stay awake for much longer periods now; my headaches were still there, but the level of pain was nowhere near the height it had reached when I first woke up. That meant the painkillers I was on were no longer at a constant high dosage, which I was thankful for because all they did was kill the pain by making me numb and drowsy enough to fall asleep. I was never a big fan of using medication for every little twinge of pain I felt, and I wasn't about to start now.

I had awoken from my first nap of the day, and I hoped it would be my *only* nap until I went to sleep that night. I found myself wondering if Anderson would drop by again. I hadn't mentioned his visit to Elliot or my parents because I wasn't sure how they would take it. Elliot didn't like him just as much as Anderson didn't like Elliot, and mentioning either one in the other's presence didn't seem like a very good idea. So since Elliot was with me nearly every waking moment, I kept it to myself.

It was interesting how I was able to cope with Anderson's existence now. The situation I was in was slowly becoming my new normal. Having a husband who I didn't remember didn't seem as shocking today as it had ten days ago when I awoke from my coma. I wondered how I would view it in ten days from now. I hoped things would only get easier from here on out and my understanding of things would become clearer, because as of right now, my brain was still warped.

I had a lot of things I needed to get to the bottom of. I needed to know why Elliot and I were no longer together; I needed to know more information about the car accident I was in. I needed to know why my parents were scared to let me make decisions for myself and why they kept referring to never letting us drift apart *again*.

Whenever I mentioned any of the above, my parents, Elliot and even AJ would shut me down. I was always told we'd talk later when I was stronger, when I could stay awake for longer periods, when my brain could deal with more unsettling information. I was being treated like a child, and after my conversation with Anderson I had reached my breaking point. He'd given me information the second I asked for it – he'd told me about a little bit of my past that

I had forgotten without overwhelming me, and I wanted everyone else to do the same.

The time for silence had gone; it was now time for talking.

I looked to my left, found the spot empty, then looked to my right and saw him.

"Don't you have a job, paddy?"

Elliot's eyes darted up to mine, then he grinned as he pocketed his phone.

"I'm on . . . extended leave."

"Why?" I frowned. "Are you okay?"

"Yup," he answered as he leaned forward and took my hand in his, brushing his fingers over my knuckles. "I hurt my back on watch a few weeks ago. I'm on leave until I get a physical at the end of the month."

Having no reason to doubt him, I nodded.

"Does it hurt?" I asked. "Your back?"

"Nah," he said. "But you know my job – you have to be physically fit otherwise it can mean someone's life."

I was very aware of how dangerous his job was. I had always been so proud of him, but I had been terrified every time he was on shift. I was always sure I'd get a call or a senior officer would show up at my front door to give me the news that would cause my heart to stop beating.

"Hey," Elliot murmured. "What's wrong?"

"Nothing." I cleared my throat. "Just remembering that your job scares me."

Elliot didn't have to say a word; he knew what I was talking about and he understood.

"Where's Mum and Dad?"

"I made them go home for a few hours. They were tired but wouldn't admit it, so I sent them packin'."

I snorted. "'Cause you're bossy."

Elliot's answer was a wink.

I shifted as I stretched. When I dropped my arms back to the bed, I smiled when Elliot retook my hand in his. Every single time I woke up, he held my hand. I think it made him feel better to know I was awake and okay. It made me feel better too, but every time he touched me, I wondered what had happened between us that would have caused me to no longer want his touch. It was a constant reminder that the person I was had not chosen Elliot to be my forever person, and each time I realised this it made my stomach churn.

"I'm bored," I said to him. "I think I have the beginnings of cabin fever; this room looks the same as my room in ICU."

Elliot snickered. "D'ye wanna play a game on me phone?"

"What am I? Five?" I rolled my eyes, then after a few seconds I grumbled, "What games d'you have?"

He laughed again as he took out his phone and gave it to me. It was the first time I'd looked at it closely and it was one that I'd never seen before.

"What the heck is *this*?" I said, turning it over in my hands. "Is that *three* cameras?"

"It's the new iPhone," Elliot explained as he scratched his neck. "There's been a bunch of upgrades since you last remember havin' one."

I blinked. "It's fucking huge."

"Tell me about it. Ye get used to it though."

"I don't have a phone, or at least not with me."

"I'll get ye a new one."

I arched an eyebrow. "I can buy my own phone – or at least I think I can. I have no idea what my finances are like." I paused. "Where do I live if not with you?"

Elliot leaned back in his chair. "With him."

His mood changed like a switch had been flipped.

131

"You don't like Anderson, d'you?"

"No, Noah. I don't."

"Because of me?"

He nodded and my belly erupted with butterflies.

"Are you . . . are you jealous of him, Elliot?"

He ground his jaw. "Yeah, I am."

I raised my eyebrow but he said nothing else on the matter; he changed the subject instead.

"Did ye have Instagram when ye were twenty-four?"

"Obviously, but I hardly used it. I had nothing interesting to take pictures of."

"The majority of people use it now," Elliot assured me. "How else would people survive without takin' pictures of their meals or lettin' everyone know they're in the gym?"

My brow furrowed. "Huh?"

"Never mind," he chuckled. "Wanna get in a picture with me?"

My heart jumped. "I look disgusting."

"Horse shite." Elliot rolled his eyes. "Ye look beautiful."

Pleased with the compliment, I looked away as I smiled with warm cheeks.

"Ye never could take a compliment without gettin' all embarrassed."

"Shut up," I mumbled.

He smiled and took his phone from my hands.

"If ye don't like the photo, I'll filter it."

"What will that do? I never liked any of the filters Instagram had."

"Oh, honey," he laughed. "There are likely seventeen thousand feckin' filters out there now to choose from. They have apps to change the colour of your teeth, eyes, hair colour, smooth wrinkles; they can even change your face shape with the littlest tap of your fingers. No one actually looks like they do in their pictures on IG."

That made me pause.

"*D'you* look like yourself in your pictures?"

"Me? Yeah. I don't care about none of that bollocks, I like the way I look."

"Me too."

"Then take a picture with me."

He was daring me; I could see it in his eyes.

I sighed, long and deep. "Don't get me hair or stitches in it, and if I look sick, just delete it. Promise?"

With a roll of his eyes, he muttered his promise then leaned over the bed and held his phone in front of us. I stared at the camera lens instead of the screen. I pressed my face to Elliot's and smiled, and he snapped the picture then stared at it for a few seconds.

"Are you gonna filter it?" I questioned. "If you are, get rid of any wrinkles I've collected over the last few years."

Elliot either didn't hear my teasing or chose to ignore me. He was staring at the screen of his phone, then he tapped on it a bunch of times and looked up at me.

"What'd you do?"

"Posted it and put it as my screensaver."

"You're so cute."

I asked to see the picture and he showed it to me. I didn't hate it, but I didn't love it either. I had seen my face in the mirror and saw my body whenever I looked down. What I thought was swelling from my accident wasn't swelling at all. I had got fat. It embarrassed me, and while I hoped no one noticed, I knew they weren't blind and could see the difference. I felt badly about myself, but when I went into Elliot's Instagram account and saw the caption for his picture, I smiled.

"'My *sasanach*'," I read out loud. "I always loved when you called me that."

Elliot took his phone back when a young nurse entered the room after knocking twice.

"Afternoon, Noah." She smiled and nodded her head in greeting. "I'm Sara, I'll be looking after you today."

She moved her eyes to Elliot and did that thing a lot of women did when they saw him. They paused whatever they were doing – usually breathing, like this nurse did – then snapped back into focus when they realised he was real. Elliot was, without a doubt, gorgeous. The wife of one of Elliot's friends once said that he looked like Thor with dark hair, and now that he was rocking a maintained beard, he definitely looked the part.

I'd never admit that he looked like Thor though; his ego would never deflate.

"Hello." The nurse smiled at Elliot. "Are you Noah's brother?"

Ouch. That was a kick to my confidence, I was sister-zoned based on my appearance. I didn't hold it against the woman, I wasn't at my best and Elliot was always at his.

"No," Elliot answered, his deep voice making the woman bite her lower lip. "I'm her . . . person."

I looked at him and smiled. He was definitely that. My person.

"Oh," the nurse said, then cleared her throat. "Noah, how are you feeling? Do you need a top up on your painkillers?"

"I'm okay for now," I answered. "The last dose still seems to be working."

"Fantastic," she said as she picked up my chart and made a note. "You're doing beautifully – only ten days since you woke up from a coma and look at you, flying along."

I was glad she thought so.

"I have a question."

She put my chart back down. "Shoot."

"Can I shower?" I enquired. "There's only so much wet wipes and the sponge bath my mum gives me can do. I really need to give myself a good scrub-down."

The woman laughed. "Of course you can. I'll grab some towels and help you with your shower."

Out of the corner of my eye I saw Elliot rise to his feet, and before I could stop myself, I looked back at the nurse and smiled.

"No need." I jabbed my thumb in Elliot's direction. "He'll help me."

The "he" in question stumbled back into his seat, and without looking his way, I knew he was staring at me with wide, unblinking eyes. I could sense his stare as if it were burning a hole in the side of my head.

"No problem," the nurse continued, unaware that Elliot was having a mental breakdown. "I'll get you some towels and—"

"My mum has a whole bag packed for me with everything I'll need," I interrupted with a chuckle. "She's well prepared."

The nurse grinned. "I'll still grab you the towels, just so she doesn't have a load of washing to do."

"That's kind of you, thanks so much."

She spun on her heel and left the room as my eyes moved to Elliot. He still hadn't moved, and he was still staring at me. I lifted my hand and waved it in front of his face. The movement jolted him from his trance, and he suddenly jumped to his feet.

"Maybe the nurse should help ye, Noah."

He was scared – of what I wasn't sure.

"You're stronger than she is; if I fall, there's a better chance that you'd catch me."

I was manipulating him a little bit, and he looked so stressed out over it that it made me grin.

He scowled at me. "Why're ye smilin'?"

"Because you look scared to be locked in a room with me while I'm naked."

He sat back down and swallowed. He clasped his hands together on his knees and I noticed one of his legs was shaking.

135

"I'm terrified, and excited, and worried, and a bunch of other emotions," he admitted as he ran his hand through his dark hair. "I haven't been close to you without clothes on in *years*."

I reached over and grabbed his unsteady hand.

"I need you, Elliot. I need *your* help, not a stranger's."

He exhaled a breath. "You're a little witch. I know good and well ye just want me alone. Don't even try and deny it, I can see it in those pretty greens of yours."

Unashamed, I shrugged as my grin deepened, making him laugh. He got to his feet, placed his hands on his hips and nodded once.

"Let's get ye washed now, because if we wait until later, I'll drive meself insane thinkin' about it. I may run all the way home, so let's get to it."

I laughed as he helped me into a sitting position. Then, with him supporting me, my feet touched the floor with the intent to walk for the first time since I'd woken up from my coma, and though putting any weight on my leg felt a little strange, it felt good. It felt like I was truly getting better physically. Dad had told me to take things day by day, and though I wished for the days to pass me by so I could leave the hospital, I found myself not minding being so helpless when Elliot was next to me.

I didn't need the aid of a crutch; Elliot took the majority of my weight as I hopped on one foot to the other side of the room. My strength wasn't close to being back, but I managed to get into the bathroom and sat down on the fold-down seat under the shower head without collapsing from exhaustion. I was out of breath and it worried Elliot, so he crouched down next to me and searched my eyes for signs of pain. I wouldn't put it by him to pick me up and put me back in bed if he thought I was hurt in any way.

"I did it." I beamed as joy bubbled up inside my chest. "I got in here."

I was glad I was seated because the smile Elliot shot my way would have knocked me off my feet otherwise.

"Stay here," he said. "I'll get the towels off of the nurse."

I nodded, and when he left the room and closed the door behind him, I began to undress. After moving out of the ICU, I'd started wearing pyjamas instead of hospital gowns. When I began to strip out of my top, my arms got tired when it was halfway over my head. It was ridiculous what a little movement did after being bedbound for so long.

"Shite, sorry!"

I removed my top huffing and puffing and found Elliot in the bathroom. He was facing the closed door with his back to me.

"Elliot." I stared at the back of his head. "You can't help me if you're all the way over there."

"Right, sorry."

He put the towels on the hooks on the back of the door, then turned and crossed the room. I was shirtless and had to use his body to pull myself up. He saw how I was struggling to balance myself in order to remove the rest of my clothes.

"You're making things awkward for yourself. Unstrap your boot first. Sit back down."

I did as I was told, and sat back while Elliot undid the strap on my boot and removed it. The compression of the boot disappeared and my leg felt so weird without it. It had been taken off a few times over the last week, but I still frowned when I looked at the brand-new scar on my leg. The scabs had fallen off and now it was just a big, chunky, jagged red line.

"My poor leg," I sighed. "I'll never be a footballer now."

Elliot snorted and helped me up. I placed my foot on the ground but didn't put a whole lot of weight on it. I was awkwardly trying to tug down my shorts and underwear with one hand as I used the other to hold on to Elliot to keep my balance. He helped me without a word.

"This is absolutely mortifying." My cheeks burned. "I didn't think you'd have to do this, I'm sorry."

Elliot didn't answer nor did he drop his eyes once as he removed my shorts and knickers. He grabbed my top from the ground and then placed my clothes on the far side of the room. When he came back, he put his hands on my waist and said, "Turn the water on."

"No," I gasped. "You'll get soaked."

"I'll get a little wet." He shrugged. "I'll angle myself away from it as best I can."

And then he could catch a chill and get sick.

"Or you could just take off your clothes, and that way they won't get wet?"

Elliot's eyes locked on mine, and he didn't blink. I heard how my words sounded, and my cheeks continued to burn. I was making a fool of myself.

"I mean down to your boxer briefs, not na-naked," I stammered. "I'm not trying to get you naked, I just don't want you to get all wet and—"

"Noah," Elliot interrupted with a slow smile. "I know what you meant."

"I'm sorry." I looked at my hand on his arm. "This is harder than I thought it would be."

I wasn't talking about showering, and I think Elliot knew that.

"I'll take off my top and jeans." He helped me lower myself back down on to the seat. "Don't move."

He removed his clothes slowly, and I knew he didn't mean it like this, but Christ, it was like a slow striptease. I swallowed when his torso was exposed. He was so physically fit it was ridiculous; he was incredibly sexy. I always thought he fit the description of a

Greek god – I remember being proud that I had someone as gorgeous as him on my arm.

I looked down at my naked body, and humiliation scalded my cheeks. He'd been with me when I was healthy and slim and didn't have a gut that could rival Buddha's.

Elliot was down to his boxer briefs and didn't look below my neckline as he approached me, but I didn't have that restraint. My eyes lowered to his chest as he helped me back to my feet, and I couldn't stop myself from lifting my arm and brushing my fingers over the hair on his skin. It was a surprise to see him with chest hair because he normally waxed or shaved it . . . then I remembered why. He knew I loved to sleep with my head on his chest but his chest hair tickled my face, so he'd removed it . . . for me.

I guess since we weren't together, he didn't have a reason to remove it any more.

"Noah," he said, his voice strained.

I didn't look up at him, I was in a trance staring at the body I was once so familiar with. He had four new scars on his torso – not big ones, just a few lines. I ran my fingertips over each of them.

"What happened?"

"Little knocks I picked up on a few watches over the years, nothin' major."

Elliot was breathing heavily and his body was so incredibly tense that his veins stood out in his arms. My eyes dropped lower and I gasped when I saw he had an erection. The bulge was straining against the fabric of his underwear.

"I'm sorry."

I looked up at him and found his cheeks burning with . . . shame?

I flinched. "Why? Are you embarrassed you have an erection for someone with a body like mine?"

I recoiled away from him, but his hold on me tightened.

"What?" he asked, his voice holding the hint of a warning. "*What* did ye just say?"

"Let me go." I struggled. "I'll shower myself—"

"What did ye mean?" he interrupted gruffly. "What d'ye mean, someone with a body like yours?"

I was mortified.

"Don't pretend like you don't know," I said, lifting my chin. "I saw your eyes, you wouldn't look below my face. I'm different than when we were together. I'm bigger."

Elliot took a moment, then he cursed.

"I didn't look at you because I didn't want to make ye uncomfortable," he stated. "I'm lookin' at you now, and I'm *still* hard. *So* fucking hard. If I wasn't physically attracted to ye, that wouldn't happen."

He was telling the truth – Elliot was never one for telling lies. He was always so forward about his thoughts and feelings; it was a trait I'd always admired. I hated liars, I hated when people chose not to be honest with a person, especially their partner. Elliot's honesty was something I'd always valued.

"But . . . but . . . why would you looking at me naked make you uncomfortable?"

"Noah." He exhaled a breath. "You're *married*."

The reminder was like a punch to my gut.

"I don't know him." I swallowed. "I know I'm his wife, I know it . . . but he isn't in my heart like you are, Elliot."

"Christ." He squeezed his eyes shut. "You're making this even harder."

I didn't want to tease or mislead Elliot, and I repeated his words in my head until I felt dizzy. I was married. Married to another man, and even though I didn't remember a life with him, how I felt for Elliot was disrespectful to my husband. My behaviour at this moment was inexcusable.

"I miss you," I said to him. "I miss your kisses, your touch, your arms around me, the feel of you inside of me. I hate that I'm married to another man . . . how can I be his wife when my heart beats for you?"

Elliot lowered his head and pressed his forehead against mine.

"I can't imagine how much this hurts you, sweetheart. Ye look at me like you used to . . . I can see it in your eyes what ye feel for me. I won't lie either, I'm *happy* you're feeling the way ye are . . . but we have to be realistic, Noah. Ye could get your memories back tomorrow and any feelings ye had for Anderson could come pourin' back."

His words scared me because I couldn't imagine feeling for another man what I felt for Elliot, and a huge part of me didn't want to.

He kissed my cheek. "I can't let us cross that line, no matter how much I want, need and crave ye, green eyes. I'm terrified that when you wake up from your next nap, ye'll have all your memories back and ye'll hate me if we do this. What if you love Anderson and this is cheatin'?"

I felt my eyes burning with tears.

"You have to tell me why I'm with him, why we broke up. I'm done waiting, Elliot. I have a right to know what's happened in my life, and you owe it to me to be the one to tell me."

He looked down at me, made eye contact and nodded once.

"After ye bathe . . . we'll talk."

I nodded. "Okay."

"Turn on the water," he urged. "I'll just bin me underwear and put me jeans back on once I'm dry."

I looked back down at his body and licked my lower lip. My head was conflicted about my situation, but my body was not. I was still so insanely attracted to Elliot that simply looking at him aroused me to the point of pain.

"Turn around," Elliot suddenly growled. "I'm tryin' me fuckin' hardest to do the right thing, but don't push me, Noah. There only so much restraint I can have when I know ye want me like I want you."

Not wanting to tease him and cause further hurt, I did as he asked and turned around. He helped me, his hands holding me tightly by my waist so I wouldn't fall.

"Christ," he hissed. "I've missed your arse. Do *not* complain about it bein' bigger. I love it."

I could practically feel his eyes burning a pathway on my behind.

I clenched my jaw. "I may be married, Elliot, but I can't deny that I want you, so don't say another bloody word. I've never wanted you to touch me as much as I do right now, so let's just focus on getting me showered. Please."

I felt him kiss the back of my head. "You're the boss."

He turned the showerhead away from us then turned the water on. When the temperature was just right, he turned it back and the water washed over me like a dream. I couldn't contain the groan that left me.

"Fuckin' hell, Noah."

I held on to the support poles on the wall while Elliot got the shampoo, conditioner, shower gel and a washcloth.

"I'll wash your hair," he told me. "I can see your wound. You can't."

His voice had an edge to it, like he was angry, so I didn't question his decision. I had twenty-six stitches that stretched back from my temple to behind my ear. They had been removed, but the jagged line was there and was no longer scabbed over. The hair on that side of my head was shaved, and that still horrified me but I reassured myself that it would grow back eventually. I leaned back against Elliot as he poured shampoo on my head and gently massaged my scalp, cleaning away weeks of dirt, grime and dried blood. My lips parted and another moan escaped me.

"That feels *so* good."

Elliot didn't reply to me, he just continued with his massage, and after several long minutes he rinsed my hair until the water ran clear. He repeated the steps for me two more times when I asked him to. I told myself it was because my head hadn't been thoroughly scrubbed in weeks, and while that was true . . . it was his touch that I was trying to prolong.

When my hair was conditioned and rinsed, I took over. I took the soaked washcloth that was coated with shower gel and I scrubbed my skin until it came up pink. I bent over to wash down my legs and Elliot cursed. I looked back and found his eyes on the ceiling. After that, I quickly washed the rest of my body. When the water was shut off, I sat back down on the seat while Elliot got me a towel.

I squeezed water from my wet strands, then got to my feet with the aid of the support poles as Elliot held open a large bath towel in front of me. I smiled when he wrapped it, and his arms, around me.

"Thank you."

He kissed my head. "You're welcome."

I hobbled over to the sink with his help and wiped away the steam. My towel fell down a little, and I gasped as I looked at the first true reflection of my new body.

CHAPTER FOURTEEN
NOAH

"What the fuck *happened* to me?"

I wasn't asking Elliot, and I think he knew that because he didn't answer.

"This body is mine but it's not at the same time," I continued. "How could I let myself go like this?"

My stomach was destroyed with stretch marks, some light pink and others dark purple. My breasts were the same, and from what I could see of my thighs, they were there too. With a lump in my throat, I covered myself up with my towel and turned away from the mirror, not wanting to see myself any more. Elliot stood before me, dripping wet, with a big frown on his handsome face.

"You're beautiful, *sasanach*. Just a different beautiful than what you remember."

His sweet words were the crack that broke the dam. I burst into tears, and in seconds he had me gathered up in his strong arms and was whispering beautiful words in my ear that I needed to hear. I leaned against him heavily, until my sobs turned to sniffles. I felt like a train wreck.

No matter what Elliot or anyone else said to me, I was living in a body that I didn't recognise. I had felt conflicted and out of place as I tried to come to terms with my new life, but seeing first-hand how different my body was made me feel even more disconnected to who I was as a person. I was in the body of the 2020 version of myself, I was living her life, married to her man – but I didn't want it. Any of it. I wanted things to go back to the way they were, but I couldn't live in denial; I had to accept that this was my new normal even though this new normal hurt my heart.

"Come on," he murmured. "Let's get ye dressed before ye catch a cold."

I nodded and secured my towel over my breasts, then with the help of Elliot, I hopped back out into my room. When I sat on the bed, Elliot was quick to lock the door just in case I got any unexpected visitors. He mopped up the water that had dripped from my body on to the floor and audibly scolded himself for not placing a towel down on the floor ahead of time.

"Calm down, Mary Poppins." I wiped my cheeks. "A bit of water never hurt anyone."

"It could hurt *you* if ye slip."

"Fair point."

He returned to the bathroom to dry and dress himself, and I used this time to dry myself down. Then I wrapped my towel back around me, stood up and was just about to hop over to the tiny wardrobe that each hospital room was equipped with, to get fresh underwear and a set of pyjamas. When the bathroom door opened, I froze as Elliot glared at me from the doorway. Instantly, I smiled at him.

He looked like an angry papa bear.

"Nu-uh," he growled as he crossed the room with my boot tucked under his arm. "We aren't kids any more, ye don't get away with things by smilin' at me."

I clicked my tongue. "You've gone and grown up on me . . . old man."

145

The corners of his eyes creased in amusement.

"Old man? I'm *two weeks* older than you."

"Technically, yes, but mentally I'm still twenty-four and you're pushing thirty, so like I said . . . *old man*."

I squealed when his fingers suddenly pressed into my sides, over and over. He made sure to grab me when I fell, and hauled me up against his hard body.

"Mercy," I pleaded. "Mercy, Irish."

He righted me, then nudged me backwards until I sat back down on my bed. Then he got to work putting my boot on and securing the straps.

"*Don't* call me Irish."

"Huh?" I looked at him as he stood up. "Why not?"

"Me friends call me Irish, and you're not me friend. You're more."

My heart clenched at his words.

"Eli then."

"Nope, ye never called me that either," he mused. "I kind of miss ye always callin' me 'paddy' and 'ocean blue', if I'm bein' honest."

I burst into giggles. "You *are* my paddy with those big ocean blues. Always will be."

I held my breath when Elliot's eyes dropped to my mouth. For a moment, I thought he was going to abandon his morals and kiss me. I desperately wanted him to, but I knew what I wanted didn't matter right now. I had to think of the bigger picture and that picture included Anderson. I had to respect him, if not as my husband then at the very least as a person. Until I figured out who I would walk my path with in life, I had to keep my lips to myself.

Elliot's thoughts seemed to mirror my own because he licked his lips and, at the last moment, jerked back.

"Pyjamas," he blurted. "Underwear. Ye need those."

"I want to brush my hair first."

He grabbed my hairbrush and didn't hand it to me, but brushed out my hair instead.

"Ye know," he murmured. "The half-shaved-head thing on you is sexy."

I rolled my eyes. "Rubbish."

He placed a kiss on my now-buzzed scalp and whispered, "Sexy."

I shuddered as he detangled my shorter locks until the brush ran from root to tip with ease. Then he grabbed the hair dryer my mum had packed for me and proceeded to dry my hair. I felt like a pampered princess. Sooner than I would have liked, my hair was dry. I ran my hand through the soft, thick strands.

"When I leave here, I'll need to get a new style so the regrowth doesn't look ridiculous."

"We'll cross that bridge when we come to it."

Elliot moved to the wardrobe and grabbed a set of black pyjamas and a white pair of knickers.

"Are those *granny* knickers?" I asked, horrified.

He held them up with a grin on his face, enjoying my obvious distress.

"Give me those." I scowled as I reached forward and snatched them out of his hand. "I thought you were a gentleman, and here you are, waving my delicates around for all the world to see."

Thoroughly amused, Elliot moved the chair until it was in front of me, and stared at my knickers without blinking.

"*Elliot!*"

He laughed when I hid them from his view.

"I *love* how ye say me name like that."

"I know," I grumbled. "You've told me once or twice. I sound all prim and proper, blah blah blah."

He winked. "Come on, ye have to get dressed. A doctor or nurse could come in."

"You locked the door."

"They can be opened from the outside for a patient's safety."

I made him stand in front of me just in case someone came into the room. Elliot made a show of helping me get my knickers over my injured leg. I slapped his hands, making him laugh as he tried to tug them up my other leg like I was a toddler. I grumbled about how hairy my legs were but a glance from Elliot had me clamping my lips together. By the time I got my underwear on, I felt about ninety years old.

"This should be considered exercise," I said as I reached for my pyjamas. "I'm knackered."

We got my shorts on, and just as I picked up my top, I caught sight of the tag and nearly died.

"A *sixteen*." I blanched as I tugged it on over my head. "Elliot, I'm a size sixteen . . . and it's a snug fit!"

"I know," he answered. "I heard your ma tell your da what size pyjamas to get ye yesterday, she made a guess by lookin' at ye."

He looked completely unbothered and unaware that I was having an internal crisis.

"Elliot!" I stressed. "I've *always* been a size ten, even an eight in some jeans! A sixteen is plus-size!"

He looked down at my body then back up to my eyes. "It's not that different – I dunno why it's considered plus-size. It's a few extra inches, no big deal."

"Not that different? No big deal?" I repeated, dumbfounded. "I have *love* handles and *back* fat. I've never had either of those. My thighs barely touched before and now they practically clap with every step I take."

Elliot put his hand over his face to cover his smile. I didn't feel like laughing, I felt like crying.

"I'm fat."

"You're chubby."

I shook my head. "I don't need you to make me feel better by choosing terms that aren't as harsh. I need you to understand what I'm saying. Being fat isn't the issue, it's the fact that I don't know this body. Nothing feels familiar, nothing feels like what I've always known. I'm not comfortable in this skin. I don't feel like me at all, Elliot." I felt his arms wrap around me and I was so relieved that they still fucking *fit* around me. "I know how it must sound. Like I'm having a meltdown over being fat, but being heavy isn't the problem, it's being in a body that I don't know that's really hard for me to come to terms with. D'you understand?"

"Yeah, Nono. I know what you mean."

I pressed my face against his chest. "Elliot, I have a FUPA now."

"Honey," he laughed as he hugged me tightly to him. "Ye sound like havin' a tummy is the saddest thing in the world."

"It's not. It's just a shock to suddenly be in a body that has things I've never had before. I wouldn't expect someone who has a body like *yours* to understand," I grumbled as I leaned back and looked at him. "With your eight-pack and your pecs, and those lines on your hips . . . d'you still have those?"

"Ye saw in the bathroom that I do."

"Did I?" I blinked. "I can't remember. I have amnesia, you know? Show me."

With a grin, he lifted up his T-shirt and showed me that he did, in fact, still possess everything I'd just mentioned.

"Cover up." I gulped. "This is a hospital, my heart rate will go up. That's not a good thing here."

He laughed and let his shirt fall back into place, but before I could say another word, he crouched down, placed his hands on my hips and gave me a big kiss on the stomach.

"I like your FUPA," he said, standing up. "I like your bum, your love handles, your back fat and everything about your beautiful new body. I like it all."

I turned my head away from him as I smiled, and he snorted and turned me back to face him with a simple touch of his fingertips on my cheek.

"Tell me ye like your FUPA too."

I blinked. "Are you serious?"

"Think of body positivity."

"Give me *one* positive thing about this body!" I demanded. "Go on, give me one!"

"Your tits and arse are bigger." He grinned. "That's two."

"*Elliot!*"

I swung my hand at him as I laughed, and he caught my arm and tugged me against his chest. All laughter fled when Elliot leaned down and rested his forehead against mine, and he closed his eyes as if savouring the moment.

"I've missed this. Doin' silly things like this with ye." He squeezed me. "I've really missed you, Noah."

My heart hurt for him, and it struck me that he would never have been the one to break up with me. He had always loved me like a man was supposed to love his woman. He was the man you read about in books or saw in films. He was one of the good ones.

"I hurt you, didn't I?"

He didn't answer.

"Was I the one to leave?"

Elliot kissed my forehead. "Yes," he whispered.

"Oh, love, I'm so sorry." I lifted my hands to his face. "I'm so sorry, I wish I could take it back. Please, forgive me. Please. I love you, Elliot. I love you so much."

I made a decision then that changed everything. Up until that moment, I'd been reminding myself of Anderson, of who he was to me, but no matter how many times I told myself that there was a reason I was with him and not Elliot, I couldn't change how I felt about Elliot. I loved him so deeply that I was hurting myself by stopping myself from being with him.

I hurt for Anderson and I felt horrible for him, because while the 2020 version of myself had chosen him, he didn't stand a chance with the 2015 woman I still was deep down. My heart was Elliot's, and if I woke up tomorrow and got my memories back, I would deal with the consequences of my actions then. My accident had taught me that nothing was permanent, and that life was promised to no one. I wanted to live the remainder of my life on *my* terms.

I wanted Elliot.

Elliot looked into my eyes, and when I slid my arms around the back of his neck and tugged his face down to mine, he didn't offer me any resistance. I crushed my mouth against his and all thoughts of him rejecting me fled when he groaned into my mouth and plunged his tongue inside. He hands tugged me into a standing position so my body was fully pressed against his. I gasped when his hands moved to my behind, and he palmed my flesh like he'd never get the chance again.

With one arm supporting me, he moved one hand around to my front and slipped it under my top. I gasped against his lips when his large, warm hand cupped my right breast. He made a sound dangerously close to a growl in the back of his throat, and it awakened my body as desire rippled through me. I kissed him harder, bit his lower lip, and gripped the bulge of his cock in his jeans.

"*Sasanach*," he snarled against my mouth. "If ye don't stop, I won't stop at just tastin' these lips."

I gripped his arm, my knees suddenly going weak.

"Yes," I panted. "Yes, please. I want you so much."

"How much?" he teased, licking my lower lip. "Tell me how much ye want me, gorgeous."

"I want you more than my next breath," I groaned as his thumb circled my pebbled nipple. "I want to feel your hands all over me while you suck on my cli—"

The handle of the door jiggled, and Elliot sprung away from me like I was scalding-hot coal. I lost my balance and fell back on to the bed.

"Noah?" a voice called. "I'm just checking that everything went okay with your shower. Are you in any pain?"

The nurse. With my eyes on Elliot I breathlessly shouted, "I'm fine, just getting dressed."

"Okay. I'll stop back again later with your medication."

Elliot had his hands on his hips, his eyes on me as he breathed heavily.

"Are you mad at me?"

He shook his head. "I want to touch ye, to kiss ye . . ."

"But you wanna make sure I'm in the right headspace because of Anderson?"

"Because of him, and other things."

I swallowed. "Sit. Talk to me."

He sighed, then helped me into bed and made quick work of covering me with my blanket. After that, he sat on the chair next to my bed, leaned forward and rested his elbows on his knees.

"What d'ye want to know about first?"

"Us," I answered. "Tell me what happened between us."

He exhaled a deep breath and started talking.

CHAPTER FIFTEEN
ELLIOT

Twenty-five years old . . .

"Irish, are you *crying*?"

I cut AJ a glare as he fell on to the sofa next to me with a wry grin on his face.

"Don't start," I warned. "I'm wound up tighter than a slag in a confessional."

AJ laughed. "What's wrong?"

I didn't answer.

"Let me guess," he said, stroking his imaginary goatee. "Your parents' divorce is eating at you again?"

I glanced at him. "How'd ye know?"

"Because you haven't been yourself since they told you and Bailey about it. I'm more than a pretty face – I tend to see what's right in front of me."

I sighed. "The whole thing has fucked with me head big-time. I want me ma and da to be happy, I do . . . but I never thought that them bein' apart would be their solution to findin' that happiness. I can't imagine either of them bein' with other people. I knew they were havin' problems but *divorce*? It's caught me off guard. I'm kind of bitter about it."

I was more than "kind of" bitter, I was a whole fucking lot bitter. For as long as I could remember, I had idolised my parents' relationship, their marriage, their love . . . I'd even told Noah on the day I loved her for the first time that I wanted us to have a love like my parents did. A love that had since fallen apart and ended.

My parents were together for ten years before they became man and wife. When they told me that they were getting a divorce, I asked my father when he and my mother's problems began – and he laughed and said their wedding day. I knew he'd said it as a joke, but it stuck with me and had been on my mind for the past six weeks.

I couldn't shake it off.

For as long as I could remember, my parents had been in love. They were a team, they tackled everything in life as partners. They never made decisions without the other's input, they were a unit and I loved that about them. I loved that they had so much trust, love and respect for one another. Learning that their love had come to an end made me question everything I thought I knew about them. My dad saying that their problems had started the day of their marriage had hit me like a brick. It meant my perception of their marriage, of their love, was completely and utterly wrong.

The more I thought about that, the more I thought about my relationship with Noah. I'd wanted a relationship like my parents', but now that relationship was dead and not what I thought – and it made me question everything. I loved Noah and she loved me, I knew that, but now that the worry and doubt had crept into my mind, I wondered if my relationship was really as perfect as I thought it was.

It was all fucking with my head.

"I don't blame you for being angry," AJ said as he handed me the can of cider he'd grabbed from my fridge. "Have you talked to your parents about it since they told you?"

"No," I grunted as I cracked open the can. "Bailey was so acceptin' of it. She was completely understandin'. I just stared at them both until dinner ended, then I came home to Noah. I've been avoidin' both of their calls because I know they'll just want to talk about it. I've only seen them a couple of times over the last few weeks, and that's only because Noah insisted we drop by for a cuppa. Neither of them would risk upsettin' her so I've yet to hear what they have to say about me silence on the matter."

AJ snorted. "Everyone loves Noah."

"Tell me about it." I took a swig of my drink. "She's easy to love, but fuckin' hell, AJ, she just keeps talkin' about weddings."

"In what way?" he asked with an eyebrow raised. "Other people's weddings?"

"*Everyone's* fuckin' weddin'," I grumbled as I shook my head. "She's bought every bridal magazine ever published, and leaves them in places I'll have to move them. She left one on the toilet seat the other day, mate."

AJ snickered. "She was never good at being subtle, not even when she fancied you but pretended she didn't."

I rubbed my face with my free hand. "AJ, I don't want to get married. She does."

There was a period of prolonged silence as we drank our drinks and concentrated on the half-time analysis of the Man City versus Man United derby.

"Tell her," AJ said during the next advert. "You have to."

"I know." I leaned my head back against the settee. "I'm gonna break her heart."

"Maybe you won't. Maybe she'll understand."

I shook my head. I knew in my heart that I was going to hurt Noah when I told her of my decision, and hurting her was going to hurt me. She wanted to get married – she'd always said so, but for the past year she'd been more vocal about it.

"I could just do it, y'know?" I thought out loud. "I could just ask her to marry me and get it over with."

"You could." AJ nodded. "You could do all of that, but I don't think it's going to make your worry go away."

"Fuckin' hell," I groaned. "Maybe I'm just thinkin' crazy because of me parents?"

"We've never talked about either of us getting married, but were you open to it before?"

"Well, yeah. I figured that at some point I'd get married, I just never put a massive amount of thought into it like I am right now. Noah's pressure on me over the last few months about marriage has been a bit of a strain, and now with me parents' divorce . . . it just feels like something I don't want to do right now."

"*Right now,*" AJ said. "Meaning it might be something you want in the future?"

"I don't know, man. Maybe."

"You're twenty-five – you don't have to get married right this second. Taking a step back to figure your head out is perfectly okay. Being married doesn't change how much you love Noah, man."

I felt my entire body deflate with his words.

"Right." I bobbed my head in agreement. "I love Noah to pieces, she's the only one I want . . . but I want things to be like they are now. We don't *need* to get married."

"You should talk to her about it. Don't shut the idea of marriage down completely because, like you said, you don't know if it's something you might want in the future. Explain it's something you don't want right now, tell her what's going on inside your head."

I exhaled.

"The thought of it is just too much right now. Whenever I think of it, I feel like me head is being held underwater. It makes me feel sick."

I'd wanted a love like my parents had, and I'd thought I had that with Noah, but their love was over and so was their marriage. It probably sounded stupid, but I believed that if I married Noah, it'd jinx what we had together. I was terrified that I'd grow to resent her or she would realise I wasn't husband material, and everything would just fall apart around me. Just like it had for my parents. I couldn't risk it . . . I just couldn't.

"I have to say, Elliot, I never thought imagining me as your wife would make you feel sick."

I froze as her voice drifted into the room like an icy breeze. Dread washed over me as I quickly replayed everything AJ and I had just spoken about, and my hands clenched into fists.

AJ looked over his shoulder and his eyes widened.

"Ah, bollocks. Noah, he didn't mean any of it, he's just under stress—"

"Please, AJ." She cut him off shakily. "Don't make excuses for him."

No. No. No. No.

This wasn't how I was supposed to tell her. I jumped to my feet, turned to face her and my stomach lurched when I saw her red-rimmed eyes and tear-stained cheeks. She'd heard everything I said. Everything. She wouldn't have been crying otherwise.

"Noah." I looked at her as helplessness filled me. "I'm sorry, sweetheart. I'm so sorry—"

"AJ," she said, offering our friend a small, sad smile. "Can you give us a minute?"

"Sure, Nono." He seemed to tighten his hold on his can. He glanced my way then left the room, kissing the crown of Noah's head as he passed her by. I heard the kitchen door close moments later, and I suddenly felt trapped as my girlfriend – the love of my life – stared at me with those green eyes I loved; but for once, they seemed to look right through me.

"Please," I gulped. "I'm sorry. I didn't mean for you to hear any of that . . . I thought ye were at work."

"I got off early," she answered robotically, her stance shifting. "You didn't say you're sorry you said it, or that you didn't mean to say it. You're just sorry because you didn't mean for me to *hear* it."

I had never seen that expression of hurt on Noah's face before, and it prompted me to move to within touching distance of her. But she held up her hand and brought me to a halt right in front of her. I didn't know what to do. She didn't want me to touch her and that was all I wanted to do.

"I'm sorry."

"Stop fucking *saying* that!"

I wasn't surprised by her shout – she was upset, but she was becoming angry too. That was Noah's way. She was always upset before she ever got truly angry.

"I can't believe this," she said to herself. "I can't fucking *believe* this."

I stared at her like a bloody eejit. I didn't know what to say, what to do, so I stood there, unmoving, feeling like a clown, as she broke down in front of me.

"*Sasanach*—"

"Don't," she suddenly screamed, and this time I jumped. "Don't *ever* call me that again. Ever."

My lips parted as shock rippled through me at her declaration. I had always called her *sasanach* as an endearment and she loved it. For her to tell me never to call her it again made fear crawl down the length of my spine.

"Noah."

She was staring up at me, tears on her face as she breathed heavily. With a shake of her head, she suddenly turned and stormed down the hallway towards our bedroom, with me following her.

"What're ye doin'?" I shouted after her. "Talk to me, for God's sake."

"Like *you* talked to *me*?" she snapped, throwing a hand up into the air. "You told Ajax everything that I should have heard first. D'you have any idea how much of a fucking idiot I feel?"

She swung the bedroom door open, not caring when it slammed against the wall. I watched as she grabbed the duffle bag she used when going away for spa weekends with her mother, and my heart just about stopped. She threw it on to the bed, yanked it open, and began to grab random items of clothing and shoved them inside. I was next to her in an instant, grabbing her hands.

"Let me go!" she screamed in dismay. "Elliot, stop it!"

I wasn't her hurting her, I knew I wasn't, but I did as she asked.

"I'm leaving."

"What?" I asked, dumbly. "*What* did ye just say?"

"What's the point in us being together?" she shouted at me, throwing her hands up in the air. "Elliot, I thought you were going to propose to me soon."

I felt my jaw drop. "What the hell would give ye that impression?"

"Other than the fact we've been together for seven years? Or that we love each other?"

"Yeah," I snapped. "Other than those things."

Her entire body seemed to jolt at my words, like they'd physically hurt her.

"I thought we were ready," she said, her voice barely above a whisper. "I thought you wanted to make me your wife."

I couldn't believe she was saying these things.

"Noah . . ." I ran my hand through my hair. "Just stop for a second. Marryin' you . . . it's not something that I can do right now. All of this shite with me parents has really fucked with me head."

"My parents are still married and in love. Just because your parents didn't make it doesn't mean that we can't."

I heard what she was saying but the doubt still had hold of my mind.

"I can't," I managed to say around the lump in my throat. "I can't marry ye, Noah. We're still kids, we have years to get married. Can't we just stay as we are right now?"

She stepped back from me as tears fell down her cheeks. I reached for her but she recoiled from me, so I let my arm drop numbly back to my side. I didn't know what to do. In the seven years we'd been together we had never encountered anything like this. We fought, and I'd had to sleep on the sofa a few times, but she'd never packed a bag to get away from me.

"Why isn't it enough to just *be* with me?" I asked, clenching my hands into fists. "Why do we hav'te get married?"

"Because I *want* to be your wife," she screamed, her voice suddenly a little hoarse. "I wanted to stand in front of our friends and family and choose you before God as my one. It's important to me . . . I've dreamed of marrying you for years, Elliot. You *know* I have!"

I rubbed my eyes with the backs of my hands when they began to sting with tears.

"I can't give ye that right now, Noah. Maybe in the future I can."

"Can you say that for certain?"

"I . . . I . . . No." I swallowed. "I can't say for certain that me feelings about it will change."

Her lower lip wobbled, her tears coming fast and furious.

"Then that's it," she said on a choked sob. "That's it. There's nothing more to say."

I wanted to go to her, to comfort her and make her tears stop, but I couldn't. I had to make her understand that I couldn't relent on this issue; she didn't understand that I was terrified of getting married. The practice felt jinxed to me now.

"I love you," I stressed to her. "I love ye with everythin' in me, Noah. Why isn't that enough for ye?"

"Everything about you is enough for me, it always has been and it always will be, but you're only saying all of this because you're scared."

"Yeah," I snapped. "I'm fuckin' scared. Me parents have been together for thirty years and married for twenty. I told ye when we got together that I wanted a love like theirs, and now that love is dead. Me da said everythin' went wrong when they got married. I don't want anythin' to go wrong for us . . . why can't we just stay as we are?"

"Because I want *all* of you. Your heart, your last name, your kids. All of it, and I won't settle for less. I love you, God knows I do, but I'll *not* settle for less."

She grabbed her packed bag and hung the strap over her shoulder.

"We're done, Elliot."

"Done?" I said as the ground fell away beneath my feet. "Just like that, Noah? Seven years together and we're fuckin' *done*?"

She lifted her chin. "I won't settle for less . . . we're done."

I stared in disbelief as she walked right by me.

"Fine," I shouted after her, suddenly furious with her for not even *trying* to see things from my point of view. "Leave, Noah. See if I give a fuck!"

The only thing that answered me was the slam of the front door. The silence that followed was almost deafening. I stumbled,

161

the backs of my knees hitting the bed, and I dropped into a seated position and stared at the floor. My head fell into my hands, and I tried to breathe normally. I heard the kitchen door opening, then footsteps followed by a long sigh.

"Eli, I'm sor—"

"She'll be back." I cut him off with a shake of my head before he could say anything further. "She didn't mean what she said, she's just upset with me."

I looked up at him. AJ stared at me – then, as if on autopilot, he crossed the room and held out a hand that gripped an unopened can of cider. I took it, opened it and drained it in seconds. My friend sat next to me and watched me, concern marring his features. With a wave of my hand I said, "Don't look at me like that."

"Like what?"

"Like I'm a drowned puppy or somethin'," I grunted as I crushed the empty can in my hand. "I'm fine . . . she's just upset. She loves me, mate. She's not gonna leave me over this. She wouldn't do that to me."

AJ didn't agree or disagree with me, but he still looked at me like I was the saddest thing he had ever seen, and suddenly I felt like a weight was sitting on my chest as the realisation of the situation dawned on me. Noah had broken up with me; she'd said the words though I could tell it was the last thing she'd wanted to do.

That was the only piece of comfort I had. She didn't want to leave me . . . but she still had.

For as long as I had known Noah, she'd made it clear that she valued commitment. Before we got together properly, she'd loved me but was willing to step back from me because I hadn't asked her to be my girlfriend. She knew what she wanted, and like she said . . . she didn't settle for less than what she wanted. She wasn't the kind of woman to play games, and she didn't say things she didn't mean in order for me to chase after her.

She said what she meant . . . and that meant she was really done with me.

"She'll come back to me," I said again to AJ, but a silent panic had settled over me. My hands began to shake as doubt curled around me, draining me of life. "She will."

No, a voice whispered in the back of my mind. *She won't.*

CHAPTER SIXTEEN

NOAH

Present day . . .

"That's what Anderson meant on the night I woke up." I clasped my hands together. "He said you broke my heart . . . that's what he was talking about."

"Yes, honey."

It had felt as if all the air was being sucked from the room as I listened to Elliot explain why our relationship had ended. My emotions were running high and my heart pounded inside my chest. Marriage. That was what broke us up. Elliot's inability to commit to marriage. Out of everything I had considered, what I'd just learned wasn't something I'd seen as a factor.

"You didn't want to marry me."

I couldn't look at Elliot as I spoke the words, because my heart was hurting. I had listened to every word he'd just said, and by the time he finished, what I'd felt was a deep hurt. The only memories I had of Elliot and our relationship were good ones. We'd never had a downward spiral like other couples who'd had to fight for their relationship; we'd never had trying times where either of us felt like the other wasn't the person for us. I'd always believed we were the lucky ones – until now.

I had always believed that marriage would be on the cards for us, and I had always made that known. To hear this was the reason I ended my and Elliot's relationship was like being doused in ice-cold water. Part of me felt angered, but mostly I just felt saddened and I didn't know what to do about it.

"I was scared," Elliot said, covering my hands with his. "I was goin' through a lot once me parents told me they were divorcin'. Ye know how much I idolised their relationship, Noah. The second doubt creeped into my mind about us, it was all over. It poisoned me mind."

I found myself nodding because, even though my heart hurt, I could understand his point of view.

"I can grasp fear wrecking your train of thought but, Elliot, surely talking to me about it, instead of keeping it all bottled up, would have helped?"

"I know." He hung his head. "I thought I could figure it out in me head, but the longer I didn't speak to you about it, the worse I felt."

I swallowed. "I never made it a secret about marriage. You knew it was something I wanted."

"I know, and up until that shitstorm, it was something I wanted too."

I looked at him. "You should have told me the second you had doubts. You said I was leaving bridal magazines around as hints, always talking about weddings . . . why did you allow me to plan and envision a future that would never happen? That was cruel of you, Elliot."

"I was stupid," he sighed. "I never factored in things like that. I was only thinkin' of how I could tell ye without hurtin' ye. I didn't think beyond that. I truly believed that things wouldn't end the

165

way they did, even though I lied and kept how I felt about marriage from ye. There's no other way to put it other than I fucked up, Noah."

I cleared my throat. "Your honesty was something I always valued because you were the only person to ever give it to me fully. My parents were overbearing when I was younger and kept things from me, believing it was for my own good, but you never did that. I think . . . I think that was part of the reason I left you."

"I'm sure it was." Elliot ran his fingertips over my knuckles. "I don't know meself because I left it too long to go after ye. I figured ye'd need some space, and when I realised ye weren't comin' back, it was too late. I believed ye'd come back even though part of me knew ye wouldn't."

"I'm sorry that I didn't come back and at least have a proper talk with you. Hearing this hurts, I won't lie, but I know you were dealing with a lot at the time with your parents' divorce. I think I let hurt and anger consume me to the point where I made decisions that hurt you. I never want to hurt you, Elliot. You know that, right?"

"Yeah, green eyes. I know."

"You're taking the blame for our relationship ending, but I want you to know that it was both of us. At the time it was wanting different things that broke us apart, and you shouldn't feel guilty for that. You felt how you felt and so did I."

Elliot didn't answer me, but I saw him process my words.

"I never thought we'd turn out like this." I exhaled a shaky breath. "I thought you'd be my forever person."

His eyes locked on mine. "I wish I could take it all back, but I can't."

I blinked. "Meaning you'd never have told me you didn't want to get married, or—"

166

"Meaning if I knew what life was like without ye, I'd never have come to the conclusion about marriage that I did. I was scared that our marriage would be jinxed and our love would be ruined if we got married, but how much more wrecked could things have got than they already are? I fucking lost ye, honey."

I removed my hands from Elliot's and placed them over my face.

"I want to believe you, but it's hard now."

He was always the one person who gave me blatant honesty, but now my trust in him was shattered and I didn't know if it was beyond repair. Maybe that honesty I'd lost in Elliot was what I'd found in Anderson? I didn't know.

"What happened next?" I mumbled into my hands. "When you tried to speak to me?"

"Ye had already moved on," Elliot answered. "I left it too late to fix everythin'. Ye never spoke to me again until after ye woke up from your coma."

My stomach churned. I knew I was still hurt by his decision about marriage and about him keeping it from me – I was experiencing that hurt right now. But it was very hard for me to imagine that I'd just shut Elliot out of my life completely without even trying to resolve matters between us. I stared at him, shocked to find that I was gauging whether or not he was telling the truth. That was something I'd never had to do with Elliot before.

Then I looked into his ocean blues and felt a weight fall off of my shoulders. He wasn't lying to me. I had to look a little longer, but I saw truth in his eyes, not deceit.

"I don't know why I didn't give you a second chance." I lowered my hands from my face. "Maybe my hurt turned to anger, and it fuelled how things panned out. For that, I'm so sorry."

"Don't be," Elliot said. "Things likely would have been different if I was honest with ye from the jump. Maybe we could have worked through my doubts or maybe we still would have spilt, I don't know. Hindsight is a great thing; I know things now that I didn't then."

"Like what?"

"That losin' ye broke me."

I bit down on my lower lip to keep from crying.

"But you still came to me when I called for you, even though my decision broke you."

"I'll always come runnin' when ye need me, *sasanach*." His gaze softened. "You're my person."

I tried again to think of why things had played out the way they did. I squeezed my eyes shut, trying to force the memory to the surface, but then I screamed out as sudden agony slammed into my head and I felt my body go tense and rigid as pain crippled me. I felt stuck.

I heard voices, felt hands on me, and the pain eased back as numbness spread over me like a veil of feathers. Then there was silence – mind-numbing, blissful silence.

◆　◆　◆

"El-Elliot?"

"I'm here," his voice answered. "I'm here, Noah. I'm not goin' anywhere, honey . . . I'll get the doctor, he wanted to be called when you woke up."

I drifted back into sleep for a few moments but then decided that I wanted to wake up. It took a few tries, but I managed to open my eyes – and instead of Elliot's face hovering over me, I was staring up at Doctor Abara. I felt myself blink very slowly as I stared up at him. He smiled down at me. "Hello, Noah."

Oh, no.

"Did I forget everything again?" I rasped. "Is it the year 2030 now? Do we have a new prime minister?"

I thought I heard Elliot curse as he laughed, but I wasn't sure. It sounded kind of distant, but at the same time not. My head felt foggy, like I was tipsy from a few drinks.

The doctor grinned. "Nope, still 2020 with the same PM."

Relief filled me.

"What happened?" I questioned as I flexed my fingers. "How long was I out?"

"A few hours or so."

"I was talking to Elliot then my head just . . . burned."

"Yes, Elliot told me what happened." Doctor Abara frowned like my dad had when I was being naughty as a child. "You are in no condition to be frolicking around with your man, no matter how well you *think* you are, Noah."

I furrowed my brow in confusion.

"*Frolicking?*" I repeated in bewilderment. "I wasn't frolicking – oh my God! Elliot told you I tried to *seduce* him?"

Memories assaulted me and humiliation reddened my cheeks.

Doctor Abara raised an eyebrow. "Yes."

"I'm gonna bloody kill him."

I heard a couple of snickers and tensed.

"Is he here?"

"Yes," the doctor answered. "Your parents too."

"*I beg your pardon?*" I asked, raising my voice only to wince as my head ached. "I'm really gonna kill him. My dad knows what I did?"

"Yes," the doctor answered casually, like we weren't having the most mortifying conversation in history. "Any double vision?"

"No," I answered. "Your voice sounds a little distant though, and I feel a little dizzy."

He nodded. "Your pain levels?"

"Low right now," I answered. "Was I given morphine?"

At his nod, I sighed. "I don't like that stuff. It makes everything all foggy and it's hard to think."

"Try thinking a little *less*," the doctor suggested. "You may feel like you're recovering fast, but it'll take your brain a very long time to be back to full functionality."

"That's just great," I sighed when he frowned. "I'm sorry, I'm being grouchy. Sore head and all."

Doctor Abara's lips twitched. "Take care of yourself. The next time I see you I want to be discharging you. I don't like getting emergency pages that one of my patients who was in the ICU just a few days ago has collapsed."

His scolding was gentle, but very effective.

"I understand, sir. Thank you for coming by and taking care of me."

He gave me a nod and a smile, then disappeared from view. I heard him talking in low tones with Elliot and my parents. I didn't ask what they were talking about because, for once, I didn't want to know. What I wanted was for the ground to open up and swallow me whole. I closed my eyes, wishing I could forget the conversation that had just taken place, but I couldn't.

"Is there any point in me pretending to be asleep in the hopes that you'll all leave me to die in this bed of shame and humiliation?"

Chuckles filled the void.

"Not a chance, *sasanach*."

I refused to smile. I was mad at him.

"You, get out," I grumbled. "I'm not talking to you, big mouth."

I opened my eyes and Elliot's face grinned down at me. "My bad. I got scared and just told the doctor everything. I thought maybe all that kissing messed with your head."

"Your kisses aren't *that* amazing, paddy."

He laughed, leaned down and kissed my cheek.

"Ye scared me, green eyes," he whispered in my ear. "Me heart just about stopped when I couldn't wake ye up. Ye screamed so loud."

I frowned. "I'm sorry, I didn't mean to."

He straightened up and used the remote to raise the top half of my bed when I asked him to. My parents were next to me then, and I felt horrible when I saw tears on my mum's face.

"Mummy," I said into her hair as she hugged me. "I'm sorry, I didn't mean to scare you. I'm okay."

She held me for a very long time, and Dad held my hand, squeezing it. I knew I hadn't chosen what was happening to me, but I still felt horrible that I was putting them through all this worry.

"I'll do what the doctor says," I assured my three keepers when they each took a seat. "I promise."

"We know you will," Dad said sternly. "Because we'll make sure of it."

I wondered how they intended to do that.

"Elliot told me about how we broke up."

"*Don't* think about it," Elliot chided. "That conversation is what made ye collapse. I should have never opened me bleedin' mouth."

I looked at him. "It wasn't the conversation; I was trying to think of why I did what I did when I strongly disagree with how things turned out. I was just . . . I was just pushing my brain a little too hard, I guess."

"Ye know why we broke up," Elliot grunted. "We don't need to talk about it any more. Ye can't change what happened even if ye could remember it, which ye can't."

It sounded so simple when he put it like that, but it was far from simple and far from being resolved. We had a lot to work through and, deep down, he knew it.

"I need to know these things, Elliot," I countered. "I won't hurt myself again, I'll just listen."

"Noah."

"I feel like I'm a book that's filled with blank pages . . . I need words to make me complete."

"No."

For a moment, I was rendered silent.

"Are you afraid that every bit of information I learn will cause me to collapse?"

"Yes."

"So you're gonna withhold things from me, things that I *need* to know?"

"Yes," he stated, more firmly this time. "Don't test me on this. Ye were overwhelmed and it hurt ye. I won't be tellin' ye a thing until you're stronger."

"Elliot, honesty means a lot to me. I can't even trust my own memory because my mind is stuck in the past. This is important to me."

"Look at me." He moved closer. "I hurt you. I know I did, and I'll always be sorry, Noah. I'm not here for the sole purpose of gettin' you back. If ye tell me right now that ye want Anderson over me but still need me as your friend, I'll be here as your friend. I'm here for *you*. I would never go out of me way to hurt and confuse you; I've learned my lesson. Can't ye trust me, love?"

"I want to, I do, but everything is different. I need the truth about everything." I looked at my parents. "Tell him."

"We agree with him," Dad replied, shocking me.

"But Dad—"

"I said no, Noah."

I snapped my gaze to Elliot and was tempted to shove him.

"Who made you the boss of me?"

"*You* did," he answered. "When ye told me you still love me."

I went silent as I remembered the words I'd spoken before I kissed him, just hours ago.

"Just because I love you doesn't mean you get to dictate everything I do."

"I'm not tryin' to dictate anythin', Noah. I swear to God, I'm not tryin' to upset you, but I'm terrified that learnin' something too soon could *kill* you. So be mad at me if you want, but until the doctor says you're healthy, we're keepin' our mouths shut."

I was furious with him and with myself, because even through my anger I could see his fucking point.

"The bloody audacity!" I spluttered, feeling powerless and unheard. "Dad! Are you *listening* to this?"

"Yup." He nodded, completely unbothered that I was being bossed around like a kid. "You'll listen to Elliot more than you will us."

My jaw dropped. "That's *not* true, Dad."

I looked between the three faces I had always loved and admired, and I felt like they were caging me in with their decisions. They barely took my feelings into consideration about what was best for *me*, and it made me feel helpless. I found myself wanting Anderson here to be in my corner. He seemed to be the only person who was willing to tell me about my life, even if it was only snippets.

"Mum asked you to wait until she was here to bathe, yet you got this one" – he jabbed his thumb at Elliot – "in that room half-naked with you in no time. His word is law until you're better."

Horrified, I looked at Elliot.

"You told my *parents* about what happened in the bathroom?"

"I was scared." He locked his hands behind his head and avoided everyone's eyes but mine. "Once I started talkin', everythin' that happened spilled out. I couldn't stop meself."

I lifted my hands to my face and groaned. "You're unbelievable, Elliot."

"Sorry."

He *was* sorry, I could hear it in his voice. He actually sounded embarrassed.

"My leg hurts." I blinked sleepily. "And I'm so poxy tired. I hate the morphine."

"Go to sleep," Mum prompted.

"I will when you all go home," I challenged. "Sitting here while I'm sleeping is stupid. I'll be out until morning now that I've got morphine in my system."

My parents shared a look. They didn't want to leave me.

"Just come here earlier tomorrow," I reasoned. "I hate when you're all stuck here with me all day doing nothing."

Dad acquiesced. "Fine, we'll leave and be back in the morning."

"I'll do your washing," Mum said. "Elliot, go get me her dirty clothes from the bathroom, please."

My parents stood up, and both of them hugged and kissed me and told me that they loved me. Elliot put my dirty clothes into one of the smaller bags Mum had packed for this kind of situation. Dad took the bag from him, then my parents left the room.

"You go with them."

"I'll leave when you're asleep."

"Elliot."

"Noah."

"You can't just sit here with me all the time." I scowled. "You have a life."

He shook his head. "Work was my life, and now that I'm on leave I'm not doin' anythin' else. I *want* to be here with ye."

Arguing with him was hard when he was being so sweet and selfless. Staying mad at him was something I had never been very good at anyway. I didn't hold grudges; I'd always believed that a person should never go to bed angry. My situation was unique, but I was glad to find that my principles hadn't changed – no matter how much everything else did.

"Don't you want to go to the pub with AJ, Stitch, Tank and Pretty?"

"Stitch, Tank and Pretty are married with babies. They don't know what a pub is now."

I sucked in a breath of shock and joy.

"They're not!" I squealed. "They're all married, and they have babies? Oh my God!"

Elliot smiled at my obvious delight.

"Ye'll see them all once you're better. I've spoken to them and they all send ye their best wishes."

I knew they did. I'd had a beautiful flower wreath sent to me from the station – Mum had taken it home once the flowers started to die. I couldn't believe Elliot's friends were married and had children, and it made me curious about something.

"Elliot?"

"What?"

"Why aren't *you* in a relationship?"

He shifted. "Pretty hard findin' a woman to deal with me when it's never goin' to be a secret that I love another woman."

My breath caught in my throat. Part of me was elated that he was still in love with me – even though he'd not actually said I was that woman, I knew he was talking about me. The other part of me was heartbroken for him, even though I was hurt over our break-up too.

"You've been all alone since I left?"

He stared at me for a moment. "I don't want to hurt ye, Noah."

"I know," I said. "You'd never intentionally hurt me."

175

Elliot had changed from how I remembered him – all the things I'd learned since waking up proved that – but I knew his heart, and I was sure that hadn't changed.

"I also won't lie to you," he continued.

I swallowed. "You haven't been all alone . . . have you? Do you have someone new that you're seeing regularly?"

When Elliot shook his head, I was so relieved that I couldn't contain it; my shoulders sagged as I lost my stiff posture. The panic that had been quietly building faded until I could breathe again.

"It's okay." I attempted to smile. "I got married; I have no right to harbour any jealousy about you being with someone else."

Christ, just the thought of it made me want to vomit.

"It's not like that," he sighed, and leaned in. "I've never been in a relationship with anyone other than you. I slept around a lot during an angry phase not long after ye got married, and I had sex with women I met in pubs or clubs over the last few years. But it was just sex, just something to make me not feel so empty."

Pain sliced through me.

"I wish everything had happened differently."

"Me too, *sasanach*," he said, smiling sadly. "Me too."

"I love you, Elliot," I said. "I do, but we need to put a pin in us until I can process all I've learned today. Okay?"

"Okay," he agreed. "We'll go at your pace."

"Will you hug me?" I asked. "Today was . . . a lot."

Without another word he leaned into me, allowing me to press my face against his neck. I inhaled and felt him tense ever so slightly. He placed his hand on my back and began to stroke up and down, relaxing me even more.

"I'm scared," I whispered. "I'm scared because I don't know how life will be for us."

"That feeling you're experiencing is how I felt when I thought of us being married back before we broke up. I was so sure we'd crumble like my parents; I was terrified of the unknown."

I wrapped my arms around him.

"How did we get here?" I mumbled. "I mean, I know how we got here, but how did it all happen like that? I never thought we'd break."

"I know, gorgeous. Me neither."

I surprised myself and Elliot when I kissed his neck. I felt a shudder run through him.

"I'm struggling with a lot on my mind right now that I need to figure out for myself. I won't lie to you, part of me is conflicted about trusting you after everything you've just told me, and since I can't trust my memory, I have to go with the only thing I have left – and that's my gut. I truly believe that I need you by my side as I go through this."

I felt Elliot relax completely, and he began to sway us from side to side, lulling me further into the arms of an exhaustion that was desperate to claim me in its embrace. On the brink of sleep, I flicked through my memories of the day. I felt like a rag doll being pulled in a hundred different directions, and even though part of me couldn't completely trust Elliot – or my parents – I had to believe that what they were doing by keeping things from me was for my health.

If I believed anything else, my head would split in two.

Learning about my past should have given me perspective to help me figure out my future, but I would have been lying if I said relearning the things I had forgotten was easy. It was trying, heavy, and more than I could handle at times. I needed Elliot, and my parents, to help shoulder the weight.

I prayed that this would be the biggest hurdle I would face – because if it wasn't, I knew that my weakened body, and fragile mind, wouldn't be able to take it.

CHAPTER SEVENTEEN
NOAH

It wasn't uncommon for me to wake up in the middle of the night, but it was when I had been given morphine for pain. Normally, my mind was so foggy on it that I was in a constant state of droopiness for well over twelve hours. My body had never taken all that well to morphine, and I didn't think it ever would.

I felt a touch on my wrist and I instantly thought of Elliot. But when I opened my eyes, Elliot was not the person I was looking at. Staring back at me were eyes like black dahlias.

"Hey, baby. I didn't think you'd be awake. I missed you . . . I just wanted to see you."

I found myself smiling as I pulled myself into awareness.

"Hi, Anderson." I rubbed my eyes with the back of my hand. "I haven't seen you in a while."

It was only two days since I'd seen him last, but two days in a hospital felt like two weeks. I pushed myself into an upright position and stretched. A glance towards the window of my room showed it was pitch black outside. It was the middle of the night, and my body knew it because I was exhausted.

"I told you that I'd come back and see you."

"I know." I yawned. "Time passes by so slowly in here. Hours feel like days. How are you?"

I looked at him and was surprised by what I saw. He looked like an entirely different person. His dark circles were gone and so was his scruff, and his tired eyes were no more. His hair was styled, and his clothing was fresh.

"I'm better," he answered, drawing my attention back to his face. "How are *you*?"

"You look better." I smiled. "I'm doing good, slowly getting there. My memories still haven't returned, and at this point I'm wondering if they ever will. It's frustrating."

"It's frustrating for me, so I can only imagine what it's like for you," Anderson said as he reached over and took hold of my wrist. He pressed his fingers against my skin – and when I smiled at him, he returned it.

It struck me as odd that I realised in that moment how attractive he was. I couldn't help but compare him to Elliot. Elliot's very essence screamed masculinity, and while Anderson was very much a man, he appeared to be much more tame than wild. I still felt dominance radiating from him though, which I found odd. I'd never liked men who were the "me Tarzan, you Jane" type, but maybe I'd changed my mind . . . or maybe Anderson had changed it for me.

"I'm sorry," I said to him, hoping he would hear the sincerity in my voice. "I know I've said it before, but I'm sorry about this whole situation. I can't imagine how you must be feeling. I wish I could remember something about you, about our time together, to give me something to go off – but it's all blank."

"Don't worry, baby." His hand on my wrist tightened ever so slightly. "We have all the time in the world for you to get to know me again."

He wasn't wrong, but I knew that wasn't something I wanted to explore. I was wholeheartedly in love with Elliot, and I wanted things to go back to the way they were . . . but a part of me also felt responsible for Anderson. I suddenly wished he had never come to visit me. Things were easier to dissect and think about when I wasn't face-to-face with him. It was simpler to imagine getting on with my life without him in it when I didn't have to speak to him or see him.

It felt less personal, less like he was a real person.

"Have you spoken to Doctor Abara?" I quizzed.

"Yes," Anderson said, leaning back in his chair but never taking his hand off my wrist. "I speak to him every evening; he's kind enough to give me updates on you. Most recently was on the phone earlier tonight. He told me you had an . . . episode."

I tried to keep my expression neutral, but I couldn't control the pounding of my heart. I knew Anderson could feel the change in pace of my pulse; his fingers were rested right on my wrist. He looked at my wrist, then back to me with a raised eyebrow. My stomach churned. Had Doctor Abara told him that Elliot and I had kissed? Or that he'd assisted me in the shower? I didn't know this man from Adam, but I couldn't control the sense of fear that filled me as I wondered if he'd found out. He would think I'd cheated on him even though, to me, he was still very much a stranger.

"It was scary." I cleared my throat. "I've had headaches constantly since I woke up, but I hadn't had an episode like that since the first day or two, where the pain was so bad that it caused me to collapse."

"You're okay now," Anderson assured me. "Just take it easy – the doctor said you were overdoing it . . . trying to heal faster."

I practically deflated with relief.

The doctor hadn't told him anything private, and I was glad. I didn't want to hurt Anderson; I needed time with him so I could eventually let him down easy. It occurred to me then that I had already made up my mind, with no room for argument. I wanted Elliot. He was my one. I was heartbroken for Anderson, and I felt awful knowing I intended to end our marriage, our entire relationship, but I couldn't be with someone I didn't know or care for. I didn't even *want* to get to know him, which made me feel horribly cruel. But the fact was I didn't want him.

Not when I had Elliot . . . No man compared to him in my eyes, or in my heart, and no one ever would.

"Yeah." I nodded. "I guess because my headaches aren't as bad, and my body is healing, I was getting restless here. It was a reminder than my brain is still hurting and I've a long way to go until I'm better."

"Do you remember what you were doing to bring on the pain?"

I hesitated for a moment but didn't see the point in hiding a conversation.

"Elliot told me about why we broke up because I have no memory of it. I guess I was trying to remember what he told me for myself and my brain just checked out. One second I was talking and the next I was lying down with Doctor Abara leaning over me. He scolded me for not taking care of myself."

Anderson kept eye contact with me as I spoke, so I busied myself with fixing my blanket. His hold on my wrist didn't hurt, but it was bothering me. His touch didn't soothe me like Elliot's did when he held my hand and brushed his thumb over my knuckles.

"Elliot has been here a lot."

A statement, not a question.

"Yes, along with my parents," I added. "My mind is stuck in a period when they're all I remember. Surely you understand that their presence comforts me, right?"

"You left Elliot," Anderson said bluntly. "You wanted more from him than what he could give you. You told me you had never loved anyone the way you loved me."

I felt like I couldn't speak.

"When I met you, we just clicked. Once we started talking, I soon found out that you were . . . depressed," he said tentatively. "You don't like medication so you didn't want to see a doctor about it, but you were hurting in your mind. You had pulled away from your parents, your ex's family, and it got so bad that you even quit your job not long later."

I stared at Anderson with my mouth agape. I'd left my job as a florist . . . something I adored and which brought me joy outside of all my relationships. My heart clenched with pain.

"Oh my God," I whispered. "No one told me any of that."

"They probably didn't know about your depression." He shrugged. "It's just been you and me for the past few years. We've been together nearly four years and married for three."

I suddenly felt sick to my stomach.

"I was depressed?" I blinked, bewildered.

It made sense. After leaving Elliot I could imagine myself going into a pit of loneliness and sadness . . . but I'd never have pushed my parents away. I tensed when I suddenly remembered my mother speaking to me on the night I awoke from my coma. She'd said she was never letting us drift apart *again*.

"Very depressed," Anderson answered. "You were sad . . . but then we got close. We fell in love fast, and when I asked you to marry me, you said yes. We married ten months after we met. A whirlwind romance."

I felt like my heart was about to burst. I had left Elliot after being together for seven years, and jumped into a new relationship and married ten months later. That was beyond crazy to me. It didn't sound like something I would do . . . but then again, neither did leaving Elliot because he didn't want to get married.

I tried to imagine myself entering a relationship with Anderson while I was still dealing with the hurt from breaking up with Elliot, and it dawned on me that Anderson must have been someone I felt a deep connection with in order for that to happen. I had always wanted security in my relationship, and since I'd lost that in Elliot, it made sense that I'd moved on with Anderson if he was someone I believed I could depend on.

"This is . . . a lot to break down," I said, lifting my hands to my head. "*A lot.*"

The door to the room suddenly opened and I heard a female voice say, "It is *way* past visiting hours, sir. It's three in the morning."

"I'm her husband," was Anderson's reply.

That didn't appease the nurse in the slightest, and I closed my eyes.

"You'll have to leave, sir. Now."

"Okay," Anderson grunted. "Allow me to say goodbye to my wife . . . she's hurting and wants me here."

I couldn't speak; an ache was forming and I was trying not to think too hard, but how could I not? Anderson had just told me a secret about myself that I would have preferred remaining ignorant of. When I opened my eyes again, the nurse was gone, and I was alone with Anderson.

"She's getting you painkillers; she'll be back soon."

"Not morphine," I said. "I hate that stuff, it makes me feel sick. I don't take to it well. A little bit of it and I'll be drowsy for hours."

Anderson nodded, slowly.

"Try to relax," he soothed, his thumb moving back and forth across my wrist. "I wasn't supposed to tell you things from your past that could upset you . . . the doctor said information like this is overwhelming and could harm you, but you had a right to know, baby. It's only been the two of us . . . now *they* want to keep you away from me. My own wife."

My head was hurting, but through the fog of pain I could hear the anger in Anderson's tone, and to an extent I could understand it. He felt ambushed by Elliot and my family, who had apparently not been in my life for the last few years. Some of this new information was clearly among the things that Elliot had decided to keep from me for my own good. I couldn't lie, I was somewhat angry at him for leaving out that I'd jumped into a brand-new relationship not long after I left him.

That was something I'd *needed* to fucking know.

"I'll hold off on visiting you again for a while." Anderson gained my attention once more. "The doctor wants me to wait until your mind is stronger to merge our lives back together, but your family, and *him*, are making things difficult, so I want you to memorise my number and our home address. When you learn the things that are being kept from you, you can come to me. You'll be safe with me and I'll be honest with you . . . like I always have."

I groaned. "What things?"

"You'll learn," he answered gruffly. "Your parents, and *him*, will fill in the blanks for you."

I felt like the years I couldn't remember had been lived by a stranger inside my body, because the things that I had done, the decisions that I had made, were just not things that I could imagine doing in my current frame of mind. I couldn't believe that I had done the things people had told me about and I found myself wishing it was all a big lie or a horrible nightmare, but I knew it wasn't. This was my life now . . . and I somehow had to figure it out without making any more dire mistakes.

"Anderson," I said, licking my lips. "This is really a lot for me to deal with."

His anger suddenly vanished, and an expression filled with concern came over his features.

"I know, baby," he murmured. "But I'm going to help you get through this, okay?"

I didn't want his help, but how could I turn him away? The man was innocent in all of this; he'd done nothing wrong other than love and marry me. It wasn't his fault I was in an accident and had lost my memory.

"Okay," I answered, my eyes feeling heavy.

We spent a few minutes with him telling me his phone number and home address, and when I could say them by heart he gave me a smile. I couldn't hold my eyes open any longer and allowed them to drift shut.

"You're mine, Noah," his voice whispered. "I'll not let them take you away from me."

I hummed in response – not really hearing his words, only the sound of his voice, which was soothing in that moment.

"Sleep," Anderson said softly. "This will all be over soon."

CHAPTER EIGHTEEN

ELLIOT

"Well, slap my arse and call me Daisy! Irish is here!"

I heard shouts, laughter and whoops from all corners of the station as Pretty jumped to his feet and crossed the common room. He embraced me in a hug and patted the hell out of my back. I stepped back and grinned as he scowled at me.

"You're not allowed around my wife." He roughly shoved my chest, sending me stumbling backwards. "She thinks you're 'ruggedly handsome' without your ten-inch homeless-man beard. Why'd you have to go and get all groomed?"

I snorted. "Noah's orders."

"Her word was always law with you." His lips twitched. "How is she doing?"

"She's getting there, she's on the mend."

I didn't mention about her collapsing the day before, because I was still reeling from the shock of it. Explaining it to my friends would be like reliving it all over again, and I was doing my best not to think about it.

I smiled when my other buddies filed into the room. Tank, Stitch and Texas were walking behind AJ, laughing at something he'd said. I got fist bumps and manly hugs with a lot of back-patting before everyone took a seat.

"How's the watch goin'?" I asked.

"Not a peep so far," Pretty answered. "I never really *want* the siren to go off because I don't want people hurt or worse, but days like this drag."

Tank rolled his eyes. "Hit the gym with me then. You don't *have* to sit on your arse."

"I'm not working out with you," Pretty grunted. "I nearly *died* the last time. Not everyone can lift what you can, you fucking mountain."

I looked between them, grinning. The banter between my friends was one of the reasons coming to work on days that were rough were worth it. I had known these guys for years, and they were truly a good group of men even though no insult was too far for them when it came to giving me stick.

"Frenchie, Wilds, Tune, Pops and Boyo are out in the drill yard. If you don't want to go join them, you can help me clean the kitchen and maintain some equipment when Irish leaves," Stitch piped up, his rank as watch manager clear. "You'll become a part of the sofa otherwise at this rate, mate."

Pretty made the motion with his hand to suggest he thought Stitch was a wanker, making me snort.

"How's Noah?" Tank asked.

"She's orderin' me around, so she's back to her old self."

The lads snorted.

"How are *you* dickheads?" I looked around the room. "Families all good?"

I got a chorus of "yes", which pleased me, and they all began to talk over one another.

I glanced around at each man and found myself thinking of the times I'd spent with them. Losing my sister, and almost losing

Noah, had made me sit back and reflect on the life I'd led over the past few years. There were many drunken nights in clubs and pubs that had ended with me having meaningless sex with women whose faces blurred together, and for a long time I'd thought that was what I was living for: the bliss of a night out and the company of an unknown, willing woman to force the hurt I felt from my heart and mind.

I looked at my friends as they spoke about something their wives had done that was funny or how their babies had had a nappy explosion at three in the morning, and my priorities suddenly shifted. I listened to their stories and saw the happiness on their faces as they spoke, and things I was once scared about didn't seem scary any more. Marrying Noah had terrified me because I was scared that our relationship would end like my parents' had, but I realised that my and Noah's relationship wasn't like my parents', or her parents', or anyone else's.

It was entirely unique to us, and the comparisons I'd once made suddenly held no merit.

The realisation of this was like being doused in ice water. What now seemed like such a trivial thing to be scared of had changed my entire life for the worse. At the time it was such a massive struggle for me, but in this moment, being surrounded by my friends, it felt like a blindfold had been removed and I could see things clearly again. For the first time in a long time, my thought process wasn't dominated by fear of the unknown, heartache from my break-up or the pain of losing my sister.

The idea of marrying Noah and her having my children was something I could envision . . . it was something I wanted.

"I'm glad Noah is back to her old self, Eli," AJ said. "She's helping you massively by keeping your mind focused."

On something other than my sister being dead, he meant.

"Yeah," I agreed. "Everythin' has changed with her back in me life. Things aren't bleak any more. I have somethin' to look forward to when I go to see her every day. Even though what happened the night of the accident is constantly on me mind along with Bailey, Noah is front and centre because I can actually *do* somethin' to help her."

I wished I could snap my fingers and get to the bottom of that night, but the key factor in that was Noah's memory. She might possibly never get it back, and what happened the night Bailey died would forever remain a mystery. I wasn't going to give up though – I'd promised my sister that I'd find out what happened, and I would.

"When are you gonna tell her that Bailey died? She has to be asking all sorts of questions."

"She is," I answered Tank. "She's doin' well but her brain is so fragile still. If I tell her about Bailey it might . . . it might kill her. She'll blame herself. I know she will."

"Christ." Pretty scratched his neck. "Poor girl is going through it."

"Yeah," I agreed. "She's stuck on her differences now too, which sucks."

"What d'you mean?"

"She's really upset about her body. In her last memory she was slim, and now she has weight on her. I hope she doesn't linger on it because I'm fine with how she looks. When I was helpin' her shower and she bent over, I was *glad* her arse got fatter. Christ, I could have cried."

"Hold up." Texas sat upright. "You helped her *in* the shower. She was naked?"

"She was showerin'," I deadpanned. "Of *course* she was naked."

"Rewind." AJ held his hand up. "She has a fractured leg . . . *how* did she get naked?"

189

"I undressed her." At the widened eyes and happy smiles I received, I shook my head, laughing. "It wasn't like how you're all thinkin'. She said she needed *me* to help her, not the nurse. I didn't touch her, but the way she looked at me may as well have been strokes to me cock. I thought me balls were goin' to explode."

Snickers filled the room.

"Sounds to me like she was trying to get some." Pretty grinned, waggling his brows.

"She was," I laughed. "She wants me, she told me she loves me."

"Mate," AJ said with a smile. "That's brilliant."

"Yeah . . . until she gets her memories back."

"She's been awake almost two weeks now and hasn't had so much as a flashback." AJ looked at me pointedly. "Don't be worrying so much. She wants you; you want her. Stop making it complicated."

"It *is* complicated though," Tank chimed in. "She's married."

Like I could forget that important detail.

"Yep," I sighed. "That prick is never far from me mind."

"She can't remember the man." AJ shrugged. "She's fair game in my book."

"I'm not sympathising with the man 'cause I know he's a wanker," Pretty said. "However, if it were *my* wife in Noah's position, and her ex knew good and well she was mine, and he was *still* trying it on with her . . . I'd kill him."

"Me too," Tank and Stitch said in unison.

I scrubbed my face with my hands.

"I don't care about *him*," I stated. "I care about Noah. I already kissed her senseless, but I won't let it get that far. If she does get her memories back, I want to have a fightin' chance with her. I don't want to take advantage of the fact that her mind is stuck in the past when she loved me."

190

There was a moment of silence, then Pretty clapped his hand against my back.

"You're a good man, Irish."

"He's a better man than me," AJ snorted. "I'd have fucked her seven ways to Sunday by now . . . you should *see* how deliciously thick she's gotten. Thighs and tits of a goddess, boys."

I was on my feet and swinging at AJ before his last words left his mouth. The fucking lunatic laughed when I landed a right hook to his jaw, followed by a solid punch to his stomach. He didn't even attempt to fight me off; he had our buddies there to save him. Tank, the monster that he was, had easily wedged himself between us, and shoved me a metre or two away from a now-groaning AJ.

"Cool off," Tank said, but he was grinning, thoroughly amused. "You got your hits in."

Not nearly enough of them, if you asked me.

"Arsehole," AJ shouted, then laughed. "Why'd you have to hit me in my face?"

"It was warranted – you talked about his missus."

"I'm *joking*!" He paused. "Okay, I wasn't, but still. Ow!"

I scowled. "Ye know better. I'm wound up over her right now. Don't be given me reasons to attend another funeral!"

"You're *so* rude!" AJ grumbled as he got to his feet. "And fuck you lot for sitting there – are you *recording* this, Pretty?"

"Hell yeah I am," he snorted. "I wanna show my wife what I have to put up with in between calls."

Amused, I signalled to Tank that I was calm. He returned to his seat and I crossed over to AJ and peered at his face. His jaw was slightly swollen and red, but other than that, he was fine.

"Ye'll live."

"If it hurts me to kiss Dani later, I'm decking you."

I grinned at his grouching.

"When are ye gonna ask her to be your girlfriend? You're actin' like a clown with that girl."

"For your information" – AJ looked me up and down – "I asked her last night. I am now, officially, no longer a bachelor. I've got me a missus, a ball and chain, a bed-warmer if you will."

"If you listen very closely," Pretty said, squinting his eyes as if that would help him hear better. "You can hear a collective sigh of relief from the women of London."

"Bullshit." AJ waved his hand. "A collective cry as hearts break everywhere is what you'll hear. Women love me."

"I'm honestly so fuckin' glad." I patted his shoulder. "You havin' a missus will be like a dog gettin' neutered. Ye'll finally calm the fuck down."

We all laughed at AJ's expense, and he did too because he never took anything too seriously. None of us did when it came to insults.

"Irish, when are you coming back from compassionate leave?" Stitch asked me. "We miss your ugly mug."

"Ugly, ay?" I smirked. "Pretty here told me his wife thinks I'm handsome when I'm all cleaned up . . . And didn't *your* wife tell me I looked like a dark-haired Thor before? Will she like my new look?"

"I changed my mind." Stitch glowered. "Quit. We all hate you here."

Laughter filled the room once more.

"I have to see a counsellor first, obviously. I'll be back . . . a couple more weeks, maybe. I can't get much more than that without riskin' me job," I answered honestly. "But Noah needs me right now."

"Get your missus better and *then* come back to work," Pretty suggested. "Life was always safer when you were dating Noah."

"I disagree," AJ chimed in. "He was the shittest wingman *ever* when he was with Noah, but luckily I no longer need a wingman. Did I mention that Dani is my missus now?"

A collective groan echoed throughout the station.

"Is this all we're gonna hear now?" Texas sighed, running a hand through his black hair. "I'm the only single one left. Jesus. I never thought I'd want a steady girl at twenty-seven, but y'all are makin' me jealous."

I didn't remind him that I was technically still single, because I didn't want to be. I wanted to be back in a relationship with Noah more than anything. But I had to remember that baby steps were the way to go, even if the slow pace was killing me. Having her in the end would be more than worth it.

"Dani has an Irish cousin who just moved here." AJ grinned knowingly. "A sexy redhead. You like those, Tex."

Texas raised his eyebrows. "What's the catch?"

"She's crazy, just like Dani, *that's* the catch. She has that fiery Irish temper."

AJ showed Texas a picture of the redhead. I caught sight of it and whistled.

"She's fine-lookin'."

"Our kids will be beautiful," Texas said, earning a laugh and a pat on the back from every man in the room.

"I've got you, bro," AJ said as he tapped on the screen of his phone. "Double date tomorrow night?"

"If she likes the look of me, hell yeah."

"Mate." AJ rolled his eyes skywards. "Why d'you think I pitched her to you? Dani already pitched you to *her* and told me to get us a double date because you're apparently 'sex on legs' and your Southern cowboy accent induces 'fanny flutters'. That was a direct quote from Dani's cousin, none of that was improvised on my part. I think you're ugly and sound like a dumbarse when you speak."

I shook my head in amusement as they exchanged insults and worked out the details of their upcoming double date. When my phone rang and I saw it was Mr Ainsley, I answered it right away.

"Mr A," I greeted him. "Everything okay?"

"No," he sighed. "Anderson was here last night and he had a long talk with Noah. She's very upset and doesn't want to speak to us. She wants us to leave, but we're not going anywhere. She doesn't want to see you either. I don't know what the son of a bitch told her but get over here now. She needs you."

I was already jogging out of the station before I hung up the phone, shouting to my friends that everything was fine when everything was definitely *not* fucking fine. I jumped in my car with my heart pounding. What did Anderson tell Noah? If he'd told her about Bailey, if he'd told her what should rightfully have come from me, West Norwood Cemetery would need to open a new plot immediately.

CHAPTER NINETEEN

NOAH

"Are you gonna make me call the nurse to ask you both to leave?" I demanded of my parents. "Because I can do just that if you want me to."

They had been here close to an hour, and they were refusing to leave until I had a proper conversation with them. But I didn't want to. When I'd awoken early that morning, alone, my conversation with Anderson had replayed over and over in my mind then anger had set in. I'd never liked being kept in the dark about things, but this took the cake.

"Stop being so stubborn, Noah Ainsley."

It was on the tip of my tongue to correct her with my married name of Riley, but that was only frustration wanting to rear its ugly head. I couldn't claim Anderson's surname when I felt no connection to it. To him.

I frowned at my mother. "You let Dad phone Elliot when I made it clear I don't want to speak to any of you right now, and you're calling *me* stubborn?"

Mum sighed. "I don't know what Anderson told you—"

"*He*," I interrupted, "a man who is a stranger to me, told me things that you should have told me. He told me I cut you both – and everyone else – out of my life. I had to hear that from *him*."

Dad's face turned purple. "He had no right, no fucking right."

"No right?" I repeated, bewildered. "Dad, I'm married to the man. I may not remember him, but he was with me throughout the period of my life that I can't bloody remember. A life none of you were involved in. He is the *only* person who can tell me what the hell happened, because neither of you, nor Elliot, trust me with the information."

We all looked at the doorway when it was flung open. It was Elliot and he was breathing heavily, sweat glistening on his forehead. I wondered if he'd run all the way up the stairs from the car park, but I didn't ask because deep down I knew the answer to my question. He had.

"Get out."

He crossed the room. "Make me."

"Make you?" I sat upright. "You pig-headed bastard. Get *out*!"

Elliot ignored me, looking from me to my parents.

"What'd he tell her?"

"How they got together, and that she pushed everyone away . . . that's all."

I gaped at him when Elliot appeared to be . . . relieved. His shoulders sagged as he placed his hands on his hips and blew out a big breath. I glared at him.

"You've some fucking nerve to look *happy* about this, Elliot McKenna."

His expression hardened.

"I *am* glad," he replied, his tone clipped. "I'm glad he didn't overwhelm ye and hurt you!"

I looked towards the window. "I'm not as fragile as you think I am."

"I don't think you're fragile, Noah. What I *know* is that you're recoverin' from a brain injury and I'm heedin' the advice of medical professionals who agree that takin' things day by day is best. Ye *collapsed* yesterday, for fuck's sake!"

He was right of course, but there were times, like now, that I didn't feel as broken as I was. I wanted to scream. I knew that keeping information from me was logically the best thing for anyone to do, but when I craved honesty, it made accepting that very difficult.

"Treating me like a piece of glass won't protect me from shattering, Elliot."

He shook his head and sat down in the chair to my left. He wasn't happy with me; I didn't even need to look at him to know it. My parents were the same.

"I'm going to find this stuff out eventually," I said. "Who knows if my brain will ever be able to handle it?"

"No one knows," Elliot snapped, making me jump. "But what I *do* know is learnin' about stressful things when you're as vulnerable as ye are right now is *not* the way to go."

He was right, but I also didn't regret finding out about the things that Anderson had told me, now that I had time to think about it. The more I learned about the last few years, the more I was certain that I didn't want to know, because it only led to more questions. But what I *wanted* wasn't important. I *needed* to know what I'd done in my life, in order to figure out how I could move forward on the new path that I was on.

"What's done is done," I said, resting my head back against my pillow. "I know what I know so there's no point in you being angry about it."

"How did he even get in here?" Elliot asked my parents.

"Because he's my *husband*, maybe?" I hissed, sitting back upright. I ignored how rigid Elliot went with my emphasis on the word. "He has a right to visit me, no matter how damaging you all

197

think it may be for me. Why would you all be so cruel to him? Do you have any idea how he feels? To be told it's better for his wife *not* to see or speak to him?"

No one said anything in reply, but I didn't expect them to.

"He's angry and upset with you all, and you'd be mad to say you couldn't understand why. He told me he understood the doctor and that's why he stopped trying to come by, but the two times he's come were because he missed me. He said he thought I'd be sleeping and that he just wanted to sit with me for a while. He wasn't expecting me to wake up."

"Two times?" Elliot raised an eyebrow. "He's been here twice?"

"Last night, and a couple of nights ago. We just spoke, and both times I was fine. He understands Doctor Abara's orders."

"If he understood what the doctor said, why did he talk to you about things you can't remember?"

"Because I asked him questions and he answered." I shrugged at my father. "I know I'm not supposed to know this stuff yet because of what happened with Elliot yesterday, but this is so hard for me. I keep learning things that *are* hurting me."

"Which is *exactly* why ye don't need to know about them," Elliot interrupted. "Not yet, anyway."

"I don't understand any of it though." A lump formed in my throat. "What frame of mind was I in to cut you all out of my life?" I swallowed. "What was going through my head to think that that was the best poxy option for me? Anderson said I was really depressed, but why did I turn away from you all?"

"We don't know," Mum answered. "We tried to contact you, but you quit your job and moved in with Anderson within days of knowing him."

"My God." I shook my head. "Right after I leave Elliot, I get with a stranger and move in with him? Who *does* that?"

I could understand moving on with Anderson after Elliot because he'd provided me with what Elliot couldn't give me at the time, but to move in with him after a few days was drastic – and I didn't agree with it.

"I thought the same," Dad grunted. "I showed up at Anderson's flat with the intention of bring you home, but you told me that you wanted to stay. You were twenty-five. I couldn't drag you out kicking and screaming, though the thought did cross my mind."

Elliot leaned forward and took my hand in his. He rubbed his thumb over my knuckles, but even his touch didn't bring me comfort in that moment. I felt distraught.

"I feel so . . . so upset with myself." I looked towards the window and out at the swaying branches of a nearby tree. "I don't know why I did what I did . . . but I'm so sorry to you all. I'll never be able to forgive myself."

"Well, ye better," Elliot said gruffly, causing me to look up at his face. "Me, your parents, our friends . . . we forgave ye years ago."

I covered my face with my hands and willed myself not to cry. When Elliot's arms came around me, I knew I was fighting a losing battle.

"I can't keep crying," I whispered as I slid my arms around his body. He sat on the edge of my bed and held me. "Nothing changes, no matter how many tears I shed."

"Cryin' can sometimes help people feel better. It's not like ye can help it anyway."

Once again, Elliot was right.

"Was he here long?"

It didn't go unnoticed to me that Elliot rarely called Anderson by his name, and now that I thought about it, Anderson did the same thing when referring to Elliot. They both really hated one another, which didn't help the situation I was in at all, because I was connected to them both whether I liked it or not.

"I don't know how long he was here. When I woke up, he was sitting next to me and he was still here when I fell back asleep. We just sat and talked a while." I shrugged as I pulled back from the hug before looking down at my hands. "I feel so cruel."

I bit the inside of my cheek to keep from crying any more than I already had. I wiped my tears away, feeling frustrated.

"Why?" Elliot quizzed. "You've done nothin' wrong."

"I talked with him for a good while, and in my head I compared him to you without being able to stop myself," I explained, not looking up at him. "He was saying all these things to me and I couldn't make sense of any of them in my mind. He's my husband but I feel nothing for him, I don't even *want* to get to know him because I want you and only you. That's why I feel so cruel, Elliot. Anderson did nothing wrong, and he'll be the one who gets hurt in the end because of me."

Elliot's touch on my knuckles finally helped me start to relax, and I found myself thinking of Anderson's touch on my wrist. This was how his touch should have made me feel, but it hadn't.

"Ye don't *want* to hurt him," Elliot stated. "Sometimes hurtin' people can't be helped when puttin' ourselves first."

"Putting myself first distanced me from you all in the first place, Elliot."

"How can ye be mad at yourself for things ye have *no* memory of?" he asked me. "How?"

"I don't know. This whole situation . . . it's so messed up."

More poxy tears fell.

"I feel like I've cried all the tears a person gets for a lifetime. I wish I was like you." I wiped my cheeks again. "I can't ever remember you crying."

"Just because someone doesn't cry doesn't mean they aren't broken, just like when someone smiles it doesn't mean they're happy." He kept stroking his thumb over my knuckles. "When you left me,

I was devastated. I couldn't function for a long time, and even when I developed a new routine without you, nothing felt real."

"I'm sorry."

"*Don't* be," he said. "I'm past it, I'm here right now with you. If cryin' helps ye move forward, then cry."

I sniffled. "I guess I'm just more prone to emotional outbursts compared to normal people."

Elliot's lips twitched. "Maybe."

"Still . . ." I shrugged. "Somehow I'm coping."

"You're not copin', Noah. You're drownin'."

My breath caught. "I don't know what to do."

"I do," Elliot said. "We'll take things *slowly*; we'll communicate and decide together when we should discuss the past few years in more depth. Sound like a plan?"

I looked from Elliot to my parents – they agreed with him whole-heartedly, I could tell from one glance. They had always trusted him, they had always loved him, and it seemed that was something that had remained the same.

"Okay." I nodded, looking at back him. "Anderson told me I wouldn't see him for a while. He's doing what the doctor wants."

I left out the part about him wanting me to go to him when my family – and Elliot – filled me in about the blank spaces in my memory. I was surprised to find that I could still remember his phone number and home address. I hoped I would never need to use either.

"Good," Elliot said. "We're going to focus on getting you better. No more talkin' of the past for the time bein', or the future for that matter. We're only goin' to be takin' things as they come. Day by day."

"Day by day," I echoed. "Together."

Elliot leaned in and kissed me in front of my parents, claiming his right to do so with pride.

"Together."

CHAPTER TWENTY

NOAH

"Noah, can you stop fidgeting for *two* minutes?"

"No, Mum," I answered, as I used my crutches to hop over to the window so I could peer outside at the world I'd been caged away from. "I can't. I've been in this hospital for six weeks. Six weeks of being stuck in a bed, six weeks of nurses coming in and out to check on me, six weeks of you, Dad, Elliot and sometimes AJ, sitting and staring at me. In twenty minutes, I'll be discharged and *free*. I cannot sit still; I don't even *want* to!"

I felt good. *So* fucking good.

A month ago, I had decided that I would do what my family, Elliot and Doctor Abara wanted. I would take things day by day and focus on getting better. Of course, there were times when I slipped and wanted to speak about the things I'd been told about – like mine and Elliot's break-up, and how quickly I moved on with Anderson – but each time I was shut down by Elliot or my parents. And I didn't fight with them – I may have got snippy once or twice, but I let it go and remembered my goal.

I wanted to go home.

I hadn't established where that home would be yet, but my parents had taken it upon themselves to ready my old bedroom for my impending arrival. A massive part of me wanted to return to the flat I'd once shared with Elliot, the flat where he still lived, but I was nervous about it, so going home with my parents was the right call. I didn't say it out loud, but I felt some worry about going back to the way things were with Elliot, because things would never really be as they once were – and that was something I had to get used to. Elliot was a gentleman about the whole living situation, and he wanted me to file for divorce from Anderson and tell him that I had no interest in continuing my marriage with him. Those were his conditions before we could be properly intimate again.

His conditions didn't extend to kisses and light, innocent touches though – he said was he was only a man, not a saint, which thoroughly amused me.

My time in the hospital had been an experience, one I wanted to put behind me. I would be lying if I said I wasn't nervous about leaving the safety that these walls had provided me over the last few weeks. It was in here that I'd regained control of a life that had got away from me; it was here where Elliot and I had reconnected and I'd found out I had managed to fall even more in love with him. It was here that I re-established my bond and trust with my parents. I had learned to walk again, through hard hours of physical therapy; and in many ways, I had become a new person.

So leaving the hospital had me a little on edge.

My headaches had been more annoying than really painful since I'd collapsed in front of Elliot after he helped me shower, but I was always paranoid that one would suddenly strike me down and that I'd be rendered useless again. Knowing I was going home and away from the nurses and doctors was daunting, but I reminded myself not to think negatively. I had to think of things as they came and stop getting ahead of myself.

It had helped me get this far, and I hoped it would help me get a lot further too.

"Elliot is sad he isn't here, isn't he?"

I looked at my mother.

"Yeah," I said. "But I'm glad he's gone back to work; he was here so much they may as well have given *him* a bed."

Mum chuckled. "How have his first few days been back on watch?"

"As good as can be," I answered. "A couple of small fires, a minor car accident, and I think he said they had to help get a cat out of a tree yesterday."

"No!" Mum laughed.

I smiled. "He says he misses me."

"Of course he does." Mum rolled her eyes. "And you miss him."

"Of course I do," I mimicked her, chuckling. "But he finishes his second night shift at nine a.m. and then he's off for four days. He says he's spending them with me."

"I'm not surprised," Mum said, winking. "You're both acting like you did when you first began to date, always wanting to be around one another."

I felt myself blush. "I love him."

"I know you do," she said warmly. "Which is why I made an appointment on Monday morning with a solicitor . . . so you can start the divorce process."

I felt terrible whenever I thought about Anderson, I truly did, but I had to do what was best for me – and that meant cutting off all ties with him.

"Good." I exhaled. "I'm ready for that."

"When will you speak to him?"

"I'll phone him on Sunday and meet him somewhere in town." I gnawed on my lip. "I don't want to do it publicly, but I'm also not going to his home. I lived in that place, and I just feel weird about going there."

"I don't blame you."

We both looked up when Doctor Abara entered the room. I returned his happy smile.

"Ready to go home?"

"Born ready," I answered.

He laughed. "I've a prescription here for you. These tablets are only to be taken as you need them. When you get a headache, take them, Noah. No trying to hold out and hoping it goes away. You take the medication. Understand?"

"Yes, sir." I saluted him. "I'm not a fan of taking tablets, but I'll do it. You have my word."

"Good. You'll come back in six weeks' time to outpatients for a check-up, and we'll decide then when your next check-up should be. But if everything is well with you, I'm thinking six months from that day."

I bobbed my head. "Sounds good to me."

"As I said yesterday" – he looked at me and my mother – "any double vision, dizziness or signs that you might be having one of your bad headaches, you come straight into Casualty. No exceptions."

"She will," Mum answered. "The three of us will make sure of it."

And that was the God's honest truth.

I thanked the doctor, and it turned out my mum had brought him chocolates, a bottle of wine and a thank-you card, which caught him off guard. He assured her he was just doing his job in taking care of me, and Mum reminded him that by "just doing his job" he had saved her child's life. He accepted the gifts with thanks, told me to take care of myself, and said his goodbyes and that I was free to leave.

Dad caught the doctor in the hallway, thanked him and shook his hand before venturing inside my room. "Ready to go?" He rubbed his hands together. "All of your things are packed into the boot of the car."

I grabbed my crutches as Mum straightened down the back of my dress.

"Let's blow this joint!"

My parents laughed as we left the room and said goodbye to the many nurses we'd come to know by name. Mum had gotten them gifts too. We wished them all the best as we left the hospital with smiles on our faces. Dad didn't want me walking far, so Mum and I sat and waited at the entrance while he hurried to retrieve the car. When he pulled up, he helped me into the passenger side while Mum hopped in the back.

I drummed my fingers on the dashboard, making Dad laugh as he climbed into the driver's seat.

"Let's go home!"

Mum reached over and squeezed Dad's shoulder, a moment passing between them that brought a smile to my face. As we drove we talked, and I tried to figure out how to work the new phone my parents had bought me. It was an iPhone, like Elliot's. I had been an Apple user back in 2015 but things had really changed, and I found myself playing around with it to get accustomed to it.

I jumped when the phone rang and Elliot's name appeared on the screen.

"Hello?"

"Hey," he yawned. "Are ye still at the hospital?"

"Nope, I'm free! Freeedddoooommmmm!"

Elliot's laughter was masked by my parents' as they shook their heads, amused.

"I'm on my way to my parents'," I said. "You go home and sleep. D'you hear me?"

I could almost hear the pout in his voice as he said, "But I wanna see ye."

"You can see me later, *after* you sleep. Come by – Mum's making a pasta bake for dinner tonight."

"I'd argue with ye, but I'm feckin' knackered."

I chuckled. "Sleep. I'll see you later."

"I love ye, *sasanach*."

"I love you too, paddy."

When the call ended, I relaxed for the rest of the drive home. When we finally got inside the house, everything was still the same, much to my relief.

"Thank God," I breathed as I hobbled over to the flower-filled vase on the coffee table and admired it. "I was so worried that everything would have changed."

"Like your mother would allow that," Dad joked.

We spent the entire morning sorting through the clothes I had there that definitely did not fit me any more, and would go to a charity shop. I helped my mum rearrange my room until I was happy with the placement of everything. I whiled away the rest of the day watching films, reading some of a book, and constantly checking my phone to see if Elliot had texted me. He was asleep – he had just come off a night watch – so there wasn't a chance in hell that I was calling him and waking him up.

He needed his rest, and when five o'clock rolled by, so did I.

I went upstairs intending to nap for an hour – two at most – but when I felt soft touches on my cheek, I groaned and flicked my eyes open for a moment to find that my room was coated in darkness. I was tired and couldn't fully rouse myself from my sleep. I didn't want to.

"No," his voice murmured, sounding far away like in a dream. "Rest. I'll see you first thing tomorrow, okay?"

I hummed in response.

"I love you, green eyes."

"Love you too."

I felt lips brush against mine, then the sound of a door clicking shut. I fell back asleep in seconds but awoke when I heard a car horn honking. I reached up, rubbed my eyes and stretched. I relaxed for a second, then quickly darted upright when I thought of Elliot.

I frowned.

I lifted a hand to my lips and wondered if I'd been dreaming of him or if I'd really missed him when he stopped by. I grabbed my phone and clicked on a text I saw he sent me.

> I stopped by, but you were snoring and looked so cute and peaceful. I didn't want to wake you up. I had dinner with your parents then came home so you could rest. See you first thing tomorrow. I can't wait. Love you.

I covered my face in annoyance, I'd have to wait until tomorrow morning to see him now. I checked the time and saw that it was only half nine. I lay back on my bed and shook my head.

"This is stupid," I said to myself. "Why am I not with him right now?"

I loved Elliot and he loved me. I wasn't staying apart from him when I didn't have to; it didn't feel right to be separated from him. I was nervous about how our relationship would pan out now, but I was doing what Elliot had said and taking it day by day.

With my mind made up, I got up and looked at the new clothes and underwear my mum had bought for me. I settled on wearing black leggings, a black T-shirt and a light grey jumper.

I grabbed my old duffle bag from my wardrobe and packed a change of clothes along with clean underwear and socks. I pulled one of my white Vans on to my right foot, then put my boot cast back on my left. I packed some toiletries for myself, since I knew I had none at Elliot's, hooked the bag over my shoulder, grabbed my crutches and slowly made my way down the stairs.

I paused by the sitting room when I saw Mum knitting.

"Mum."

She looked up at me and an amused smile stretched across her face. "Is your father going to owe me twenty pounds?"

"Depends." I raised an eyebrow. "Did you bet on something?"

"Yup." She grinned. "I bet you wouldn't make it past ten p.m. without coming down and telling us you wanted to go and be with Elliot; he bet eleven."

I glanced at the clock and saw it was twenty to ten. I looked back at my mother and laughed.

"You win, I want to go and be with Elliot."

"Figured as much," she chuckled. "Come on, Dad will drive us."

My dad grumbled as he put my bag in the boot of the car. He wasn't upset that I was leaving, only that he'd lost the bet he made with my mum, which cracked me up. The drive was quick and uneventful. When we got there, Dad waited in the car while Mum carried my bag on her shoulder as I hobbled inside.

We shared the elevator with a pizza delivery boy. I glanced at the receipt on the box and grinned when I saw it was for Elliot. He had had dinner with my parents a few hours ago, but was obviously still hungry. I borrowed money from my mum, told the boy I'd bring it to the flat because it was my boyfriend's, and paid him. Mum took the box from me and we quietly made our way down the hallway until we stopped in front of my old flat.

"I'll phone him and pretend I'm at home, then I'll ring the bell and he'll think it's his pizza."

Mum kissed me goodbye, gave me a thumbs up, then ran back to the elevator giggling the entire way. I balanced the pizza box in one hand, and dialled Elliot's number and put my phone to my ear with the other.

"Hey," he answered on the second ring. "Are ye okay?"

"I'm fine," I answered. "I just missed you."

Elliot's low laughter made me smile. "Ye saw me three hours ago."

"Three *long* hours ago . . . I thought I dreamt about you. I forget what you look like. I forget if you have a six-pack or an eight."

Elliot's laughter became louder. "Witch, don't be teasin' your man right now. It's not nice."

"Want me to make it up to you?"

"With what?" he joked. "Phone sex?"

"You read my mind . . . You know I'm in bed, alone, right?"

Elliot groaned so loud I could hear him through his front door, and I had to bite my lip to keep from laughing.

"*Sasanach*," he growled. "What're ye wearin'?"

"Tiny red shorts . . . maybe I'm topless."

I think Elliot whimpered. "I can imagine ye—"

I picked that moment to press his doorbell. Part of me wanted to draw out getting Elliot hot and bothered, and part of me just wanted to be next to him, touching him. Teasing him meant teasing myself.

"Fuck. One sec, gorgeous," Elliot grunted. "I think that's me pizza at the door." The door swung opened seconds later, and before Elliot even looked my way he said, "Ye have shitty timin', right when me missus was—"

"One large meat feast, sir?"

CHAPTER TWENTY-ONE

NOAH

Elliot stared at me, shirtless with his phone held to his ear by his shoulder, cash in his hand. His lips were parted, but no words came out.

"Can you take the box?" I laughed as I hung up and pocketed my phone. "My leg is stronger now but standing on it for too long makes me tired."

Elliot seemed to snap back into reality, grabbed the box from my hand and then guided me into his flat. I grabbed my crutches but didn't use them to walk – I just took my time as I went into the sitting room and glanced around.

"You painted," I said, smiling. "I like it – grey is very modern."

I looked over my shoulder when Elliot didn't reply; he was still standing in the hall staring at me. I snorted and shook my head.

"Close the door, go put your pizza on a plate, then come in here and join me."

I placed my crutches against the wall and then walked over to the sofa to sit down. I sighed as I lifted my leg and rested it on a beautiful coffee table that was new to me. There were also new cabinets in both corners of the room, and the television on the wall was new – and bigger too. The sofa was still the same, which didn't surprise me; it had cost us a good chunk of money and still looked to be in great condition.

"Elliot," I called. "Can you get me a glass of water, please."

He didn't reply, but instead of shouting again, I prepared to get up and get it myself. But then he suddenly appeared holding a glass in one hand and a plate stacked with pizza in the other. I smiled at him.

"Thanks, hon." I took the glass and drained half of it. "I feel better now."

Elliot sat down, put the plate on the coffee table, then turned and stared at me. He was freaking me out with his strange behaviour, and just as I was about to call him out on it, he leaned over and crushed his mouth again mine. Instantly, I put my arms around his neck and moaned into his mouth. I squealed against his lips when he tugged me against him. It resulted in me half-straddling him, which made him laugh.

"My boot will have to come off otherwise—"

There was a sudden rip of one of the straps as Elliot made quick work of removing my boot and letting it fall to the ground, and then he sat back on the sofa and eased me into a sitting position on top of him. It didn't hurt my leg, but I knew if I stayed that way for long it'd go numb and later it would hurt.

"Are you surprised to see me?" I whispered against Elliot's mouth. "You seem surprised."

"I am." He flicked his tongue against my lips. "I'm so happy you're here, but Noah, ye can't stay."

"I *am* staying," I said firmly. "I'm not leaving you again. I told you this."

"Sweetheart." He lifted his hands to my cheeks. "I know ye aren't goin' anywhere. I know."

"Then let me stay," I almost pleaded. "I was at Mum and Dad's and my heart hurt for you, Elliot. I don't want to be apart from

212

you when I don't have to be. Please, I'll beg you if I have to. Don't send me away. Please."

He kissed me deeply before he responded.

"I want ye next to me, always," he said, rubbing the tip of his nose against mine. "But, Noah, you're askin' a lot from me. I'm gonna be blunt, I wanna fuck ye into next week. Makin' love to ye is all I can think about lately. You bein' here will tempt me beyond measure, green eyes."

"I want that too." I rolled my pelvis against him, drawing a groan from his lips. "You *know* I want that."

"I'm tryin' to be a decent man by waitin' until ye at least file for divorce."

I didn't want him to think about Anderson; the man had no place in my life any more. It wasn't fair on him, but I'd chosen Elliot and that decision wasn't changing.

"Consider me and Anderson separated, because we *have* been since my accident. I. Do. Not. Know. Him. I am never going to be with him, *only you*. You're denying yourself the chance of having me right now by being so damn sweet. Would he do the same for you?"

"No" – the answer was a growl – "he wouldn't."

I gasped when Elliot suddenly stood up. My arms and legs wrapped around him. Before I had a chance to speak, he was walking out of the room and down the hallway and into the bedroom. My back hit the mattress before I could blink.

"Elliot!" I gasped. "I'm too heavy for that!"

"And yet I carried your sexy arse in here," he said, looming over me. "How much weight have ye lost in the last four weeks?"

"A stone and a half." I swallowed. "I'm a size fourteen now."

"Keep this arse fat for me," he practically snarled. "*Please*."

He gripped the waistband of my leggings, and my knickers, and slowly slid them down until he could toss them over his

213

shoulder. I worked on removing my jumper and T-shirt, but I got myself tangled up, and when I laughed, Elliot laughed too.

"See what happens when you're too eager and don't take your time?"

His cool fingertips brushed over my bare thigh, making me gasp.

"Boy, if you don't get these clothes off of me and love me in five seconds flat, I'm gonna *bite* you!"

He removed the rest of my clothing with a few tugs and a flick of his wrist.

"That took me three seconds." He grinned. "Still bite me though."

"And you say *I'm* sinful."

His eyes lowered to my body and he swallowed.

"Beautiful," he said, slowly raising his eyes back to mine. "Every inch of ye is beautiful."

I loved how his eyes roamed over me. It made me feel beautiful in a body that a few weeks ago had felt like it belonged to a stranger. As the days passed, I'd come to respect my new body and love it, because though it was different from what I remembered, it was strong. It had got me through my accident.

"Prove it." I leaned back. "Love me."

"I do love ye," he said, removing his clothes, liking my eyes on him as he stripped for me. "I need to take me time with ye, Noah. It's been so long since I've had ye . . . I want it to go slow but me body is screaming for me to go fast. You're too perfect for me to hold back."

"Sweet-talker," I hummed. "Come here and I'll take the edge off for you."

He moved to stand in front of me, and I sat up on the side of the bed, facing him. I clasped my hand around his throbbing length, giving it a gentle squeeze, and Elliot's legs seemed to buckle at the

214

contact. He cursed, tilted his head back and groaned low in his throat before he lowered his gaze back to me. His breathing was laboured, and I had barely touched him yet. I looked up at him as I opened my mouth and placed my tongue against the head of his cock, closing my lips around him then gently suckling. Pre-cum leaked into my mouth. His eyes almost instantly rolled back and his lids shut.

"Christ," he rasped, a hand blindly finding its way to my hair, fingers grasping the strands tightly. "*Sasanach* . . . I missed this mouth *so* fuckin' much."

I wanted to tease him, to have a little fun, but that could happen later . . . right now I needed to please my man.

My response was to close my mouth around the head fully and suck. Not too hard, just a gentle bit of suction to get his heart pumping. Elliot moaned out loud, and his reaction sent shivers racing up and down my spine. I removed my lips from the head and kissed the base, then licked it from root to tip. When Elliot hissed God's name, I took the head of his cock back into my mouth and sucked again. He whimpered. I tentatively began to bob my head, testing how much of him I could take in my mouth.

I had done this so many times to him before, but I could tell my body was out of practice. The sounds my mouth made while I sucked and licked seemed to add fuel to the fire in turning Elliot on. The sounds *he* made and how hard his cock was in my mouth caused a pulse to throb between my thighs. He opened his eyes a few times to look down at me, so he could watch my mouth sucking him, but when he found my eyes were locked solely on his, his eyes rolled back in his head again and he bit down on his lip as if he were in pain. He knew how much I loved sucking him, and his reaction always made me hot.

I *loved* it.

I loved that I made him feel so good and that he reacted in such a way. Elliot was usually calm, collected and the one in charge, but when I had my hands and mouth on him, he was at *my* mercy and he knew it. He liked it. When I reached up with my free hand and cupped his balls, his entire body jolted. The hands in my hair tightened their hold and his hips began to buck back and forth. I kept my touch light and where I knew he liked it, and if his vocals were anything to go by, I'd hit the mark.

I hummed around him, letting him know just how much I was enjoying myself, and the vibrations from my throat were too much for him to handle.

"Noah." His lips were parted. "Fuck. I'm gonna come."

I smiled around him and the sight seemed to be enough for him, because his hips jerked suddenly and I felt hot spurts of salt-iness coat my tongue. Elliot's groan was low, like it was almost stuck in his throat. I milked him dry and swallowed every drop. He always loved that part, when I swallowed and showed him that I liked it.

"*Sasanach.*" He was breathing heavily, his eyes were still closed and his hands were still in my hair as I let him slide out of my mouth. "I've been waiting *years* to feel that again."

I tilted my head. "You never let another woman—"

"No." He cut me off. "I never gave, or received, head. I never kissed anyone either."

I was surprised to hear this, but my heart thrummed with delight. I was glad that those things had been saved just for me.

"Let me take back something else that belongs to me too." I reached for him. "Play with me."

He pushed me back on to the bed.

"I wanna kiss ye."

My body tensed. Elliot's "kiss" during sex meant an entirely different thing, and when I grinned, he lowered his head to my stomach and kissed it.

"My FUPA."

"Shut *up*," I laughed, slapping his shoulder. "It's nowhere near big enough to be called that any more, you fuck – *Elliot!*"

He chuckled as he slid his hot tongue up through my wet folds, and my body bucked. He found my clit immediately and placed a kiss on it before he sucked it into his mouth and ran his tongue back and forth. His hands drifted over my body, squeezing my flesh here and there. My eyes crossed when he tongued me to the point that I could hardly draw in a breath. When he suddenly moved down to my labia and sucked on my lips before dipping his tongue inside me, my body twitched.

"Elliot!"

He moved upwards, back up to where I needed him most. As soon as his warm tongue returned to lapping at my swollen bundle of nerves with zest, my legs began to shake.

"My . . . *God!*"

Elliot made a sound in the back of his throat as he hooked his arms around my thighs and pressed his hands at the base of my stomach. He always did this when my body began to move of its own accord so he could keep me in place. He inhaled a deep breath, then curled his tongue around my clit *slowly*. It felt so good that it almost hurt. I reached down and tangled my hand in his hair as jumbled words left my mouth at a fast pace.

My body was like a live wire as I twitched and bucked with every swipe of Elliot's tongue. My flesh was flushed with desire, and my skin burned with need. I was drunk on his touch, and I wanted, needed, more.

"Right there," I gasped. "Yes, Elliot. *Fuck!*"

His hands flexed against my stomach in response.

Jolts of pleasure became more constant, and with an abundance of attention focused on my clit, an orgasm began to build. I couldn't focus on anything but Elliot's touch, and I quickly lost myself to it. My body felt like it was on fire, and my thighs were quivering. The second he scraped his teeth over me, my body began to convulse.

"El-Elliot!" I stammered. "Don't st-stop."

I screamed, then drew in a sharp breath and held it for a moment.

Time, and life itself, fell to the back of my mind, and I became pure sensation. My breath came out in rough pants, and my heart beat uncontrollably as I felt something sharp almost like pain before an inexplicable wave of bliss touched my every nerve ending. It spread out from my clit, and it felt heavenly.

I hissed as jolts of what felt like electricity shot up and down my legs. For a moment, my eyes rolled back, my spine arched and my lips parted as I let out a scream of raw pleasure. My lungs burned for air, so I inhaled greedily. I bucked against Elliot's face as he continued to lap and suck on my now-oversensitive clit. I turned my body, forcing him away as I continued to twitch in the aftermath of my orgasm.

"I can't move," I panted. "Oh my God."

Elliot chuckled and tugged me up the bed, then covered us with a blanket. I was embarrassed because I was tired, and Elliot knew it.

"I need to join a gym," I told him. "My stamina is *awful*."

He kissed my shoulder and settled in behind me.

"Sleep," he told me with a chuckle. "Ye'll need your strength for when we wake up, because I intend to love ye good and proper."

"You already do love me good and proper," I hummed. "Elliot, I'm so happy with you. I truly am."

"Me too, Noah." He kissed the back of my head. "My person."

I snuggled back into him, closed my eyes and sighed in delight. This was where I was meant to be, cocooned in Elliot's arms. This was my space with my person, and it always would be.

CHAPTER TWENTY-TWO
ELLIOT

"How many times?" AJ continued to ask. "Two whole days is a *long* time to be holed up with a woman, so don't be acting dumber than usual. How. Many. Times?"

I put down the weights in my hands, wiped the sweat from my forehead and looked at my oldest friend, momentarily wondering why I didn't punch him in the face more often.

"If I give ye a number," I said, blinking, "will ye shut up?"

"Yes. Once it's an *honest* number."

"Nine," I answered. "And a half."

"And a half?" Pretty shouted from the treadmill. "Did he say nine and a *half*?"

"He sure did, Pretty." Texas grinned from the bench press. "What does the 'and a half' mean? Is it a language barrier? Because I feel like it is."

"Come on, lads," Tank snorted as he spotted for Texas. "'And a half' means oral without sex to follow it up . . . right?"

I winked. "Right ye are, big man."

Tank grinned and focused on the task at hand . . . making sure Texas didn't get choked if he couldn't lift the barbell.

"I haven't gone nine rounds in two days since . . . no, since never." Pretty shook his head as he ran. "I was never with the same girl long enough, until I met Louise and married her. Even then, I think the most was on my honeymoon. Four times in the one day, and she walked funny for most of the trip. I'm still proud of that, three years later."

I grinned. "Ye should be proud, you're an old man now."

"I'm thirty-seven." He flipped me off. "Watch your mouth."

"I'm thirty-six," Tank chimed in. "I don't feel old."

He didn't look it, and neither did Pretty – or Stitch, who was the same age. Pretty still looked in his mid-twenties, for God's sake. I looked my age, and Texas looked his. AJ too.

"All I can say is if I was still at home with her, that number would be *much* higher." I placed my hands on my hips. "She's like Viagra to me. I look at her and *boom*, instant wood."

I had spent two full days of sex-induced bliss with Noah. I had intended to spend the entirety of my four days off with her, but Frenchie, a co-worker, shot me a text at six this morning and asked if I could cover his watch at nine, because his twins had been up puking all night and so had his wife. He needed to take care of them. I'd wanted to say no – I desperately wanted him to text someone else – but when Noah rolled over and saw the text, she encouraged me to help him, so I swapped a watch with him for later in the week and here I was.

God, but I missed my woman. And she was my woman again.

Not Anderson's, *mine*.

"I feel like I'm eighteen all over again." I pounded my fist against my chest. "I was showin' no signs of slowin' down, and bless her, she was tryin' her hardest to keep up with me. The last round I could have sworn she rolled her eyes when me hands went to her arse."

"Maybe *that's* why she told you to cover Frenchie's watch," Texas shouted with laughter. "To get a break from you and your cock for a few hours."

I tipped my head back and guffawed, and so did everyone else.

"She knows what to expect when I get home tonight, so she'd better enjoy the next few hours of peace."

My friends shouted their encouragement as AJ and I left the gym so we could shower. I finished before him, dressed and headed into the kitchen. He followed not long after, complaining about being hungry.

"There's pasta or somethin' in the fridge," I said, eating the portion I'd scooped out for myself. "I think Stitch's wife made it, it's fuckin' amazin'."

"*Yes!*" AJ all but danced on the spot. "That woman knows how to cook. If she wasn't Stitch's wife, she'd at least be my baby's mum by now."

I snorted. "If Stitch heard ye talkin' like that, he'd kill ye."

"What'd he say about my wife?"

AJ froze and looked at me when Stitch's voice filled the room. He was like a ghost – he appeared and disappeared at will. I looked from AJ to him and grinned. "He said if your missus wasn't your wife she'd be his baby's mum because he loves her cookin' so much."

"Rat!" AJ hissed. "You're a fuckin' *rat*."

I sniggered as he turned and smiled at Stitch. "He's a barefaced liar, and I wouldn't trust him as far as I could throw him, Stitch. You shouldn't pay him any attention."

I continued to eat my pasta as Stitch advanced on AJ, who actually began to scream as he dodged to the left and fled the room. For someone who hated fighting, he always let his mouth get him into trouble.

"Fuck you, Irish . . . I'm still starving!" I heard him say.

Stitch grinned. "She *is* a good cook though, huh?"

221

With my mouth full I bobbed my head, and my friend left the room, thoroughly amused.

I checked my phone as I ate and sent Noah a text when I saw she hadn't messaged me yet.

> Are you still sleeping, green eyes? It'll be great for my ego if you are.

My phone buzzed within seconds.

> I'm awake, but you'll be happy to know . . . I can practically feel you with each step I take.

Amused, and very much filled with pride, I tapped a text out on the screen.

> Stroking my ego will get you everywhere with me.

I washed my dirty plate and fork before placing them on the drying rack. I checked my phone when I was done, and grinned when I read Noah's reply.

> I'd rather stroke something else . . . text me later, I'm researching flower shops to see if anyone is hiring. When I get my boot off in a few weeks I should be ready to get back working. No harm in looking. Wish me luck.

As long as she was just looking and not planning to march off to a job tomorrow, I was happy for her. I knew how eager she was to have some semblance of normality back in her life.

Good luck, I replied. Love you.

Her reply was instant.

Love you too.

"Why're you staring at your phone with that creepy smile?"

I looked up. "Stitch let ye live, I see."

"No thanks to *you*." AJ glared, rubbing his stomach. "Move away from the fridge. I took a solid to the gut to get some of that fucking pasta and I'm having a big plate."

I stepped away and gestured for him to have at the fridge.

"You didn't answer my question."

I hopped up on to the counter and watched AJ move about the room.

"What question?"

"Why were you smiling at your phone like a creep?"

I snorted. "I was textin' Noah."

"Sexting?"

"No, perv." I grinned at his frown. "Just regular textin'. I told her I loved her and she said she loved me too. I'm still gettin' used to hearin' it again. Makes me feel all special and shit."

AJ didn't tease me; he surprised me by nodding.

"I'm happy for you, brother," he said. "You and Noah deserve the best."

"Thanks, man." I patted his shoulder he passed me by to heat his food up in the microwave. "How are things with Dani?"

"I told her to move in with me and she said okay," he answered. "She was sleeping over at my place five nights a week before we even made things official. It makes sense just to move all her crap in."

He said this so casually that I thought I'd misheard him.

I stared at him in disbelief. "You *want* her to move in – you'd have never brought it up otherwise."

AJ scowled. "Don't overanalyse things, fanny boy."

I widened my eyes when he appeared . . . flustered.

"You're in love."

"I am fucking not."

"Ye are." I hopped down from the counter. "You're in love with Dani and you're havin' a silent panic attack. I can see it in your eyes!"

"You shut your whore mouth!"

"Admit it!" I demanded. "Admit you're in love with Dani."

"Okay!" AJ shouted, his hands flying up in the air. "You're right, I love her. I am a man in love. Christ, help me. I'm freaking the fuck out. I only realised it this morning when I caught myself smiling at her like a fucking creep while she slept. What do I do? She can't know; the power it'll give her over me will be a force to be reckoned with."

I burst into uncontrollable laughter.

"Me boy is a man, he's in love."

"Stop smiling at me like a proud mother and help me. Slap this out of me! Do your duty as my brother!"

I hugged him instead, making him curse me as he gave my back a rough slap.

"Tell her," I said, ruffling his hair like he was a kid. "Trust me. Tell her all the time, she'll love hearin' it and ye'll feel good sayin' it."

"I'm shittin' it . . . What if she laughs at me?"

"You just echoed exactly what I said back when I told Noah I liked her on me eighteenth birthday . . . Ye told me then that ye *know* women, so why are ye askin' me?"

"'Cause Dani's not just *any* woman, she's *my* woman, and I love her so much it scares the shit outta me."

I snapped my fingers. "Repeat those exact words to her. That was gold."

"I have to time it right," AJ said, scratching his chin. "How did you tell Noah?"

"She was actually in the middle of breakin' up with me when I told her, and then we had sex for the first time in her parents' house right after."

"You're no fucking help, Irish." My friend looked me up and down. "None at all."

I was chuckling as my phone began to ring. It was my mother, and I answered it straight away.

"Heya, Ma, I'm at work—"

"Elliot!" My mother's voice sobbed through my phone, pulling the smile from my face. Suddenly I got a feeling in the pit of my stomach of sickening dread. "Oh, Elliot. Noah knows . . . she knows about Bailey! Please, come! Oh, Elliot. *Please.*"

CHAPTER TWENTY-THREE
NOAH

Three days had passed since I was discharged from the hospital, and I had been in a bubble of love with Elliot for two of them. We were holed up in *our* flat just enjoying being with one another. We ate together, watched films together, showered together and made love to one another every chance we got. I was happier than I had ever been, and the only thing that was stopping me from throwing myself into my new life was Anderson Riley. The man deserved better than what he thought I could give him, and I hoped that, with time, he would understand that the divorce I wanted would be as much for his benefit as it was for mine.

I just had to get up the courage to tell him.

Elliot was supposed to have four days off work. That was how his shifts worked – four days on with two day shifts and two night shifts, and four days off – but a friend of his on a different watch had poorly twins and an ill wife, and had asked if Elliot could cover his watch today. Elliot had been reluctant but I encouraged him to go – and to get out of the flat we had been locked inside for more than forty-eight hours. He'd kissed me senseless before he left and told me all the things he was going to do to me when he got home that evening, making me tingle with excitement.

In the meantime, I wanted to get some fresh air . . . and visit a flower shop. I missed being around the scent of them – and being surrounded by them. I knew I was likely to get a telling off for going into town by myself, but I needed the time outside and some alone time in general. I just wanted to take a stroll . . . or as much of a stroll as I could take while walking with the aid of crutches.

I had been cooped up in the hospital for so long that two days inside of a flat was killing me inside. I was desperate to develop a somewhat normal routine where I wasn't staring at walls every hour of the day. I was very conscious of not overdoing it, but a little fatigue was worth it in order to feel like I was living again. I had always been quite independent, and after the last couple of months of being helpless I wanted to prove to myself that I could be alone and still be okay.

Once I knew I could tackle a stroll, I wouldn't feel as worried when I eventually told Elliot about my little adventure. He worried over me constantly, so showing him – and myself – that I was truly on my way to being physically healthy again was important to me. As much as I loved his help and attention, I didn't want to become a burden to him or a responsibility. I simply wanted to be his partner and his equal – and once I was better, he could step down from the twenty-four-seven Noah care service he was currently offering.

I dressed with ease, pulling on a sky-blue sundress that fell to my mid-thigh to reflect the warm May day. After I put my sock and shoe on to my good foot, I put my hair into two French plaits, and popped on some mascara and lip balm. I didn't look like anything special, but I felt like a million quid. With my boot securely fastened, I made sure I had the key Elliot had given me to the flat, as well as some money and my new phone. Then I hooked the strap of my bag over my head and left the flat, locking the door behind me before making my way outside and to the bus stop.

I was going to All in Bloom, the flower shop I'd worked at in Tulse Hill. It was only a ten-minute walk from my and Elliot's flat, but that ten-minute walk could easily turn into an hour with how slow I was moving these days, and how many breaks I knew I'd need to take. The bus made the journey less than a couple of minutes long, and the shop was within sight of the bus stop at the other end.

With a smile on my face, I took my time as I walked down the street. Not much had changed on this particular road since I remembered it last, and I was pleased about that. But as I got on the bus and gazed out the window, the entire neighbourhood looked different. It was astonishing to see how much even little changes could alter my impression of a place. I noticed so many new things that it was both astounding and somewhat disturbing. When change happens gradually, people tend not to notice it. But when you're disconnected from a place during the time of that change, you notice the differences right away. Or at least I did.

And that was how I felt when I entered All in Bloom, my old place of work. I noticed everything that was different. The floor space was bigger, and I recalled that the owner, Helen, had briefly talked about expanding the shop once she got planning permission for an extension from the council.

There were thick, dark wooden ceiling beams and the walls were a bright, crisp white with colourful decor. The shop itself had a whole new layout that took customers on a little path as they browsed. It was beautiful . . . It was also my idea.

I had drawn up a plan of what I wanted my own flower shop to look like in the future. I had never kept it a secret that one day I wanted to run my own place, make my own rules and bring to life a vision I saw in my head. I felt my heart pinch knowing that Helen had obviously taken a liking to my plan and put it to use herself. I didn't feel angry though, just disappointed. And that disappointment quickly changed to motivation. The plan I'd drawn up wasn't the only one I'd thought of – it was simply one of many. I was confident that, when the day came for me to design and open my own shop, it would be with more thought than what I'd put into the design Helen was currently using.

I wished her all the best.

Wanting to view the entire shop, I began to walk the flower trail. Lesley, who'd been the manager when I worked in the shop, wasn't around from what I could see, and I didn't know either of the two middle-aged women who were currently working in the shop, so I didn't strike up conversation. Once I told them I was just browsing, I took my time looking around the arrangements, pieces and loose flowers on display. The smell of all the mixed scents was like a drug. It always brought a smile to my face; it was a scent that made me feel very much at home. I'd missed it.

I couldn't *wait* to get back to work.

Excited that I hadn't lost my love for flowers and the desire to work with them, I wondered when I could realistically look into flower shops that were hiring. I mean, as soon as I got home I would be researching my arse off, but I had to think of when I would be ready to work again. The only thing holding me back right now was my leg. Normally wearing a boot cast was only a six- to eight-week ordeal, but as I had fractured the same leg in two places once before, the newest fracture was even more severe and had required more screws, pins and metal plates to repair it – which left me wearing the boot for at least ten weeks.

I had another four weeks of wearing the boot, and I had eight physical therapy sessions left during that time that would strengthen my leg and get me walking crutch- and boot-free. As much as I didn't want to wait until then to get back working, maybe it was what was best for me. I was still fresh out of the hospital, and a few more weeks of taking it easy and adjusting to a regular life again would be good for me.

It would be good for Elliot and my parents too. When I took on a responsibility that would allow me to be left to my own devices all day, with only myself to depend on, it would be an adjustment for them too.

I took my phone from my bag when it pinged. It was Elliot messaging me and asking if I was awake. I suddenly felt like a little kid who'd been caught with their hand in the cookie jar. I wasn't going to tell him I was out and about in Tulse Hill at my old shop. He would probably have a heart attack out of fear I would suddenly collapse or something. So I played it cool as we sent texts back and forth. I couldn't text and walk at the same time due to my crutches, so I wrapped my conversation up with Elliot and left the shop.

There were no signs I could see that the place was hiring, and I wasn't sure if I'd left the shop on good or bad terms with Helen the owner, but I thought I would add it down as one of the shops to check when I eventually applied. It had been a few years since I'd worked there . . . Helen probably wasn't even the owner any more.

I walked back towards the bus stop, but I felt like skipping. My little adventure was rewarding, thoroughly enjoyable, and had given me a plan for the future and the determination to go with it. Having my drive back and something to look forward to would make the next few weeks more bearable. I had a goal, and I knew that once Elliot could see that I was getting stronger, he'd support me and help me in whatever way he could. My parents too.

I had to walk uphill to get back to the bus stop – in reality it wasn't much more than a little incline, but my body was beginning to feel the ache that all this movement was causing. I paused and leaned against a wall, just to catch my breath. I frowned as I stared at the scene before me. There were piles of flowers against a partially damaged building wall – so many that the pathway was almost obstructed for pedestrians who were passing by. My heart hurt when I realised that someone had died there. I wondered what had happened, and before I knew it I was in front of the flower pile, to read one of the cards attached to the mountain of bouquets of flowers. Many of the flowers were bloomed pink lilies that were at different stages of dying.

I leaned forward and read the first one I spotted.

Rest easy, angel.
xoxo

Quick, simple and very sweet. I moved my eyes over more cards, but many of them were without the usual plastic sheets to protect them from being exposed to the weather and had been damaged. My eyes found a huge arrangement of pink lilies in the shape of a butterfly in flight – it was beautiful. I carefully lifted it up with one hand, squinted and began reading.

Sleep tight our darling Bailey girl.
Watch over us, and wait for us, beauty.
Love you always,
Da, Ma & Elliot xx

I stared at the card, reading it three times before I slowly lowered the flowers back down to the ground. *Bailey girl. Da, Ma and Elliot.* I blinked at the coincidence of the girl who had clearly died being called Bailey and having someone close to her – maybe a brother – with the name Elliot. I looked to my right when an older gentleman paused, like me, to peer at the flowers and read a couple of cards. He glanced at me, noticed I was looking at him, and smiled in greeting.

"Very sad." He nodded to the flower pile. "The poor kid was only starting her life."

"A child?" I asked, horrified. "The girl who died was only a child?"

I would have been sad for a person's passing at any age, but there was something about a child losing their life before they had a chance to live it that struck me as truly tragic.

"To me, yes." He nodded. "To you, not so much."

I frowned. "She was an adult then?"

"Twenty-one or twenty-two, I think. I speak with her father every so often, he's an Irishman. He owns McKenna's pub."

I stared at the man as a cold, painful sensation of dread churned in my stomach. His words were almost impossible for me to comprehend.

"Bailey?" I almost whispered. "Bailey McKenna? She . . . she died?"

"Yes." The man nodded. "Poor kid. She's buried over in West Norwood Cemetery; her brother was on duty when the accident happened, I heard. He's a firefighter, he got a woman out of the car but the car was engulfed in flames before anyone could get to the girl. It's horrible."

I felt like I couldn't breathe.

The man said something else to me, but I could no longer hear a word that came out of his mouth as his earlier words repeated over and over in my mind. An ache formed at my temples, and I lifted my hand to my forehead and closed my eyes. I focused on breathing in and out. It helped. When I opened my eyes, the man was staring at me, concern plastered all over his face.

"Mister, *listen* to me," I said, an edge to my voice. "Are you sure it was Bailey McKenna? Maybe another Irish family owns a pub in town?"

"I'm sure they do." His brown was furrowed. "But McKenna's has been owned by the same man going on eleven years now. Seamus McKenna."

Elliot's father. I bent over as pain erupted in my stomach. My heart beat wildly within my chest and my head started to kill me. I felt a pulsing in my left temple, but I didn't have a second to focus on it because through the haze of physical pain and fear I felt, I heard my name being called.

"Noah?"

I turned as Elliot's parents, Mr and Mrs McKenna, got out of a car. Both were staring at me with wide eyes. It felt as if everything had slowed down. I stared at them and shook my head.

"It's not true," I said, raising my voice. "Tell me it's *not true*."

Mrs McKenna promptly burst into tears, and my chest tightened to the point where I rubbed it hopefully to relieve the ache. It didn't help.

"No!" I shouted. "Where is she? Where *is* Bailey?"

Mr McKenna approached me slowly.

"Noah, darlin', look at me."

I groaned as my head exploded with pain. My mind was racing a mile a minute as I tried to make sense of what was happening.

"She's in Australia," I said, my hand on my temple. "She's in Australia with her boyfriend. This is another Bailey McKenna."

A range of emotions passed over Mr McKenna's face and I quickly identified one of them as pity. I had been given that look enough times in the hospital when I couldn't do something for myself. People couldn't stop that look from forming in their eyes when they felt pity for a person, no matter how much they tried to contain it.

"Ye shouldn't be here, kid," he answered me. "Ye should be at home, Elliot will worry if he knows you're out here all alone. Ye know how much he worries over ye. Come on, let's go and give him a visit at the station. I spoke to him earlier, he should be there if there hasn't been a call."

He was talking to me like I was a crazy person, and it was making me panic.

"*Tell me* she's in Australia."

Mrs McKenna came to her ex-husband's side, and I watched as she slid her fingers between his and gripped his hand so tightly that her knuckles turned white. I looked from their hands to their faces, and my gut twisted.

"Please," I pleaded, my voice cracking. "*Please* tell me that she's in Australia."

Mr McKenna shook his head. "I can't do that, honey."

With shaking hands, I dug my phone from my bag and dialled Bailey's old number. It went straight to voicemail, and logically I knew it was because it was a dead number. Elliot had said she didn't use the number any more, but I was in a panic and needed to speak to her.

"Hey," Bailey's voice chirped. "This is Bailey, I'm busy right now, *obviously* . . . or maybe I'm just starin' at me phone and waitin' for ye to hang up so I can text ye and see what ye want. Hint hint."

When I heard the beep, I began talking.

"Bailey, it's Noah. I want you to ring me as soon as you get this message, okay? I really need to speak to you, baby. I love you. Ring me straight away. I'm not joking, Bails. Call me. Please, please, *please*, call me."

Mrs McKenna was crying so hard that a few people had stopped to stare. I couldn't move, I could only look between the pair of them. My mind refused to let me process what they were saying, so the only thing I could do was fight their words with my own.

"She's fine," I snapped. "She's okay."

"No, honey." Mr McKenna swallowed. "She's . . . she's gone, Noah."

I stumbled back and managed to catch myself with my crutch before I took a tumble on to my backside. My breathing was irregular, and loud to my own ears.

"Where is she?" I screamed over the pain in my head. "Where the *fuck* is she?"

"West Norwood Cemetery," Mrs McKenna blurted out on a choked sob. "Row twenty-three, ninth plot from the left in the lawn cemetery."

I felt like all the blood had drained from my face.

"Liar!" I snapped. "You're . . . you're *lying*!"

Both of Elliot's parents shook their heads, and I suddenly felt helpless as pure panic flooded me. The old man's words echoed in my head. He'd said the brother was a firefighter who was on duty and had pulled a woman from the car that had crashed, but before he could save his sister the car had been engulfed in flames and she'd died. Who was that woman he saved?

You, a voice whispered in my head. *It was you.*

"This is wrong!" I screamed. "This . . . this . . . this wasn't the accident I was in. It wasn't."

"It was, honey." Mrs McKenna was trembling. "You and our Bailey . . . ye were both in that same accident. Elliot saved *you*, Noah. Bailey . . . she was beyond help. He made up the Australia story because he was terrified the news might kill ye."

I felt like I was being shaken from the inside. I wanted to run, to get as far away from the flowers, the McKennas and this conversation as possible. I spotted a car driving down the road that made my heart jump.

"Taxi!" I shouted, and waved it down. "Taxi!"

The car pulled up right next to me, and I clumsily climbed inside, pulling my crutches with me. Mr McKenna was trying to keep me from closing the door as I was talking to the driver, telling him where I wanted to go.

"West Norwood Cemetery," I demanded. "As fast as you can."

"Noah, honey, don't do this alone. Please, sweetheart."

I felt like I couldn't breathe.

"Elliot!" I heard Mrs McKenna cry as she fumbled putting her phone to her ear. "Oh, Elliot. Noah knows . . . she knows about Bailey! Please, come! Oh, Elliot. *Please.*"

I pulled the door shut and locked it as the car pulled away from the kerb. The driver didn't say anything to me, but I saw him glance back repeatedly in the rear-view mirror. I didn't realise I was breathing heavily until then. My hands were shaking, and I felt like I was going to be sick.

Row twenty-three, ninth plot from the left.

I could barely form a coherent thought. All I knew was that I had to get to the cemetery and prove to myself that this was all wrong. Bailey was okay, she was. I physically couldn't believe she wasn't – my body, and mind, refused to do so. My head throbbed and it was a fight to keep my eyes open, but I somehow managed it. Quicker than I expected, we came to a stop.

"West Norwood Cemetery," the driver said with a heavy accent as my phone rang. "That'll be six pounds and seven pence . . . Miss, are you okay?"

Without answering, I pushed a twenty-pound note blindly at the driver and all but fell out of the car. He didn't call after me; he barely waited more than a couple of seconds before he drove off. I didn't look at him go; I was too busy glancing around. The cemetery was huge – there were over forty thousand graves in the place. I thought of what Mrs McKenna had said – she'd mentioned the lawn cemetery, and I knew that was the modern section away from the historic sections and the catacombs.

236

I followed the signs, and numbly made my way to where I needed to go.

As fast as I could, I hobbled through the cemetery and ignored the pain in my leg. Mrs McKenna's directions were forgotten in my panic and I lost count of the rows. I looked from left to right, looked for graves that had freshly upturned dirt, indicating recent burial. I saw three, and the first two I checked were for men I had never heard of. As I approached the third, I spotted a bunch of pink lilies sitting prettily in front of one of the small wooden crosses that every grave had until a tombstone was made and installed.

"No," I said out loud.

I dug out my phone again, rejecting Elliot's call, and tried to ring Bailey again. It went straight to her voicemail once more, and I felt myself choking on air.

"Phone me back, Bailey!" I demanded angrily. "Right when you get this message, you call me straight away. No messing around! Baby, *please*. Please, phone me back."

I tried to put my phone back in my pocket, but I fumbled with it and it fell to the ground. I didn't look at it or attempt to pick it up. I couldn't take my eyes off of the pink lilies. They were Bailey's favourite flowers. I was too scared to walk forward so I could read the name on the golden plaque on the cross, in case it was her name printed on it.

"Please be okay, Bails," I said, finally shuffling forward one step at a time. "Please, please, *please*."

I kept my eyes on the lilies for ages, so long that I heard my name being shouted from a distance. The touch of a cool breeze startled me into reacting. I looked up in that moment and the second I read the name and date of birth on the plaque, I dropped to the ground and screamed.

CHAPTER TWENTY-FOUR
NOAH

"Noah!"

I could barely hear his voice over my cries.

"No!" I fought against the arms that suddenly surrounded me. "No! Let me go! Let me *go*!"

The arms around me tightened as I screamed in emotional pain. My heart felt like it had been ripped out of my chest and torn apart in front of my very eyes.

"Not Bailey," I sobbed, my fingers digging into the dirt. "Please, not my Bailey."

I heard Elliot's choked intake of breath as he pressed his face against the back of my head. I cried until my throat went raw with pain and until no more tears fell from my eyes. I had stopped struggling against Elliot, because I could no longer move. I felt numb to everything except the pain in my heart.

"No! Please!" I pleaded. "This isn't real! It's not! It's *not*!"

"I'm sorry," he said against my ear. "I'm so sorry."

I didn't know what he was apologising for. I couldn't think.

"I can't breathe."

Elliot pulled me to my feet and looked at me. His eyes were glazed over with tears, but none fell. I stared up at him as my body trembled with fear, pain and heartache.

"Focus on me," he said, placing his hands on either side of my face. "Just look at me, green eyes. Okay?"

"She's gone," I whispered, not being able to accept it. "How can she be gone?"

"She just is." Elliot swallowed. "It doesn't make sense, Noah. None of it does; nothin' will ever make sense to me. She shouldn't be buried here but she is, and there's nothin' we can do about it, honey."

I lifted my hands to Elliot's wrists, and held him tightly to keep from falling over. My leg was hurting me, and my body thrummed with pain from my head all the way down to my injured foot.

"Australia," I blurted. "You said she was in Australia and . . . you . . . you lied to me."

"I'm so sorry." He exhaled. "Ye were so vulnerable, I was terrified ye'd up and die on me too if you knew. I had to lie to protect ye . . . I'm so sorry."

He was sorry, I could see it in his eyes. He was sincere and he was hurting, likely more than I was. Bailey was his little sister; she was a massive piece of his heart.

"I should have known." I was shaking. "I should have known that you were lying . . . How could I believe that she wouldn't call me when I almost died? How could—"

"Sweetheart, *don't*," Elliot interrupted. "Ye had no reason *not* to believe me. Ye have no memory of the last five years, and ye were strugglin' enough with the changes in your own life that ye didn't need Bailey's death on top of that."

I could feel each beat my heart took, and it made me feel sick knowing mine was working and Bailey's was not. It killed me that

I was so close to her, but so far away. I'd never be able to cuddle her or laugh with her ever again.

"What happened?" I asked as I squeezed his hands. "And don't tell me you can't say or make an excuse . . . I want to know what happened."

Elliot's gaze bored into mine, and when he breathed out, I knew he was going to answer my question.

"The night of the crash, there was a London-wide blackout because of a storm. It was uncommonly cold for March – it was below freezing and the roads were a danger because of ice. You and Bailey . . . she was drivin', she lost control, and the car flipped a few times before it hit the side of a building in Tulse Hill."

I tried to remember what he was telling me, but there was nothing in my head, only darkness.

"I was on watch, and when we got there . . . she was already gone. The coroner's report said she died on impact, the driver's side hit the wall of the buildin' first and she wasn't wearin' her seat belt. I didn't care about anythin' other than gettin' both of you out of the car. Ye were conscious, but barely. There was blood all over ye, and you were in so much pain, honey. I thought ye were gonna die in me arms."

Tears slid down my cheeks, and he leaned in and kissed them away.

"I got ye out of the car, ran with you away from the flames so the paramedics on scene could take care of ye. I went back for Bailey but it was too late, the car was engulfed by fire and any chance I had of gettin' her out of the car died with her."

My legs went from under me, and Elliot quickly enveloped me in his arms and held me against him as the weight of his words descended on me.

"Elliot?"

I didn't turn or react to his mother's voice, but he did.

"She's . . . she's okay. Just lemme talk to her."

I wasn't okay. I felt like I would never be okay again.

"You said I pushed you all away after we broke up and I got with Anderson."

Elliot's arms tensed around me. "Ye did."

"Did I push Bailey away?"

"Yeah."

"Then why was I in her car with her?" I asked, not understanding. "Why?"

"I . . . I don't know," he said, sounding as lost as I felt. "None of us know. Ye rang me from Bailey's phone, ye left me a voicemail as you were in the car with her, but it's only left me with more questions than answers."

I leaned back and stared up at him with wide eyes.

"A voicemail?" I repeated. "I left you a voicemail. D'you still have it? Let me hear it!"

Elliot hesitated for only a moment before he removed one arm from around my body so he could take out his phone. He looked from the phone to me, then back to the phone as he tapped on the screen. He put it on loudspeaker, and we listened.

"Elliot? Elliot? Shit, shit, *shit*! It's his voicemail!"

I jolted the second my voice sounded.

"Help us," I sobbed, clearly terrified. "Oh God. Please, I don't know what to do! Bailey, what're we gonna do? It's so dark, put the high beams on."

I stared at the phone, a feeling of helplessness filling me. It was my voice I was hearing, mine . . . and I had no memory of ever speaking these words that I was saying with such fear.

"Oh God, oh God!" my voice continued to sob. "Bailey, you're going too fast!"

The line began to break up somewhat, and it made me tense.

"Tulse Hill," I said on the call. "Elliot, we're on – Bailey, *slow down*!"

"I'm tryin'!" Bailey's sweet but scared voice screamed. "I can't stop, it's black ice! We're slidin'!"

"Elliot!" my voice blared as the line began to break up. "Elliot, help us. Tulse Hill . . . Please, please . . . going to kill . . . Bailey! Look out!"

A scream from Bailey made my blood run cold. The call ended and I looked up at Elliot.

"Was that when we crashed?" I asked, hearing the worry in my own voice. "Was that . . . was that the moment we crashed and Bailey di-died?"

Elliot was shaking now too as he nodded.

"Elliot," I whimpered, "what the fuck happened? Why did we sound so scared? I said the words 'going to kill' . . . what the hell does that mean?"

"I don't know," he answered, his voice filled with frustration and devastation. "I don't know what *any* of it means. I don't, Noah."

Shame filled me, and so did self-loathing. This was my fault. I had pushed Bailey away along with everyone else in my life, and the one time I got back in touch with her, she died. I broke out of Elliot's hold and stumbled away from him. I took a few steps back so I could see them. All three of them. Elliot's parents were staring at me, and so was Elliot. Pity. Each of them looked at me with pity.

"How can you look at me?" I screamed at him, at his parents. "How can *any* of you look at me? I killed her. If she wasn't with me, she'd be here and not down there! It's *my* fault. I killed Bailey!"

"No!" Elliot bellowed. "It's not. None of this is your fault."

"How do you know?" I cried. "You can't answer because you don't know, Elliot."

"I know *here*." He smacked his hand on his chest. "Me heart tells me it's *not* your fault."

I lifted a shaking hand to my throbbing head as I began to break everything down.

"This is why Doctor Abara never told me about the accident, why he said it wasn't his place . . . he knew Bailey was . . . he knew she was . . ."

I couldn't even say the word.

"Yes," Elliot answered, taking a small step towards me. "Doctor Abara had been monitoring ye for a while. How ye reacted to things ye couldn't remember was so dangerous, Noah. He feared ye'd have an aneurysm and die. He decided it was best to keep ye in the dark as much as possible . . . we all agreed with him."

"Ye should've told me," I said, looking back at Bailey's cross. "I should've known so I could . . . so I could . . ."

"Ye were so vulnerable when ye woke up, honey," Mrs McKenna said. "It's why we never visited – we both knew we couldn't look at you, or talk to ye, without breakin' down. Elliot is stronger than us . . . he never left your side."

I looked back at them, and Elliot must have seen something in my face, or in my eyes, because he was in my space in seconds.

"No," he said gruffly. "You're not leaving me."

I banged my fists against his broad chest.

"I've been angry with her for not calling me! I've been angry with her and she's been *dead*!"

Elliot allowed my assault on his chest to continue uninterrupted.

"My Bailey," I choked. "She died next to me and I didn't even know!"

I pushed away from Elliot and placed my hands on the back of my head.

"This can't be real."

"It is real," Elliot said. "We're livin' in a nightmare, Noah. All of us."

I looked back to the pile of dirt and my heart pinched.

"I'm sorry," I whispered. "I'm so sorry, Bailey. Please, please forgive me."

I turned from her grave and looked for my crutches. I stumbled over to them and picked them up. Mrs McKenna approached me, holding out a phone in her hand. My phone, the one I'd dropped. I took it from her and placed it in my bag blindly.

"I'm so sorry."

"Stop." She shook her head, her eyes red-rimmed and swollen. "Sweetie, we could easily be standing here next to you and Bailey both being under this ground. None of this is your fault . . . don't apologise for livin'."

I wasn't apologising for surviving; I was apologising that I somehow caused Bailey's death. I didn't care what Elliot said, I could feel it deep inside my chest that this was down to me. I just didn't know why or how, but I planned to find out.

"I need to go," I said, leaning on my crutches. "I need to find out what happened. I need to speak to Anderson."

Elliot was in front of me in seconds.

"Don't go to him," he said, trembling. "Noah, don't."

"Maybe he knows why I was with Bailey that night." I wiped my face. "I *lived* with him. Maybe he knows why I was with her when I'd ignored her for so many years."

"He doesn't know *anythin'* though! The police already questioned him about that night, but he said he didn't even know that ye left your flat."

Elliot was breathing heavily.

"I have to find out for myself," I said, peering up at him, hoping he understood. "I have to hear it from him, Elliot. This guilt will eat me alive unless I know what happened."

"What if he doesn't know?" he demanded roughly. "What if he doesn't and ye never know?"

The thought of it made my knees week.

"Don't say that." I was shaking. "How can I go on knowing she died because of me?"

"You didn't cause this!" he shouted. "There was a blackout, she was driving fast and there was black ice—"

"I heard the voicemail," I interrupted. "Something scared us both. She was driving fast for a reason. If Anderson has an idea, it'll help."

"Help how?" He blinked. "Bailey is dead. Nothin' can bring her back."

I gripped the handles of my crutches.

"It'll help *me*," I said, my tone hushed. "Elliot, if I don't find out something, I'll die inside. I love that girl with my whole heart . . . I'll be broken if I never know, so please don't stop me."

"I'm askin' ye *not* to go to that man, Noah. You're mine."

I couldn't believe he wanted me still; the possibility that I caused his sister's death had to be lingering in his subconscious somewhere. How could he still want me? Still love me?

"I'm not going to Anderson because I want him." I searched his eyes. "You know I'm yours. You *know* I am, paddy. I'll always be yours, as long as you'll have me."

The muscles in Elliot's jaw tightened. He was struggling with what I wanted to do.

"Look at me," I said softly. "Please."

His eyes moved to mine and I saw fear in them, and my heart thumped with pain. He thought he was going to lose me to Anderson again. I didn't need him to confirm it, it was as plain as day in his ocean blues.

"I love you," I told him. "I love you so much that it scares me, Elliot."

He lowered his head to mine as I heard the soft cries of his mother off to our left.

"What if he knows something that he doesn't think is important, or something he doesn't even realise is important?" I quizzed. "You might be right, he might know nothing . . . but if he can tell me something, anything, that will help me figure out why I was with her, then it'll be worth visiting him."

"I want to take ye home and keep you with me." Elliot closed his eyes. "But I know this is somethin' ye have to do . . . even if I don't understand it, or agree with it."

"Thank you, honey." I leaned up and gently brushed his lips with mine. "Thank you for trusting me."

"I'll always trust *you*."

It was Anderson he didn't trust, but Elliot didn't have to worry about me losing my heart to him – because Elliot owned my heart, and he always would.

"You'll get in trouble over me." I glanced down at his uniform. "You didn't have extended leave because of a back injury, did you?"

"No," he said, frowning. "Compassionate leave for Bailey's death. I was on scene when she died, so missing a few weeks' of work is standard. I've been meetin' with a counsellor as ye recovered over the last few weeks in hospital. It was one of the requirements before I could be approved to go back to work."

"Really?" I blinked. "You obviously got the approval . . ."

Elliot nodded. "I'm fit for work. I'm just in a boat that's shared by a lot of other people who've lost someone they love. I found a new way to cope."

"How?" I asked, suddenly desperate to know. "How d'you cope?"

He brushed stray hair out of my face. "By takin' things one day at a time."

I let his words sink in. Taking things day by day had been our method since I got hurt . . . maybe when Elliot had said he was

246

taking things day by day, he'd been talking about way more than just my recovery – and I was glad of that.

"I feel like I'll never get to a place where I want to take it day by day," I admitted, tears still lingering on my cheeks. "I feel like I can't breathe with the pain in my chest. I miss her so much, Elliot. Even more now because I know I'll never see her again, never talk to her again. We'll never get to call her 'baby' and listen to her give out to us."

Elliot wrapped his arms around me and held me as I softly cried against his chest. This hurt. This hurt so much more than any physical pain ever had, because there was nothing – no medicine – that anyone could give me to make it better. The ache in my head was nothing compared to the hollow feeling in my chest.

"Are you in pain?"

"Yeah," I answered. "But not the way you think. My head is fine."

It wasn't fine; it just didn't hurt nearly as much as my chest did.

"I'm sorry, sweetheart."

"*I'm* sorry." I brushed his hair away from his face. "You lost your baby sister."

"We both lost her," he replied. "Ye loved her like a sister."

I did, I truly did. That girl had meant the world to me.

"Will you drive me to Anderson's place?" I tentatively asked. "I don't want to go alone, not with what I just found out."

"I was takin' ye whether ye liked it or not," Elliot replied. "And I'm waitin' for ye there."

I didn't argue with him, because that was what I wanted too.

"Good."

Elliot stepped back from me, and the second he did, his mother took his place and gathered me up in her arms. She squeezed me so tightly it made me gasp, but I returned her hug and held back more tears. She had lost her daughter – her pain trumped mine and I didn't pretend otherwise. I couldn't imagine how much she and Mr McKenna were hurting. Their baby girl was down in a hole, covered in dirt, and the only thing they had of her now was memories.

"I love ye, Noah," she said into my hair. "I love ye so much, honey. I always have."

"I love you too, Ma," I whispered, using the term she'd always asked me to call her. "I swear I do."

When we separated, Mr McKenna stepped forward and gave me a tight hug too. He kissed the top of my head and patted my back. He was massive, just like Elliot. He was a warm man and I loved him dearly. He and his wife had always been somewhat of a dream to me. To love the parents of my partner so much and to have them love me in return was special.

We all turned towards Bailey's grave and I suddenly grabbed Elliot's hand, needing to feel his touch and closeness. Just looking at the mound of dirt made me feel like I was being crushed on the inside. Elliot squeezed my hand as he moved behind me, wrapping his arms around my body.

"I'd give anything just to hear her have a go at you, Elliot," I said, my lower lip wobbling. "She could always give as could as she got. I swear she defined the term 'firecracker'."

Elliot and his parents chuckled.

We stood in silence for a while, just being in the moment and thinking of Bailey. I was very aware that I was in a different stage of grieving compared to them – this was so fresh for me. I was still having trouble believing it was real and not some sick and twisted joke that the fates were playing on me. I looked from Bailey's grave to Mr and Mrs McKenna. For a moment I stared at them, then I realised they were holding on to each other intimately.

"They never got divorced," Elliot whispered in my ear, startling me. "They planned to and were separated for years, but at the start of this year, they got close again. Da asked Ma on a date, and they've been together ever since."

Wide-eyed, I looked at Elliot.

"I know." He smiled. "They caught us off guard again."

"They're still married." I blinked. "Wow."

"I told you I didn't want to get married because what happened to them scared me, but I'm not scared any more, Noah. Even if they did get divorced, I wouldn't be scared. I was comparing our love to theirs when I shouldn't have, because our love is ours and no one else's can ever touch it."

I swallowed and didn't reply as his words sank in.

"I want it all with you," he murmured. "I've lived without ye, *sasanach,* and they were the bleakest years of me life. You're my happiness."

My heart pounded, but I couldn't think too much about what he'd just told me. I had too much to think about as it was.

"We'll talk about everything, just me and you later, but right now . . . will you bring me to him?"

"Yes," he replied gruffly. "I will."

We said goodbye to his parents, and Elliot let me have a moment where I simply bathed in Bailey's presence.

"I'll find out what happened," I whispered to her. "I promise, Bails."

I hoped it wouldn't become a promise I had to break, for everyone's sakes.

I righted my crutches and Elliot and I walked away, leaving Mr and Mrs McKenna to spend time with their daughter in private. Elliot hovered close to me – I could feel his eyes on me and I knew he knew that I was physically hurting, but because I didn't mention it, neither did he. We came to the end of the pathway that led to the car park and I blinked when I saw Elliot's car parked up on the kerb at an odd angle. I looked at him.

"I was in a hurry to get to you," he explained with a shrug. "I didn't have time to park properly."

There was a warden or security guard of some kind who Elliot spoke to and he explained our situation. I got into the front of the car with a murmur of apology, and not a few minutes later he joined me.

"Are you in trouble?"

"No." He shook his head. "He saw you when ye arrived; he saw your face and knew somethin' was wrong. I didn't tell him everythin', just that ye learned of me sister's passin' and were distraught."

"Well, you didn't lie."

"No," Elliot answered solemnly. "I didn't."

We drove out of the cemetery, and before I could blink we were on the road. It was a few minutes before I realised that I'd never told Elliot Anderson's address. I glanced at him.

"You know where he lives, don't you?"

"Ye lived with him, Noah," came the response. "Of course I know."

A feeling of warmth filled me.

"I love you," I told him. "I was with another man and you still looked out for me, didn't you?"

"I tried," he admitted. "There was little I could do. I barely caught a glimpse of you . . . but a few times I drove by and parked out front just so I could be close to ye."

"Elliot," I whispered. "I'm so sorry."

"Don't be," he replied, glancing at me. "You're mine again."

"I am," I said. "I am yours."

We pulled into the car park of a block of flats, and came to a stop. I breathed deeply as I gathered my crutches, grabbed my bag and climbed out. Elliot got out too and came around to my side, and before I could say a word he lowered his head and captured my lips in a kiss that both surprised and relaxed me. I returned the kiss until we both pulled apart, breathless.

"I'll wait down here," he said, shifting his stance. "Take as long as you need, but when I text ye, reply so I know you're okay. Understand?"

I nodded. "I love you."

"I love ye too, *sasanach*," he said, running his finger down my cheek. "So much."

"I don't even know if he's here," I said with an exhale. "He could be at work . . . I don't even know what he does."

"He's a graphic designer, he works from home. He'll likely be here."

"Oh, okay. I'll be back soon."

I gripped the handles of my crutches, and walked across the car park, up the steps and into the building without pausing or looking back. I remembered the flat number Anderson had told me, and the floor. I entered the elevator, and hit the button for the fourth floor. When the doors opened, I made my way down the hallway, counting the numbers on the doors as I passed them. When I came to 406, I came to a stop.

I put my phone on silent just in case the noise of it interrupted an important conversation. I sent Elliot a text that I was okay and would speak to him soon, then I put my phone into the pocket of my dress, lifted my hand and knocked on the door. There was a period of thirty seconds or so where I felt like I couldn't breathe, then the door opened and I inhaled.

"Noah."

"Anderson," I said, swallowing. "Hi."

He tilted his head to the side and watched me with his dark eyes. I wondered what was going through his head at my unannounced arrival.

"Bailey is dead."

Anderson blinked, then stepped aside without a word and waited as I silently passed by him and entered his home. There was a short white hallway that I walked down, and at the end was a kitchen that was paired with a large, open sitting room. There was another hallway to the right of the room that I assumed to be where the bedroom and bathroom were. I had no way of being sure, because I had no memory of the place.

"Do you recognise anything, baby?"

I looked around the strange place once again and then shook my head.

"Nothing," I answered. "I can't remember anything."

"That's okay," Anderson said from behind me. "You don't need to remember it."

I couldn't help but tense when his hands touched my waist, simply because he wasn't my partner.

"You've lost a lot of weight," he said, leaving his hands in place. "Are you sick?"

"No." I cleared my throat. "I'm just eating the diet I normally did – the one I remember, at least."

"You don't need to lose weight," he said, his face moving to the back of my neck as he inhaled my scent. "You were too skinny when we met."

"I didn't think so. I was just slim."

Anderson hummed but didn't reply. Then, "Sit," he said, "I want to talk."

Good, because I did too.

I crossed the space and sat down on the sofa, not being able to help the sigh of relief that left me. I was exhausted, both mentally and physically. My leg hurt like hell.

"Can I put my leg up on your coffee table?" I asked. "It's throbbing."

"Of course." Anderson pushed it closer to me, and helped me lifted my leg up.

"Thank you."

"Want a cuppa?" he asked with a wink. "Two sugars?"

I found myself smiling as I nodded. "Yes, please."

He entered the kitchen and put the kettle on while I looked around the room. I gasped when I spotted pictures of myself decorating the wall. I was smiling in every single one, but I didn't look happy. I knew what I looked like when I forced a smile, and that was exactly the expression on my face in each picture. My stomach clenched. If I wasn't happy in these pictures . . . maybe I hadn't been happy with Anderson like I thought I was.

I was planning on divorcing him, but the knowledge that I may have been unhappy in my marriage to him shocked me. For some reason, I'd believed if I got my memories back that I would find myself in love with Anderson, and that had scared me because of how much I loved Elliot. But as I looked at my smile, at my eyes, in the pictures around me, I was starting to believe that may not have been the case.

I looked at Anderson as he walked towards me with two steaming cups in his hands. He placed one in front of me on a coaster, then sat across from me and sipped from his. He watched me the entire time, and it was a little unnerving. I picked up my cup and thanked him. I blew on the steaming liquid, then took a gulp. I smacked my lips together, tasting the sweetness of the sugar and the slight bitterness of something else. It wasn't bad, just a faint taste. I drank some more, then placed it on the coaster next to my leg.

"You look like your health has improved."

"It has," I said with a nod. "My leg is the only thing giving me a spot of trouble right now, but it's healing, and that's the important thing."

Anderson took another sip of his tea.

"I rang the hospital this morning," he said casually. "They told me you were discharged a couple of days ago."

"Yeah." I licked my lips. "It's been kind of hectic, I've been settling back into . . . life."

"Are you here because you're ready to come home?"

Christ. My heart hammered against my chest as I tried to figure out how I was going to end my marriage to him.

"Anderson," I began, shifting in my seat. "We have a lot to talk about, but first I want to talk about Bailey. She's gone."

Anderson said nothing.

"You knew."

It wasn't a question and he knew it.

"I wanted to tell you ages ago, but your parents and Elliot were dead set against it. They didn't want you to know, for their own selfish reasons."

There wasn't anything selfish about Elliot or my parents keeping Bailey's death – or anything else – from me . . . they'd done it to protect me. I wanted honesty from Elliot, but it wasn't something I could cope with just after my accident. I was barely holding it together now.

"I feel like *everyone* should have told me," I replied, emphasising the word. "Everyone. I understand why no one did though. It's killing me to learn about it now . . . I wouldn't have been able to handle learning of her . . . of her death when I woke up."

"I only got to speak to you one-on-one on two occasions," he said. "You don't know me like you once did, so how would you have reacted to news of Bailey's death coming from me compared to him?"

I blinked.

"You have a point," I said. "But either way, I didn't know and now I do, and it's killing me inside."

Anderson sat forward. "I'm sure it's distressing – in your mind you were still close to her, but the fact of the matter is you weren't close to Bailey, or him – or anyone except me. You *never* spoke of them at all."

I flinched at his words. They were so abrupt, cruel and completely unnecessary considering the topic. I had only spoken to Anderson twice before, like he said, but both of those times he'd been upset and sweet and someone who I wanted to take care of because my situation was hurting him. His coldness while talking about Bailey upset me.

"Can I use your bathroom?"

"Of course," he said. "It's *your* bathroom too. Down the hallway, first door on the right."

I got to my feet and, without my crutches, made my way out of the room and towards the bathroom. When I was inside, I locked the door. I felt sick at how dismissive he was being about her death and how I felt about it. He was my husband; he should have been comforting me, or at least understanding of how I felt. I wanted to leave but I couldn't; I hadn't found out anything about Bailey yet and I needed answers. I took out my phone and saw a text from Elliot that he'd sent just two minutes ago.

Everything okay?

I swallowed.

Yeah, it's a bit awkward, but I expected that. He made me some tea and we're talking now. I'm waiting to broach the subject about Bailey. If I don't reply, it's because my phone is on silent.

I sent the message, then relieved myself in the toilet before I washed my hands. I checked my phone and read Elliot's return text.

> Okay. I'll be out here, so don't worry.
> Love you.

I pocketed my phone after I'd thumbed out my reply, and returned to the sitting room where Anderson was staring into space.

"How have you been?" I asked as I retook my seat. "Anderson?"

His eyes moved to mine. "Not great."

I frowned. "I'm sorry."

"For what?"

"For everything," I said. "None of this is your fault and you're suffering because of it."

He didn't reply; he just took a gulp of his tea before placing the cup on another coaster on the table.

"You came here to see me?"

I blinked. "Yes."

"Why?"

I shifted. "I wanted to ask you if you know why I was with Bailey that night? Like you said, I pushed her away and had no contact with her. Why was I with her?"

"I have no idea," he answered with a blink. "I've been wondering that myself. I didn't even know that you'd left the flat that night. There was a blackout and I went to bed early . . . I awoke to the police at my door informing me of the car accident."

My shoulders slumped as his words sank in.

"You have no idea?"

"None."

My gut twisted. "I was hoping you'd be able to shed some light on it . . . I can't remember anything. I've had no flashbacks, no dreams of things I don't remember. Nothing."

"Don't beat yourself up about it," he said, as if things were that simple.

"How can I not?" I questioned. "My entire life is different, Anderson. I feel like a stranger in my own body. I've been making progress but today has knocked me back massively."

"You'll get past this," he said with a small smile. "I'll help you, baby."

A shiver of discomfort ran through me every time he called me that word. I had never liked it; it was the reason Elliot never called me it. I'd made it clear years ago that it was an endearment I didn't care for. Why hadn't I made that clear to Anderson? Unless I had and he'd disregarded it.

"When are you coming home, Noah?"

I felt my body go rigid.

"Anderson." I clasped my hands together, realising this was the moment I needed to tell him our marriage was over. "Don't you feel a change in me when you're in my presence?"

"Yes," he almost growled. "I do."

I stared at him, surprised at his sudden anger.

"Surely you understand that because I don't know you . . . it means I have no feelings for you."

He cracked his knuckles, the action drawing my attention.

"Anderson," I continued after I cleared my throat. "Do you love me?"

"More than anyone has ever loved another person."

I wasn't sure why, but I didn't believe him. He was acting strange, not like the times he'd come to the hospital late at night to visit me. He was being blunt and somewhat rude now, but what I noticed most of all were his black dahlia eyes. They were cold, hard, and if I was being honest with myself, they made me very uneasy in that moment.

"When . . . when I look around this flat and I see images of our life together, it doesn't seem real," I admitted as softly as I could. "The last thing I want to do is hurt you, Anderson, but this place . . . this life I had with you, it's not my home any more. I'm truly sorry."

He said nothing, he only watched me with a calm that caused tingles of worry to dance up and down my spine. I stared at him, then a small dizzy spell struck me and made me shake my head. I raised my hand to my head and rubbed. It felt foggy and I suddenly felt tired – really tired.

"I came here to ask about Bailey, but you don't know anything," I heard myself almost slur as I clumsily grabbed my crutches. "I'm sorry. I don't want to hurt you but I don't feel anything for you. I have to leave, I have to go home."

I stood up, my legs shaking. Then I turned and stumbled forward.

"We have to get a divorce, Anderson. It's the only thing I can think—"

My words were cut off when something slammed into the back of my head and sent me spiralling into a dark void of loneliness.

CHAPTER TWENTY-FIVE

NOAH

Twenty-nine years old . . .

I can't do this any more.

I sat cross-legged on the floor of my bedroom, flipping through a picture album that was filled with lies, pain and fake love. I stared at my wedding photos; I was standing next to Anderson and smiling, but I could see the pain and uncertainty in my eyes. It was just the two of us at our courthouse wedding . . . one of the biggest mistakes of my life. I flicked through a couple more pages and with each photo that my eyes slid over, I felt less and less upset and more and more angry.

I closed the book, picked it up, got to my feet and put it back on the table of Anderson's office. He always kept it there within touching distance, and I didn't know why. I didn't look happy in any of the pictures even though I was smiling from ear to ear. He was too stupid to see what was in front of him, or he simply didn't care. I turned and left the room I was not allowed inside, and walked down the hallway and into the bathroom.

I stared in the mirror at myself, and when my eyes took in the swollen flesh of my cheek, the usual monologue that had replayed in my head the past few years didn't start. The reasoning I automatically made up on behalf of my husband never began. The excuses I made for why Anderson did what he did never formed and didn't make it to front and centre in my mind. The realisation of this made me gasp. I put a hand over my mouth.

"I'm done," I said to myself in the mirror. "I'm so fucking . . . *done*."

I began to cry and laugh as soon as the words left my mouth, even as my body began to tremble.

I'd given up my entire fucking life for this man, and for what? For him to beat me whenever I questioned him or did something he didn't like? For him to control every little thing I did, from who I spoke with to the activities I took part in? Somehow, he had even convinced me that having a relationship with my parents was toxic for me, and that cutting them out was the only option if I wanted to have an open, healthy mind.

"Stupid," I snapped at myself. "Stupid, stupid, *stupid*!"

I had options; I didn't have to do anything that I didn't want to . . . I just hadn't realised that until now.

I wasn't sure what had brought on this frame of mind. This thought process had never occurred to me before, I had always been so scared. Scared and never angry. Today, I was angry. Maybe the punch Anderson had landed on my face had knocked some sense into me. I'd allowed him to hurt me and drain me for far too long. He was evil. He'd manipulated me when I was at my most vulnerable. He'd used the heartache of the end of my relationship with Elliot against me so he could worm his way into my life and take over every little aspect of it.

At the start he was so wonderful – my knight in shining armour. He came to me when I was at the lowest point in my life, when getting out of bed became harder and harder to do every day. Everything I had lost in Elliot, I seemed to have found in Anderson.

He worshipped me, told me he loved me, that he wanted to marry me, to have a family with me and be with me forever. I could now see that I was severely depressed and only saw the things I thought I wanted to see in Anderson . . . By the time I found out who he truly was, it was too late. I felt broken inside whenever he laid his hands on me, but once his anger subsided, he would return to the wonderful, kind man he was when we first met, and he would cry and cling to me as he apologised and swore it would never happen again.

But it would *always* happen again.

I dropped my hands and examined my face. The swelling and reddening of my flesh were nothing compared to injuries I had sustained before. I glanced at the white scar that cut through my eyebrow and recalled one of the first times Anderson hit me – he'd punched me so hard that my eyebrow busted open and I was knocked unconscious. That injury was the first time I'd woken up in a hospital because of my husband – the man who was supposed to love, cherish and protect me.

"Bollocks," I grumbled. "What a load of fucking rubbish!"

I left the bathroom and headed straight for my bedroom. I felt myself begin to rush as I realised what I was doing. I was leaving. I was leaving Anderson, this flat, this godawful life I had with him, and I wasn't looking back. I felt sick to my stomach as I kept jumping at every noise. I grabbed a bag and shoved some clothes inside, followed by my purse and a spare pair of shoes. My gut was churning, and I looked over my shoulder every few seconds out of blind fear.

After our fight Anderson had left the flat, saying he needed to cool down before he did something he would regret. Punching me in the face and making me cry were apparently not things he regretted doing, but he would regret them later. I knew what was going to happen next. He would come back to me with a gift, likely flowers, and he would be on his knees, crying, as he apologised for hurting me. But this time he wasn't getting my forgiveness.

When the small bag was packed, I got dressed. I changed out of my pyjamas and put on a pair of thick leggings, a T-shirt and a hoodie, followed by my coat. I slid my feet into socks and my trainers, and put my hair up into a bun on the top of my head. I didn't need anything else, but I hesitated because I had nowhere to go. I knew in my heart that my parents would come for me, but I couldn't trust my father not to attack Anderson if he showed up. I couldn't risk him getting arrested, because Anderson would spin the situation in his favour. He was a master manipulator; he could argue with God that He was really the Devil and he would somehow come out on top.

"Elliot," I whispered.

I had no right to call him. Just the simple thought of him caused my chest to ache with need. I loved him – I loved him so much and I always had – but I'd ruined everything with my own stubbornness. I couldn't call AJ as I'd cut him off too. I'd cut everyone off, because Anderson made me. He was the only person I needed – that's what he'd said. And I'd believed him too. I shook my head as I left the bedroom and then paused by the house phone.

"Bailey." I blinked. "*Bailey*."

I hadn't spoken to her in years, but she would help me, I knew she would. I picked up the phone and dialled the number I remembered, and hoped it was the one she still used. The phone rang a few times, and I held my breath as I waited for an answer.

"Hello?"

"Hey." I cleared my throat. "Hey, Bailey?"

"Hiya," came her response. "Who's this?"

"It's Noah," I said. "Noah Ainsley."

Using my maiden name felt good, and also like a big fuck you to Anderson.

There was a pregnant pause, then a whispered, "*Noah*?"

"Yeah," I answered. "It's me, Bails."

There was a rustle on the other end of the line as if she was moving, then I heard her breathing.

"Ye haven't phoned me in years," she said. "Ye don't even look at me when ye see me on the street."

There was no hate in her voice, no accusation or bitterness, only hurt.

"I'm so sorry, Bailey," I said, my voice cracking. "I've been . . . I've been stuck for a very long time. I've been trapped in this world with Anderson, and I'm finally seeing now that it's not a world I have to remain part of if I don't want to. And I *really* don't want to."

I heard Bailey's gasp. "You're leavin' him, aren't ye?"

"Yes," I answered. "But I need help. He's out right now and I have nowhere to go. This is my only chance."

"I'll come for ye," Bailey announced. "I'll come and pick ye up, Noah."

I released a nervous breath. "Really?"

"Of course, but why d'ye want to leave, tonight of all nights?" she demanded, and when I didn't answer right away, she cursed under her breath. "Has he hurt ye, Noah?"

"Don't tell Elliot," I blurted. "He'll kill Anderson."

Things had ended badly between us but I knew him . . . he was a real man. He'd go ballistic if he knew how Anderson had been treating me all these years – how he'd abused me in more ways than just physical. Even though I'd hurt Elliot and hadn't given him the chance to speak to me when I should have, I knew he would still come to my aid. That was the kind of man he was: a gentleman.

"Son of a bitch!" Bailey snapped. "How long has this been happenin'?"

I looked down at my feet. "A very long time."

"Fuck, Noah, I had no idea. I thought . . . I thought ye were just so hurt by your break-up with Elliot that ye just pushed us away, I never imagined *he* was the reason why."

My hands were shaking. "You have absolutely nothing to be sorry for. I ruined everything. I'm so sorry."

"*You* have nothin' to be sorry for," she stressed. "Don't even think of takin' any blame upon yourself for what this scumbag has done to ye! D'ye hear me? He's abused ye. Your silence in that situation isn't silence, it's a scream that only *you* can hear."

I began to cry. "I miss you so much, and Elliot. God, I ruined everything when I left him. I was so upset and angry with him at the time that I just couldn't go back to him, but I wish I did."

"Shhh," she soothed. "I'm on my way right now, literally leaving the house and running to my car."

"Be careful," I sniffed, wiping my nose. "The roads may be dangerous, so much of London has no power. It keeps coming and going here. Watch out for ice too."

"I will, Noah," she assured me. "Get whatever you want to bring with ye, I'll be at your place in a few minutes. I know the buildin', just not the floor or flat number."

"Fourth floor," I said as I glanced out of the window. "Flat 406."

"Got it. I'll be right there, I promise."

I put the phone down and noticed my hand was trembling. I jumped with fright when the lights knocked off for the fifth time in two hours. The darkness scared me. I felt trapped in the flat in which I was forced to spend nearly all of my time. I was here all day every day, but I'd never felt more stuck inside of these walls than I did right now. I looked around and felt nothing but emptiness. There were no happy times here – even the times I'd thought were happy were really sad. I just hadn't been able to see it through the web Anderson had woven in my mind.

I could see now, though. And I hated what I saw.

As the lights came back on I began to rip the photo frames from the wall and threw them on the floor, feeling powerful when each one of them smashed. I ran into Anderson's office, grabbed a crowbar he once hit me with and smashed all of his belongings. His prized computer, his precious drawing materials, I slammed the bar into everything. Then I dropped it and focused on the photo album that Anderson kept so close to him. I ripped out all of the pictures and shredded them into pieces, and threw them around the room as if they were confetti.

"Good fucking riddance."

With a grin of delight, I turned my back on the room, grabbed my bag and walked out of the prison that had kept me caged for far too fucking long. I unlocked the door and stepped into the hallway, shutting it behind me as firmly as I could. I hurried towards the stairwell and ran down them as fast as I could without tripping and falling. When I reached the bottom floor, I slowed my movements way down. I opened the door to the entryway slowly. I heard nothing, not a single peep, so I walked briskly out of the building, relief slamming into me as a rush of freezing cold hit me. I carefully descended the steps, wary of the ice.

I looked around, my eyes wild as I tracked any and every bit of movement I could see. My heart jumped when a small car pulled into the car park of the building and came to a stop right in front of me. I gripped the strap of my bag, and I burst into tears when Bailey jumped out of her car and hurried around to me.

"Noah!"

I wrapped my arms around her and cried.

"I love you." I hugged her tightly. "I love you, I always have."

"I love ye too, Noah," Bailey said, her voice cracking. "You're me sister."

I whimpered.

"I'm here," she said, squeezing me. "I'm here, it's okay."

"You're all grown up now." I pulled back, sniffling, and looked at her. "You're so beautiful."

She smiled at me, but that smile faded when she squinted and leaned in to look at my face. I watched as her eyes of ocean blue, ones identical to her brother's, scanned my face from top to bottom. I saw the worry, and anger, that glowed within them.

"The fuckin' *scumbag*," she hissed as she lifted her fingers and brushed them over my throbbing cheek. "Look what he's done to your face."

"This is nothing," I assured her. "It's really not, I swear. Let's just go. I don't know where he is. He'll kill me if he finds out I'm leaving him. "

Bailey dropped her hand and nodded, then she grabbed my bag and put it in the boot of her car.

"Get in," she said to me. "It's fuckin' Baltic out here."

I hurried towards the passenger-side door.

"Noah!"

I got such a fright that I jumped, and for a moment my feet cleared the ground. With my hand gripping the door handle of Bailey's car, I looked over my shoulder as Anderson slammed the door of his own car shut. I wasn't anywhere near him, but I could see the anger burning within his cruel black dahlia eyes. He knew what I was doing. He knew. He had a bouquet of flowers in his hand. With his eyes on me he dropped the flowers to the ground, took a step forward and crushed them under his boot.

"Don't you *dare* get in that fucking car, woman."

I stared at him, and for the first time since I became fearful of him, I held his gaze and met his challenge head-on. I wasn't going to cower before him any more; I wasn't going to allow him to break my spirit any longer. He was nothing, and I wanted him to know that.

"I want a divorce, Anderson. I don't want to be your wife for a second longer."

"She's done with you, ye woman-beatin', no-good stream of piss!"

He didn't look at Bailey for a second; his focus was entirely on me. When he suddenly lunged and started to cross the car park, Bailey and I screamed as we rushed into the car and locked the doors behind us. I put my hands over my ears and screeched when pounding erupted on the window of my door. Bailey fumbled with her keys for just a moment before she started her car and pulled away.

"Noah!"

I looked over my shoulder, and in the moon's light I spotted Anderson running back towards his car.

"He's coming after us!" I gasped in fright. "Oh my God! Oh my God, Bailey!"

"Don't worry," she said, her voice determined. "He can't hurt ye any more. He knows that *I* know that he's been abusin' ye."

She may have known that he was abusive to me, but she didn't know Anderson or the lengths he would go to keep me. I did – I had first-hand experience of how dangerous he could be when someone tried to take away something that was his. He viewed me as his property, even though he always tried to spin a story that everything he did was for my benefit.

"What do we do?" I asked, then I looked over my shoulder and screamed when Anderson's car skidded out of the car park. "He's coming!"

"Call me brother," Bailey shouted as I struggled with my seat belt before I heard it click into place. "The dispatch grid might be busy with a lot of callers tonight. Call Elliot directly, his number is the same as it's always been."

"I don't have a phone," I said, panicked. "Anderson never let me have one, I used the flat phone to ring you."

She grabbed her phone from her pocket and pushed it at me without taking her eyes off the road. I took it and hurriedly unlocked it once Bailey told me her passcode. I dialled Elliot's number; I knew it by heart. I pressed Call just as Anderson drove directly behind us, making me scream with terror. Elliot's phone rang a couple of times, then I heard a beep instead of a voice.

"Elliot? Elliot? Shit, shit, *shit*! It's his voicemail!"

Panic gripped me as my hand grabbed on to the handle of the door. I kept looking over my shoulder, and when I realised Anderson was never going to let me go, I began to cry.

"Help us," I sobbed. "Oh God. Please, I don't know what do! Bailey, what're we gonna do? It's so dark, put the high beams on."

I screeched as the car slid slightly as Bailey made a sharp turn.

"Oh God, oh God!" I sobbed. "Bailey, you're going too fast!"

With shaking hands, I looked back at my phone and realised I was still on a call with Elliot's voicemail. I tried to hang up and call him again, but I was so distraught I couldn't make my fingers do what I needed them to do.

"Tulse Hill," I cried into the phone. "Elliot, we're on – Bailey, slow down!"

"I'm tryin'!" Bailey suddenly shouted. "I can't stop, it's black ice! We're slidin'."

"Elliot!" I screamed as the car swerved. "Elliot, help us. We're driving through Tulse Hill. Please, please! Anderson is going to kill us – Bailey! Look out!"

One moment we were sliding at an insane speed, then the next our bodies were being violently jerked from side to side as the car flipped multiple times before landing on its side and smashing into something solid and unmoving. Somewhere in the midst of this, I smacked my head against the window of my door and felt warm liquid dripping down my face, as pain unlike anything I had ever felt before spread like wildfire across my head and body.

Before I closed my eyes, I called out a name. I called out for a man to help me, but before he could answer . . . darkness had already claimed me.

CHAPTER TWENTY-SIX
ELLIOT

Present day . . .

I was going fucking *crazy*.

I hit my hands against the steering wheel of my car for the millionth time. This was the most insane thing I had ever done, and I was a fucking firefighter! Sitting in my car while knowing the woman I loved was in the flat she'd once shared with a husband she couldn't remember was like resting my balls on scalding-hot coals. I hated every fucking second of it. But I had no choice but to endure it until she heard whatever it was that she thought Anderson Riley was going to tell her.

For her sake, I hoped he had the information she believed he might.

I would be lying if I said a huge part of me wasn't curious to know if he knew anything. The police had questioned him for information about that night, but he'd said he hadn't been aware that Noah had even left their flat. He went to sleep early and was awoken by the police knocking on his door to inform him about the crash that took Bailey and almost took Noah too. They had no reason not to believe him, and though I disliked him greatly, I had no reason either.

Maybe Noah was right. Maybe there was a chance that Anderson knew something that could help shine a light on what took place that night and he didn't realise it, but I wasn't holding out much hope.

My issues with the man boiled down to one thing on my part: raging jealousy. I hated him for having Noah, and he knew it. He hated me for wanting her, because I made no effort to hide that fact. Back when I found out that Noah had moved in with the creep barely a few weeks after we broke up, I blew like a fuse. I was so furious, hurt and ready to beat the shite out of the man who had moved in on my girl. I'd found out where they lived, showed up at the place and demanded to know what was happening. Anderson had happily told me how he'd fucked Noah in every way imaginable, and planned to continue fucking her for the foreseeable future. I landed a solid to his jaw. Noah hadn't been home at the time, but Anderson made sure to let me know that she would be returning to him and to his bed.

I left the flat that day expecting to feel better after letting my frustrations out on the pathetic wankstain, but I didn't. I felt a million times worse off than I could have ever imagined. It had solidified in my mind – and heart – that Noah and I were never going to get back together. She had chosen another man over me . . . and at the time, I blamed myself. As time went by, I'd still mourned the loss of her and our relationship, and had a lot of self-hatred and blame for what had happened, but after thinking of our talk in the hospital I'd come to a conclusion.

It was no one's fault.

Noah had wanted to get married and I didn't; it was something we couldn't compromise on and it was the end of our relationship. When said like that, it seemed easy to understand and to accept, but the reality of it was very different. It had been very hard for me to accept it was the end for us because I was still so deeply in love with her. So in love that, years later when she needed me, I still came running without a second thought or a moment of hesitation. I loved Noah Ainsley, and I always would.

She was my woman.

My person that was alone in the company of her husband who she planned to divorce. It eased my nerves, mind and racing heart to know that she had chosen me over him. It was even more comforting knowing that even if I wasn't around, she would still be leaving him. He wasn't the person for her, especially in the frame of mind she was in. He was a smooth-talking son of a bitch – I had heard him spin tales so easily the night I confronted him, and I'd learned that he was very good at making people believe what he wanted them to believe *when* he wanted them to believe it.

Present-day Noah wasn't falling for his bullshit.

When he'd met her, she'd been in a low, dark place over our break-up; I didn't need all the brains in the world to know that. He arrived in her life when she was at her lowest point, and the scumbag had sunk his claws into her before I ever got the chance to speak to her. It always made me tense when I wondered if things would have turned out differently if I'd spoken to Noah before Anderson entered her life. I had no way of knowing, but I believed that we could have talked at length about what was bothering us both, and we could have come to an understanding.

I would have rather been scared of marriage ruining us than losing her . . . The pain of that hurt more than I could ever describe. My mindset on marriage had drastically changed from the night Noah and I broke up. It was stupid to me that I'd been scared that marriage would change us, when in reality, the only thing that would change was Noah's surname. Our daily lives would still continue, we would still have the future we'd planned together, and we would still love and be the person the other one kissed each night before bed.

I wondered if Noah believed me when I told her I wanted a life that involved everything with her. I wanted to stand in front of our friends and family and declare before them, before God, that Noah was the one I'd chosen to spend the rest of my life with. After bringing it up in the cemetery, I would leave her to think about it until she was ready to talk about it. Noah wasn't one to keep things bottled up, especially when she needed an answer to whatever was bothering her.

That was exactly why she was in Anderson's flat right now: she needed answers to the questions that plagued her mind.

"Me poor *sasanach*," I mumbled to myself. "How can I make this better for ye?"

I already knew the answer. I couldn't make *any* of this better for her. She had just found out Bailey had died – but what was worse, she now knew that the crash she was in was the same crash that killed my sister. I still believe that the decision to keep Noah in the dark was a sound one. If we had told her the truth weeks ago, then she would have reacted differently – and by that I mean she would have likely collapsed and maybe even died.

I could have lost her too.

Her brain was stronger now than it had been a few weeks ago, but I wasn't fool enough to think she was healed. I saw the physical pain she'd been suffering in the cemetery. I understood that the emotional pain of Bailey's death hitting her had overshadowed the pain in her head and body. I knew that later, once I had her home and alone, everything would hit her all at once. Her pain, Bailey's death, the confusion of it all. It would slam into her when she had a moment to stop and realise the weight, and truth, of it, and I would be there to shoulder the burden with her.

I closed my eyes and heard her scream in my head as I remembered running up to her on the ground by Bailey's grave. It was a wail of disbelief and raw pain, and a desperate plea for what she was seeing to not be true. I knew it because Noah had been voicing the scream that I'd been keeping inside since the night my little sister died. Noah couldn't hold her emotions in, and I couldn't let them out. Not because I didn't want to – I just had a wall built up inside me to keep everything in check. It was the only way I could function.

I was terrified that if that wall broke I would collapse right along with it.

A shout followed by a feminine scream snapped my eyes open. I jolted as my eyes sought out the source of the commotion, and I locked my gaze on the entrance to the flat building. A few people were rushing out of the double doors, almost trampling over one another to get outside, and it caused me to jump out of my car in a panic.

"What's wrong?" I shouted, rushing forward. "What's goin' on?"

"Fire," a man coughed, waving his hand in front of his face. "Fourth floor. It's bad. There are dozens of families in this building, lots of elderly too!"

I widened my eyes. "Call 999. *Now!*"

Without another word, thought or a second's hesitation, I took off sprinting towards the building. I shoved my way through the crowd of people who were pouring out of the doors clutching their children, loose belongings, pets and their sanity, as the sound of the building's fire alarms reached my ears. Nothing else mattered to me in that moment, other than getting to Noah and bringing her to safety.

Nothing.

CHAPTER TWENTY-SEVEN

NOAH

When I opened my eyes and found Anderson practically in my face, I flinched. I stared at him with slowly blinking eyes for a long moment. He was silently staring at me, as if waiting for me to do something. I tried to gather my thoughts but couldn't.

"What?" I rasped. "What happened?"

My head was sore, but only slightly. There was a heavy pressure on my wrists and hands that made me feel uncomfortable. I tried to move my arms but found I couldn't. They were behind my back and bound together. Confusion swirled in my jumbled brain. My mind felt hazy, like I couldn't straighten anything out to form a coherent thought.

"You were only out for a few minutes," Anderson answered with a tilt of his head. "That's surprising. You said that morphine knocks you out for hours."

His words made no sense to me.

"Anderson." I struggled against the material tied around my wrists and feet. My boot had been removed and I couldn't see it anywhere. "What is this? Untie me."

I looked to my left and right as he straightened to his full height, crossed the room to the dining table and sat in front of a plate full of food and a wine glass that was filled to the top. I realised that I was on the floor in a sitting position, with my back resting against the base of the sofa. I leaned my head back and groaned. I hated how fuzzy my mind was; it reminded me of being in the hospital when I was given medicine to kill my pain.

"Anderson." I swallowed, my throat dry as a desert. "I can't think."

"You don't have to think," he answered. "I'll do that for you."

I looked at him and frowned. "What?"

"Things are going to go back to the way they were," he said as he cut up his food with his knife and fork. "I promise."

I struggled against my bindings.

"Let me go!" I demanded. "What are you doing?"

He paused and glanced at me. "You know better than to raise your voice at me, woman."

I most definitely did not know better. Had he forgotten I didn't know *anything* about him?

"I'm so confused," I said, clearing my throat. "Did I collapse?"

"No," Anderson answered as he picked up his wine glass. "I drugged you, but before you fell asleep you tried to leave so I hit you. I had to protect you from yourself, so I did what I had to do."

I heard every single astonishing word he said and repeated them twice in my head. I stared at him as he calmly drank some wine, then went back to eating his food like he hadn't just said the most insane thing I had ever heard another person say. I looked straight ahead as I tried to process what I was hearing. I closed my eyes to think, and suddenly the memory of the night of the crash, of Bailey's death, resurfaced and my body jolted.

"Oh my God."

"What?"

"I remember."

The cutlery Anderson was using clanked against his plate, and within seconds I found him on his knees in front of me. His hands touched my shoulders and his fingers bit into my flesh painfully. His eyes looked wild as his gaze drilled into mine.

"What d'you remember?"

My eyes burned with tears.

"I was leaving you . . . that night . . . I was leaving you."

My husband blinked, sat back on his heels and sighed, long and deep.

"You weren't leaving me," he said, his dark eyes still boring into me. "You were just confused; you'd never leave me."

I was about to disagree with him, but fear made me hold my tongue. I couldn't remember everything about my life with this man, I could just remember the night he ruined mine and I knew it was enough for me to watch what I said to him. Anderson . . . he was abusive towards me. He'd beaten me, controlled me . . . and tried to kill me.

"Things are still hazy," I lied, swallowing. "What happened if I wasn't leaving you?"

He watched me with such intensity that it scared the shit out of me. I quickly realised that I couldn't let him know that I remembered that he was a woman-beating, abusive piece of shit, because I didn't think I would get out of the flat alive if he knew.

"Can you untie me?" I asked when he didn't answer. "I can't go anywhere with my leg, so can you just untie me, please? I can't feel my hands."

Anderson stared at me for a long moment.

"Please?" I pressed. "I'll sit right here; I just want to be free. I promise."

He got up, grabbed his steak knife and then walked back towards me. I held my breath as I eyed the knife, and when he put a hand on my shoulder so I could lean forward, my heart thudded in my chest. I released a breath of relief when I heard the knife cut through fabric. The tight binding on my wrists and feet suddenly fell away, so I pulled my hands around my body and rubbed my aching, raw flesh.

"Remember your promise."

"I will," I replied, trying to keep my voice even. "I'm staying right here."

"I know you are," he said. "You aren't leaving me. We've spent years together, just the two of us. We're in love."

I couldn't believe what I was hearing. In love? He couldn't really believe that. He'd abused me until I was so filled with terror that he could control everything I said and did. I wanted to scream at him, to attack him, to inflict some sort of pain on him for everything he had put me through, but I couldn't. I couldn't do a single fucking thing.

"So, what now?"

"Now" – he stood back up – "I finish my lunch."

I watched him as he returned to the table, sat down and resumed eating his food like he hadn't just knocked me unconscious and tied my wrists together to keep me from leaving him. After a few minutes of silence, I pushed myself to my feet and then sat on the sofa and groaned as my body melted into the cushions. I felt Anderson's eyes on me, but I didn't look at him. I was trying to think of what to do. My mind instantly went to Elliot. He was downstairs in the car park. Anderson had said I was only out cold for a few minutes. I was thinking of how I could get Elliot to come to the flat . . . but I was worried if I did that then Anderson might harm him.

I knew he was capable of it.

The back of my head ached and my wrists were sore, but nothing to the extent of what I should have been feeling. This was only a taste of the pain that Anderson could cause me, though he didn't appear to be angry and that was how I knew that I was safe for the time being. My gut told me to keep him calm, but I also needed him to talk so I could find a way to get proof of what he had done to cause the crash that Bailey died in, and what he had done to me all the years I was with him. I shifted and felt something dig into the side of my right thigh. I tensed when I realised what it was.

My phone.

"Oh my God."

My phone was in my fucking dress pocket. The loose material of the fabric made it hard to notice the pocket, Anderson obviously didn't know this, or he would have taken it away from me. I looked around and couldn't see my bag anywhere, so I knew he had searched it and taken it out of my sight.

"What?" Anderson said, his gaze on me. "What is it?"

I glanced at him. "My wrists are sore."

"They'll be fine," he grunted. "The skin isn't even chafed."

I looked down at my red wrists and realised that he was right. "They're still sore."

He didn't reply, he just finished off his food and his wine. Then he proceeded to wash and dry his dishes like it was a regular day, and not like he was keeping me hostage in his home. It hit me then that Anderson was really deranged. Not just sick, but twisted and clearly evil. He had to have some sort of mental disorder to think what he was doing was okay. It was fucking crazy. *He* was crazy.

"I'm going to the bathroom," he told me with a pointed glare. "I'm leaving the door open, so if you move, I'll know, and I will *not* be happy."

In other words, he'd beat the shit out of me if my arse left the sofa.

"My leg is sore," I said, shrugging. "I'm not going anywhere."

He walked out of the room and my mind raced with my options. I couldn't call Elliot because he would come running and probably get hurt, and I couldn't call 999 because I couldn't speak to answer any of the questions they'd have. I had to think of what I needed at the current moment, and what I needed was Anderson verbally saying what he'd done on the night I left him. I needed proof. I hurriedly got out my phone and triple-checked that it was on silent. I turned the volume up so the microphone would pick up the words more clearly, then I opened the voice memo app, pressed Record and put the phone back in my pocket.

When Anderson returned, I groaned when I reached behind me and rubbed the throbbing spot on the back of my head. It really was hurting me, but I was trying to appear to be as little of a threat as I could – so I wanted to appear as weak as possible.

"I can't *believe* you've attacked me, Anderson."

He retook his seat.

"I didn't want to hurt you, it's why I gave you some morphine. Don't you understand?"

I sat upright. "You could have killed me . . . you know I'm recovering from a *brain injury*!"

"That is the *very* reason I put morphine in your tea, so you'd just fall asleep."

"Wait." I felt my lips part as I realised just what he was saying. "You drugged me?"

I recalled him mentioning it when I woke up as well, but I hadn't focused on it until now.

"Yes, but not very well. You're still conscious. You said morphine makes you sleep."

"Yeah," I replied dumbly. "It does."

"I should've used two capsules instead of one." He shook his head.

I stared at him. "You drugged me *and* you hit me!"

"I didn't want to hit you; I never *want* to hit you."

"But yet you always do hit me." I glared at him. "You're the reason why waking up in a hospital felt familiar to me when I awoke from my coma . . . each time I woke up in a hospital, it was because *you* put me there."

"Me?" Anderson jumped to his feet. "I had no choice but to discipline you! You *never* listen to me, when all I want to do is protect you!"

I clenched my hands into fists to keep myself from screaming at him.

"Protect me?" I repeated with a slow blink. "You protect me by physically damaging my body? Is that it? You almost killed me, and you did succeed in killing Bailey. Anderson . . . you *killed* her."

My voice cracked as the weight of my words took hold. Anderson had caused Bailey's death; he was the reason we were so scared that night. He'd caused *every single thing.*

"I didn't mean to cause the crash, but she took you from me!" His hands shook as he spoke. "I just wanted to get to you, I didn't think she'd drive so fast to get away from me."

I lifted my hands to my face.

"She was only twenty-one," I said. "She had her whole life ahead of her!"

Anderson didn't reply but I didn't expect him to. He was deflecting the blame of the situation on to me and Bailey, and he wasn't going to take accountability for what he'd done because he didn't care. I wasn't sure he felt real emotions, not like a normal person did. All he cared about was having me under his spell.

"Why do you want me?" I asked, dropping my hands. "What the hell could you possibly want me for?"

"Because you're my best friend and my wife. I love you, Noah. I've always protected you from Elliot, from your parents, from everyone who has ever hurt you."

"Anderson, *you* were the one who hurt me!"

"To protect you." He rubbed his hand over his face. "If you went back to him, to your parents, you would have killed yourself. *They* caused your depression. You're still alive because I protected you. I helped you. You see that, right?"

I didn't see what he wanted me to see; I saw what he was trying to do. He was trying to manipulate me by making me feel sorry for him, to sympathise with him and accept that he hurt me to protect me. I may have believed that once upon a time, but not any more.

"I can't remember being your wife, so why do you still want me?" I pressed. "Why?"

"Because you're mine," he growled, lowering himself back down on to the chair. "I'll *never* let you go."

I bit the inside of my cheek to keep from crying. I needed to keep him talking. His mood swings were startling. One second he was trying to be gentle, and the next he was firm and had anger blazing in his eyes.

"If I'm yours, why didn't you try harder to see me at the hospital? Why did you only come to me twice?" I quizzed. "Why wait until I came to you?"

"Because your parents and that piece-of-shit ex of yours got to you first," he replied, his voice so low it sent a shiver of fear up the length of my spine. "They never liked me. None of them did. At the start, I was extra nice to them. I wanted them to like me because it makes things easier when people like you . . . but none of them ever did. It's why I stopped you from having any involvement with them."

I lifted my hand to my mouth. "You stopped me from seeing them because they didn't like you?"

"Because they would have had influence over you," he corrected as I dropped my hand. "We would have never been able to be together the way we wanted if everyone from your life was sticking their noses into our relationship. You didn't need them . . .

don't you see, baby? You only ever needed me. I take care of you, I protect you. Me, not them – and not *him*."

He words felt like a pile of bricks weighing me down.

"When I met you," he continued. "I didn't know you were the one for me, but when we started talking, I saw that we were meant to be together. I wanted someone for my own, someone I could love deeply, and I found that in you. You love me, Noah. You do."

My gaze bored into his. "It's ownership, not love. You don't hurt someone you love, not in the ways you've hurt me."

He didn't reply, he only watched me.

"I'm scared of silence because of you." I clasped my hands together. "I remember the night of the crash . . . you beat me badly. I remember you were glad of the blackout the night I left you. You wanted things silent so you could hear nothing but my cries."

"So *you* could hear them," Anderson corrected. "So you could hear yourself be disciplined for your actions. You never understand that I do what I do for your own good, Noah. Please, believe me."

My body began to shake.

"I won't be like that again." I lifted my gaze to his. "I won't be the shell of a woman you want. You can beat me until I'm dead. I don't care, I won't be that woman."

Anderson nodded his head slowly.

"I know," he answered, surprising me. "You're a different Noah from when I knew you; you're strong of mind. I knew when you first looked at me in the hospital that you were lost to me."

I frowned. "Then why keep me here? Why do this?"

"I said you were mine." He got to his feet. "You'll be dead, but you'll *still* be mine. You'll never be his. Ever. I told you in the hospital that this would all be over soon. I meant it. We're going to be together forever. Just you and me, the way it always should be."

I sucked in a breath when he pulled a piece of white material from the drawer of the coffee table and advanced on me. I screamed, but a punch to the face silenced me as blood filled my mouth and dribbled down my chin. Anderson made quick work of tying my wrists together once more, followed by feet. He pushed me on to the floor, and I stared at him as he reached behind the sofa and produced a jerrycan. I sucked in a breath and was about to scream, but one look from Anderson kept me silent. I was frozen as he uncapped the can, and the fumes of petrol stung my nostrils.

"Anderson," I whimpered. "Please, don't."

He ignored me as he splashed the fuel around the room, then he went down the hallway and I heard the petrol sloshing around as he dispensed it in each room. He hadn't poured it on me or on the part of the sofa I was near, and I wondered if he planned to do that last. I leaned forward to watch him and was gobsmacked when he went outside the flat and splashed fuel on the walls all the way down to the elevator. When he reached the door of his flat, he produced a lighter, flicked it, lit a newspaper and dropped it in the hall. The fuel on the ground ignited instantly, and it spread like wildfire down the corridor.

"Anderson!" I shouted. "Please, just talk to me. We can figure this out, things don't have to be this way."

"We can't," he snapped as he came back into the room. "I sensed the change in you the night you woke up and in the times when I finally got to speak to you. You made eye contact with me and questioned me . . . two things that you knew *never* to do. I touched your wrist and you still did all of those things. I knew your parents and that McKenna prick would never let you go this time, so I made a promise to myself that if I couldn't have you then *no one* could."

I began to cry.

"What does touching my wrist have to do with anything?"

"It was always a warning between us," he explained. "When we were out in public and you behaved in a manner that I didn't like,

284

I would touch your wrist and you knew to stop whatever you were doing. I've kept you safe so many times by doing it."

Horror filled my mind as I remembered all of the times that he'd touched my wrist when he came to see me in the hospital, and stared at me while he did it. He was trying to see if I had any memory of its significance so he could control me once again. I was flabbergasted.

"Anderson, *please*!"

"We'll go together," he assured me with a smile. "The smoke will kill us long before the fire touches us. I'm gonna carry you to our room and we're going to go to sleep together one final time. Just the two of us."

"You'll kill other families on this floor, maybe everyone in the entire building!" I snapped, trying to make him see reason. "You'll *kill* people."

"They'll get out," Anderson said. "Don't worry about them."

I jerked my attention to the front door when I heard screaming and shouts. I heard fire alarms go off, but the emergency sprinkler systems never kicked in. Anderson saw me looking at the ceiling and laughed.

"The sprinklers have been broken from the second floor up for the last week now. They've been out daily trying to fix the problem, but they haven't been able to do anything about it yet."

His words were so exact that it made my skin crawl.

"Did you somehow disable the system?"

"Maybe."

He was crazy. He was a raging fucking *lunatic*.

"I can't believe I ever felt sorry for you."

Disbelief was all over Anderson's features.

"What?"

"During my time in the hospital I felt sorry for you – I felt like I was awful because I didn't know that you were my husband.

I thought I was being cruel because I didn't want you," I said with a look of disgust. "After seeing the true you, and how completely worthless you are, the only reason I stayed with you was out of fear. That's the conclusion I've come to. You're a pathetic loser who beats me when things get tough; you may have broken my body and even my mind for a time, but no more. You have no hold over me any more, Anderson. You're a fucking *joke*."

His face turned a blistering shade of red as he reached down and grabbed a fistful of my hair and dragged me by my head out of the sitting room, down the hallway and into the bedroom. He was shouting, cursing and kicking my back along the way, and when he finally released me, he picked me up and threw me on to the bed. I sat up in time to watch him flick his lighter again and throw it out into the hall. A spark ignited, then flames spread.

I saw a wall of fire for only a moment before he slammed the door shut.

I reached for the lamp next to me, and threw it at him when he dove for me. It smacked off him but didn't slow him down. My screams were so loud that Anderson ducked his head to escape the shrill sound. When his hands closed around my throat, he stopped the sound – and my breathing – instantly. My hands went to his face and I dug my nails into his flesh, making him roar. But he never let go of my throat, and the pressure made me feel light-headed. I felt my hands drop away from Anderson's face as my chest burned for air.

Black dots danced in front of my vision and I stared up at Anderson, whose black eyes were wild and misted with fury. I was about to close my eyes and give in to the sleep that beckoned me, but one second Anderson was on top of me and the next he wasn't. I sucked in air greedily and began to cough as pain stung my throat. My body felt like jelly, but when I turned my head to the side, I didn't see Anderson. I saw him.

Elliot.

CHAPTER TWENTY-EIGHT

ELLIOT

"Keep going down!" I shouted up the stairwell as I rushed past people who were descending at a rapid pace. "Keep your children and pets in your arms to avoid losin' them. Do *not* come back into the buildin'!"

I wasn't sure if people were even listening to me, but I repeated the message three more times. I only stopped when I passed the third floor and the scent of smoke touched my nostrils. I hurried up to the fourth floor where I knew Anderson lived, and yanked the door open.

"Fuck!" I snapped.

Flames filled the corridor all the way up the walls and to the ceiling. I looked from left to right and spotted a rack of four large fire extinguishers. I grabbed the one in the middle, undid the safety clip and then checked the label to make sure it was the extinguisher I needed. I could smell petrol in the hallway; I needed to smother it with carbon dioxide otherwise the fire would spread.

The extinguisher was large, but I knew from experience that the contents of the can would run out quicker than most people would expect. I lifted it up, took a few deep breaths of clean air, then I ran. The fire hadn't spread to the entire floor or to all the sections of the walls and ceiling. I jumped and crouched and kept my body in the fire-free zones. As soon as I reached flat 406, I didn't hesitate; I kicked it open and instantly stumbled back when flames darted out of the doorway.

"Fuck!" I paled as dread slammed into me with the intensity of the flames that surrounded me. The smoke was thick and overwhelming, and breathing it in caused my lungs to burn. "*Noah!* Noah, can you hear me?"

I pointed the nozzle at the base of the flames and sprayed. The CO_2 helped, but the fire inside Anderson's flat was bad. The smell of petrol was heavier inside the room and I knew this piece of shit was the cause of it. I felt it in my bones. Using a now-fire-free patch of floor, I reserved the remainder of the extinguisher and hopped and weaved on to dry patches of floor. I dipped into the kitchen and quickly ran the water at the sink. I took my T-shirt off and completely soaked it, then I pulled it back on. I soaked my hair and body, and used a pot of water to douse my trousers in the liquid too.

I dropped the pot on the floor when I heard a scream.

"Noah!" I roared. "Noah, I'm here!"

I grabbed the extinguisher and followed the sound of the scream, spraying CO_2 on the worst of the fire in the hallway that I assumed led to a bedroom. I began to cough as oxygen around me was replaced by thick, black smoke. When I reached the end of the hallway, I kicked the door open. The second my eyes landed on what I was seeing, I dropped the can and shot forward. Anderson, that sorry excuse for a man, was on top of Noah and he was strangling her.

"No!"

My hands gripped his neck and arm and I forcibly yanked him off her. He hit the ground with a thud, and I unleashed my fury, and fear, upon him. I cracked my fists into his jaw, nose, chest, and any other piece of flesh I could connect to. My body was shaking with anger, and I only stopped hitting Anderson, who was so dazed that he couldn't even fight back, to look at Noah when she moaned in obvious pain.

She looked right at me, but then her eyes rolled back. I jumped on to the bed and gathered her up in my arms, and I almost cheered in delight when I heard the sirens of fire engines. My brothers were coming to help me.

I shook Noah and she moaned again. I could hear the roar of the flames as they ate their way through the flat, inching closer and closer to the bedroom. The smoke had already begun to fill the room, and I knew that at that very moment, it was the immediate threat.

"Noah." I shook her. "Sweetheart, wake up."

Her eyes opened, and it took her a minute to focus on me, but when she did, she gasped.

"It's Anderson," she coughed, as under her nostrils darkened with soot. "He chased me and Bailey that night, I was leaving him and he tried to kill me because of it. He forced the crash . . . he killed Bailey. I remember it, Elliot. I remember everything about that night!"

I was stunned into silence.

"I recorded it all," she said as she fumbled with her dress.

She pulled out her phone, tapped on the screen then pushed it at me.

"Keep it safe," she rasped. "Protect it. It'll put him in prison."

I looked from Noah to the phone, then pocketed it.

"You remember?"

"Just that night," she answered, groaning as her hand went to her head. "I was leaving him. I phoned Bailey and she came to pick me up, she came to help me and he chased us. Elliot, if I hadn't phoned her—"

"No," I cut her off. "Don't. This is not your fault, it's his."

I looked down at Anderson. He wasn't moving, but the rise and fall of his chest told me he was still alive.

"He beat me," Noah whimpered. "He broke me, Elliot. It's why I stayed with him and cut everyone out. He controlled everything I did. I never loved him though. I thought I did, but it was always you."

I heard Noah as if she'd screamed every word.

"He beat you?"

She nodded and began to cough once more, wincing in pain as her hands touched her throat. Her already-bruised throat. I had to close my eyes for a moment and focus every ounce of my energy on getting Noah out of the building and not putting her down to kick the fucking life out of Anderson Riley. He'd killed my sister. He'd abused Noah. I wanted to hurt him, to make him feel pain he could never imagine feeling.

"Elliot," Noah whimpered. "The fire."

"Fuck," I snapped.

My thoughts of revenge had distracted me from the danger at hand.

"I'm gonna get ye outta here, *sasanach*," I vowed. "You and me, we're going to get out of this place and go home, okay?"

"We might have to go to the hospital," she mumbled. "My head."

She tensed and went completely rigid as her eyes rolled back. I held her as pain consumed her body, then I nearly collapsed with fear when she went lax. I pressed my head to her chest and heard her heartbeat. Relief smacked into me like a tidal wave.

"Hello!" a voice roared. "Anyone in here? Hello?"

I recognised the muffled voice instantly.

"Texas!" I shouted. "Tex, in here!"

"Irish?" I heard his bewildered reply. "AJ, *Irish* is here!"

I put one arm under Noah's legs and another under her back and lifted her from the bed. I adjusted my grip on her and held her close to my body as I approached the bedroom door. The flames were everywhere, but I had no other choice. I had to get us out of there. I ran forward, heat licking all around me. When I entered the main room of the flat, I almost ran smack into one of my friends.

"Fuck," AJ's voice shouted through his apparatus. "Noah? Is she breathing?"

Flames had caught on to her hair and AJ was quickly patting them out with his gloved hands.

"Yeah, she's knocked out." I choked on smoke as I looked around. "I need to get her outta here!"

"The fire is out of containment on this floor; it'll reach higher floors soon so we need to move *now*. The others are sweeping floors five to eight."

"Help!"

I paused and looked over my shoulder; through the flames and thick veil of smoke I saw Anderson was crawling towards me, crying and choking as he tried to draw in a breath.

"I can't breathe!" he shouted. "Help me!"

He was crawling over the burning floor as if he didn't feel pain. His trousers had caught alight, and the longer I stared at him, the more he began to burn. I made a decision in that moment.

"Elliot!" AJ bellowed. "We've got to *go*!"

I turned and passed Noah off to AJ and Pretty; they both had to carry her because the weight and mass of their equipment meant she couldn't simply be thrown over their shoulder. Both of them instantly backed out of the flat and made their way to safety with her. I turned back for Anderson. I wasn't like this piece of shite; I was ten times the man he was. He wasn't getting a quick death, he was going to pay for what he did to my sister, to Noah – behind bars, where he'd have no control over anyone, or anything, ever again.

I'd make sure of it.

I rushed towards him, grabbed his arms and pulled him into the main room. I removed my wet T-shirt and smacked it over his trousers until the fire was out. Anderson screamed in pain the entire time, and I couldn't find a fuck to give. I was going to save his life, but I was happy he was suffering.

I could see the fabric of his clothing that wasn't burned away was binding into his scorched, melting skin and I was glad.

So fucking glad.

I bent down, hoisted him up and put him over my shoulder. I steadied myself, then I took off at a run out of the burning heat of the flat and the thick choking smoke. I held my breath as I ran down the corridor, and didn't suck in a breath until I was in the stairwell. I heard talking, lots of talking, and familiar voices. I left my brothers to their duty – this was their watch, and my responsibility was currently being carried down the stairs by my friends.

"AJ!" I shouted, my voice echoing. "Is she still breathin'?"

A moment passed by then he said, "Yeah! She's just out, man."

No further words were exchanged until we were outside. People were everywhere, and so were ambulances, police and the three fire engines from our station. But I paid no one any attention – my focus was on Noah, who AJ and Texas were placing on a stretcher that the paramedics had ready. I put a sobbing Anderson on another stretcher and called the police over to me.

"This piece of shit started the fire," I told them. "He tried to murder me girlfriend, and he also caused the death of my little sister on the nineteenth of March."

The policemen shared a look then looked back at me.

"I have the proof on a recording my girlfriend took," I continued. "But once an investigation is carried out, it'll show clearly that the fire was established in his flat. It reeked of petrol inside it and on the corridor of his floor."

I looked down at Anderson, and before the paramedics had even got a chance to check him over, I swung my foot and made contact with his ribs. His screech of pain told me I'd broken something and it pleased me greatly. The policemen did nothing; one of them even appeared to grunt in agreement.

"I hope it hurts, ye rotten scumbag."

The policemen moved forward to stand watch over Anderson, and I assured them that I would give a statement afterwards. Once I told them that Noah's life was in danger, they didn't question me, they just gave me a simple nod.

I hurried over to the ambulance that Noah was being loaded into the back of.

The female paramedic tried to stop me. "Sir, you can't—"

"She's my *girlfriend*!" I interrupted. "She has a traumatic brain injury, she was in the ICU a few weeks ago. She only got out of hospital three fuckin' days ago. Her left leg should be in a boot cast, it was severely fractured and had to be surgically repaired. She inhaled a lot of smoke, and the bastard who started this fire tried to kill her and beat her badly. I'm comin' with her, missus. God 'imself couldn't make me stay away. She's me whole heart."

The woman blinked up at me, then wordlessly stepped aside so I could get in the ambulance.

"Irish!"

I looked over my shoulder at AJ.

"Take care of her," he called. "We'll take care of things here."

I nodded. "Thanks, brother."

He gave me a thumbs up, then got back to work just as the doors to the ambulance closed. I moved to Noah's side and took hold of her open hand. She still had darkened soot under her nostrils and her face was bruised and swollen. Her throat was a mess of red and blue, and I could almost see finger marks imprinted on to her skin. I clenched my free hand into a fist.

"Noah?" I called. "Come on, *sasanach*, show me those pretty green eyes." I kissed her face as she moaned. "Come on, gorgeous. Look at me."

Her eyelids fluttered open, and for a long moment she stared at me like she had never seen me before, and my heart just about stopped in my chest.

"Elliot," she suddenly rasped. "Anderson did it, he caused the crash."

Relief that she hadn't forgotten any more of her life – forgotten me – washed over me.

"I know, honey." I stroked my thumb over her cheek. "I know. Look at me, okay?"

"I can't," she whimpered. "I can't see your face, everything is blurry."

My gut twisted.

"I'm right here, Noah," I assured her. "Right here, beauty. I'm not goin' anywhere."

"Elliot," she cried softly, her voice a rasp. "I love you, I've always loved you. Please, tell me you know that? It's always been you, paddy."

I laughed in disbelief. I knew this woman loved me; I felt it radiate from her in waves.

"Yeah, *sasanach*, I know. I love you too."

"I recorded everything," she coughed. "The police have to hear it!"

"They will," I assured her as I took the oxygen mask the paramedic was trying to put over Noah's face and fixed it in place. "Nice deep breaths. Slow everythin' right down for me, green eyes."

"Elliot," she whispered. "Everything hurts."

My heart ached.

"I know, beauty. It's gonna be okay."

"Please," she said as her eyes closed. "Don't leave me. I'm not scared of the silence when I have you."

I had no idea what she was talking about, but I squeezed her hand.

"I'm not goin' anywhere, Noah."

"My head . . . my head."

Her head lolled to the side, and my body tensed as the woman I loved with every fibre of my being was lost to darkness. I sat next to her, ignoring everything around me but her. Then I bowed my head and I prayed. Noah's fate was out of my hands . . . I just pleaded with all that was divine in the universe to show mercy on her because she, more than anyone, deserved it.

CHAPTER TWENTY-NINE
NOAH

When I came back to awareness, a familiar off-white ceiling came into view. I could hear a steady, repetitive beep that drew a long groan from me. That fucking sound killed my head. As a matter of fact, that groan I'd just released hurt my head too.

"Noah?" his voice said. "Noah?"

"Elliot?" I lifted my heavy eyelids. "Is that you?"

"Yes, it's me, *sasanach*." His voice cracked. "I'm right here."

When my vision came into focus, I blinked against the light in the room – but it didn't bother me once I rested my eyes on his face. I looked straight into the ocean blues I loved, and widened my own eyes when I saw they were filled with tears. When Elliot blinked, those tears fell.

"No," I whispered. "No, I'm okay. Please, don't cry, honey."

This was the first time in the many years I'd known Elliot that I had seen him cry. I had never seen him look so scared and yet so relieved in my life.

"I'm okay," I repeated. "I promise."

He held me for a long time, and after he'd wiped his eyes, he kissed me.

"Ye scared the absolute life outta me, green eyes," he said, leaning back and exhaling. "I've aged twenty years. You're awake, thank God."

I ran my eyes over his face. "You're looking like a peng ting from where I'm lying."

"My God," he laughed, tears still sliding down his cheeks, and shook his head. "I've never heard ye say those words in all the years I've known ye."

"Never had a reason to say it . . . until now."

He kissed me again and held me for a long time.

"Am I in the ICU?"

"Yes," he answered, wiping his face as he sat back. "Doctor Abara was on shift when the ambulance brought you in, and you were brought straight up."

"And when was that?"

"Ten days ago."

I widened my eyes. "Ten days?"

"Ye were in another coma – this time it was a medicated one," Elliot explained. "They've done a bunch of tests. Scans show ye have some swellin' on your brain that ye didn't have the first time so keepin' ye under helped it reduce. It's not severe any more but it's not good either. They took ye off of the drugs last night so ye could slowly come out of your coma."

I digested this information, but suddenly another thought popped into my head.

"Anderson."

"Calm," Elliot urged. "He's been arrested. He's still in the hospital, he had third-degree burns to fifteen per cent of his body. He has a broken jaw, nose and six broken ribs. He'll be here for a while but he's under twenty-four-seven police watch. He's cuffed to his hospital bed."

My heart slammed in my chest.

"My phone." I swallowed. "Did you give it to the police?"

"I did. It's evidence. He's goin' to be charged with a lot of things, Noah. Arson, kidnappin', attempted murder, physical assault, and he's goin' to be landed with a charge for Bailey's death too. Accordin' to the voice memo you recorded, he didn't mean for the car to crash, but he caused it by pursuin' you both. Me sister . . . she's goin' to get justice thanks to you, Noah."

Relief hit me, as well as pain.

"I forgot she was dead." I burst into tears. "For a minute, I forgot."

Elliot leaned down and pressed his forehead against mine.

"I know," he whispered. "There are times when I wake up in the mornin' and for a few seconds I forget, and when I remember it's like a kick in the teeth."

I nodded. "That's exactly how I feel."

Elliot kissed away my tears. "D'ye want the good news?" Sniffing, I nodded. "No one was harmed in Anderson's flat building. Me friends managed to keep the fire contained to the fourth floor before they extinguished it. Everyone was safely evacuated, right down to an old man's goldfish."

I laughed but then winced in pain.

"Yeah." He frowned. "No laughin'. Your head is worse off than before. This time, you're doin' every bloody thing that Doctor Abara says or so help me God, I'll never kiss ye again."

I closed my eyes and smiled. "Like you could manage that."

Elliot playfully growled. "Behave."

I opened my eyes and lifted my hands to his handsome face.

"I love you," I told him. "I never stopped loving you, I was just so scared of him that I couldn't leave . . . I got so lost, and I made a mistake when I left you. I'm so sorry, Elliot. I'll always be sorry."

"Don't be. I pushed ye away because of a fear that I couldn't get over at the time. Ye've always been me girl, Noah, even when ye were his."

"I was never his," I assured him. "Not really. I was broken when I met him; it's the only way he was able to manipulate me the way he did. I was vulnerable and he took advantage of me."

"I should've killed him," Elliot growled. "I should've—"

"I'm glad you didn't," I interrupted. "I'm glad you don't have to live with knowing you took someone's life, no matter how much we believe he deserved it. You *save* lives, you don't take them. That's the man you are – you're incredible."

Elliot's kiss caught me by surprise. In an instant I was in tears as he crushed his lips to mine, plunging his tongue into my mouth and claiming what was rightfully his. Me.

"I shouldn't be doin' this," he whispered against my lips. "I should be tellin' ye that this is a bad idea because your brain is still—"

"Shut up." I flicked my tongue over his lower lip. "I need you to be with me, I need all of you."

"Woman," he groaned, "sex is *not* happenin'. Ye can barely hold your head up. Your parents only went to get tea, they'll be back any minute."

I slid my hands down to his waist but froze when I heard a shout. Elliot jumped away from me like I was a naked flame. I looked towards the door and clamped my lips together.

"No!" Doctor Abara pointed at me, wagging his finger. "No! Leave that man alone, Noah!"

It hurt like hell, but I laughed.

"Stop," Elliot warned as I groaned in pain. "Stop it right now."

I closed my eyes and sighed.

"I'm sorry." I opened my eyes and looked at the doctor. "I'm not allowed to *frolic* with him . . . I remember."

"Uh-huh." Doctor Abara approached me. "You cause nothing but trouble when you're in my hospital."

"Sorry." I smiled softly. "But at least this time I remember you . . . that's an upgrade from before, right? No new prime minister for me."

Doctor Abara's lips twitched. "I'm going to get your parents, then I'm going to do an examination on you, and then we're all going to have a big talk about how this time there will be strict rules concerning your recovery. *Strict*."

He left the room and my eyes darted to Elliot.

"Kiss me quickly before he bans it during my recovery."

Elliot smiled as he moved to my side, and he bent down and kissed me gently.

"Can I ask ye a question?"

"Is it more important than kissing me?"

"Right now?" He raised an eyebrow. "Yes."

I sighed. "Shoot."

Elliot reached out and brushed hair out of my face.

"Will ye marry me, *sasanach*?"

I stared at him, then looked down at his hand, which had two silver bands on his ring finger. With my lips parted in shock, I felt like I was choking on air. He removed one of the rings and held it out to me.

"I wanna marry ye," he breathed. "I know what it's like to not have you in me life, and how much it hurt. Not havin' ye in me life scared me more than anythin' else in this world. I want ye in every single way, *sasanach*. Marry me. Be my person for life."

"Yes," I said, trembling. "Yes, yes, I'll marry you!"

With a beaming smile, Elliot slid the band on to my left ring finger, and then I took his face in my hands and kissed him until a throat was cleared.

"This is *exactly* what I'm talking about." Doctor Abara's voice carried loud and clear. "She just doesn't listen."

"I'll make her listen," my dad's amused, and very relieved, voice answered.

I opened my eyes and looked at Elliot's ocean blues as they gazed into my eyes.

"That was some kiss, Elliot McKenna."

"Ah." He grinned, rubbing his nose against mine. "That's because you're some woman, Noah Ainsley."

I kissed him again, and smiled when Elliot jumped away laughing as Doctor Abara held up my patient chart like a weapon that he was going to whack Elliot with. I closed my eyes and relaxed. I was in pain both physically and emotionally. Bailey's death was very fresh in my mind – and heart – and I knew the time to come would be a test for me. I was going to have to adapt and overcome many things. I had to somehow move on from a dark past that was filled with pain because of Anderson; I had to come to terms with the fact that the blank spots in my memory may never return. I had to move forward. But I knew I could do it all because I would have Elliot by my side.

We were going to do things in our new way . . . we would take it day by day.

EPILOGUE
NOAH

Five years later . . .

Rumbling laughter followed by light-hearted giggles – that was the first thing I heard as I entered my home after a long day at work. I'd been hired to provide flowers and arrangements for the funeral of an old man who had passed away a couple days prior, and the orders from his family and friends had me, my mum and two of my other employees rushed off our feet. I'd never had a day like it since I opened Bailey's Lily Patch two years ago.

I was certain my feet were numb from the pain.

"Do I hear something?" I said out loud as I removed my jacket and hung it up on its peg. "Huh. I was *sure* I heard something, I must've imagined it."

I turned, set my bag down on the floor, then tossed my keys on to the side table just as shouts sounded from behind me. I was expecting to be surprised, but the volume of the shouts frightened me out of my skin. I didn't have to fake it when I screamed, I bloody well near shit myself. I spun around with my hand on my chest and found the culprits. Both of them were on the floor and laughing so hard they couldn't speak.

"That *wasn't* funny!" I admonished. "If I have grey hairs, it's because of you two!"

"Aw, Mummy," my almost-four-year-old son said as he got to his feet. "You should have seen your face! It was like *this*."

He pulled a very unattractive, almost-constipated-looking face that had me placing my hands on my hips as I stared down at him. My son, my beautiful Baylor, soon stopped laughing and swallowed when he took in my stance and expression. I think two seconds passed by before he pointed to his left and said, "*He* made me do it, he planned the whole thing. I'm only a baby!"

He was only a baby when he was in trouble – every other time he was a "big boy" and most definitely *not* a baby.

"Traitor," Elliot grumbled as he got to his feet. He was trying his hardest to keep from smiling. "How was work, Mummy? How 'bout Daddy gives ye a good ol' foot rub?"

I made a mental note to scold them both later, but the foot rub could come first. I kissed my son on the head and told him to go and watch some television.

"I'll allow it," I mused to Elliot as I removed my platform heels, vowing never to wear anything other than flat, comfy shoes to work for the rest of my life. "I could actually really use a good rub-down."

I grinned as I passed by my husband, who made a noise deep in his throat that told me my feet weren't the only place on my body that he'd like to rub down. I walked down the hallway and into the kitchen. I grabbed some wet wipes, sat on a chair and cleaned off any dirt, sweat and stink left behind on my feet from my workday. I sighed as I got up and binned them, before resting my hands on the counter and closing my eyes.

"Headache?" Elliot murmured, and his arms encircled my waist.

"No," I said, leaning back against him. "It was just a long day. Mum had been taking orders for the past two days for a funeral, and I didn't realise how many we had to fulfil until I opened the shop this morning. It was non-stop all day, but it's not the work that has me feeling . . . upset. I couldn't stop thinking about our Bailey, and how there was a shop catering orders like today's for her funeral. It's just . . . it just reminded me that I wasn't there to say goodbye to her."

Elliot turned me in his arms and frowned when tears splashed on to my cheeks.

"Green eyes," he said softly as he thumbed them away. "Ye were with her when she passed away; she wasn't alone in her final moments because she had *you* right next to her. Your goodbye to her was that night."

My lower lip wobbled as I burst into sobs. "I miss her so much."

Elliot enveloped me in a warm, tight embrace, and I wrapped my arms around him as I cried. Life without Bailey was hard, but it was getting somewhat easier in the sense that I didn't always cry when I missed her. But today was one of those days where my grief struck me hard, and broke me down into tears.

"Mummy?" a small voice called. "Don't cry, we didn't mean to scare you. Did we, Daddy?"

I pulled back and smiled down at my son, and when I bent to lift him up, Elliot stopped me and picked Baylor up instead. Baylor reached down and rubbed my swollen stomach, which brought on a fresh wave of tears that had my son near tears himself.

"Mummy's okay, Bay," Elliot assured him with a cuddle. "She just misses Auntie Bailey."

"I miss her too, Mummy. It's okay."

He only knew of Bailey through pictures, videos and stories we told him of her, but that was enough for him to fall in love with his sweet auntie. I stepped closer and wrapped my arms around my boys, and the baby in my belly decided that he – or she – didn't want to be left out, and they gave me a whopping kick that Elliot felt against his own stomach. He laughed.

"This one will definitely be me footballer."

I snorted. "Maybe *she* will."

"Still stuck on him bein' a girl?"

"Yup," I answered with a smile. "Our little Bailey."

Elliot eyes shone with love, and he leaned his head down and pressed his lips to mine. We'd named Baylor after her by tweaking his name, and I'd named my shop after her because I could never look at lilies without her face popping into my mind, but I wanted a little girl that I could name after my sister-in-law too.

The kiss my husband gave me lasted no more than a second before Baylor claimed he wanted a kiss from me too. Elliot's grunt made me grin. Once Baylor heard the theme song for *Paw Patrol* play on the television, he wiggled in Elliot's arms until he was put back on the floor and then he took off running.

"That lad has the energy of ten kids."

I pressed my face against Elliot's chest and slid my arms back around his waist. While I was still hurting for the loss of Bailey, I couldn't deny how happy I was in my life. I'd gone through a hardship not many people face. I'd lost the love of my life and found him again, as I found myself. I'd married him and given birth to his son, and was a few months away from giving him a second child. I had the security, love and life I had always dreamed of with Elliot, and I had that life with my parents living right down the street.

My father had beaten his cancer and had been in remission going on two years. My bond with my parents had strengthened and our love for one another had only deepened. I couldn't imagine my life without them, and I didn't want to. Elliot's parents were still happily married and heavily involved in our lives; his mother was currently thinking of coming to work for me in my flower shop. I hoped she accept my offer, because I loved being around her.

AJ and his beautiful wife Dani had twin girls a month after I had Baylor; the two of them aged AJ by the day. He often swore he was getting the snip when he'd had one too many nights of getting nothing but a couple of hours of sleep. Those threats were clearly empty now that Dani was ten weeks pregnant with their third child. After AJ cried for a day, he started praying to God that he'd get a boy this time around because he was certain it would be his and Dani's last baby.

All of Elliot's station buddies were doing wonderfully in life. Stitch, Tank and Pretty had added two more kids – each – to their families. Texas and his girlfriend, Jodie – Dani's cousin from Ireland – were engaged and expecting their first little one. We all often had family day outings together, and we made sure whenever one of our kids had a birthday that we all made a big deal about it. Each of those men put their lives on the line every time they went to work; they knew the importance of celebrating each milestone like it could be the last.

The person who was the cause of so much pain and suffering in my life would never have the chance to hurt me or anyone else for as long as he lived. Anderson Riley had been charged with multiple serious offences, and in a trial that had lasted just a couple of weeks, a court of law had found him guilty of all charges. With his sentences all added together, he would die in prison and would forever lose the control on his life that he craved.

He'd got what he deserved, and Bailey and I got our justice.

"I miss her too," Elliot said as he hugged me to him. "But she's here with us. Ye feel her, right?"

I nodded. "I do. Today was just a day that I missed her extra."

"I know, green eyes. I had one of those days last week. I just can't believe the years have gone by so quickly without her. Think of it, this time five years ago you had no clue how much time ye had forgotten."

"There was benefit to it, though. Forgetting you made me fall deeper in love with you." I squeezed him. "I love you, Elliot. So much."

"Hey," he said, leaning back so I could look up at him. I lifted my hand to brush my fingers over the silver calla lily pendent that he still wore to this day. "I love ye too, Mrs McKenna. I'm scared of how much I love ye."

"Me too. Terrified. You'd better always be scared of how much you love me."

"Oh, I will," he said, his thumb grazing my lower lip. "I always have been."

When he kissed me this time, it was slow, intense and filled with emotion. He showed me with his kiss just how much he loved me, and I felt it from my heart all the way to my toes. A shiver ran the length of my spine.

"I think you promised me a rub-down, paddy."

"Oh, *sasanach*." He grinned, his ocean blues gleaming. "Wait until Baylor goes down for his nap, and I'll be sure to rub ye down *everywhere*."

This man had my heart; he'd given me my son and another baby that I would soon bring into the world. He'd come back to me at a time when I was lost, scared and didn't know where to turn. He'd saved me. As he slid his hand down to my behind, my laughter and his mingled together, until he silenced me with a toe-curling kiss that held the promise of so much more to come.

ACKNOWLEDGMENTS

Reaching this section of a book always seems like such a far-off point that I'll never reach when I start writing. When I eventually find myself here, with the book finished, I have a moment of disbelief. How did I get from a fleeting idea to a finished book that I love? It still blows my mind, and I think it always will.

To my sister and daughter, who give me nothing but endless support and never question why I stay holed up in my office for hours at a time, looking a fright while I get my books finished. I love you both to Neptune and back.

To my friend Rebecca Prescott and your wonderful hubby, thank you for answering all of my questions about the station life of a fireman in London. I appreciate it so much, Becks.

To Mark Gottlieb, my agent, thank you for always having my back and for all you do for me.

To my editor, Lindsey Faber, my copyeditor, Gemma Wain, and my proofreader, Becca Allen. Thank you, ladies, for going through my book with a fine comb to make the story, and its characters, as strong as they could be. I really appreciate your many hours of hard work to get *Forgetting You* to where it is right now.

To Sammia, and the team at Montlake Romance, thank you for taking a chance on a rough summary of the book that changed drastically by the time I finished writing and submitting it.

To my readers, I sound like a broken record, but you all make my world spin. I hope you enjoyed reading *Forgetting You*, because I had a ball writing it.

ABOUT THE AUTHOR

L.A. Casey is a *New York Times* and *USA Today* bestselling author who juggles her time between her mini-me and writing. She was born, raised and currently resides in Dublin, Ireland. She enjoys chatting with her readers, who love her humour and Irish accent as much as her books. You can visit her website at www.lacaseyauthor.com, find her on Facebook at www.facebook.com/LACaseyAuthor and on Twitter at @AuthorLACasey.